# Somewhere Between Love and Justice

## The Journey of Sarah Sawyer

**By**

# S.W. Andersen

**2015**

**swandersenwrites.com**

**@SW_Andersen**

ISBN-13: 978-1514370056

This is a work of fiction. Names, characters, businesses, places, events and incidents are either the products of the author's imagination or used in a fictitious manner. Any resemblance to actual persons, living or dead, or actual events is purely coincidental.

Published by S.W. Andersen

# Contents

To my wife Dianna for her love, patience and understanding and my mom, who always loved a good cowgirl story.

# **<u>Acknowledgement</u>**

So many amazing people made this happen. The last couple of years have been an incredible journey of self-discovery as I stumbled onto the path of fiction writing. I've made so many new friends along the way. I'm sad to say I can't mention everyone by name, but thank you to each and every one of you that supported and encouraged me, read my early drafts, offered feedback or help.

There is still a long road ahead and I hope to continue to grow and share these stories with you.

Alas, I must mention a few people who either helped shape my writing or contributed to the production of this book: Sabrina, Cindy, Rafi, Sam, Amanda, Candace and a nice German lady who really does rock.

Thank you to Cindy Bamford for her beautiful cover art, Beta work and patience. *hugs*

# <u>Chapter One</u>

## Somewhere Outside Red Lodge, Montana

*Kicking and screaming, I struggle to see through my tears as my fingernails dig deep into the dirt. I claw at the ground and pray for anything to hold onto. Angry hands grab at my feet, filling me with terror. I frantically kick to stay free, but their relentless pursuit seeks to prevent my escape. My heart pounds like the thunder of a hundred hooves. The tightening of my chest makes air impossible to find. Sweat and dirt cover me, crawling as fast as my small limbs will take me toward what I hope will be safety under the old house.*

*All my efforts are in vain. A claw-like grip takes a hold of my ankle and gives me a swift yank backwards. My dress slides up, my belly scraping along the rocks as I scream and flail, desperate for escape.*

*Won't someone, anyone help me?*

*The mid-day sun blinds me when I'm dragged back into the light. I scramble to my feet with the desperate need to run. A fast, hard slap to the face stings as I fall to the ground stunned. My head spins and my vision blurs from more than tears. My body is lifted upward by the arms of a faceless captor. Splatters of my own blood glistening on the orange dirt is the last thing I see before I pass out.*

My eyes snapped open wide, darting wildly into the starry night for any sign of danger. Sweat soaked from the struggle and still on edge, every muscle I had stood at the ready. A huff of hot air down my neck stopped my breath. With a shaky hand, I made a slow path for my gun. I was prepared for a fight, but a gentle nudge from behind brought me back to reality. Relief slipped through my lips in a deep, slow exhale. I slid my hand behind my neck and stroked the soft hair of my one true friend and constant companion over the last five years, Clover.

I dropped my head back and sighed. It was only a dream, again. Well, not just a dream, a nightmare. A memory of the worst day of my life that I relived over and over again in my sleep.

I was helpless back then. Even though I was only thirteen, I still harbored a deep seeded rage at my own weakness. Something I vowed never to be again.

"Thanks girl." My voice flowed thick and raspy from sleep.

Clover was more than a horse. Like a good friend she woke me from my distress. Sleepless nights were becoming more and more frequent. She served as my protector from a subconscious insistent upon reminding me of a fateful day ten years ago I couldn't change. For the third time tonight, her soft nose brushed my cheek and softened my stressed muscles.

I moved my head to kiss the gentle creature, showing my appreciation for her concern. Often I wondered how my friend got any rest of her own. She probably loved the few nights a year I sought comfort with my own kind.

As of late, the dreams had become more vivid. Some nights the same nightmare repeated until I abandoned the effort of sleep all together, but as I lay quiet, my body calmed. The cold air surrounded me and the sweat dissipated. With a blind hand, I reached for the warm covers lost during the night and pulled them back up.

I propped my head on the edge of my saddle and stared out to the horizon at the few remaining stars. The solitude of night was short lived when an inkling of light broke through the darkness and began the countdown to sunrise. For a brief speck of time I let myself imagine that Clover and I were the only ones in the world.

Like so many other nights, I found little peace behind closed lids, but I kept trying. Never one to give up, I shut my tired eyes and attempted yet again find any semblance of rest before another long day.

The sun's early light warmed my exposed skin, gently nudging me like mama's touch waking me from slumber. For a moment I forgot she was gone. I imagined her sitting on the edge of my bed smiling down at me. *"Sarah, time to get up,"* she would say. And so I did.

Stiff limbs greeted me as I slowly rose to my feet and stretched. My mind drifted back to mama and what she'd think of me these days. Her words often hung in the back of my mind, guiding my actions. She only fell silent when I exacted my revenge, though she never scolded me either. Since she never complained, I assumed she didn't hate me for succumbing to the demon within. Mama never would have guessed her outgoing, peaceful, innocent little girl would sink so low as to take another life, much less find satisfaction in the deed.

I sighed and gave Clover a pat on her butt. My mind and body were more refreshed than they had been in a long time after managing a bit of sleep. The shut eye was refreshing, even if it was only an hour or so. I'd skimmed books over the course of my travels that made note of sleep deprivation causing everything from foul mood to decreased reaction time, even mental instability.

A ridiculous laugh escaped. The foreign sound flowing from within floated into the emptiness of the valley. As if I could be any more unstable. I spent my days running around the country in an effort to hunt down the vile creatures responsible for murdering my family and making me their slave. The pursuit of revenge alone would drive a person insane, yet I found the idea oddly comforting. Insanity would suggest I lacked control of these feelings and actions, but that would be a lie. In fact, I possessed no real feelings about any of my deeds, but control belonged entirely to me. I chose when and where to collect the debt owed me from years ago. Black and white. Right and wrong. Cause and effect.

I was simply carrying out the effect of what they had caused. Nothing crazy about that in my eyes. I laughed again and shook my head. My attempts to analyze myself always provided a chuckle.

Mama always said I was my father's daughter. As a doctor, he investigated everything. He believed in a logical, scientific solution for any problems. I believed the same, even for payback.

Thin rays of sunrise glistened on the river bringing me a rare sense of serenity. The clean, brisk morning air refreshed me in those precious few moments of each day when everything began anew. Well, everything except my body, which hurt from repeated nights on the hard ground and so many hours in the saddle. This had been our longest stretch yet, two straight weeks out on the trail and I felt every minute of it.

The river called to me. I slipped out of my clothes and padded over patches of soft grass and sharp rocks to its edge, begging the bitter, cold water to numb my aching bones. The icy sting stimulated every single nerve ending in my worn body as I submerged myself neck deep. Wonderful weightlessness soothed me. Within minutes my soreness had eased as the water renewed me from the outside in; flesh, bones and soul.

My face shimmered in the crystal clear mirror. When did I last pay attention to my reflection? Months probably. My flaxen hair had grown long and unruly and my amber eyes weary. Small wrinkles perched at the corner of my eyes and mouth. The once fine features of my face appeared hardened. All signs this quest of mine had taken its toll at the age of twenty three. I needed to take better care of myself, but that could wait.

It was only a matter of time until this would all be over. In the meantime, the river made me happy, so I made a promise to myself to travel near the tranquility more often in some small effort to get an ounce of joy out of this otherwise stagnant life.

The time for pleasure was brief. We still had a good many miles to go and if we were going to get there by nightfall, we needed to get moving. On my way back to camp, I smiled at the intense watchfulness of Clover's big, soft, brown eyes. Her red hair with white blaze and socks glowed as the sun rose higher. Such a majestic creature. I was always amazed at how powerful she was, yet gentle as a mother with her newborn baby.

Wasn't that the age old question for most forms of life though? Would you use your power for good or evil? It didn't matter if it were a man, a horse or any other animal with the ability to think. The ability to choose made all the difference. The distinguishing factor in each of us came down to our choices.

Sometimes though, was it possible one really didn't have a choice, but rather a commitment? Like in the case of justice or vengeance? An eye for an eye? At least that's how I came about my "choice" when everything I ever loved was taken from me at a young age. My stolen innocence left behind an inner rage that evolved into a life of its own. The monstrous wrath laid trapped beneath a calm collected exterior, waiting for the next possible moment to escape its cage.

I ran my hand down Clover's neck in a show of affection for keeping me safe. She was the one life on this earth with the ability to bring me peace. Wait, I lied. There was another, but she occupied a mere memory in the corner of my mind, helping me through long days of an otherwise miserable existence. Our brief encounter, two to be honest, teased me with a glimpse of a normal life.

Normal for people who weren't me. There was no time for such farfetched fantasies. I needed to keep on track.

Yesterday's shirt served to dry my damp skin. One last set of clean clothes had been saved for the day we headed to town. I was no hobo. My parents taught me to take pride in my appearance.

I combed out my hair then slipped into tan corduroys, a white long sleeved button down and saddle brown vest. My boots had seen better days. New ones topped my list of things to get at the next stop. Boots were a cowgirl's best friend, well, besides her horse. I tucked my pant legs into my boots to protect them from the brush. The final touch was my favorite; my perfectly worn brown Stetson. The old hat kept me safe, providing shelter from the elements and from the eyes of strangers.

Dressed and ready to ride, I proceeded on to the daily ritual of checking my side arms. Each bullet of my Colt single action would be painstakingly removed and replaced, spinning the chamber to make sure everything operated like clockwork. Like every morning since the day I'd gotten the revolver, I wiped down the steel and polished the pearl handle before placing them back in the holster. The key to precision wasn't just practice, but maintaining the perfect working order of one's tool. That's what Henry had taught me.

I packed up my gear, grabbed my Winchester rifle and saddled Clover. Today we would continue to the north-west to meet an old friend. Last we parted, Jessie and I made a pact to get together in a little town in Montana called Red Lodge around the third day of August. If things went well, we'd arrive tonight. Our stop couldn't come at a better time. Clover and I both needed a break and I was pretty sure she wanted to get rid of me for a day or so anyway.

"Ain't that right girl? You need your own space once in a while, huh?"

She threw her head up and whinnied, making me smile. I imagined her mumbling something about owing her a decent meal and a straw bed, maybe even a gelding to flirt with for all her sleepless nights. She could be such a prima donna sometimes.

No offense to my dear four-legged friend, but I found myself eager to interact with another human. I usually preferred the company of animals, but it had been a while. Plus, I hoped Jessie had all the goods on the O'Shea gang. So far, I'd only punished the men no longer involved with the gang, but all responsible for the heinous act would eventually suffer. Soon, very soon, the old man's time would come as well. Patrick Daniel O'Shea would pay in full for his sins against my family.

Ten grueling hours later, we arrived in Red Lodge. First things first, Clover needed a place to stay. As we rode through town I kept an eye out for the saloon, making a note of its location. I'd be heading over once I met Clover's list of demands. A shot of whiskey sounded so damn good right now. I could almost feel the burn.

An old gentleman at the barber shop gave me a stall. I went right to work unsaddling, grooming and setting Clover up with a hearty helping of oats. She nudged me and voiced her thanks with a snort and a soft grunt as she packed her mouth full.

I returned my gratitude with a kiss on her muzzle. I loved to see my friend happy. In the back of my mind I hoped this would be over soon so she could relax in a pasture. I never truly thought of what my life would be like when all those bastards got their due, but I often dreamt of a better life for my best friend.

"Now, don't start any fights among the boys tonight." I chuckled and stroked her muscular neck before I turned with determination and marched toward my own reward.

I pushed through the swinging door of the old saloon. There was a good crowd inside laughing and carrying on the way a bunch of drunks usually would. At the front of the room stood a tall woman with flowing brown hair that matched her sorrel horse and cascaded down to her waist. A black Stetson set atop her head with matching boots, tight brown trousers and a black holster set on her slender hips that made her a sight to behold. There was no mistaking Jessie in a room full of dusty cowboys and gussied up barmaids. Her appearance damn sure didn't blend in with the crowd, but her brash attitude fit to perfection. She was early and I was happier than I thought I'd be to see her.

The odor of stale beer and the tinkling of piano keys were pure joy to one's senses after being alone for two weeks. The short distance between me and the whiskey seemed like miles. For days I'd dreamt of a sip. The drought was about to be over.

A deep laugh roared out from behind and a forceful hand grabbed my ass. I stopped on a dime and wheeled around sporting an amused grin. Someone seemed to think they had permission to touch me. Well...someone did not.

The tall, thick, balding man was all toothless smiles and damn proud of himself. "Hey darlin'. You're a pretty one. How 'bout you have a drink with me?"

I leaned in close and spoke low, trying to avoid trouble. "I'm sorry, but I'm meetin' a friend," I answered politely and turned toward the bar. I mean, I just got here for crying out loud. All I wanted was a shot and a warm bath. Well, maybe a little something extra if things went well.

He grabbed my arm and pulled me back around. This time he stood up, towering over me, not looking quite as pleased as he did a second ago.

Did he miss the guns on my hip? He should have picked a different woman to force himself on. On second thought, he shouldn't force himself on anyone. The slightest inkling of anger rose to the surface, but I choked the rage down and kept an even keel.

"I don't think you heard me darlin'. I want you to have a drink with me," he growled and squeezed tighter. A few patrons took notice of the disturbance.

"And I said, I'm here to meet someone." Keeping my voice low and calm was a struggle. My eyes narrowed in warning and my body tensed, prepared to deliver a beating if needed. "So I'll ask you one time to please remove your hand."

His grin broadened, but his hand stayed put.

I tried the polite approach. Polite didn't seem to be working. I hated when someone tested my limits. You'd think a woman carrying two six shooters fitting the description of the elusive "Doctor" could enjoy a drink in peace, but the identity only seemed to create a bigger challenge, especially with men threatened by my abilities. Either that or he was just a dumb ass. Looking him over, I was gonna opt for the later.

"Oh yeah? If I don't, what're ya gonna do?"

His condescending tone rubbed me the wrong way. He held such confidence that this little woman wouldn't be doing any

damage. Idiot. "Well, I won't be having a drink with you. But..."
The words flowed without distress. A flurry of anger begged to be
released.

His grip tightened even more.

In one swift motion I reached across and peeled away the
little finger of the unwanted hand anchored to my bicep. I flexed
his wrist and twisted the tree trunk of an arm behind his back.
On the verge of snapping the bones in two, I pushed him face
first to the table. "I tell ya what." Gone was any hint of nicety in
my tone as I growled through gritted teeth. "How 'bout a free
drink, courtesy of the Doctor and you leave me alone for the rest
of my stay, okay friend? Or I snap off this hand you seem so
intent on touchin' me with."

Holding back cries of pain, he wasted no time nodding in
agreement. I released him and motioned to the bartender to get
the man another beer. He apologized under his breath while he
rubbed his injured arm.

The place fell silent as everyone sat slack jawed and wide
eyed. Any other challengers? I searched the room. My glare met
with fearful eyes and carefully avoided glances until I settled on
Jessie.

She never blinked as she leaned back against the old
cherry wood bar, both elbows propped up and legs crossed with
her usual smug "don't mess with me" grin across her face. With
two shots waiting atop the bar, she threw a casual wave to the
stool beside her.

I headed toward my long awaited drink again, this time
with ruthless determination. The next person to come between
me and my shot of whiskey...let's just say bad things would

happen. I was hungry, tired and my patience had reached its end.

She didn't move as I made my approach. Her focus locked on the patrons for any other signs of trouble. "Well Doc, you sure know how to make an entrance."

"Mhm," I mumbled, not bothering to hide my eagerness as I slammed down the first shot. I closed my eyes and took a moment to savor the smooth, oaky taste. The long awaited burn hurt so good blazing a trail to my stomach before my eyes fluttered open.

Jessie spun around and signaled for another round.

With my best poker face on display I reminded her, "Don't. You know I hate that nickname. It's ridiculous." Someone gave me the moniker early on in my quest for vengeance as stories of my exploits spread like wild fire. She knew I hated the name. We did this every time. If I didn't find the game so amusing I'd call it frustrating.

Jessie never got tired of playing though. The woman loved getting a rise out of me. She snickered as she continued to peruse the crowd, who'd gone back about their business. Content no further disturbances would be occurring, Jessie turned her attention to me. "Very well Sarah, what's with all the commotion?" Her sparkling blue-gray eyes focused on me with more interest than a close friend.

The second shot followed the first in a matter of seconds. I threw a half smile her way. "He said these britches didn't flatter my backside. I didn't appreciate it. They're my favorite."

Jessie pondered for a moment before she leaned over and took a good look at my ass. Never one to worry what others thought, she ignored the confused mutterings from those around us. She tilted her head up at me with a wide grin puffing the cheeks of her round, sun kissed face. "Well, surely he's an idiot. There's not a finer backside in seven states. Some people just don't know how to talk to a lady."

I rolled my eyes and laughed at her ridiculousness. "My, aren't we the sweet talker. Flattery may just get you everywhere." My gaze drifted down the length of her body. She was attractive, but the imposing demeanor scared many people off. They'd never believe she was a caring and compassionate woman after she steeled those eyes at you.

Fortunately for me, Marshal Walker and I struck up a friendship many years ago when I first started seeking my vengeance and ended up on the most wanted list. I was one of the few people she couldn't stare down and after I saved her hide one day, she realized I wasn't one of the bad guys.

I winked, returning her blatant flirtation. All I needed tonight was a hot meal and all the new information she gathered on the O'Shea gang, but looking at her right now, a different kind of need burned deep inside. One involving her naked body on mine.

She recognized the spark in my eyes and flashed a knowing grin as she held up a key.

I couldn't help but return a flirtatious smile myself. Our times together always served as a welcomed release. Who needed food anyway? I ordered a bottle of whiskey and followed her up the stairs.

# **<u>Chapter Two</u>**

I jolted awake. Where the hell was I?

Nightmares once again racked my mind, sending me hurling into consciousness with no idea of place or time. An unknown anchor held half of my body hostage. I struggled to free its hold as my pulse galloped. There was just enough light to make out my surroundings. Scanning floor to ceiling, left to right with quick precision, I found myself naked and tangled in a mess of sheets. I wasn't alone, but there was no danger. Jessie was passed out with an arm across my waist. Her body pinned my left side to the bed.

Several seconds ticked by until I regained my senses. Slow, deep breaths brought a welcomed calm. Her warm skin pressed against mine and our bare legs intertwined. The steady rhythm of her snoring filled the room. Lucky lady. As usual sleep was scarce for me. If only I could sleep as soundly as my friend.

The beat of my heart slowed, but I brimmed with need to escape. The heat from her body made me uncomfortable. I finagled my way out, tip toed over to the table and poured some water into a glass. The refreshing liquid soothed my parched throat. I dumped some into my hands and splashed my face.

The cool night air pricked at my bare skin sending small shivers racing across my flesh. I embraced them. I greeted the cold room as fondly as the morning at the river. There was something energizing about the chill in the air and how it brought me to life in the same way as the ice pumping through my veins. When this journey ended, possibly warmth would find a home again, but I wasn't about to hold my breath. Any warmth died in me ten years ago along with my parents. Every day and night since, only frigid hate surged within, powering me toward my destiny.

I leaned back against the wall and stared at Jessie. In bed lay a beautiful woman with chiseled cheek bones, a lean body and a hint of a smile on her lips. A smart, loyal and strong woman who wanted me. If I couldn't love her, how could I be capable of loving anyone? She understood me, but wanted more. I wasn't capable of more, at least not now and not with her. The fact that my heart had made room for a trusted friend brought me a sense of relief, providing an inkling of light that almost made me believe a normal life could exist for me one day.

Almost.

Light didn't exist in me now. The darkness from my past infected me, keeping the veil of ice firmly in place. On the rare occasion a speck of light broke through, I found myself thinking of a different woman. One with dark hair, soft hazel eyes and a stunning smile that saved me from so many restless nights on the trails. A woman I'd only met twice when I passed through Ketchum, but I hoped to meet again one day.

In the corner, the half empty bottle of whiskey beckoned. Half empty or half full? Such a ridiculous question intended to reveal so much about one's self, yet either way, in ten shots I needed another bottle.

I grabbed a glass. A few more rounds might help dull the ache in my mind and my chest, but whiskey wouldn't solve anything. My family was still gone, slaughtered without mercy by a man with a god complex. I still lost whatever good was left in me while under his thumb, beaten, degraded and treated like a dog.

I threw back the first shot. For a little while, the self-inflicted burn of liquor in my throat fogged up my thoughts and served its purpose. I stood at the table with glass in hand, naked and shivering in the dark while I stared at Jessie. The relief of the alcohol was short lived as the memory of my past forced its way to the forefront yet again. Seven years had passed since I'd escaped. They would all pay for their sins. I'd make sure of it.

Downing another shot, I chased it with small sips of water, leaned my head back and sighed. I fought through the horrid images of my life to find one of my saving grace. The one of her.

"Sarah?" Jessie's rich voice held the rasp of sleep when she called out into the darkness and ripped me from my musings.

"Yeah," I answered low and soft, trying to keep the uninterested tone out of my response. "I'm here. Just gettin' a drink." I made my way back to bed and crawled under the covers.

She threw her arm over my stomach and moved in closer, letting the heat from her body warm my chilled skin. The companionship was comforting in many ways, but I wished it would still my mind. I wished it was Jo.

"Havin' trouble sleepin' again?" Half asleep and she was still concerned about me.

"I'm fine. Go back to sleep." I pulled her hand to my lips and placed a gentle kiss on her palm.

"Bullshit." She mumbled, pulling a soft laugh from me.

Even partially consciousness the woman sensed my lie. Jessie could read a person like nobody I'd ever met, but I sure hated when she used her talent on me. "Okay, yes," I whispered, admitting she knew me well. Still, she didn't know everything. "But havin' you here does help. Please go back to sleep."

In a matter of minutes she passed out again leaving me envious of her easy slumber. I brushed some hair from her face, using care not to wake her while I took in her sleep softened features at close range. In her smiling state it was hard to believe the woman was a warrior like me. We'd both seen death and caused death, but we were both in search of justice and the greater good. Two sides of the same coin, Jessie and I, only she had made her peace and I had yet to forgive.

I wanted to sleep, even bargained with deities for the damned necessity of life, but only one could settle my turmoil enough for more than a few hours of rest.

Guilt ripped through me. I was a horrible person for thinking of another woman while I laid naked with Jessie as she held me tight against her naked body. I tried to fight it, but the relentless beauty penetrated the walls of my psyche I'd painstakingly built to keep her out.

So I finally stopped fighting. They were just dreams anyway. Sometimes I found myself imagining her during a long day in the saddle. She'd find her way to me when the deliriousness of a monotonous, dehydrating ride set in. Her smile. The way her eyes bright eyes sparkled when she looked at me. The way my body came alive with the slightest touch. All of it was a figment of my imagination, but I enjoyed it none the less.

Dreams served as my only defense to keep the darkness in check. Dreams were the place where she could be mine. In reality though, a woman like her would never care for me. She was warm, loving and hopeful. I was detached and cold, a monster, a killer. I wandered this earth with one sole purpose consuming my mind, my soul.

Vengeance.

What would I do when my task was complete? When Danny O'Shea was dead this life I'd become accustomed to would end and I knew nothing else. What could I offer anyone?

I sighed hard and squeezed Jessie in tighter. My eyelids slammed shut with force in hopes sleep would take mercy on me.

Hope never served me well.

***

### Ketchum, Idaho- Jo Porter

"Hey! Hey! Nick, you either take the card you slipped up your sleeve out and play your true hand or leave right now."

Jade's usual smoky voice became firm and authoritative. She was half-Spanish and half-white, but all fire. When her anger rose up, the light hint of a Spanish accent she picked up from her mother became heavy.

The giant of a man brushed the shaggy black hair from his face and frowned as he groaned in protest.

She ran right at the man with raven hair flying and her intense green eyes piercing right through him. "Nope! No complaints. Everyone plays fair here or you leave and don't try to say you weren't cheatin', cause I saw ya with my own eyes. You can't pull one over on me Nick. Believe me, I know all the tricks. Estúpida."

"Fine," he spat and threw his cards on the table to reveal only a pair of threes.

The other gamblers laughed aloud and took his money.

Jade stood behind the towering man and rubbed his shoulders. Her small, slender frame appeared child-like even with him seated. Jade leaned over and said, "Just cause you're my gentleman suitor, doesn't mean I'm gonna let you cheat in this here establishment."

I took in the drama from my spot on the stairs. Jade had everything in hand, but I had to ask anyway. "Everything okay?"

"Sí. Don't even give it a second thought, right boys?"

All four men at the table nodded in agreement as she slapped Nick on the back and headed over to the bar. She hopped up on the end, grinned and yelled up to me, "Relax, I got it handled. Everything okay upstairs?'

I laughed. "Yeah, Lil' Jim got a little too frisky with Lanie. I put him in his place. We're all good now."

Jade glanced around the room. "Damn, must be a full moon or somethin'. Everyone's gone loco."

"Yeah." I shook my head and trailed my gaze from one smoke covered table of drunken cowboys to the next. They were rowdier than usual. "Well, let's hope we're done with all the crazy tonight."

I headed down stairs. It wouldn't be long until he arrived and at the creak of the swinging door, I knew exactly who I'd see standing there. He was right on time. I lined up a few shots of whiskey on the bar and took one myself.

*Here we go again.*

The tall, lanky sheriff strode with confidence into the saloon wearing a silver star on his dark brown double breasted vest and a six shooter on his hip ready for action. "Evenin' Jo. Someone mentioned a little disturbance here? You gals all right?"

"Yes, Carter, we're fine. You don't need to run over every time someone tries to cheat at cards." This had become a familiar scene and it was exhausting. I could defend myself, a lot better than he knew.

"Well, I am the sheriff, so I'm just doing my job," he said with a shy smile as he made his way toward me.

I smiled back. "Yes, I know and I appreciate that, but we're fine, really. Thank you. Since you're here, how 'bout a drink?"

He nodded, climbed up on the stool and removed his hat. That must have been the standard issue for lawmen, because everyone I'd ever met all wore the same square top, flat brimmed cowboy hat.

Despite being married, he had always held a soft spot for me and that carried over into this over protectiveness that annoyed the hell out of me. My interest in him was never more than friendly, but still, it was hard to ignore his good looks. The Sheriff was ruggedly handsome with a thick, chestnut handlebar mustache and smoky blue eyes that tracked my every move behind the bar.

Carter finally peeled his gaze from me and glanced around the room.

My place was your typical western saloon with dirt on the floor, a piano player, some pretty girls serving the patrons and swinging wooden doors. The difference was me. Out here it was rare for women to own a business, but I stood my ground and became a well-respected member of the town. Carter insisted on putting his two cents in whenever someone objected to my ownership and even though I didn't need his help, his support was appreciated.

He unbuttoned his vest, relaxing a little more since the saloon had calmed down. Seemed none of the boys wanted to go to jail tonight. Carter offered Jade a gracious smile and a nod as she approached. "Ma'am."

"Don't ma'am me, Carter," she said with a near perfect southern drawl as she smiled graciously. "I'm too young and pretty."

My best friend turned on the charm and the accent whenever the need suited her.

He laughed, deep and honest. His eyes sparkled in delight. "Indeed, how rude of me, mi' lady."

"That's better." Jade gave him a peck on either side of his cheeks. "How's Maggie and the kids?"

"They're good, thanks. You should come and eat supper with us one evening, the both of you." Carter turned to me. "I know they'd like to see you more often."

I looked away and fiddled with the glasses. "I know, it's just...I've been busy. Sorry."

He knew better and tried to ease the tension. "No, it's all right. I get it."

To be honest, I'd been avoiding him as much as possible. Things had been awkward since the day he tried to kiss me. When I turned him down, he apologized profusely. Even if he hadn't had a family, I just didn't share a connection with him and I wasn't one to sleep around. The Sheriff had been nothing but good to me and sometimes I felt a little guilty around Maggie, thinking maybe I'd led him on. Try as we might to move on, there had always remained an uneasiness that left us questioning how to act with one another.

Jade took the uneasy silence as her cue to leave, slipping out without a whisper while I glared at her.

"No, it's not like that Carter." I struggled for an excuse. "I'll make some time soon, okay?"

He nodded, but knew I wouldn't. "Bobby Ray's back in town," Carter said as he focused on the whiskey glass between his hands. "He's gonna be takin' over his daddy's farm. Maybe you two would hit it off?"

I slammed my hand down on the bar in frustration making him flinch. "I'm not interested, Carter. Don't do that!"

"Why?" His eyes darted up to mine. "Is there someone else? Why haven't I met 'em?"

I paused as thoughts of the mysterious blonde gunslinger flooded my memory. A small smile crept up. Though it only lasted a second, the observant lawman's eyes flashed when he caught the change. I pushed on, determined to make my point despite my slip. "No, no one else. I told you. I don't need anyone else to be happy Carter, okay? I'm happy with me and my saloon. I don't need nothin' else."

"Um, yeah, sure. Whatever you say Jo. As long as you're happy," he said. His shoulders slumped in defeat as he put his hat back on and headed toward the door.

"Oh Carter?"

"Yes Jo," he turned and replied with a softness to his voice that matched the sadness in his eyes.

"Um, any new developments?"

"One of these days you're gonna to tell me why you ask the same question every day." He forced a polite smile. "I heard some of the former O'Shea gang got killed to the east, but otherwise, nothing new."

My ears pricked up at the familiar name. "Oh yeah? Any idea who?"

"Nope, but they're doin' us all a favor and signin' their own death warrant in the process. Goodnight Jo."

***

## Red Lodge- Sarah

*Dammit Sarah, you should have eaten last night.*

A bottle of whiskey on an empty stomach wasn't pleasant and the effects were ever present as I struggled to wake. I needed food and soon. Thanks to the numbing alcohol though, I did manage get some solid shut eye. So much so that I didn't even hear Jessie leave this morning. I sat up in bed, trying to get my bearings, pulling the blanket up over my chest. The chill I usually embraced hurt a good bit in my current state.

Footsteps stopped outside. My eyes darted to the door. Reaching for my guns, I cursed under my breath at having left them lying across the room. My trusted companions fell victim to my drunken lust-filled haze of getting Jessie's skin against mine.

I should've been smarter. One mistake, even a rare one, could cost me my life. My heart hammered in my ears, making my head ache as I sat naked and paralyzed in bed.

When the Marshal poked her head into the room, my pulse settled and I let out a relieved breath. Light, awkward laughter replaced the fear holding me seconds ago. The sight was almost comical in the way she struggled to hold the tray of food and get in the door. I hopped up to help, ignoring my nakedness as the blanket fell to the floor.

She laughed at me as I carried the tray to the table. "Well, that's one way to say thank you."

I rolled my eyes. The heat her gaze stirred in me made its way up my neck as I grabbed my clothes. The way she scoured my half naked form and threatened to reignite my desire. Sex with Jessie was never dull. For the briefest of moments I actually considered revisiting the previous night's activities, but my body had other ideas. The growling of my stomach and the bit of nausea from the late night liquor said food was a priority.

"Thank you for gettin' this. I'm starvin' and I've been lookin' forward to a real meal." I motioned for her to sit.

She took a plate and dug in. We sat in comfortable silence as we devoured our food. You never realized how much you missed a home cooked meal until it was gone. Grits and the small items I carried to eat on the trail got old in a hurry, but they kept me alive.

Jessie finished in seconds and leaned back, watching as I savored every bite. "Maybe you should cut back on the long trips, Doc." She grinned wide at the narrowed eyes I shot her before continuing, "So, I hear O'Shea is adding to his territories. He's settin' up in Spokane and leavin' his number one guy in charge back in Texas."

"Hmm, I can get to Spokane before winter sets in. I got a lead on a few of the gang in these parts. Does it sound like he'll be there a while?"

"Sounds like he'll be there permanently." She shrugged. "Sarah, there is no 'I,' only 'we.' I am goin' with you, no matter how much you protest. You're gonna need help."

I dropped my fork and glared at her. "Dammit Jesse. No." The firmness in my words left no question.

"We have our plan to meet Jake. You agreed and besides, you're not the only one who wants him dead." Her lip curled up in that damned smug grin of hers.

I did agree. That was the smart thing to do, to have a plan that accounted for everything, just like Henry had taught me. Yet I still kept fighting her. I didn't want anyone else's blood to be shed. Yeah, he'd ruined many people's lives. So many could stake their claim to wanting him dead, including Jesse. Well, get in line. Either I would get to even the score or he would put the last of the Sawyer family to rest. That was the way it should be.

"This is my fight and I don't want anyone else gettin' hurt."

"For a moment it almost sounded like you cared." She studied my expression, but I didn't show my hand.

I met her gaze with defiance. "What I care about is good people bein' safe and bad ones gettin' what they deserve."

Her eyes softened. "So that's it, huh? Sarah Sawyer's just gonna roam the west alone for the rest of her life?" The hurt in her voice shone through. She put on a poker face of her own.

We were two fighters in an emotional sparring match that neither of us were trained to fight. I took a deep breath. We needed this conversation. We'd been avoiding it for too long. Communication wasn't my strong point, or hers for that matter. So similar, the two of us, our physical selves were easy to give, but emotions always proved a different story. Problem was, she seemed ready to take the next step. Me on the other hand...

"Jessie, we've been through this. You've been a great friend to me, but friendship is all I'm capable of. I don't know if I'll ever want anyone. Openin' myself up only invites pain."

She shook her head. "Damn shame you feel that way, Sarah. You'd have a lot to offer someone if you ever did let go."

"Jessie." I stared her dead in the eye. "You're my best friend. We've occasionally enjoyed one another's company in other ways and I never shoulda let that happen. Our relationship's always been based on respect and a common goal and I let those lines get blurred." I was blunt and to the point. My words cut her, but they weren't meant to be malicious. A line needed to be drawn even though the damage had already been done.

Her gaze drifted to the window as she cleared her throat. "Well Doc, one day it's gonna sneak up on you like a rattlesnake in the forest. I wish we could be more. You know that and you know that I care for you, but also know that whether you like it or not, you got me and I'm goin' along with you according to plan. It's the right thing to do." She met my eyes once again, cool and collected as always even through the sadness. "And I'm riding with you till we reach the road to Billings."

I knew she was right, but I kept holding out hope that I could leave her behind and confront O'Shea myself. Today wasn't that day. Damn Jessie and her determination. "Fine," I huffed and brushed past her, focused on the task at hand. There were more men that needed to face judgment before I got to O'Shea. "But you better not slow me down and I don't wanna hear any objections to whatever my plan is along the way. Oh, and any bounties we get are an eighty-twenty split to me."

Jessie slapped her hands together with enthusiasm. She knew what I was doing and accepted we were done with our little talk. "All right then, when do we leave?"

"In an hour. There's a few things I gotta do first." I threw on my clothes and walked to the general store for supplies. Along the way I managed to garner plenty of looks from passersby who either recognized me or feared a stranger with pistols. Intimidating them was fun. I'd glare at them from under my hat, causing women to protect their children and men to avert their eyes.

Fear was a powerful emotion and it was easy to understand how people used it as a tool. I took pleasure in the solitude it afforded me and freely admitted to feeding off it on occasion. You know, you kill a few folks, one thing leads to another and all of a sudden you're one of those mythical stories everyone tells. "A killer of many" they say, though it's only three, plus a few beatings. They made it sound like I'd toppled empires. Little did they know my true goal, I'd slay a self-proclaimed king if it was the last thing I did.

Now and again I caught an envious glance from a woman or child. They wanted to run over and shake my hand, but feared what others would think. On some rare occasion, I'd give them a knowing nod and enjoy the thrill of them trying to hide a smile. Ah, the power of being a legend in the west.

I laughed to myself, the snicker drawing concerned expressions from those nearby as they scurried away from the crazy lady with the guns.

As I entered the store and made my way toward the back, a conversation peaked my curiosity. Two men were talking about Murph, the next name on my list. Hiding behind a pile of clothes, I took note of all the details; who, what, where, how many. Best of all, Murph was coming to town tonight. Guess we wouldn't need to go far to get this one. We'd ride out and kill him in the valley where there'd be no witnesses and no innocent townspeople hurt.

I collected my supplies and waited until they left before I stepped up to pay. Out of the corner of my eye, brand new light brown boots caught my attention. I glanced down at my own worn ones that were starting to hurt my feet. I snatched new pair off of the shelf and tried them on. When I stood up I sighed, relishing the comfort they offered. I truly couldn't recall the last time I'd gotten myself something new and a rare smile crept up my face.

As I paid the man, a familiar sarcastic voice remarked from behind, "Ah, no girl can resist a shiny, new pair of boots."

My smile faded before I turned around with nothing but killing on my mind. I set my old boots out the door for anyone in need then grabbed my bags and walked past Jessie with cool indifference.

"Change of plans. Murph's coming to us."

# **Chapter Three**

Jessie followed me to the stables in silence. I was all business. My senses were tuned into the task at hand.

Murph was one of the O'Shea gang that fateful day. He laughed at us while me and my parents begged for mercy and struggled to be free. The son of a bitch took the liberty of slapping me and my mother around while Danny O'Shea tortured my father.

The rage inside of me grew the longer I thought about him. An ache in my jaw settled in as I clenched so hard I thought my teeth would crack under the strain. Murph would die today, of that I was sure. Someday soon, the evil old bastard Danny O'Shea would too.

The Marshal remained quiet. She had been privy to my mood changes before and knew better than to interrupt as I constructed a plan in my head. At least three men would be accompanying him, so we'd need to be swift to avoid getting killed ourselves. There would be plenty of cover to the west near the mountains, the perfect place to take Murph down.

We saddled the horses side by side. Jessie shot me a look, but I said nothing. I stroked Clover's neck, gave the Marshal a nod and then pulled myself up into the saddle. A moment later she did the same and we cantered off toward our next mark.

An hour or so later, we agreed on an area between two small hills where the trail to town passed through. The scattered boulders would provide cover and enable us to set up the ambush from both sides. I dissected all possible options. An old friend taught me well. Preparing for the worst kept you from being surprised. Always a sound battle strategy.

Minutes went by and they turned into hours. My mind began to drift to days gone by and the possibilities of ones yet to come. What would I have done if my life hadn't turned out this way? Would I have followed my father's footsteps and become a doctor or a school teacher like my mother? Would I have stayed in small town Texas or moved to a big city? Would I have turned to gun slinging anyway, doing it for the excitement and glory and not because someone had destroyed my life?

I chuckled a little at the absurdity. There I went, self-analyzing again. The proper, parent pleasing little book worm I used to be would never have done this. My parents taught me to cherish life, to protect it as much as possible. Now I lived hell bent on ending life, at least for a special few. I didn't wish harm on good people. No. I wasn't raised that way. Every once in a while I had to teach someone a lesson in manners, but otherwise, I only punished the deserving ones.

The rest of the time I was content to keep to myself with one good horse and one good friend. Everyone else I ever cared about was gone. Jessie was the closest I'd let anyone get to me and sometimes I even pushed her away. Letting people in only invited the chance for more pain.

Well, I liked to believe no one else had gotten closer. My short time with the breathtaking woman still lived in my mind, hitting me in a way I couldn't explain. I didn't think I could let her into my heart. Not the way she deserved anyway. Could I be everything she needed? Could she make me whole again?

Hell, I didn't even like to say her name, because that would let her sink further into my mind and heart. It was safer to refer to her as the beautiful, dark haired woman I'd slept with and let her continue to wander my dreams. That was all she would ever be anyway.

The weight of the many reasons I became this shell of a woman grew heavier. The losses didn't even truly hurt anymore, there was only a constant numbness accompanied by anger. People liked to say that all things happened for a reason, but what good came from such tragedy? I had trouble talking to God with the intense resentment I clung to over the supposed "reasons" behind murdering two good people and the untimely deaths of others close to me. I highly doubted turning me into a bitter, vengeful, killing machine was meant to be the heart of the lesson.

I blew out a hard breath and closed my eyes, attempting to refocus my mind until I picked up the faint rumble of hooves approaching. Jessie sat across the way flashing a thumbs up. Show time.

The three riders approached, oblivious to the fate about to befall them. I wanted to be sure it was Murph before I attacked, but they were still too far out, so we played the waiting game. I kept sharp focus on the potential targets as they slowed to a trot through the rocky trail. One by one I scanned them for a definitive identification. I spotted his hat. The trinket was unmistakable. The man was a sadist. He bragged of his many victims, keeping a trophy of each one with him in the form of braided hair adorning the rim of his dirty, old tan gaucho hat.

Jessie would let me take the first shot. I set my Winchester, steadied my breathing, aimed and fired.

My bullet hit dead on, passing through his non-shooting shoulder and knocking him clean off his horse. Jessie followed suit, taking the other two down before they could respond. Dropping the rifle, I hopped over the rock and sprinted down the side of the hill. I didn't kill him. I didn't want to, yet. First, I wanted to look him in the eye so he'd know good and well who I was and why he was about to die.

Murph was still getting to his feet as I reached the bottom. I smirked and stopped thirty feet away from the hefty, older man, staring him down. "Hello Murph. It's been a long time."

He raised a hand to block the sun, trying to figure me out. "Who are ya," he asked with a growl and a wince from the pain of my bullet. "Am I 'sposed to know ya?"

Maintaining calm, I kept an even tone as I fell into the controlled persona I'd come to find comfort in. The one that got me one step closer to avenging my family. My eyes locked on him as my hand readied for action. "Oh, I think you'll remember me as the little girl you abused after murdering my parents. You remember Doctor Sawyer?"

He cackled. The obnoxious sound rung loud and rubbed me the wrong way.

Did Murph think me a joke? Just some weak woman? He was in for a surprise. My concern for him as a living, breathing being dwindled more by the second. That little girl was dead and gone. What remained was the cold hearted bitch he helped create. One who planned to spit on his lifeless carcass after I killed him.

"Aw, come on now sweetheart, that was a long time ago. So now what? Ya got yourself a little gun and ya want some revenge?" Murph scoffed.

Jessie circled off to the side. I shook my head, stopping her in her tracks.

"Ain't no woman gonna kill me." He let out another laugh, growing cockier with every passing moment. "You shoulda been a better shot girl cause now ya gonna die!" He set himself upright, assuming the position as he tried to stare me down.

I didn't flinch. His words grated my nerves, but I'd wait for him to go for his gun first. My lip curled into a sneer, enjoying this way too much for a life or death situation. The beat of my heart slowed. I held no fear, only a confidence that I'd be the one to prevail. My gaze narrowed in on him with intense focus as I took in every tiny detail of movement. The rise and fall of his chest. The beads of sweat as they formed on his forehead.

One eye twitched. He went for his gun.

I drew faster, cutting him down in an instant without an ounce of mercy. He didn't even get the gun out of the holster. My hand was steady and my aim true. One shot through the heart got it done far swifter than he deserved.

Jessie trotted up to me. "Whoa, Doc! Nice shootin'. Feel better now?" She grinned wide at me, but I was in no mood.

I walked over to the body lying face down in the grass, leaned down and double checked the pulse in his neck. Nothing. My work was done. Without another thought I stood up and stretched. I wasn't at all bothered about taking his life. Instead, I delighted in a small sense of pride at my handiwork. A death delivered clean and painless was a beautiful thing, though it was far too good for him; far too good for any of them. I'd love nothing more than to punish them more severely, but then I'd be as bad as them. Looking each one in the eye as I took their lives was satisfying enough for me. With one more scratched off my list, I relaxed for a moment before nodding to the other two bodies.

"Oh, they're dead too," she said in a matter of fact tone. Jessie didn't regret killing them one bit either. "I don't think they're on the wanted list, but we can drag him back and collect." She smiled and kicked Murph's body.

Sounded as good as any other plan. I whistled for Clover. Murph's body was headed to town on the back of my horse. Then it was on to the next one.

Two hours later we arrived at the sheriff station in search of our reward. The Marshal tied up the other two kills with a cute little story about an ambush and barely escaping with our lives. How convenient to have the law working with you. Sure was a good thing I saved her skin from that outlaw all those years ago. I guess you'd say it was a bonding moment.

We walked into the street and I leaned against the hitching post.

Jessie looked over at me. A grin pulled at the corner of her lips. She slapped my eighty percent into my hand and gave me a wink. "I think this calls for a drink, Doc."

I smiled and nodded. We went directly to the saloon and took a seat at the bar. A beer sure tasted good after a victory. I was never sure if I should be enjoying it after killing a man in cold blood, but I damn sure did anyway. Like clockwork, it didn't take long for my thoughts to drift back to the one person who'd been consuming my mind the last few weeks. I came to a sudden conclusion. I needed to see the gorgeous saloon owner one more time before taking on O'Shea. "I think I'm gonna head up to Ketchum before Spokane." A slight smile tugged at the corners of my mouth. My mood lifted at the thought of seeing her soon.

Jessie's brow creased. Confusion etched itself all over her face. She knew how I worked.

I'd been hell bent on finishing this as fast as possible. Even through my protests, I'd always stuck to whatever plans were set, but now with the end in sight, I was choosing to take a detour. She'd be suspicious.

"What's up there?"

I wouldn't tell her. I merely shrugged with indifference. "Nothin' really. I love those gray, jagged mountains. Another mark on my list was last seen along the way. Maybe he's still there." I took a deep breath and sipped my beer. I hated lying to my friend, but it wasn't a conversation I cared to get into, especially with our interesting relationship. Besides, it was only a pit stop along the way to my eventual destination.

She chuckled a bit, wiping the froth from her lip with the back of her hand. "I didn't take you for the sight-seein' type."

"Well, life is short. I try to take the time to enjoy the little things." At least I wanted to start taking the time.

"Hmm, okay, I can appreciate the sentiment." She took another sip of her beer, but her eyes stayed locked on me.

I read her tone. She was skeptical. "What?" I didn't mean to come off harsh, but I did. My smile fell to a frown at having to explain my decision.

She looked around the room then spun to face me full on.

I did the same, meeting her questioning gaze.

"Oh nothin'. Just seems like there's somethin' else on your mind is all."

Damn her and her abilities. I couldn't buckle now, so I gritted my jaw and feigned ignorance. "Like what?"

She didn't like my response. Her eyes narrowed. Those soft grays transformed into the deadly stare I knew too well. "I don't know. You tell me Sarah. We're friends, right?"

"Yes, I consider you a friend Jessie." I lifted my beer to my lips and took a big gulp, wanting nothing more than to avoid talking. Her eyes bored right through me, but I refused to falter. The "something" on my mind was nothing new, but it was becoming more and more consuming as I got closer and closer to Ketchum. Part of me wanted to test out what could be, but the realist in me knew that whatever I was hoping for would never come to be. The infatuation was one sided. Of that I was sure.

"Like I said, nothin'. When this is all over I'll have to find something new to obsess over." Like a stunning saloon owner who managed to permeate the crevices of my mind. The thought of Jo brought a smile to my lips.

Jessie picked up on the grin before I could reel myself back and shook her head. She was hurt. I would be too. A twinge of guilt swept over me, but this was just one more thing I'd keep to myself.

"And this somethin' else is in Ketchum?"

I shrugged. "Who knows, but there's a little place I kinda like near the mountains. Just somethin' to consider."

"Fine, Sarah. I know you have your secrets, hell we all do, but I can tell this is different. Whatever it is, I hope it's good for you." She spoke the truth. The sincerity flashed plain as day in her eyes.

We waved the barkeep for a refill. As soon as the glasses were topped off, we toasted our new round of drinks.

"I'm gonna head up to Billings for a few days. I got some business to take care of, but despite your protests, I am goin' to Spokane with you." She raised her hand to silence me as I began to argue. "I'll meet up with you in Ketchum in say, mid-September and we'll go accordin' to plan. I trust you'll be waitin' for me, friend."

I sighed and agreed. She refused to let me take him on alone. The woman was relentless. It was one of the reasons she was so good at her job. I was reluctant, but agreed. There was no doubt I'd need a little help to get through the gang to reach O'Shea. Bad guys never fought fair.

A few drinks later, I called it a night. Jessie stayed behind saying she wanted to enjoy her drink a bit longer. I headed to the stables to check on Clover. My girl would be mad if I didn't leave her plenty of food tonight. Once she was satisfied, I grabbed my gear and made a beeline back up town to my room. One more night in a soft bed before hitting the road again sounded perfect.

On my way past the saloon, I spotted Jessie through the window. She was in a heated conversation with an unsavory looking fellow. Actually, the closer I got the more the guy seemed familiar to me. Angling to get a better look, I recognized him as one of O'Shea's gang I'd scouted back in Texas. They simmered down and she pulled him into a tight embrace that set my blood to boil.

A sudden stab through my heart and a deep overwhelming sense of betrayal rocked me to my core. I stormed past the entrance on the way to my room, making no effort to avoid being seen.

Jessie ran out after me. "Sarah, wait! It's not what you think."

She pleaded for me to listen, but I couldn't think straight. My mind raced with possibilities. Every muscle tensed as the anger spilled over at having trusted her. She was the last person I would've ever suspected to turn on me. Had she been lying all this time? Was she helping me get to Spokane only to lead me to my death? O'Shea had his hand in everything. Did he have her too?

"Jessie, all I know is I trusted you and now you're rubbin' elbows with the enemy. There's not much left for me to know about where your loyalties lie." It took all I had to hide the hurt in my voice. I refused to crumble in her presence, turning away as my eyes began to well up. I balled my fists to fight my emotions, rushing to my room before I lost it in front of her.

Her pleas to stop fell on deaf ears. I couldn't imagine any good excuse for what I saw that didn't include me getting double crossed. At the crack of dawn I'd get out of this town and far away from her. The only person I could trust was me. I would take on O'Shea alone, just like I wanted.

# <u>Chapter Four</u>

**Spokane, Washington- O'Shea Ranch**

"Excuse me, Mr. O'Shea, sir?" The timid young man used caution as he stuck his head into the room.

A short, stocky older man lay back in a wooden barber's chair. Foam coated his neck below his neatly kept beard. A blade was angled against the old man's throat, a second away from dragging the sharp edge up his skin with the grain of his whiskers.

He wasn't supposed to disturb the boss during his afternoon shave, but the news seemed important. He weighed his options of punishment for not telling him right away versus disturbing him now. Neither was a more pleasing option, so he opted for sooner rather than later.

The barber's face dropped. His hand froze in place as the old man frowned.

Without so much as a glance at the messenger, O'Shea spoke. "I'm sure you know I'm not to be disturbed during my shave, so why on earth would you do such a thing?"

The deep, authoritative voice dripped with contempt, the powerful aura made him cower. He pinned his eyes to the floor and shifted his weight as he replied, "I'm sorry sir. I know. Um, we got news of several men once associated with you bein' killed the last few months between Kansas and Montana. I thought you should know."

O'Shea motioned to the barber who pulled his seat upright. He turned and considered the sandy haired boy. With brows knitted in anger, his dark eyes burned holes through him. "I don't pay you to think, son. What's your name?"

"Um...Mi...Mike, sir," he stuttered, keeping his eyes anywhere but on the wicked glare bearing down upon him.

Danny O'Shea smirked, clearly enjoying the power he held as Mike shriveled in fear. "All right Mike. Since you've already interrupted my personal time, any word on who did the killin'?"

"N...no sir, but some bounties were collected. A guy named Murph was found about a week ago."

O'Shea let out a hearty laugh, shifting from intimidating to joyous in the blink of an eye. "Old Murph! He was always trouble. Hell, his own mother probably put a mark on his head. It's somethin' worth paying attention to though. Last few years we lost a few in Texas and Oklahoma that were still with me. Some lady killed both of 'em, but I figured it was a lover spat since those two were always the cheatin' kind. Keep an ear out son and let me know if you hear of anythin' else."

Mike perked up a little a having been given a task by the boss himself. "Yes sir. I will." He turned to leave, letting out a breath of relief, but before he got away, O'Shea called him back.

"Mike?" The old man lay back in his chair again.

Deflated, the young man turned back around. His voice and posture echoed his feeling of dread. "Yes, sir?"

"For interruptin' me, as you were specifically instructed never to do, tell Brandt to just smack you around a little. Nothin' too severe like broken bones, all right? I gotta keep a tight ship and anything less than an attack on the farm does not warrant disturbin' me, you understand?"

Mike nodded.

"Good. Now consider this your one warnin'. I think you're gettin' off easy, but at least the news was interestin'. Now get your ass outta here."

Well, it could have been worse Mike thought. "Yes, sir. Thank you sir," he said as he took his leave.

***

## Challis, Idaho-Sarah

I took my time stopping in various towns such as Bozeman and Dillon on my way to her. After two weeks, I was beginning to lose hope of finding Earl until I stumbled upon him outside the Challis general store. I leaned back against the wall of the saloon directly across from him. From under the brim of my hat, I kept watch as old Earl packed up his saddle bags. He seemed to be alone, making this one easier than the rest. My plan was the same as always, follow him away from town and take him down.

He took his time conducting business. Patience was a virtue when it came to killing. There was nowhere else I had to be anyhow.

As I stood there, several men passed by throwing me awkward glances. A couple of women actually gave me a wink. I tipped my hat and hid my grin. For most, a woman in britches was a rare sight to behold, but a woman with a side arm? We were almost non-existent. Always seemed funny to me the way my guns intimidated a lot of men, but attracted the ladies. I guess they liked bad girls.

Earl finally exited the store and mounted his horse. He headed out of town in no particular hurry. I gave him a head start before climbing into the saddle and trailing him.

A few hours later I pulled ahead of Earl. A wide berth allowed me to circle around without being noticed. I scouted a wooded area fit for a take down and stashed Clover a safe distance out of sight and out of the line of fire.

"Relax here a bit girl. I'll be back soon." I pet her on the neck and pulled my rifle from the pack.

My usual plan of attack would work fine. Get the jump, knock him down and close the deal face to face. After finding the perfect cover, I waited for the right moment to clip him.

Earl rode in, oblivious to my ambush. Most men like him traveled in groups. With all of their indiscretions, they expected people to be gunning for them sooner or later. He seemed unfazed by the idea of anyone daring to challenge him. Was that a sign of arrogance or ignorance? Only time would tell.

Smooth and slow I squeezed the trigger. The moment the bullet left, I dropped the rifle and started running toward him.

Earl was a big man, slow to get up, but he saw me coming. He tracked my movements as he struggled to his feet. He leaned on his knees until I was standing before him. A flash of metal shone in his hand right before he came up throwing.

In my haste, I got sloppy. I missed the part where he reached for the knife in his boot, but somehow I managed to avoid being hit. The dangerous blade flew past far too close for comfort and the momentary lapse left me vulnerable. My heart raced. Adrenaline pumped through my veins.

BANG!

The rush of it all dulled the burn in my side. I glanced at my stomach, thankful he was a bad shot. With lightning quick speed, I drew my own pistol. All three bullets hit him dead in the chest.

Earl fell to his knees and dropped on his side in the grass. With my focus on the blade hurling toward me, I'd missed him pulling his gun until it was too late and it nearly cost me. Now that the threat of life or death had been decided in my favor, I took a better look at my wound. The bullet went clean through. Thank goodness I wouldn't need to worry about removal. Blood oozed out from the hole in my flank. I was fortunate he missed all vital parts.

A short whistle brought Clover trotting over. Slow steps carried me to Earl's body where I reached down with caution and checked for a pulse. As usual, he was dead. Unlike my other kills,

I didn't get to identify myself as his messenger of death. It disappointed me. That was the one downside to being the best gun in the west.

I pulled the extra bullets from his holster and kicked his lifeless body. "That's for yankin' me out from under the house. Rot in Hell, Earl."

The excitement of the showdown wore off fast. My brain and body began to register the gunshot wound. The throbbing pain in my side offered a not-so-subtle reminder of my failure to account for all the possibilities during my attack. I was damn lucky to survive. I couldn't afford to slip again.

My shirt soaked through with my own blood as the sticky liquid spread across the soft cotton threads. The shock dropped me to a knee as the stress of almost being killed flooded my system. I'd never been shot before. Beaten, whipped, stabbed and emotionally broken sure, but not shot. It hurt like a bitch.

Clover gave me a nudge, urging me to hurry as I reached into my saddle bag for the medical kit. I'd learned many useful things helping my father and keeping a small kit handy was one of them. Unfortunately, I'd slipped up on refills. There was nothing left to use as a sterilizer, but at least my supplies allowed me to stitch the hole and stop the bleeding. Ketchum wasn't too far away. I could deal with it later.

For now, I'd ride on until nightfall and camp near the river where I could clean up and burn my ruined button down. The smell of blood on you in the wild was never a good idea. Damn, I was gonna miss that shirt.

***

**Ketchum, Idaho- Sarah**

I was glad to get to Ketchum by the first week of September. The winter weather would move in soon and if I wanted to get to Spokane, I needed to pick up my pace. The trip took longer than expected due to my stupid mistake. I passed out not long after setting up camp the night I got shot and slept the next day away. The pain weakened me and forced me to travel slower. The hole in my side wasn't looking too good either. I needed to clean the wound out before I left. But first, I had a stop to make.

Clover and I rode into the bustling town. People milled around from shop to shop. I was glad they paid me no mind. God only knew what I looked like, but I didn't have the energy to get fancied up for them.

We went right to the stables where I tied Clover up next to the trough before heading uptown. The only sounds were the clink of my spurs and scuff of my boots on the dirt as I stumbled onward. The effects of the blood loss and infection had taken hold and sapped my strength.

The lights of the saloon shone up ahead as I limped my way along the street. I wanted to get to her faster, run to her, but my body was shutting down. It was a miracle I'd made it this far. The smart thing would've been to seek out a doctor first, but sometimes I wasn't as smart as I'd like to believe. I came here for one thing, to see her and that's what I was gonna do before anything else.

Only a sliver of the sun remained above the horizon as darkness began its reign. I stopped outside the old saloon and peered through a dust covered window, scanning for the one woman who'd been a constant source of inspiration and pain. She was the sole reason I stopped in Ketchum even though it diverted my path to Spokane.

I wondered if the fact I'd deviated from plan meant something, like I was afraid of confronting the man who ruined my life or that I wasn't ready for this life as I knew it to end. Deep down though, I felt like I was being called here. Something kept steering me back and I couldn't comprehend the reason. All I knew was my subconscious beckoned for me to return, so here I stood in hopes of catching a glimpse of her.

My intention was to take a long, hard look and then go back about my business, but I couldn't tear myself away. There was no chance of leaving once the magnificent, dark haired beauty lifted her head and flashed the gorgeous smile that was forever burned in my brain. I had to go inside.

My feet refused to move as my body ignored the will of my heart, so I stood a moment longer, taking in every detail of the woman previously living only in my dreams. Porcelain skin, a doll face and shapely lips. She was exactly as I remembered, the most breathtaking woman I'd ever seen with a smile brighter than the sun on a midsummer day.

In secret, I hoped that if I ever came back to her, she wouldn't be with anyone else. It was unfair of me to wish her unhappiness or an unfulfilled life given my own story, but when the idea did cross my mind, it accompanied a twinge of jealousy. I had no right, no claim. We rarely even spoke during my visits. We just took care of our needs physically in a way I'd never experienced with anyone else. I clenched my hands tight and mustered the strength to go inside.

As if she possessed a sixth sense, she stiffened and looked around the room.

With a quick move, I ducked aside, groaning from the flash of pain. The discomfort was short lived though, as I thought about what just happened. Did she know I was near?

My heart pounded like a quarter horse at full gallop. I closed my eyes and breathed in deep. Any attempt to straighten up failed miserably as I doubled over from the excruciating pain in my side. With each passing moment I grew weaker. I sucked in a ragged breath to dull the pain and peered inside again.

Her back faced the entrance as she busied herself with drying and stacking glasses. Thankfully, there were few patrons to derail my focus.

I dragged myself around front, through the swinging doors and straight toward her, stopping a few feet from the bar. I stared, almost awe struck from being this close again.

Her body tensed. The air in her lungs hitched. She dried her hands and pushed her hair back behind her ears in a nervous motion. "Sarah." Her voice hung in the air, barely audible, but clear enough.

The perfectly timed beat of my heart jumped erratically when she breathed my name.

She turned to face me. The sight froze me right where I stood. Nearly nine months had passed since last we met and seeing her up close again took my breath away. Something in her soft, adoring eyes twinkled in a way I couldn't place. The energy between us surged, sweeping over my body like a wave.

Did I haunt her dreams the way she did mine? Could it even be possible?

"Hello, Jo," I croaked out with my voice weak, but my expectations hopeful. Every ounce of strength I had was needed to steady myself as I stood before her and awaited the verdict. How would my reappearance would be received? Would she be happy to see me? Would she be angry? Her pause was agonizing.

Jo's look of utter surprise shifted. Those full lips pulled up into an endearing smile melting my insides as her cheeks dimpled just for me. Stunning was the only word to describe her in dark trousers that flaunted her curves, black boots and a red button down adorned with white pearl snaps. She wore her hair back in a loose ponytail exposing her slender neck. A few trundles of dark hair surrounded her shoulders.

I remembered our last meeting. Oh how I loved to kiss my way down that neck line and all along the silky skin of her collarbone.

"Hey." She never lost the smile I adored so much. "I was beginnin' to wonder if you'd ever come back here." Her eyes sparkled. She waved me over to a seat, but once again my feet defied me.

My brain was still mesmerized by the exceptional beauty of the woman whose eyes refused to leave mine. Maybe she worried I'd disappear the moment she reached for the whiskey. Given my history, it was a valid concern.

She raised her brow, questioning the awkward silence and why I was still standing there staring instead of accepting her invitation.

In truth, I didn't know why. After a few months, Jo seemed like some grand idea rather than a reality. I still didn't understand why I'd been so compelled to come back here, but here I was none the less.

She grinned a little, no doubt reading my apprehension. She almost seemed to enjoy my discomfort. "Come on, Sarah. Take a load off. I'm sure you're tired."

I let out a deep breath and wobbled. The room spun as I turned woozy. The combination of the infection, the long trip and the overwhelming feelings from seeing her again were too much and I stumbled on my way to the stool.

"Whoa, whoa." She bounded over the bar and raced to my side, catching me with her strong arms before I hit the floor. Her eyes blazed full of concern as she helped me sit. "Are you okay?" She checked me over, looking for signs of injury.

"Um..." My head kept spinning. I couldn't think with her hands all over me. I wanted to hold her, kiss her, but my body had reached its limit. Sweat formed on my skin. My heart skipped a beat. Was it the effect Jo had on me or the stress of my wound? I resisted the urge to pass out, if only for a moment. Maybe a drink would help.

Reaching for the shot glass with a shaky hand, I threw the drink back and pushed myself up straighter. In my stubbornness I managed to suppress a groan, but the piercing stab in my side forced my eyes shut for a second. I swallowed hard and took a shallow breath before speaking, "Nothin' but a little flesh wound. I'm okay. Maybe a little tired." A brave smile forced its way across my face as I held her worried eyes with my own weary ones.

Jo frowned as she stood back and crossed her arms like a disciplining mother. "Well, lookin' at you right now, I'd say it's a lot more than being tired. You're coming home with me. I'm gonna take care of you."

Whiskey on an empty stomach wasn't my best idea. Like I said, sometimes I wasn't as smart as I liked to believe. The room began shift like a boat in a heavy storm. "No. Give me a room here like before. I'll be fine, Jo. I don't need a keeper." I tried to argue, but my words fell on deaf ears.

Jo wasn't even listening to me anymore. She trotted over to the petite, Spanish girl who ran the place when she was gone.

Through blurred vision I barely made out the two of them looking at me and nodding. The girl punched her on the arm and smiled. Jo waved her off and shook her head.

What they were talking about? I only wondered for a second before my mind went blank again.

"Sarah, where's your horse?"

I didn't respond. I recognized her voice, but I was lost in a haze.

Jo grabbed my shoulders and shook me awake. "Sarah, stay with me." Her prodding grew more urgent. "Where's your horse?"

I pointed down the road.

"The stables," she mumbled. Jo eyed me up and down before motioning for her friend to come over.

The next thing I knew I was on Clover with no idea how I got there or who I was with. A warm body pressed against my back and a pair of arms straddled me as they held the reins.

"Hang on, we're almost there," she soothed.

It was Jo. Her soft voice in my ear brought a smile to my face. My eyelids grew heavy and fell shut once more.

When I opened my eyes again, she was pulling me from the saddle whispering, "Sarah, I need you to help me for a few minutes."

I mumbled something and tried to find my legs while Jo helped me up the steps. Even in my current state she affected me. Every touch left behind a trail of tiny tingles. I regained my strength long enough to get inside where my exhausted body hit the bed. Then there was darkness.

# **Chapter Five**

By the angle of the sun, it was late afternoon. The insistent rays made it impossible to shield my eyes from the glare of the blinding light as I struggled to regain my bearings. What day was it? Where was I?

I vaguely remembered seeing the woman who'd become something of an obsession, but was it only another dream? Actually, I didn't remember dreaming at all. Well, at least there were no nightmares. Guess I was in bad shape.

As my eyes grew accustomed to the brightness of the room, I glanced around and smiled at the quaintness. White cotton curtains adorned the windows. The wood of the floor and walls was newer which meant the house was probably built in the last year or two. A few small painted pictures of mountains and horses hung opposite my bed. There were fresh cut wildflowers on the table beside some gauze and medical supplies.

My hand ran across the top of the colorful homemade quilt in search of the edge. I pulled the cover back to find myself in clean sleep wear. Heat rose up my neck and cheeks. I was embarrassed and violated at having been undressed by a stranger. In a panic I yanked up my shirt, cringing as the stitches pulled against my skin. A new dressing with ointment surrounded the wound.

The need to know where I was drove me crazy. I shoved myself upright wanting to get out of bed, but my tired body had other ideas. My arms wobbled under my weight and the pain that accompanied moving was severe. I fell back and groaned. Damn that hurt.

The rattling door knob drew my attention. My gun was nowhere to be found. The only protection I could find were the scissors on the table. Before I could grab them, a woman entered the room and all thought faded. I couldn't believe my eyes. A dream no more, Jo stood before me smiling brightly with a tray of supplies accompanied by food and water.

"Hey Sarah, glad to see you're finally awake. You've been out a couple of days."

My mouth was dry as cotton and kept me from uttering a word. She waved me off and handed me the glass of water. I stared at her over the rim still muddled in disbelief while I took slow sips. The refreshing liquid soothed my parched throat, but nothing compared to the way the warm smile directed at me soothed my heart.

I handed the cup back and forced a weak smile. A twinge of regret passed through me. My imagination planned a different reunion in my head, but I guess my subconscious led me back to her for more than one reason. I would've been dead by now if I'd stayed out on the trail. If not from the infection, then I'd have been torn to shreds by coyotes after passing out.

She took the glass and brushed some hair back from my eyes. Her touch left a burning trail across my face as she continued to smile at me with a certain sparkle to her eyes.

Baffled. That's what the unexplained adoration did to me. Not knowing the meaning or the source made me uncomfortable. I hated not knowing things, but I knew I wasn't worthy of her affection.

Jo's hand pulled back, but I moved fast enough to catch it. Thank goodness for my quick reflexes. "Thank you Jo." My voice trembled, raspy and weak from days of silence. I almost didn't recognize it myself. With a gentle squeeze of her hand I relaxed back in the bed again, allowing her to slip free of my grasp. My strained muscles thanked me for their release.

The burning of her eyes on me still seared even after I closed my own. I wanted to pull her down on top of me, kiss her everywhere, but my damned body refused to cooperate, so I pushed down my desires for the time being. I prided myself on control and no one made me struggle with control the way Jo did.

After a moment to collect myself, I sighed and reopened my eyes. She was still in the same spot staring at me with a longing that made my insides ache. The lingering gaze did nothing to help curb the war between my raging libido and my weary body.

Jo's lips fidgeted and her brows narrowed in indecision, as if she had something to say. She bit her lip and then let out a hard breath, looking back at the tray. "I brought you some soup. You wanna try and eat a little?"

I nodded, studying her expression for any clues as to what she decided to keep to herself, but there were none.

Jo attempted to spoon feed me. I objected and took the bowl from her, having far too much pride for that kind of thing. The unsteadiness of my hands made it a challenge, but I refused to be treated like a child. My actions drew a little chuckle, to which I gave her a half grin in return.

"So stubborn." She shook her head. Jo lifted the corner of my shirt and pulled the bandage back. Her finger tips grazed my skin.

Did she do that on purpose? Was she trying to kill me? Her touch electrified me and it took everything to steady the hot bowl of soup in my hands.

She smiled at me with complete sincerity. "I'll be back shortly to change your bandage." She placed a soft kiss on my forehead and walked out the door.

In a matter of no time I finished the soup. I didn't realize how hungry I was until the first spoonful, but then again, I hadn't eaten real food in days.

Several minutes passed and Jo hadn't come back. Then, several strange voices filtered through the door. Curiosity got the best of me. I willed my aching body into action. Stifling a scream of pain, I swung my legs over the side, intent on listening in. Using the chair to stabilize myself, it took more than a few tries before my legs bore my weight safely enough to shuffle toward the door. Stealth was difficult in my current state.

I reached the wall and winced, leaning against it for support as my angry body protested my actions. With my ear pressed against the gap of the door, I strained to comprehend their words. There was Jo, another woman, maybe the girl from the saloon and a man. Jo didn't sound too pleased by the conversation. I pressed harder in hopes the voices would become clearer.

The deep voice of the man spoke with authority. "Jo, you know nothin' about her. Her type always ends up bringin' trouble."

"I'll have you know it's not the first time we've met and there's never been any trouble. Is she wanted for somethin'?" The irritation in Jo's voice at being challenged came through loud and clear.

"No. Not that I know of," he replied. "But if she is who I think she is, you gotta be careful."

"Yeah, Jo, we only want ya to be safe," the other woman stated full of concern.

"I know, Jade and I love you both for it, but I'm a big girl. She won't hurt me. Carter, I know you're the sheriff and it's your job to look out for everyone, but believe me when I say I'm fine and I'll let you know if I need you."

Jo's used such softness when she spoke to them. They must've been close friends or something more. She cared about these people and they cared about her, but still, she stood her ground. Jo was a strong woman and she followed her gut.

"Fine," Carter huffed. "Just don't say I didn't warn ya."

"I wouldn't dare," Jo said with a light chuckle in her voice. "Goodnight Carter."

The door closed, followed by silence. I leaned back and steadied myself, exhausted from the strain of spying.

Jade was the girl from the saloon and Carter was the sheriff. If memory served correct he was a tall, thin man with dark hair and one of those ridiculous twisty mustaches. He didn't care for me and his tone toward Jo sounded like more than concern for a casual resident.

A jealous twinge flared within me at the thought of him with my Jo.

Did I call her my Jo?

I was getting so far ahead of myself. I didn't understand these thoughts and emotions. She couldn't possibly share them. Who in their right mind would? We didn't know one another and for all I knew she had someone in her life by now, maybe even him.

More movement in the other room carried through the door as voices rose and fell according to their distance. The sound of Jade's voice again caused me to press back up to the door frame.

"So, how's your pretty little cowgirl doin', anyway?"

"She's not MY cowgirl," Jo answered, lacking any hint of offense at the question. "And she finally woke up, so she's gettin' better."

With Carter gone, Jo's tone held a touch of relief as she interacted with her friend.

"Say what you want, but I saw the way you looked at her the other night and you haven't been the same since the last time so..."

"So, nothin'. Yes, I like her. There's somethin' about her. I can't explain it."

"I can. El amore." Jade giggled, but Jo fell silent. "Do you think she's an outlaw? A bad girl? That would be sexy."

My interest piqued at Jade's suggestion and my heart stopped at the notion of Jo loving me. More so than the words,

I'd be on the lookout for any nuance in Jo's reply that would give away her truth.

"Don't be ridiculous, Jade. She's not a bad girl or an outlaw or else she'd be on the wanted list and I'm not in love with her."

I expected to be relieved by her answer. Instead her admission caused a deep aching pain in my chest and a sting from tears that threatened to fall. Her denial fueled the thoughts already circulating through my head. She couldn't possibly have feelings for me. I was a monster who didn't deserve her anyway.

Deep breaths calmed me and I allowed my full weight to rest against the wall. Why was I reacting so harshly? I didn't want anything serious. Jo took care of people and her actions toward me spoke of her warm heartedness. No need to make anything more of the situation.

Once I forced the idea of us ever being more from my mind, I was relieved. I never wanted to cause her pain and that's exactly what would happen if she fell for me. Love was something I couldn't return. That part of me had died. In a matter of days I'd be gone anyway, maybe forever. I was better off alone.

"Maybe, but there's definitely somethin'. I've known you too long. Just be careful. I don't want to see you get hurt."

"Thanks. You're like my sister and I know you watch out for me, but believe me when I say I can handle myself. Can you manage the saloon for a few more days? I'm gonna stay with her and make sure she's okay."

"Yes ma'am. I'm here to serve."

"Yeah, yeah. Stay out of the whiskey. We got a business to run."

"Okay, fine! I'll do it cause you're my best friend and I love you. Now go on and check on your cowgirl."

"I love you too. Thanks Jade."

Issuing their goodbyes spurred me to move. I didn't want Jo to catch me up and about. I pushed my body to its limits as I tried to get back to bed, knocking over the chair in the process and grunting from the extreme discomfort.

*Shit. Stupid. Clumsy. Hurry up Sarah, before she finds you snooping.*

Jo called out from the other room, "Sarah, you all right?"

I managed to get close to the bed by the time she came through the door. I stood winded with a light sweat breaking out, but forced a smile. "Sorry, I wanted to wash up a little." I lied, but she seemed to accept it.

Her concern eased as she wrapped an arm around me and helped me over. "You shoulda asked for help. You're stubborn as a mule." She laughed and set me down.

"Sorry." I lied again, trying to hide my smile. I'd do it all over again to get her body against mine. When she put me back to bed, I kept a hold of her hand. "Will you sit with me for a while?" I patted the spot beside me.

Even her half smile sent my pulse sky high. My insides turned to jelly when she cupped my cheek with a tender touch. I closed my eyes at the gentle contact and pressed into her hand.

"Of course." Jo smiled and pulled the sheets back on the other side. Once she climbed in, she tugged me in close and slipped her fingers through my hair.

We'd only been together twice, but they were probably the only two nights in the last many years where I slept in peace. I couldn't explain it, but looking into her eyes felt like home. Well, at least how I tried to remember home feeling...safe and warm.

"Mm, that feels good." I let my eyes fall shut as her touch soothed my pain. "Thank you for all you've done for me. Any chance you know where my horse is?" I slurred a bit with sleep overtaking me. The exertion of sneaking around mixed with the emotions about Jo exhausted what little energy I had left.

"A true cowgirl through and through." Her words held a smile in them. "Clover is out in my pasture and lookin' quite happy about it." She kissed my head. Her hand still moved in slow circles through my hair, stilling my mind.

"Good," I mumbled. "She deserves it."

Her laugh flowed like music to my ears. The wondrous sound vibrated through my body as she tried not to shake the bed. My one thought before sleep prevailed was this gentle moment with her and how I'd cling to it for the rest of my days.

If she only knew how much I didn't deserve her kindness.

✳✳✳

Well, I'd made it another day or maybe couple of days? I had no idea how long I'd been out cold or what day it was, but this time I was waking much earlier than before and my strength had improved since the last time. I pulled back the bandage and the wound also appeared to be healing well. Jo must have changed it again after I fell asleep. Neat stitches replaced my callous ones, but how well could you stitch yourself with a fresh bullet hole in you and the rush of almost dying coursing through your veins?

I sat up and swung my legs around with much more ease bringing a victorious smile to my face. When I stood and walked across the room by myself, my smile grew wider, almost giddy. Sitting still was never a strong point, but my body obviously needed the rest more than I cared to admit. Getting shot merely sped up my eventual crash.

Through the window I spotted Jo out in the pasture. She brushed Clover who shamelessly flirted with the other horses in the field. I laughed out, "Such a prima donna."

I turned my attention to the face in the mirror. I cringed at my reflection. This is what Jo's had to look at for days? "Goodness, I look like death," I muttered with disgust as I poured water into the basin to freshen up. Some days nothing soothed as well as cool water against your skin and today topped the list.

Good thing I had some clean clothes in my pack. I decided on black corduroys with a white and yellow long sleeve button down. Pain still grabbed me when I bent over, as well as a few other movements. Sharp twinges made it difficult to dress, but by going slow, I managed to get into my pants. I walked out of the bedroom finishing the last of my shirt buttons.

The sight of her standing in the kitchen stopped my feet and my heart. Jo was breathtaking. I'd said it before, but it never rang more true than right now. The rays of light cascaded around her making it seem as if she glowed. The outline of her voluptuous body etched a barely discernible line through her canary yellow dress. Her dark hair flowed down today, falling freely along her back and shoulders as she washed dishes in the basin and hummed to herself.

I tip toed closer without a word. My gaze locked on her. I couldn't bring myself to turn away. I couldn't speak.

"You're up," she said without a glance.

I thought I was quiet enough, but apparently not. I cleared my throat and swallowed hard. "How did you know?"

She shrugged. "I can just sense when you're near. Like the other night when you came back to town. I knew." Even with her back to me, the way she spoke gave away her smile.

I stepped closer, still doing my best to be silent.

Jo kept to task, never ceasing her movements. "You should be restin'. A wound like that and the amount of pain...you need time, Sarah."

Did she have eyes in the back of her head? Like a doting mother, she reminded me I should be in bed, knowing darn well I'd be too stubborn to listen. I didn't say a word as I stopped and admired the woman who stood with her back to me just inches away.

Kind, gentle, caring, Jo encompassed everything that I wasn't. Maybe that's what kept me coming back. I'd never be like her, but when we were together, at least I experienced true compassion in my life again, if only for a few moments.

My arms slid slow and gentle around her waist. My body pressed against her back, enjoying her warmth against me.

She tensed a little in surprise, but quickly relaxed and folded back into me. She fit to a tee.

I nuzzled my nose into her hair, closing my eyes for a moment as I inhaled. As if the feel of her beneath my fingers didn't please me enough, her infectious lilac scent drove my senses wild. Every little detail found a place in my memory for when we would be apart.

My hands traveled across her stomach and down her hips. Her breath caught as I kissed and nipped my way up her neck. I paused at her ear and whispered, "It's more painful bein' so close and not touchin' you." Nibbling her lobe buckled her knees. I loved being able to do that to her.

Jo pushed back into me harder to steady herself.

The contact pulled a moan from me. I wanted so much more from her and I tried my level best not to rush it. With Jo, every second was to be savored. I didn't know when or if, another chance would come again.

Her hand trembled as she reached up and pushed the basin toward the wall. She spun around and leaned back against the ledge. Jo pulled me in and draped her arms around my neck. Her hands tangled in my hair, sending a shiver down my spine.

For the first time in a long time, I allowed myself to truly smile. My eyelids fluttered shut as I let my head fall back, enjoying everything about the moment before bringing my eyes to meet her shimmering ones once more. They filled with questions, concerns and something more than lust.

In a snap, her eyes turned dark and hungry. Like my last visit, the time apart affected us both. She craved me every bit as much as I did her.

I leaned back in her arms, allowing my eyes to travel the length of her and land on her breasts. My blatant desire to have her brought a blush to her cheeks.

She sighed and tipped her forehead to mine, breathing out a ragged breath. "How do you do always do that?"

My brows pressed together, confused by her question. "What?" I studied her expression, curious of her meaning, but she just closed her eyes and smiled.

Jo moved closer, her lips brushing ever so light against mine. "Look at me and make me feel like the most beautiful thing in the world."

Her innocent reply struck something deep inside. How could this perfect creature be so unaware? The need to make her believe consumed me and I wanted her to feel the truth in my words.

"Because you are, Jo. I've traveled sea to sea, but you...you are without question the most beautiful thing I have ever laid eyes on. You are beautiful inside and out." My lips met hers in a tender kiss. She felt so right.

Jo pulled back, sending me into panic. Did I do something wrong?

She peered deep into my soul and said, "That's how I feel about you, too."

What? No. I couldn't believe what she said. She didn't know me, not the real me. I shook my head in defiance. The kind words pained me. This soul had been shattered. I didn't deserve her. I wanted to run away, save her from the heartache I would cause.

Jo fought me, denying me the chance to break free. She held on tight and forced me to look at her. "You are, Sarah. You are beautiful and good. I don't know what happened in your life or who made you think otherwise, but I can see it here," she touched my face, "and here," her hand came to rest on my heart.

Tears welled up in my eyes, falling victim to emotions I'd long since thought extinct. Long ago my mind fractured. One small part lived in the dream of a little girl still with a family and the other as an adult in the cold reality of an unforgiving life. Now this woman stood strong, trying to piece me back together again, if only for a brief moment in time.

"You don't know me Jo. You wouldn't say those things if you did." I continued to fight her. I had to make her understand. What she believed didn't exist. I didn't want to hurt her later when she realized the truth. I wasn't caring like her. I killed for vengeance and I had no regrets about it. What kind of truly good person does that? Shouldn't you feel something for taking a life? I didn't know what it meant to let someone in, or to trust, or to love.

The pained expression from my inner struggle drew her attention. I couldn't seem to hide anything from the woman. Her hand moved to my cheek, gracing me with a gentle caress. The small touch did so many things to me.

"We're more alike than you know and I see through you, Sarah. I see what's inside if you ever allow yourself to be set free."

Her eyes always did me in. They could see into my soul and made me feel stronger. Maybe I could be the person she thought I was one day, but I wasn't now and might not ever want to be.

She kept her intense gaze on me as her thumb chased away an escaping tear. "Sarah, I know bad and it's not you. The way you look at me, touch me, I can feel what you are deep down. You couldn't make my heart quiver or my knees weak if you were bad."

I swallowed hard and closed my eyes. Jo's thumb continued to brush back and forth across my cheek. My head dropped as I processed what she said. Her words rained down like a priest giving me penance. They didn't change who I was, what I'd done or what I'd do tomorrow, but for a brief moment in time, I felt a little bit better about myself. Her belief comforted me, even though I would let her down later.

I'd never wanted anyone the way I wanted her. Want didn't even fit the description. Need would be more accurate. I needed her like my body needed water or air. Everything in me screamed to have her body against mine, to prove to myself that she was real. My head, my heart, every single cell, all requested physical proof that I was alive and Jo wanted me, Sarah Sawyer.

With a gentle touch she lifted my chin, urging me to open my eyes. We met with the same deep longing in our gazes. No further prodding was needed to act on the one thing my entire being had screamed for since last I left her. I threw all thought and fear and pain out the window.

One hand grabbed her behind the neck and the other captured her cheek as I crushed our lips together in a furious, passionate kiss. Our mouths melted into one another, moving in rhythm as if we'd practiced this a million times. Beneath my touch her pulse pounded every bit as hard as mine.

My hands found their way along a familiar path sliding down her back to her thighs. Determined fingers took their time inching up the cotton dress. Every one of her muscles strung tight as I took my time getting to know them all. She pressed for me to go faster, but no, I wanted to make this last.

I couldn't bring myself to leave her lips. The need for air was overridden by months of pent up desire begging to be satisfied. With a swipe of my tongue she proved just as anxious when she opened wider. I would gladly take all she offered, basking in the taste and explosion of sensations that came with exploring Jo.

She sucked my bottom lip between her teeth, the sweet pain drawing a sound from me I never thought possible. Pleased with herself, she smiled into our kiss and rocked her hips against mine.

The subtle, yet possessive move drove me mad with hunger for her, turning my slow purposed movements frantic. I worked her dress up and peeled back her petticoat enough to graze the skin of her inner thigh.

She pulled back with a gasp. The picture perfect view of her aroused and panting with kiss swollen lips sent my need sky high as the passion between us flared.

I studied her expression while my fingers traveled along the inside of the waist band, noting the tiny trembles of her lips when I brushed a sensitive spot. I reveled in every little response. Her eyes offered a silent pleading for me to take her the way we'd both been dreaming since our last meeting. But this wasn't like our last time. This was like nothing I'd ever experienced before.

She dropped her head back, giving herself to me of her own free will. Her submission lit a fire in me. My mouth wasted no time finding the sweet spot on her neck before traveling along her collarbone in a frenzied mix of licks and nips. I smiled at the sound she made when my hand slipped between her legs. Her breath hitched as I dipped into the heavenly abyss awaiting me.

"God Jo," I moaned against her skin. Her flood of desire for me coated my fingertips. I nearly lost myself on the spot. She undid me so easily. Some might be ashamed, but I chalked it up to whatever special hold she had on me, happy and willing to succumb any time she willed.

She moved against my fingers, pleasuring herself and making me weak-kneed in the process. A jolt traveled right to my core. I loved being at the mercy of this amazing woman. If she were a trained killer, I wouldn't even put up a fight.

She flashed a devilish grin, slowly removed my hand and pulled me to the bedroom. Laying me down with care, she began to undo my pants. She pulled them off in one swift move as I looked on in silent awe. Jo's smile had never been brighter than when she straddled me and attacked the few buttons on my shirt. With the final one freed, the fabric fell open, exposing my breasts to the cool air pricking at my flushed skin.

"You're so beautiful," she whispered. Her tongue teased my scorched flesh while her hands explored my body, taking care to avoid my wound.

I arched into her, allowing her to have anything and everything she wanted. My hands slid up her dress and gripped her hips, earning me a soft whimper and a bite on the neck. The reaction brought a smile to my face. "Take these off," I whispered and tugged on her undergarments.

Jo hopped off the bed to grant my wish.

I pushed up on my elbows to enjoy the view while she worked them down in a seductive dance, biting her lip with her eyes locked on mine. When the show came to an end I took her hand and pulled her back to me. I lifted the dress up, removing the final obstacle between her skin and mine.

With wide eyes I admired every inch of flesh revealed. My God, it seemed like forever since I last laid eyes on her fully. Large, perfect breasts I longed to touch, creamy skin I couldn't wait to have against my own and a wanting center begging for my attention, just like in my dreams.

I licked my lips and pushed myself further up the bed inviting her on top of me. I sighed, relieved to finally get lost in the wondrous sensations of her naked body against mine. My mouth covered her breast and my fingers dipped inside, igniting a furious pace of push and pull between us.

Like a wildfire I burned for her. No one did what Jo did to me. Sure, I've had the company of others, even Jessie on occasion, but there wasn't even a competition. I didn't experience the same warmth, safety or peace within my body, mind and soul like I did with Jo.

What it meant in the grand scheme of things, I couldn't say. But what I could say in all honesty was that I had no desire to figure it out. For once I didn't want to think. I'd have plenty of time for thinking later. Most times, real life couldn't compete with our imaginations, but as Jo and I kept our gazes locked in the throes of passion and my name echoed through the silence of the house in a breathless release, I let go. For a brief moment I gave myself to her and it was so much better than even my wildest of dreams.

# **Chapter Six**

I groaned and threw an arm over my eyes. The excruciating brightness of the afternoon light forced its way through with a vengeance. I was angry the rays deemed it necessary to disturb my slumber knowing how little I truly slept, even though this was the most time I'd spent in a bed since before my parents were killed.

The simple act of shifting my weight on the bed made every muscle hurt. I over did myself, but several, intensely passionate exchanges with Jo would do that to a person even in the best of health. The forces within wanted the woman more than rest.

Completely worth every bit of pain.

With a lopsided grin on my face, I rolled over. Jo lay passed out beside me. If I thought she was spectacular before, the sight of her right now rivaled the Mona Lisa. Naked on her belly, head turned toward me with both arms overhead and her long, dark mane splayed over her back. She wore an easy smile on her lips that hinted she knew a secret no one else did. Her brows twitched a little as I continued to take her all in.

I ached to reach out and touch her, but I didn't want her to wake up. I draped my arm across her back and simply stared. This moment would burn into memory for those long nights on the trail. My body and mind eased for the first time in a long time as I drifted back to sleep and dream.

*The week before Christmas on the year of my sixteenth birthday, I managed to escape from O'Shea. I was cold and hungry, seeking cover in random barns each night for warmth. I avoided people as much as possible, suspicious of everyone for fear they'd return me to him. I had no plan, nowhere to go, but I'd rather freeze to death than go back.*

*On a frigid, gray morning, an old couple found me. I sat huddled in a corner with a feed sack for a blanket and a piece of bread thrown to the dogs. My appearance didn't deter them. After a lot of coaxing on their behalf, they took me back to the little cabin on their modest farm. They never had any kids of their own. The joy of experiencing one Christmas with a child shone in their eyes. I'd only been there a few days, but they got me gifts and treated me like kin.*

*Mary Johnson was a fragile looking older woman with long gray hair always up in a bun. Everything about her emanated warmth, from her eyes to her smile to the way she spoke. She made me a sweater to cover my frail frame. Back then I didn't welcome the cold, so the wool kept the chill away. I appreciated every loving stitch.*

*Her husband, Henry, was a tall man with thinning white hair. Anyone could tell he used to be muscular in his younger days. He still maintained an ominous appearance, though he was nothing but gentle. He bought me a little doll, explaining as he handed it to me how he had no idea about an appropriate gift for child my age. He seemed embarrassed. I didn't understand why. The gesture alone meant more than they knew. I hadn't spoken much since they took me in, but I softly voiced my thanks. Their effort to bring me joy brought a touch of a smile across my lips for the first time in years. It was a good day.*

Lost in a slumber of days gone, my head filled with pleasant memories instead of nightmares for a change before movement of the bed set off my inner alarm. My eyes shot open, darting side to side and body tensed, ready to take on any threat. All I found was Jo lying on her side facing me.

Her eyelids fluttered and a raspy voice spoke up. "Sarah, you okay?"

Barely awake and already worried about me. I didn't realize I needed such looking after. My muscles eased as I sighed. "A little sore." I chuckled. "But I'm good. How are you?"

"Mm. I'm good since you're still here." She smiled a sleepy smile.

The two times we met previously, I was hot on someone's trail and left long before she awoke. Deep down, I didn't want to wake up next to her for fear of this exact feeling. Never wanting to get up.

Now that she was awake, I let a finger glide down her back, enjoying the shiver my touch elicited. A low moan slipped through her lips making my core ache. Jo's smile, already in full force, never failed to make my stomach flutter.

She blinked away the sleep and peered up at me with light, sparkling eyes. Her arm draped over my waist and pulled us closer together. "I don't think your body needs to handle another round Sarah. I'm actually surprised we did as much as we did."

"Yeah well, you know us cowgirls. Tough as nails." I laughed even though it hurt. Jo caught me wincing and kissed me on the shoulder.

She stroked across my belly, careful to avoid the wound in my flank.

I closed my eyes and released a sigh at her tender touch.

"I guess I know I need to shoot you to get you to stay for breakfast," she smirked.

"Nah, I'll get back on my horse and pass out a few days later," I returned. My tone reeked of sarcasm.

"True. So, what were you thinking about before?"

"Hmm?" I tried to deflect her question.

"A few minutes ago when I woke up, you were somewhere else. Where were you?"

"Oh, nothin' really."

She sat up and commanded my eyes with hers. There was warmth and sincerity in them mixed with a pleading to let her in, but I wouldn't. "Sarah, you know you can trust me, right?"

"I do, but this has nothin' to do with trust." It didn't, but the honest truth was I didn't trust anyone. I'd come to believe in Jessie only to find out she was involved with the men we were wanted to take down.

"Okay, well if you ever wanna talk about anything, I'm a good listener. Besides, I'd like to know a little bit more about the mysterious Sarah Sawyer." She smiled a soft smile and kissed me on the lips. "I'm gonna feed up, then make us some supper."

"I'll help." I rolled to get up, but the pain stopped me in my tracks.

"No Sarah, I think we've done enough damage for one day."

I flashed a mischievous grin back at her. "I'm glad you're sharin' the blame."

When she headed out, I tried to get out of bed again. The task was neither easy nor pleasant, but finally, I succeeded and somewhat dressed in sleep clothes. I couldn't manage much more after all the physical activity.

Catching me on my feet when she returned earned me a hard glare. I gave her a stubborn grin and swallowed down any fatigue or discomfort. My nature didn't include lying in bed and waiting. The quicker I got my body going, the better.

For dinner we ate a light meal and enjoyed some casual conversation about crops and business. It was nice for a change. We avoided anything too serious, for which I was thankful. She wanted to learn more about me, but I didn't care to share much.

Still healing and exhausted from the day, I turned in early. Jo sat beside me on the bed running her fingers through my hair. The repetitive swirling along my scalp was soothing, like a child being rocked to sleep. I closed my eyes and hoped for pleasant dreams.

*My father came from the house with tears in his eyes. Mom rushed up and wrapped her arms around him in a comforting hug. He explained to the men that he'd done all he could to save the young woman, but she hadn't survived her wounds. They were furious, grabbing my father and shaking him roughly while my mother yelled at them to let go. I had no idea what was happening, but I was scared. I cowered in the corner trembling in fear, hoping he wouldn't be hurt by the angry strangers.*

*After several minutes of threats and yelling, they rode off. He broke down in my mom's arms. I ran to him, tears spilling from my eyes. He hugged me tighter than ever before and I hung on for dear life.*

*His compassion and love for helping others was something I envied. The sight of him so upset over losing a life filled me with overwhelming pride at having him as my father and a doctor. All he ever wanted was to help as many as possible. When the men had gone, he had the body hauled off in a carriage.*

*That was two days before they were killed.*

\*\*\*

Today I was feeling much better, both mentally and physically. I always seemed to have a brighter outlook when I had good dreams of my old life, though I knew Jo played a part in it as well. I walked to the window smiling at the sun. A perfect day weather wise. Jo collected eggs outside, so I decided making breakfast for the two of us would be a good way to thank her.

I rarely cooked, but it was something I rather enjoyed. A simple act that brought about a sense of normalcy. I heated up the stove and warmed the oven, throwing together the ingredients for an omelet with bacon and biscuits.

Jo entered the house with a full basket in her hand. She sniffed at the air, taking in the aroma wafting through the room that had overwhelmed her senses. "Wow, that smells wonderful, Sarah. I didn't know you could cook." Her smile pulled high, making tiny creases around her eyes.

"I've picked up a few things over the years."

She removed each egg and cleaned them to store. "You should be resting," she said idly without looking up. "But I appreciate it. I'm starving. Did you sleep well?"

"Yes. Thank you for everything, Jo. I'm feelin' much better."

She was still smiling, but sadness washed over her, wiping the gleam from her eyes. "I'm glad." An uneasy pause filled the air between us. Something else weighed on her mind. She glanced up then returned to her chore.

I held still in silence.

"So um," she broke the uncomfortable moment between us, but proceeded with caution, "does this mean you're leavin', cause you're more than welcome to stay a while?"

Jo tried to maintain a brave front, but her eyes gave her away. She wanted me here. While I had to leave at some point, I did enjoy my time with her. A little while longer wouldn't hurt, besides I needed to heal more before I faced the man who took away my life. I wished I would've met Jo as the caring person I once was instead of this shell of a woman I'd become. She deserved better.

"I do have somewhere to be, but I think I need to rest a bit longer, so I may take you up on the offer. You sure it's all right?"

Her eyes sparkled in delight and her smile, well it was something I'd never tire of seeing. Those adoring glances caused my heart to race like crazy.

"More than. You can stay as long as you like Sarah." She walked over and kissed me on the cheek. "Honestly, I like having you around."

I couldn't help but smile back at her unexpected words. They took me by surprise. I stared at her in disbelief, still unsure of why anyone would want a broken soul like me around.

She caught my questioning gaze and shook her head. "Yes Sarah." She took my hand. "It is possible for someone to enjoy your company. You're smart, funny, beautiful and passionate."

Her compliments stirred something inside me. Something I hadn't felt in a long time. Something I didn't want to acknowledge I still possessed. The feeling made me uneasy.

I moved away, pretending to need my hand for cooking. I was none of those things she said. Well, maybe passionate, but only in my pursuit of killing O'Shea.

Jo recognized my mood change when I decided to focus on the eggs. I was never able to hide from her. She frowned as she moved to the cabinets where the dishes were kept and pulled a couple out for breakfast. "I know. You're bad. Not worthy of being happy. Not capable of lovin' anyone or anything."

The words made me pause. I turned to meet her eyes as she walked back to the table.

"You can be bad all you want, just keep bein' who you really are with me. Like yesterday. I told you once, I know you Sarah. I was you at one time and it's okay to let someone in."

I tore my eyes from her intense gaze. My hands trembled and my nerves hung on edge. Sometimes it was like she could read my mind and it scared the hell out of me. She made me so vulnerable, yet so at home. It was uncanny. It was unsettling. "Can we talk about somethin' else?"

She nodded without another word and set the table.

The tension in my body relented and my pulse slowed back to normal. There was silence, though to my surprise, it didn't feel awkward.

I served up the food. We both dug in, stealing quick glances at one another as we ate. I still had my walls up.

She offered an apologetic smile as she walked the line between my emotions. "So Sarah, is it okay to ask where you're from?"

A half grin formed on my lips at her need to ask my permission. I didn't want to talk about me at all, but I had to give her something. "Yes, it's fine. I grew up mostly in El Paso. What about you?"

Her eyes lit up. "Wow! We weren't too far apart. I'm from Amarillo. Have you ever been there?"

I cringed at the memory of my time in there, but I forced it back down. "Yes, for a short time as a young girl."

"Maybe we've seen one another at some point. Wouldn't that be funny?"

"Mm, I don't think so. The people I stayed with didn't exactly allow me a normal childhood." I kept it short. I didn't care to revisit the past any more than I already did.

"Oh. I'm sorry." Her face dropped. She felt bad for bringing it up.

I'd never spoken about my childhood in any capacity before, but for some reason I could talk to Jo. I did want to know more about her though. "How'd you end up here?"

Right before my eyes, my innocent question turned her usual sparkling eyes cold. My insides shivered. It was a side I'd never seen of her and I immediately regretted asking. "I'm sorry, you don't have to answer, Jo."

The words she spoke earlier finally registered. She said she was once like me and at the time I'd wondered what she meant. Was it related to her family? I'd never push, though. I believed some things were best left unsaid.

"Um, no. It's all right. It's uh...it's been a long time since I talked about it to anyone." She pressed her lips together, forcing a tight smile. "You might say my family and I had a fallin' out over a difference in opinions. When I was eighteen, I ran away and for a few years I roamed the country workin' odd jobs until I found this prospering town in the middle of nowhere. I met Jade and stayed. I bought the saloon with money I had saved up." She took another bite and smiled sadly. "You did great with this breakfast, Sarah. It's delicious."

I didn't say a word. I returned the gesture and finished off my plate, realizing both of us had less than story book childhoods. Still, here she was, the picture of a loving, caring woman, so vibrant and full of life. Amazing how things changed you for better or worse.

When we were done eating, Jo took up the plates and began washing them. She moved with such grace and ease, like she floated around the room. I admired her from afar, much the way I planned to do the night we first met. She smiled over her shoulder at me, surely feeling the weight of my gaze on her.

Shaking old memories from my head, I excused myself and took my leave to the bedroom for my boots. I hadn't been outside in days and I needed to see my best friend.

It was a beautiful late summer day in the mountains with the sun shining, a light cool breeze and clear enough to take in the sharp contrast of color between the dark gray jagged tops and the bright blue sky I loved so much. The sun was nice on my skin after being cooped up for so many days. When you're used to being outside all the time it's easy to go stir crazy inside four walls. Not that having a soft, warm bed and a home cooked meal were bad, but there was an attraction to being out in nature.

Clover grazed way out in the pasture with the other horses and cows. I'd seen her with Jo the last few days and for a horse that didn't like strangers, she sure did warm up to that stranger in a hurry. I guess no living creature was immune to the woman's charm. I whistled and her ears perked up as she turned my way. She threw her head up and whinnied before galloping back to me.

"Hey girl. You look happy out there." I stroked her blaze and kissed her muzzle. "I'm almost worried you didn't miss me."

Clover nudged me with her nose and searched my hands for goodies.

I chuckled at her. "What? Seein' me isn't present enough for you?"

A soft laugh behind me drew my attention from Clover. Jo approached with a few carrots in her hand. She was a vision of loveliness with her hair pulled back, old Victorian pants, black boots and a light colored shirt. She let her hand slide down my back as she stopped beside me leaving a trail of goose bumps behind.

A smile hit me in an instant. Seemed like all I did in her presence was smile like an idiot, but her touch made me feel lighter somehow and I couldn't help myself.

She held up the carrots and Clover stretched her long, muscled neck as far as possible, working her lips in an attempt to grab one. Jo handed one over so I could feed first. "I think she missed you," Jo said as she stroked Clover's neck.

"I don't know, she sure cozied right up to you. She doesn't like anyone. What did you bribe her with?" I winked.

"I didn't have to. I think she knows I care about you." Jo's gaze met mine. There was an intensity in her voice that rolled through me.

Out of nowhere I was nervous again. I couldn't give her what she so desperately wanted. I looked away and cleared my throat. "Jo, I--"

"Sarah," she interrupted. "You don't have to say anything. I know what it is you can't bring yourself to say and its okay."

"No Jo, it's not. You deserve more. Someone who will stay and be here with you, not run around the country on some personal mission. I don't want to make a promise I know I won't keep."

I averted my gaze as I focused on petting Clover.

"I'm a big girl, Sarah. I know what I need and what I will or won't accept in my life. I don't know what it is you do or where you're headed, but all I need is one person who I know is looking up at the same starry sky and thinkin' of me the way I think of her. The universe will take care of the rest." She paused. She was looking for a reaction, but I offered none. "By the way, there's a big difference between won't and can't. Honestly, which one is it for you, Sarah?"

Her words had bite. She wouldn't let me out of this one, keeping her gaze locked on me as I searched within myself for the answer.

Wouldn't or couldn't? I knew I couldn't stay here with her, at least not until I finished what I'd sworn to do, but would I stay afterwards? There were so many things about Jo I couldn't explain. I was drawn to her by an invisible force, like destiny, but then there was me and my inability to let destiny or anybody else, in. With complete honesty I answered in sadness, "I don't know."

She flinched at my reply.

I knew what she was really asking. She wanted to know if I would come back here for good when I found what I was searching for. It pained me to hurt her, but in all truth, I couldn't answer right now. I let my eyes fall away from hers, swallowing hard before I mustered the courage to speak again. "Maybe it's best if I leave, Jo. I don't want to complicate things for you or us."

She shook her head and took my hand into her own. "No way. I said you can stay and I meant it. I want you here as long as I can have you and after, well, I'll deal with it. I almost lost hope you'd come back here at all." Her eyes began to glass over.

I started to realize the words she'd spoken to Jade were not spoken in truth. My heart fluttered. Any question I had about her feelings for me were now answered.

# **<u>Chapter Seven</u>**

For the first time in a long time I truly enjoyed my day. I helped Jo in the garden and out in the barn as much as physically possible. We indulged in idle chatter about the town and things in the news. She refused my help with dinner, saying I'd already done too much today and would pay tomorrow. She was probably right.

Jo made a delicious roast chicken with mashed potatoes and carrots. All day she'd steal glances at me. She thought she was being slick, that I didn't notice, but I did, every time. Truth was, I did the same thing and rather liked the feeling it gave me.

I couldn't deny Jo was something special. We had a deeper connection, even if I kept resisting the urge to let her in like she wanted. I'd put the pieces together. They all added up to her having deep feelings for me. The blinders were off and I could finally see the longing in the way she smiled, the little glances she'd cast and in her touch, even in casual exchanges.

The attention was nice. I could almost let myself explore more with her, but I knew what would happen.

Jo said she was happy to have me as long as possible. She was lying or perhaps trying to convince herself. My distance wasn't fair to her, but was it right to build something knowing I'd be leaving? I would only break her heart and I had no idea how my story would end. I was doing us both a favor by not complicating our relationship. I appreciated what she did for me and we enjoyed an amazing afternoon in one another's arms, but all I'd ever done was share my body and then ride off into the horizon.

As we sat on the porch swing staring at the night sky, Jo slipped her fingers between mine. Her skin was so warm. I didn't look at her or our hands, but enjoyed the moment, never letting on how much her companionship meant to me. Seemed I missed being around people more than I thought. Maybe I wasn't meant to be a loner forever. I could have a little farm like this. I had enough money to buy one, but I couldn't start dreaming yet. No, I had to keep my eye on the prize and live to enjoy the old man's judgment day.

An hour passed and my energy waned. The night was young, but the effects of a day's work and the stress of keeping my distance from Jo kicked in. I gave her hand a squeeze, thanked her and went to my room. I lay in bed, my eyes closed; tired but unable to sleep. Too many thoughts ran through my head and too many emotions filled my heart. Such a tedious practice to resist temptation with her nearby. Even more so when she wanted me to touch her, to give in to her.

Deep, calming breaths relaxed my sore muscles. Soft footsteps at my door ceased the rambling of my tired mind. I focused on the form appearing before me as the door inched opened. Any other time I'd go for my gun.

The bed moved beneath me as she climbed on, but I remained still. "Jo," I whispered and tensed in anticipation of her next move.

"Yes," she answered softly as she snuggled in beside me. She made a slow path of kisses up my neck. Her lips on my skin jolted every nerve awake on contact.

My eyes rolled back. A sharp intake of air acted in defense of the moan wanting to escape. Instead I choked out, "What are you doing?"

My body trembled as her hand slipped under my shirt, brushed across my stomach and found its way to my breast. Her warm breath tickled my skin as she breathed out, "Complicating things."

Earlier I was strong, but this time I was too weak to resist. I arched into her and allowed my moan the freedom it so desired. Fire coursed through me, bringing a throbbing ache to areas desperate for her touch. My need to have her overcame my need to protect her from the certain heartbreak I would cause.

Searching fingertips found her chin in the darkness to bring her mouth to mine. I sucked her bottom lip between my teeth then deepened the kiss, making her whimper.

She climbed atop me, straddling my hips.

I pulled back, admiring her silhouette above me. Her eyes were cloaked by the night, but the scorching heat between us burned without question.

"I know you want this Sarah. Your body is screaming for me, so why deny this? Why deny us?" She rocked her hips against mine.

Sliding my leg between her thighs was my only reply. The first reason, as usual, I couldn't form words when she was touching me so intimately. Second, because I had no legitimate reason beyond my own emotional incompetence. Third, um...I knew there was a third. Dammit, she won that round.

Pain never had a chance as my passion overrode my frazzled nerve endings. I rolled her over, pinning her to the bed and stared down at her. Shadows danced across her face. A light reflection of the moonlight glistened in her eyes. Every time she gave herself to me, only one word came to mind. Breathtaking.

"This doesn't change anything, Jo. I can't make you any promises." I wished she understood how much I wanted her to give up, to leave me be so I couldn't hurt her any more than I already had, but she was so damn stubborn.

She cupped my face in both hands. "I told you, I'm not askin' for a promise. I'm only askin' for all of you, as long as you're here with me. However long..."

"Jo--"

Her lips met mine with a tenderness that brought tears to my eyes. It shouldn't be this hard, should it? I should spill everything and let go of my burden; stay here for the rest of my life with this caring, beautiful woman who saw me for what I could be, but I couldn't or wouldn't. I didn't know which.

My eyes drifted shut as her thumb brushed across my cheek. "I will try Jo, but there are things...things I can't talk about. I have never talked about. I--"

She shushed me with another tender kiss, this one needier. "I understand," she whispered between kisses. "Let's just start with tonight."

I said nothing else, only nodded my head and lunged forward, claiming her lips in a searing kiss. My tongue sought hers in desperation. I pushed her nightgown up, running my hands down her outer thighs then up along the inside.

She hissed as my nails dragged across her heated flesh. Jo writhed underneath me in hopes I'd take her not so subtle hint during our moment of passion. "Sarah, please," she begged.

I enjoyed the game, but how could I say no when she said my name so full of desire? In a flash our clothes were shed. The quickening beat of her heart matched mine as I pressed our bodies together, dissolving all space between us. My hands slid up to knead her breasts as my mouth worked down between her thighs, settling on one spot that proved without a doubt how much she craved my touch.

"Yes Sarah," her soft moan filled the quiet room.

I smiled against her skin at the audible approval. The sound was all it took to do me in. Not a single thought filled my mind, only an intense need to fulfill her request.

She rocked hard into me. I gave all I had, taking her to the edge before pulling back again and again until she cursed me for denying her the satisfaction she yearned for. We both knew it would be worth it in the long run.

When I dipped inside matching her rhythm, not another second was wasted as her body arched up. Every muscle locked tight as she shuddered through her release.

My mouth found hers, devouring her screams with as much desperation as the desert sand soaked up drops of rain. The final waves rolled through her as I slowed my movements. Stopping took every ounce of will I possessed, but control was merely an illusion when she screamed my name in such bliss.

Without hesitation I went back for more, blazing a trail from her lips to her navel. Not an inch of scorching flesh was missed. Her soft whimpers were a delight to my ears as I settled back between her thighs, enjoying the fruit of my labor. The taste of Jo was like nothing else in this world and I wanted to enjoy every bit.

"Uncle," she gasped, jerking and twitching at even the lightest contact.

I needed more. Climbing the length of her in a snap, I captured her mouth in a hard, deep kiss, refusing to bend to our need for air. Finally, I mustered the strength to pull away. We lay skin to skin, sweaty, satisfied and completely spent. I rested my forehead on hers and gazed into darkened pools. What this woman did to me defied all logic.

Jo licked her lips, tasting herself on them. She smiled at me so wide, so bright, that I filled with emotion I never believed I possessed.

I left a tender kiss on her forehead and collapsed beside her. I stared at the ceiling. That was amazing. She was amazing. She made me feel amazing. It didn't change anything. I had to keep telling myself that.

***

The days seemed to fly by since I came to. So much about a settled life seemed foreign to me, but waking up with Jo in my arms was something I could force myself to get used to. There truly was no more magnificent sight to see when I opened my eyes. Who was I kidding? I was already used to it and couldn't imagine it would ever get old. I was all too aware I'd be leaving her soon. Every sense in my body stole any little detail about Jo to press into memory.

As much as Jo began awakening parts of me I didn't know I still had, deep inside my gut burned with the need to finish what I started. Jo said I was stubborn, but the bull headed brunette was intent on breaking down my walls and turning me into a homebody. Staring at her beside me, I could almost let her do it too. Almost.

I smiled as I rolled to wrap around her. Even in sleep her body reacted to mine as she pushed back into me. Slivers of sunrise peaked through the window. My eyes fell closed. There was a little more time to rest and enjoy the safety and comfort Jo's warmth gave me.

## Six years ago- Outside Amarillo

*I rode beside Henry on our way to the valley. We stopped in a clearing along a steep hill and he handed me a pistol. I never held one before. My father was a peaceful man who didn't believe in guns or taking a life, so we never kept one around the house.*

*Henry looked at me and said, "A lady should know how to protect herself."*

*Though I never revealed what I'd been through, he sensed giving me some idea of control in my life would be helpful. The eighteen-nineties were crazy times after all, where innocent people were killed every day for land or gold and women were often treated as possessions.*

*The cold metal felt so good in my hand. An instant smile pulled at my lips. It was a perfect fit, like an extension of myself. He showed me everything. How to shoot, clean, what each piece did and why it was important to keep it in perfect working order. Most of all he taught me to respect the weapon.*

*"If your life is going to depend on it, you can't afford a misfire," he said as he stared into my eyes with a seriousness I'd never seen from the loving old man.*

*After the first few apprehensive shots, Henry laughed and called me a natural when I started hitting near the bulls eye on a consistent basis. I stood in awe of the power within the object. Not only the explosion when I pulled the trigger, but the ability to defend myself, to take a life when my own was threatened.*

*Foreign feelings swarmed me knowing I finally had what I so badly wanted. Strength, confidence and control of my future. It meant the world to me after the last few years where I sat helpless as my parents were murdered and I became slave labor.*

*My life changed. I vowed to never be weak again. Tears welled in my eyes when I hugged him and from the way he embraced me in return, he knew what he'd done.*

*For months I traveled to the field to practice my technique. It didn't take me long to become a skilled shooter, but I wanted to be fast. Faster than anyone. Not only did I want to be faster, but I wanted to be able to hit my target with extreme precision. I practiced for hours on end every day after that first lesson. So much like my father, I studied endlessly, searching for patterns, nuances or any little advantage. I examined everything about whatever topic I pursued to become unbeatable.*

*In the back of my mind, a plan took shape. Outlining my revenge took a hold of my subconscious and began to rule all thought. With every draw of the gun I pictured the face of Patrick Daniel O'Shea, imagining how it would feel to bring forth my vengeance on him.*

I laid in bed half asleep and half awake, yet dead to the world. That time when your body hung heavy and restful, but your mind still registered things around you. Stuck between dream land and reality, I lost track of where I was laying.

The floor creaked and the bed moved beside me. I jumped up startled and ready for a fight, grabbing the intruder tight with one hand while the other drew back in a fist. My mind glazed over. My pulse raced in surprise. I ran on instinct, but her yelp brought me back to reality as I stared into hazel eyes peeled open wide and fearful.

I was quick to release her from my grip. "I...I'm sorry, Jo. I was having a dream and you startled me. Are you okay?" My heart sunk at the alarm in her eyes, reinforcing to me why I should leave sooner rather than later. I had issues to work through.

Sometimes my dreams triggered something in me. Even good dreams apparently. I swung my legs over the edge of the bed and turned away from her, ashamed of my actions.

"You caught me by surprise is all. I shoulda known better than to sneak back in here. Must be odd for you to have someone walk in on you in the mornin'."

She did her best to relieve my guilt, but I wouldn't look at her. I couldn't. "I would never intentionally hurt you Jo, it's just sometimes," I sighed and ran my palms over my face to wipe the sleep away, "sometimes my dreams are emotionally intense."

The bed sunk in behind me. Her comforting arms snaked around my waist. Jo straddled me from behind and leaned her head against my back.

The tension melted from my body, replaced by soothing warmth. It truly was unbelievable, the effect she had on every part of my physical and emotional being. I'd never experienced anything like this with anyone else. I didn't know the right word for what she did to me, but the more time I spent with her, the more I wanted to lose myself in her.

"I know you wouldn't, Sarah. I trust you completely."

Her somber voice vibrated through my rib cage, giving me an odd sense of comfort. She wrapped around me like a cocoon, protecting me and I never wanted to come out. My hands traveled up to cover hers, holding them tight to me.

"If there's anything you want to talk about, I'm happy to lend an ear," she said soft and sincere, but her tone was all knowing.

I squeezed her hands tighter and shook my head, looking down at our hands. "No, not right now, but can we stay here for a few more minutes?" I couldn't believe how vulnerable she made me. This wasn't something I'd normally do; not part of the detached, calculating persona I'd worked so hard to fortify in my desire to live life without emotional connections.

Jo read between all the lines, saw past every guise. She could see deeper within me than I could myself. She didn't make me feel weak by letting her be strong. Not that she was in any way a mother figure to me, but I think a part of me missed having someone to offer up a strong, silent security. With no one else to depend on for years, I handled everything alone. I'd come to enjoy it, but she was changing the way I thought. Jo was changing me.

"Of course. We can stay here as long as you like."

We remained still for the next twenty minutes. No words were exchanged. There was only the two of us, breathing in and out as one, wrapped in her strong embrace.

When I settled down, we unraveled ourselves. I refocused on my plan for the day before the emotional ride that became our morning took over. Life sure was easier when I didn't let those parts of myself escape into the light of day.

It'd been a while since I'd been in the saddle or handled my weapons, something I'd done on a daily basis for years now. I felt a little lost without them, naked. Besides, you had to build up stamina to ride on those long trips. There was no way I was going to let myself slip now.

Her eyes were on my every move as I gathered my things and dressed. I offered her a soft smile, thankful for her understanding this morning. Now, I had to get out and do what I knew how to do best.

"You can quit staring." I chuckled. "I'm not runnin' away yet." The assurance eased her immediate concern, but her wheels still turned. The onslaught of concerns were evident in the expression on her face. If only I possessed her other talents, I could read her like she did me. "What?"

"Nothing. I um, should go to town and check on my saloon and Jade today." She paused stuck in thought, keeping her focus on me.

That wasn't all. She had something else on her mind, because she was chewing on her lip again. Somewhere in the back of my mind the answer struck me. Her biggest fear was never if I cared for her, it was only ever one thing. The thing I'd already done to her twice.

"And you're worried I'll be gone when you come back," I said more as a statement than a question.

I hit the nail on the head, because she blushed and shied away. Maybe I was better at reading her than I thought. She was embarrassed and worried I'd think her needy. Quite the opposite actually. I was still amazed anyone would want to keep me around, but if it had to be one person, I was glad it was her.

Slipping my arms into my shirt, I buttoned up as I approached her.

Jo took my hands and with a gentle touch she removed them from their chore. She smiled and took over for me. I think she did it to ignore my gaze, but the gesture was sweet none the less.

"Jo, I don't usually make promises, but I'll make you one." I tilted her chin up towards my face, holding her solemn eyes with my own. "I promise you I will not leave without lettin' you know first. Okay?"

The concern in her eyes eased, replaced with a welcomed sparkle. She finished the buttons and stood, putting us face to face in close proximity. She placed her hands on both sides of my face and gave me a soft kiss on the lips.

"Yes. Thank you. Now what are you plannin' to do today, my beautiful cowgirl?"

Ah, right back to fun Jo. Much better. I hated for her to worry, especially if it had anything to do with me. I never wanted to be the one causing her pain, even if it was an inevitable fact of us being together.

"Well, my beautiful saloon keeper, I'm a itchin' to get back into the saddle and my trigger finger is getting twitchy, so I'm takin' Clover for a ride and a little target practice. You're welcome to come along. We can go to town after. That way you can keep an eye on me." I winked, grabbing my hat and holster.

"I think I'd like that," she said. Her eyes lit up with excitement. "I want to see if those hands of yours are as good with those guns as they are with other things." She flashed a devilish grin.

The heat rose up my neck, surely turning my cheeks beet red. Clearing my throat and head of the images of said things I'd done with my hands the last few days, I nodded and headed out. Unable to look her in the eye without blushing, I stared at the wall and stammered, "I'll uh... just...I'll be out at the barn."

The sound of her laughter filled my ears as I walked out. One more thing to store in my memory for later.

# **Chapter Eight**

The crisp mountain air was exhilarating on a picture perfect day for a ride. I grabbed a few things for targets, packed up my rifle and extra bullets and whistled for Clover. About the time I got her saddled, Jo strode from the house.

I'd never seen her in a cowboy hat before. Not that she'd ever look bad in anything, but the black hat with her light skin and dark features gave her a dangerous, yet sexy appearance. I swore she put a little extra sway in those hips of hers. She definitely knew how to flaunt her many appealing attributes.

I bit my lip and enjoyed the view as she approached. "Killing me," I whispered under my breath and turned my attention back to Clover. "You like her don't you?"

Clover looked at me and threw her head up. She knew exactly what I said. When Jo reached us, she greeted my girl, who acted like a love sick puppy around the woman.

I rolled my eyes. "Since Clover here seems to have taken a likin' to you, has she shared her talents yet?"

Jo quirked a brow, her interest piqued. Her eyes moved between me and my four legged friend. "No, what talents?"

"Well I am glad you asked." I smiled wide, unable to hide my enthusiasm of showing off the parlor tricks I'd taught her. I turned to my old friend and met her eyes. "You've been suckin' up to Jo all week and you haven't pulled out your best stuff yet? I'm shocked."

When I asked Clover to shake with her, Jo stared at me like I was crazy. I motioned down at Clover's hoof raised high for her to take.

"Wow, thank you Clover." Jo smiled and took the hoof.

Clover put it back down. With a wide sweep of my arm, she bowed down before Jo.

"Geeze Sarah, do you ride side saddle and do tricks too?" She laughed.

For some reason I felt awkward and was surprised at my own behavior. Maybe because I let myself open up for a moment, offering her a glimpse of what Sarah Sawyer could be if I let the bad parts go. "Yeah well..." My gaze trailed away from her. "We have a close relationship and I gotta do something to pass the time out on the trail."

"I guess so. Thank you for sharing your talents with me Clover." She addressed my girl directly, earning her a happy whinny in return.

Oh yes, my friend was every bit as taken as I was with Jo.

"You are full of surprises. Tough as nails Sarah Sawyer teaches her horse circus tricks. How delightfully unexpected." She ran her hands down both of my arms with a wide grin.

Clover and I sat patiently as Jo saddled up one of her horses. Her touch left me flustered, but her words hit me deep. The woman really did love any new detail I revealed about myself and never once judged me. Even still, I was unsure if my idea was a good one. I was a little nervous for Jo to see me shoot, somehow believing she'd think less of me when she realized I'd actually used the guns before. A silly notion. Surely she knew I'd shot people before, but to have an idea was one thing. Witnessing an act firsthand often changed your feelings. Hopefully, it wouldn't be for the worst. She never mentioned knowing about my alias as "the Doctor," but I was sure the sheriff would've clued her in at some point. He didn't like me.

We enjoyed a peaceful ride with comfortable silence and random chatter. She looked so natural up on a horse. She fit in anywhere, but out here she had an air about her. An aura beckoning back to whatever history she kept hinting.

One thing had always been obvious to me. Jo was more than some small town farm girl who owned a saloon. No, something deeper, more powerful and dare I say dangerous, remained hidden behind those caring eyes. Something inside made her strong enough to break through the barriers of women and own a business in the west. Not only that, but some very special gift had been bestowed upon her the ability to recognize and understand my pain and make me believe I wasn't alone.

"Sarah, you got any brothers or sisters," she inquired with hesitation. Her fear of me withdrawing into my shell fell short of her desperation to know more about me.

The funny thing though? I didn't have to know more about Jo. I knew all I needed to know about the woman riding next to me. Any who's or what's about her prior life didn't matter. Only the present mattered. Whatever she kept hidden, she'd been successful at pushing down to become the most compassionate person I'd ever met.

My pause made things awkward, so in the spirit of sharing, I choked down my desire to hide and answered her. I even went so far as to attempt a conversation by returning a question of my own. I guess it was supposed to work that way, right? "None. You?"

The one thing about riding with Jessie? She never asked me about much. Then again, she had similar emotional issues as me. Two people with walls up did not a deep conversation make. We had a common goal in the pursuit of justice for those who deserved it. Jo, however, wanted to share. She wanted to know things. Little things and big things. Things I didn't think I could divulge, but Jo held a certain quality that made me want to try.

"My sister died when I was eighteen and I have an older brother, but as I said before, I split from my family years ago." There may have been a hint of regret in her voice, but mostly, she sounded quite pleased with her decision.

I didn't usually pry, but given my story I had to wonder. "Do you miss them?"

My question met with silence. I didn't know how to recover and I didn't want to stir up her past. I should've shut up. These uncomfortable moments solidified the reasons I avoided conversation. The fact I mostly traveled alone or trapped in my own thoughts also played a part. When she began to answer me, I breathed a sigh of relief.

"I miss the idea of a family, but no, I don't miss them. It wasn't a healthy environment. I'm a better person now."

I didn't say anything.

"Sarah," she started in a soft tone. "Would you be willin' to tell me about your parents?"

I had hoped she wouldn't ask me another question, but those things tended to happen when you conversed freely. Curiosity just opened it up to so much more. Another reason I never got too involved with people.

"They were murdered." I blurted it out harsh and fast.

She gasped at my words. Her head snapped toward me. "I'm so sorry, Sarah. I shouldn't have pried. It's none of my business."

"Well, now you know why I don't talk much about the past." I didn't mean to be so short with her, but my anger still boiled over whenever the topic came up.

"I really am sorry. I hope you're not mad." She panicked at the sting of my words.

"No Jo, I'm not mad at you, but I'm still angry as hell at the people who saw fit to needlessly kill two people who only ever tried to do good in this damned world."

"I understand. It explains a lot. I won't push you anymore, but..." she released a tired sigh. "I can tell you have a million stories and I'd love to hear them." She looked to me, her eyes glassy and apologetic.

"Maybe one day, but I'm not ready. I'm sorry." I kept my tone even and breathed deep to relax the painful memories in my mind.

"Don't be. I know how hard it is for you to open up. Thank you for sharin' a little with me, as hard as it was."

We continued on for a spell in silence until I spotted an area perfect for target practice on the backside of the hills similar to the one in my memory. "Let's stop here."

I slid out of the saddle with a little stiffness after an hour ride, but not too bad. My body still had some healing to do. I lacked my usual strength, but my limbs moved with more precision than a few days ago. "Are you any good with a gun?" Certain she'd used one before, I didn't know if she was comfortable with one.

Jo shrugged at me as I pulled out the random targets. "I can use one. I'm better with a rifle, but honestly," she pulled a knife from her boot, "these are more my thing."

Surprised would've been an understatement. For someone who always looked at all of the angles, Jo sure threw me for a loop. I quirked my brow and couldn't resist the half smile from creeping up. "Really? Knives are a bit of a lost art, but they're deadly in the right hands."

Jo smirked at me and rolled the small pumpkin from the garden which came to rest roughly fifteen feet away. "Oh, they're in the right hands."

She turned on a dime, throwing the razor sharp blade with perfect form. It impaled the small gourd right in the center. She spun back to me with a proud grin as I looked on in awe.

Okay, that was pretty damn sexy. I didn't think it was possible for Jo to be any more exciting, but I stood corrected. Knife skills certainly answered the "dangerous" vibe I noted earlier. She had a past, but now I couldn't help wondering how knives fell into it.

"Damn impressive, Jo. How'd you learn to throw?"

"Eh, well my father wasn't a good man. He always used guns to show his power. I learned how to shoot, but I didn't want to be like him, so I took up knives." Something inside her flipped, the normally bright eyes succumbed to a darkness I hadn't seen before. She continued, "Besides, if you really want to intimidate or kill someone, isn't it best to do it up close and personal?"

The look in her eyes nearly made me shiver. I was shocked. I only knew Jo to be warm and caring. There was pain in her expression when she mentioned her dad, but something in the cold tone of her voice when she spoke of killing up close said she'd had the experience before. The thought of Jo ending a life in such a violent manner both chilled me to the bone and intrigued me.

A burden like that being carried by someone as genuine and loving as her though, pained me to no end. But things also made more sense. When she said she was like me, she meant on an intimate level. Not many people were comfortable staring someone in the eye while they killed them. I believed you had to be a little bit dead inside to do such a thing. Jo, however, had done the deed and still lived a happy, productive life. Maybe there was a little hope for me yet.

"I feel the same way, but you can be up close with a gun." I walked away from her, stopping to pull her knife out on my way past. I set my items up on the rocks and stepped back about twenty feet. I removed my left pistol, checking it over and judging the balance. Since it had been a while, I needed to reacquaint myself with this very important part of me. I holstered it and repeated my ritual with the other. Finally getting back in my element gave me a sense of normalcy. This was my comfort zone.

In my periphery, I took note of Jo following me with an intense focus. Squaring up to the targets, I nodded to her and said, "Say when."

Hope I wasn't too rusty.

She laughed. "Really Sarah?"

I glanced back at her and reinforced my request. "Really. You give me the go."

She shrugged with a smile. "Okay." Silent seconds passed before she shouted, "GO!"

The word had hardly escaped her lips before my right hand hit the butt of my pistol, drawing at the hip and putting three holes in the center of each of the two large pumpkins. Like a flash, I holstered the right while drawing the left. I used my free hand across the hammer and blasted three bottles with three shots. I returned the second gun to its resting place and let out a breath in relief. That could have gone a whole other way.

"Holy shit, Sarah! I had no idea! How did you learn to do that?"

Her shocked expression was exactly what I was going for. I gave myself a pat on the back for knocking her socks off, but now I was in a spot. I didn't think about having to explain my skills, but Jo revealed a dark piece of her past, so I could manage it as well.

"Um, a nice family took me in. The old man showed me how to use a gun. I studied and practiced for hours a day to perfect the draw and improve my speed and accuracy. I wanted to be the fastest and the deadliest. I swore I'd never be weak again."

Our light moods turned heavy as we both opened our not so pleasant past up to the other.

"Sarah, I knew you were good with your hands, but wow!"

Jo's effort to relieve the tension in a way only she could made me laugh and her dual meaning sent a flush right through my body. "How do you do it Jo?"

"What?"

"Make everything you say have a whole other meanin' behind it?" I still reeled from the innuendo. She knew exactly what effect she had on me.

"I think it's because you're thinkin' the same things I am." She strolled up to me with a seductive smile.

My insides quaked like a herd of buffalo.

She stopped millimeters away. Her breath brushed my face as she ran her fingers over the collar on my shirt. "Know what else I think, Sarah?" The volume of her voice dropped, like telling a secret not even the birds and insects around us were allowed to hear.

My mind stuck itself on wanting to take her right out in the open. It took everything to whisper one word with her this close. "What?"

She whispered hot against my ear, "I think we're two very good looking, very dangerous women, who're very good together." Jo brushed her lips against mine.

My eyes fluttered shut at the light, enticing touch.

She pulled back, leaving me questioning.

I expected her to follow through and kiss me, but there was nothing. I opened my eyes. My gaze drifted down to her delicious, full lips just a wisp away, waiting for me to close the gap and taste them.

So I did. Gentle at first, but the passion between us flared like a bonfire as our kisses turned feverish. Impassioned moans and whimpers smothered out by one another's mouths as we both searched for more. I dropped my holster and laid her down in the grass. Two sets of hands moved in a blur, yanking and pulling at clothing with a burning need to be closer than the thin fabric allowed.

This morning I never imagined wanting her more than I did already. This new side of her however, brought on a whole other level of desire. Jo was this beautiful, amazing, mysterious, deadly woman and it was as exciting as hell.

# **<u>Chapter Nine</u>**

Minutes before dark we arrived at her saloon. I took my seat near the end of the bar and smiled when Jo hopped over the top to get me a beer.

She leaned forward, giving me a good view down her shirt and served it up with a wink. "I'm gonna go talk to Jade."

"I think she's already found you." I nodded behind her to the dark haired girl making a beeline towards us.

Before Jo even had a chance to turn around, Jade wrapped her up into a big hug. "I have missed you my little Jo!" She hung on for a few seconds, drawing a big grin from her friend.

"I missed you too, Jade. You can let go now." Jo chuckled through her words.

The two women enjoyed a wonderful relationship. I was a little envious they both had someone close to confide in.

When Jade pulled back, she started picking things off of her dress, then off of Jo. "What the--? Why's there grass in your hair?" She spun her around "And all over your back?"

My eyes darted to my beer in a poor attempt to hide under my hat. The harder I tried, the more the heat rose in my cheeks. I couldn't keep my grin hidden at the memory of the two of us making love in the valley or the way Jo looked on her horse as we cantered back toward town. Peeking up from under the brim, I winced at scrutinizing glare of her best friend.

Jade's examination shifted to Jo. Her eyes flashed when the light went on in her head. She placed her hands on her hips and raised a knowing brow. "Oh, I see. You've been out wranglin' your little cowgirl over there. Is that what you two have been doin' all this time?" Her eyes narrowed when she glanced between the two of us like a mother catching her children in a fib.

My beer needed my full attention. Seemed my feelings for Jo made me an easy read, a problem I'd never had before. I didn't know I could even be embarrassed. That hadn't happened in my adult life. Oddly, as mortifying as it was to be under the inspection of Jo's best friend, it was every bit as exhilarating having been with Jo in the intimate matter we were earlier.

I hoped to get another opportunity again soon. In her arms was the only time I truly found peace. With every experience, I wanted her more and more. As much as I tried to fight and keep her out, Jo kept breaking down my walls, getting me to expose more of myself to her. I might be in big trouble.

I peered up at the pair again, never able to keep my eyes off of her for long.

Jo caught me stealing a glance when her eyes flashed to me as she spoke to Jade. She let a sly half grin creep up her lips and Jade froze.

Jade shot a quick look at me and then back to Jo. "Okay you two, enough. I'm standin' right here."

"What? No! God Jade." Jo huffed, pretending to be appalled, but doing a horrible job.

She loved it, unlike me. I cleared my throat, hoping to relax the uncomfortable tightening accompanying the conversation. A conversation involving my very private and intimate activities.

"Can we not talk about it," Jo plead on my behalf, reading my discomfort.

"Sure. We can 'not talk' about it," Jade answered as she walked past me. Her reflection in the glass showed me everything as she motioned they would indeed be talking about every detail later.

Jo shook her head. "Sorry Sarah. You can't keep a secret from her."

I offered her an appreciative smile for ending their little conversation, at least in front of me. "Does she know about the knives?" How much did her best friend really know about her?

Jo leaned both elbows on the bar. "That's how we met. So yeah, she knows. But don't worry, I won't tell her about you."

"Won't tell who, what?" A deep voice called out behind us.

I stiffened at the sound. I turned around to Carter standing in the doorway. I never sensed him coming. Jo would definitely be the death of me. She commanded the focus of all my senses when she was near. Every detail about her bombarded me, leaving no room for anything else. Clear thought went right out the window.

Jo winked at me before turning her attention to him. Grabbing a towel to wipe down the bar, she addressed the sheriff. "Hello, Carter. I won't tell Jade how good Sarah is with her hands," she said with a small laugh and walked away, leaving the two of us alone.

Thanks a lot, Jo. Mental note, make her pay later in the most pleasurable way possible. I cleared my throat again, not at all happy with her dropping him in my lap. Carter also appeared to be less than pleased with the situation.

He didn't look at me, just motioned for a beer. "Sarah, I see you're feelin' better."

"Yes, thanks to Jo's hospitality." His statement seemed to hint at something other than his obvious observation, so I kept my response cold and flat and my focus on my glass.

"She's different than any woman round these parts."

The tone of his words made me squirm. He had feelings for her and a big distaste for me. I'd be damned if I'd let him see any signs of weakness. After all, I got the girl.

"Mm," I hummed and sipped my beer, trying not to get into a conversation. I was as suspicious of him as he was of me. I didn't think him a bad person, but I did believe his feelings for the woman I held dear might cloud his judgment.

The two of us had yet to look one another in the eye. Carter took a big gulp of his beer. "Some people try to take advantage of her generous nature. I won't stand for it."

Ah, there it was. The air between us grew colder. I knew sooner or later he would get to his point. "Well, I can tell you it won't be a problem Sheriff."

"We'll see. I don't want her to get hurt by anyone." He grew more insistent as I refused to back down.

As if I'd ever leave her to satisfy him. I braced my hands on the edge of the bar. My patience wore thin in a hurry. He wanted to protect her. I understood and respected his loyalty, but I didn't respond well to bullies and that was the vibe he sent out. Since I learned to defend myself, I swore I would never be pushed around again.

I spied Jo keeping an eye on us with concern while stocking her bar. I responded to Carter with absolute certainty in my tone. "I would never hurt her."

"Humph. You may not, but I've known people like you, Sarah." He turned, our eyes finally locking.

I met his determined gaze with a steeled jaw.

"You attract trouble. I don't want either of these fine ladies to get caught up in your mess."

I saw his point, but I would never let anything happen to Jo. "Understood. Anythin' else I can do for you Sheriff?"

"Nope, that's it Doc." He flashed a sideways grin, watching for my response.

I gave him one, flinching at the name. Dammit! I should've seen that coming. I needed to get back on my game.

Carter must've been counting the days to drop it on me. His smirk of satisfaction made me sick. He tipped his hat to me.

I narrowed my eyes in return as he took his leave. When the coast was clear Jo hurried over, catching me in a rare moment of trying to contain a violent explosion. His insistence I leave her hit an unexpected nerve. I admit I'd end up hurting her emotionally. Heck, I'd been telling her as much the whole time, but I'd give my life to protect her physically. There was no doubt something more personal was behind his request. It was about him, not Jo and I didn't like it one bit.

"Is everything all right, Sarah? You look a little tense? What'd he say?"

I swallowed hard and calmed myself with a deep breath. "Nothing Jo. It's fine. Everything's fine." I swung back around and forced a smile.

The sideways glance she gave me said it all. She knew I was lying. I had to come clean if I was to honor her request. She wanted everything while I was here and she would get it. "He's not a big fan of me with you is all."

She searched my expression until she was satisfied, then sighed, "I'm sorry." She placed her hand on mine. "He's always like that no matter how much I ask him to stop, but only my opinion matters here and I'm your biggest fan."

Her bright smile was an instant cure for the storm brewing inside of me. No one could soothe my demons like Jo. Her hand slid up my arm, giving it a little squeeze. In the blink of an eye I went from a raging Grizzly to a cub. "Just give me ten more minutes and we can head home."

What else could I do but nod, finish off my beer and be the lucky lady escorting the lovely Jo Porter back to her place? A sadistic grin stretched across my face. Let the Sheriff simmer on that all night.

***

The horses were tended to, supper was done and Jo and I finally settled in after the long day. We sat on a bench near the fire pit enjoying the cool night air as the stars came up. This truly was relaxing. Having a place you could call home, kick back, look over your fields and be comforted by one who cares for you had an appeal after all. For years I wondered what all the fuss was about.

Jo snuggled into my side. She looked down at my hand in my lap. Always craving contact, her hand covered mine, warming it in an instant and bringing about an involuntary sigh.

Smiling or sighing seemed to be my body's normal response to her touch. Jo's silhouette against the shimmering flames was something to behold and I couldn't resist stealing glances at her.

"Sarah, do you remember the first time we met?" She stared out at the horizon and rubbed her thumb over the top of my hand. Jo tilted her head up at me with a curious quirk of her brow.

The memory rushed to the forefront of my mind making me smile so big my face hurt. "Mm hmm." I nodded and glanced down at her. Her eyes sparkled up at me with the flicker of the fire reflected in them. "Perfectly." I smiled wide in return and brushed stray hair from her eyes. I turned my hand over, mingling her fingers with mine.

She turned her gaze back to the glowing pit. "You sat there alone for over an hour, just nursin' your beer and hidin' under that hat of yours. You were so strikin' in your brown Stetson with long blonde hair fallin' out from underneath, a crisp white shirt and matchin' brown leather vest." The broad smile on her face spilled into her words. "I got a little nervous when you left, thinkin' I shoulda gone over to talk to you and I had missed my chance. After a few minutes you returned. You stood out from the crowd like a sore thumb. So beautiful and with a certain air about you. Even Jade noticed." She chuckled at the recollection.

The last comment struck me as odd. The question in my mind coming through with the tilt of my head.

"Relax." Her hand gave mine a soft squeeze. "Jade doesn't feel that way about women, but she's right, you were quite the looker." She patted my leg and continued, "Anyway, when you came back, I watched you from the corner for a few more minutes then decided it was now or never. I had to meet the mysterious cowgirl, because the moment you looked at me…" A heavy sigh slipped from her lips. "I felt somethin' I never did before. It was scary, but at the same time, like a missin' piece of me had been found."

Jo locked her eyes with mine. "The next mornin' when I woke up, you were gone. I'll be honest, it hurt a lot. I figured it was the single best night of my life. The way you touched me Sarah..." She swallowed hard and looked away, unable to maintain contact while she bared her soul to me. "You made the beat of my heart race with a touch and stop with a kiss..." Her eyes fell to our hands before she returned to me.

I was shocked at her confession. I never realized she was just as enraptured with me as I was with her since the very first night. Our encounter was meant to be just another release, an escape, a moment of companionship to help me forget I was alone. Instead, the woman had an earth shattering effect on me.

My night with Jo blindsided me physically and emotionally. Seemed I'd done the same to her.

Leaving the next morning had never been a problem for me, until Jo. Other women never got a second thought when I walked out the door, but Jo marked me in one night of passion. Before I walked out the door, I couldn't help looking over my shoulder at her sleeping with a content smile. Resisting the urge to run back to her was one of the hardest things I'd ever done. Now I knew she'd been equally affected. Leaving her this time would be infinitely worse.

Jo gave me a gentle nudge. "I'm just glad I mustered the courage to talk to you or we woulda never met."

The impact of our initial meeting aside, her version made me chuckle. The truth? I was the one trying to lure her in. Luckily I played it right. "I remember things a little differently." I laughed harder and shook my head.

Jo shot me a perplexed look.

"See, when I rode into town, I stopped at the general store to rent a stall for my horse. On my way in, I caught a glimpse of this bewitchin' brunette. There was something about her, an undeniable pull to follow her, so I did."

Her eyes glued themselves to mine as she took in every new detail I offered about our first meeting.

"You were stunnin' in your deep burgundy dress and your long, dark hair pourin' down over your shoulders. You had the brightest smile for everyone you passed. You were a shining beacon amongst the tattered dresses and solemn faces that lined the street. Not to mention those gorgeous dimples. Those had forever found a home in my memory."

For a moment, I couldn't think. The sight of her often took my breath away at the most unexpected times. With a twinkle in her eye and those very dimples making themselves known as her smile continued to grow, all my thoughts stopped in their tracks.

"Um," I stammered, making her grin impossibly wider. "Anyway, I stood against the wall with my head down until you went into the saloon and by the way you made your rounds, I could tell you worked there. I took a chance you'd be around a while as I put up Clover. I came back and settled in, hopin' you were into the quiet, female, gunslinger type. I knew it was workin' when I finally excused myself and caught the despair in your expression. I waited long enough for you to worry you missed out, but not enough to lose your attention and to my delight, it worked." A wide grin stretched across my face watching her process my words.

"You sly devil you." She slapped me on the arm and grinned. "Then why did you run out afterwards?"

My behavior still embarrassed me. Never mind the fact I'd done the same to countless other women, doing it to Jo just seemed wrong. I really didn't know what to do that day. I didn't understand the feelings coursing through me at the time, but I knew I had to catch Bill Martin, my next mark, so I continued on with the one thing I did understand.

I shook my head, still not able to fully grasp the way I reacted to her from one brief encounter. "I never had any kind of feelin's for anyone I'd been with. You took me by surprise, Jo. I didn't know what to do and I was headed somewhere. I had a job to do. I was leaving the next day anyway. I figured it would be much easier if I didn't have to say goodbye to you. I just didn't know I'd never really be able to say goodbye to you. You lived in my heart and mind each day since. That's why I came back. I'm sorry I did that to you."

Jo pushed herself up and away from me. I missed the warmth of her body against mine. She didn't seem to be mad, more like trying to comprehend the reasoning behind my decision to leave her the way I did. "Why didn't you come back sooner?"

A very valid question to someone who had any idea of what it meant to care for another person, which was not me. "Again, I'm not used to havin' any emotions for anyone and I was in the middle of some business. I guess I kinda thought the feelings would fade after a while, but they never did. I'm sorry it took me six months to get back to you. I didn't know you were hoping to see me again."

We sat side by side. Neither of us looked at the other. We stared off into the darkness beyond the fire pit.

"Yeah, but then you ran off again the next mornin'. I never thought I'd see you again after the first time, but when you came back, I was hopeful, thinkin' surely you felt the same." Her tone grew desperate. She spoke faster with each word, relieving herself of the weight she'd carried from those painful days.

"I was so upset to find you gone again. Every day since you vanished I waited and hoped. Each new face that came in, I prayed it would be yours. I almost gave up."

The lingering pain of the second time I left let itself be known in her mournful eyes and defeated posture. I hated what I had done to her and I didn't want to think of how much worse she would hurt the next time.

She tipped her head to me as she continued, "Jade told me to move on, but I couldn't. Then nearly a year later, you appeared a third time out of the blue and my heart stopped, not knowin' if it should beat faster in excitement or prepare to be crushed once more."

"I'm sorry Jo. I didn't know. I never meant...I had no idea you felt that way. I thought I was the only one..." I tried to explain, hoping the sincerity rang true in her heart and mind. My hand found hers, claiming it once again in a gentle embrace. The need to console her drove my actions.

"I don't know how you couldn't tell I was head over heels for you." A pained smile tried to force up the edges of her lips through the hurt we'd dug up. "Had you stayed till mornin' you woulda known. I swore if I was lucky enough to see you again I wouldn't let you go without telling you."

This conversation was long overdue even if it hurt us both. "I care for you Jo, like no one else, but you know I gotta leave again soon, right?"

There was no way I could make her understand. Hell, I didn't even understand why I kept running from this amazing woman. Why couldn't I abandon this whole mission I created and be happy here with her? Hell that one fact alone told me I wasn't of sound mind. No one in their right mind would make that decision once, much less three times.

"I do, but I wish I could get you to stay. I don't know what you do when you're gone, but I know it's not healthy. I hear stories, but I ignore them, believin' you'll tell me when you're ready."

"Jo, it's complicated, but it's somethin' I just have to do. I did promise not to leave without tellin' you and I meant it."

"Does this have anythin' to do with your parents?"

My lack of response gave me away. My eyes darted from her as I forced down the anger once again from the mere mention of them.

"Sarah, do you think they'd want you to spend your life lookin' for revenge? Worse yet, for you to die doing it?"

I still wouldn't look at her. What they wanted didn't matter anymore. I was lost to any hopes they ever had for me anyway. There was only what I'd become and what I believed without question needed to be done. I let go of her hand, plunging mine into my jacket pockets.

She flinched at my abrupt move, her brow creased as she struggled to figure me out.

"Jo, I know you think you know me, but do you really? Do you know the things I've done? Do you know my reputation?"

She offered only a blank stare.

"Have you ever heard of the Doctor?" I didn't want to tell her, but better she heard it from me than some convoluted version from someone like the sheriff. He had it out for me.

Jo nodded. She had indeed heard stories. "You are the Doctor," she stated under her breath as if she suspected it to be true and now her suspicions were confirmed.

"I am," I affirmed with sadness. I wasn't proud of the reputation I made as I set out on my path to avenge my family. While it was a relief having one less thing to hide from her, I worried about what she thought of me.

"Why do they call you that, Sarah?" She didn't seem upset or disgusted, which surprised me. Instead, Jo seemed more curious to learn more, to dig deeper.

I huffed at the question. The Doctor was one thing I always hated to talk about, besides my parent's death anyway. "I hate the name, it's silly, but it all started when a man decided to slap his wife around in a store. I was there and I couldn't bear anymore, so I asked him politely to stop. He told me, in rather unpleasant language, to mind my own business and how women had no place tellin' a man what to do. I introduced his face to the table, breaking his nose in the process."

I paused, checking for any sign she might be disturbed by my actions. "Everyone was stunned to see a woman act out, but his wife gave me an appreciative nod and that was all the acknowledgement I needed. My father was a doctor and I'd picked up a few things while helpin' him out. I grabbed the sobbing, apologetic man a cold rag and reset his nose. I proceeded to let him know, rather curtly, that if he ever touched his wife again I'd be back to break his arms."

Jo sat in silence. She seemed unfazed and urged me to continue with a gentle squeeze of my knee.

"There was another guy who wouldn't keep his hands to himself. Earned himself a stab wound in a rather unpleasant place, which I stitched up for him accompanied by a lecture in manners."

"So you're not a bad person, just teachin' lessons to those in need of learnin'." She half smirked at my scrunched brow.

A rather interesting analysis of disturbing behavior, but a spin I rather enjoyed. "Well, there's also those who're meant to be killed." I met her eyes with an intense stare. I wanted her to see the cold killer in me, to know I wasn't the kind, caring woman she built me up to be. I kept trying to maintain a distance, a wall, but she wouldn't allow it to stand.

"Apparently, there was an audience when I used my six shooter to nearly amputate one man's shooting arm. I took out both knee caps first so he couldn't get away. I knew from studyin' my father's books where to hit him to inflict great pain and slow death. I watched him bleed out as he begged for help."

With a steeled jaw, again I tried to gauge her reaction. I saw no fear, no judgment. I'd been prepared for a look of disgust or for her to scoot away like I was a deranged stranger, but again, nothing.

"Did this someone cause enough harm to feel he warranted such a punishment or was it just fun for you?" Jo still held a neutral expression; no emotion what so ever, but there was a distinct shift in her eyes similar to the one in the valley when she spoke of killing.

"Oh, it was well deserved," I answered with certainty. A small grin still tugged at the corners of my mouth when I thought of him begging for help. I laughed at him the same way he laughed at me when our roles were reversed. "Though I can't say I didn't find joy in it."

"Well, if you believed it in your heart, then it musta been bad and I can't fault you for doin' what you thought was right. Is that what you do when you travel?"

I was expecting a different reaction. "Kinda." I shrugged and pushed forward. "From there the stories grew, some of them true and others exaggerated. I killed a few, even ended up on the wanted list for a short time. So you can see, I'm not a good person, Jo. I don't know why you want to be with someone like me."

Why wouldn't she just accept who I was? She always tried to justify my sins and it drove me insane.

Jo stood up from her spot on the bench and stepped in front of me.

I looked up at her. She was so frustrating. I needed to make her see things my way, but she didn't give in. This woman was a stubborn mule, albeit a gorgeous one.

"Sarah," she let out a tired sigh, "as I've said before, I've done things I'm not proud of, things that made me think I was a monster and didn't deserve happiness, but I was wrong and so are you."

Jo straddled my lap, pulling herself in close to my body, letting her finger trail down my jaw. "You didn't have to help the people you hurt. Whatever your reason for killin' the others, I know it wasn't just for the heck of it. You weren't stealin' and hurtin' innocent people. Will you tell me who you're after?"

I shook my head. "No, I don't want you involved and if they ever figure out who I am, you could be in danger. That's another reason I never stay put for long or get attached to anyone."

"So, why are you still here now," she asked with her eyes full of emotion and desire, causing a shiver to run down my spine.

I tried to turn away, but her hand held me still. "You." It took all my strength to choke out one word. I couldn't look at her, even though she demanded it. My gaze drifted to anywhere but her as I spoke, "It's so hard to leave you, almost painful. I've never been so drawn to anyone before. I still can't believe you really want to be with me. I can't understand it." I finally forced my eyes back to her. "It doesn't make any sense why someone like you would want someone like me."

I traced along her collar bone, drawing an inner satisfaction at the tremble I evoked. "You reach something deep inside of me, Jo. I can't even make sense of it, but my body and my soul surrendered to you against my will."

"The heart always knows." She leaned in and whispered against my skin before sucking my bottom lip between her teeth.

God, how all I ever wanted to do when I was in her presence was possess her, and in turn, let her possess me, over and over. It was all I could do to think or speak. My mind reeled with the task of sorting out what it all meant for me.

"How can it know? I don't even know who I am, much less what I want, besides..." I trailed off, my eyes searched for something in the distance.

Jo stared at me, her breath halting as she awaited my next words, but I didn't finish the thought. I sensed she already knew I'd bring up leaving again, that I would embrace the urge to run from her and my heart once more. But I wasn't just running from her, I was running toward the finish of a ten year journey of heartbreak and pain.

She took my hand, entwining our fingers so tight I couldn't escape. "Sarah, you may not know yourself, but in spite of everything you think you are, I know better and I love you." Her eyes widened in surprise when she said the words.

My breath caught at her honest confession. I'd not heard those words directed at me by anyone other than my parents and I'd never uttered them since. I wasn't capable of them anymore. My mind raced. My heart ran away with it. Panic swept over me. This was bad. She shouldn't love me. I tried to push her away. "Jo I--"

She held me down and shushed me with a finger over my lips. "Sarah, don't. Don't say anything. I don't want you to feel obligated to anything. Lovin' you is my burden to bear. I know what's involved, but it doesn't change what my heart wants. I wouldn't change it for all the money in the world."

Her words stunned me to silence, able to do nothing but stare at the heartfelt emotion in her eyes. Mine own filled with disbelief and pain. Pain at hearing she'd given her love to me and in return I would hurt her. I didn't deserve such a blessing and I hated that such a precious gift was wasted on this lost soul. Yet, the confession filled me with thoughts and feelings I couldn't explain. Nothing about our lives made sense. I was a drifter and she'd planted roots. I was a killer, while she had compassion. Still she was perfect for me in so many ways.

I couldn't say for sure the nagging feeling in me was love, but the place she held in my heart and soul was reserved only for her, never to be replaced.

Tears welled up in her eyes and I knew the cause. None of this was fair to her. She'd put herself out there knowing the cost and not hearing me return her feelings...

I wanted to say it, if only to make her smile, but I couldn't. Not now. Saying those words would make everything so much harder. I never wanted to be the source of her pain, even though it was inevitable. Once again I was reminded of why I always ran away from her, why I should have left sooner.

My struggle carried through every muscle in my body. Eyes darted. Arms tensed. Should I run? Should I stay? Through my conflicted haze, nothing made sense.

She looked into my soul like no one else and waded through the torment of emotions without fear. Her hand cradled my cheek and thumb traced the edges of my mouth. My quivering lips parted, tempted to suck and tease, but opted instead to nip softly at her finger tip.

She flashed a small, endearing smile. With one hand still locked in mine, she led me inside.

"Jo, I don't think it's a good idea." I managed a whispered protest. My body still had other ideas. It screamed to follow her, battling my mind that kept reminding me how this would only make matters worse. I didn't want us to dig a deeper hole and yet, as wrong as it was, I also couldn't leave without feeling her one more time.

"I want to show you what my love for you really feels like." She never sounded so fragile, yet she tugged my arm with insistence and gazed at me with complete adoration.

My stomach fluttered in anticipation. Every cell in my body ached with the burning need for her touch. I wasn't one to cry, especially after sex, but I could feel every bit of emotion Jo held for me. Every touch, every kiss, branded me as hers and brought a tear to my eye. The love, the pain, the heartbreak, the desire, all unleashed itself upon me. It was the most amazing thing I'd ever known. Jo was the most amazing gift I'd ever been given and I was a fool.

Screaming her name out into the darkness, all I could focus on was the inevitable breaking of her heart that was soon to come again. I wouldn't expect her to forgive me a third time. I wasn't worthy. But how on earth would I ever get her out of my mind, out of my soul?

# **Chapter Ten**

Jo's arm draped across my bare stomach to hold me close. Darkness still ruled the hour, though the moon hung high and its beams shined into the room casting a light over the two of us.

I couldn't have been out for too long. My chest rose and fell in quick breaths. The ramblings of my unconscious mind once again deprived me of precious shut eye, but for the first time in a long time, my dream was different.

My mother was smiling at me, but this time I was an adult. Instead of El Paso, we were sitting on the porch together here in Idaho as we looked across the pasture at Clover. Mother seemed happy for me and squeezed my hand tight. I was at peace.

Jo walked out the door, exchanging smiles with us as she announced lunch. She walked back inside the house. My mother and I stood and headed for the door. When I turned to look for her, I was thrust back into the same old scene, cowering alone and helpless as my mother was murdered before my very eyes.

Daniel O'Shea laughed at me. A gun sat on my hip and I drew fast, but before I could fire, he was gone.

Soothing breaths slowed my heightened response to the memory of my dream. Relaxing was difficult even knowing I was safe. It was rare I dreamt of their murder when I was with Jo. This was the first time the dream had changed, like my parents wanted me to find peace, just like Jo said.

I couldn't though. Not as long as he was alive. Mom, dad, Jo…they'd all have to understand that he'd always haunt me. I couldn't say how I'd feel after I killed him, but I was sure I'd find a deep satisfaction in the deed. Maybe then I could come back to her, to Jo.

"You okay?" Her voice was raspy from sleep.

My arm laid across the pillow over her head. I suddenly realized I'd been running my fingers through her hair in a subconscious attempt to calm myself. "Um, yeah. Just a dream. Go back to sleep," I whispered and let out a deep breath as I glanced at the beautiful woman snuggled against my side.

"I won't let anyone hurt you" she muttered and pulled me in tighter.

The sentiment was appreciated and sounded so good falling from her lips. It had been a long time since anyone protected me, but it wasn't me I was worried about.

Why on earth couldn't I be happy here in her arms? Why? Because my damn scars ran too deep. There'd be no happiness, no settling down, no closure until I finished this insane mission.

I decided on the spot to leave in two days. The time had come to put it all behind me and move on with my life.

I squeezed her tight and kissed her on the forehead. I was gonna make the best of the time we had left. Jo smiled a sleepy smile, making the thump of my heart pound like a herd of wildebeests. Content for the moment, I closed my eyes and hoped, as usual, to find sleep.

***

I cooked breakfast and stared out the kitchen window. A storm brewed over the mountain tops making everything gray and damp. Days like this I didn't miss the trail. No one could say in honesty that they loved being out in the rain, at least not for a whole day. You were stuck in soggy clothes, chilled to the bone and everything you owned was wet no matter how well you tried to protect it. Your horse sure wasn't happy either. All you really wanted was a warm, dry room with a fireplace and some whiskey.

I was happy today. I had all of those things and a warm body to keep me company. This was the type of life I could have when I was done wrestling my demons. There were some days I wished it would come sooner than others.

I sighed and flipped the sausage around, returning to the view outside. A smile crept up my lips at Clover running around with a few of the other horses having a grand time.

That warm body just pressed up behind me. Her arms snaked around my waist, holding me in a possessive embrace. Soft lips pressed to my neck and she whispered into my ear, "Whatcha thinkin'?"

Her breath tickled my skin causing me to smile wider. My eyes fluttered shut. "Nothin', watchin' Clover. She's so happy out there." I took a deep breathe in a feeble attempt to settle the ache within. The ache I was coming to know all too well. The one that grew whenever she touched me like the way she was now.

"I see a few fence posts leanin' and boards missin'. I'll go fix 'em after I eat. Do you have extra posts?" I sighed as she brushed her lips along the nape of my neck.

"Yes I do, but you don't have to. It's about to start rainin' and I'm sure there are other things you could do in here," she husked in a seductive tone followed by a devilish giggle.

My insides fluttered in anticipation of the "other things" as her arms squeezed me tighter. Deft fingers slid under my thermal shirt and grazed my stomach. I gasped at her touch. Supple lips that I loved to taste pulled into a smile against my skin. It really was hard to leave her embrace.

Evil temptress!

"Don't ya have to go to work today?" As soon as I asked the question I realized how it sounded and I cringed.

"Why? Ya tryin' to get rid of me?" Jo chuckled and released her hold. She moved to the stove to pour some hot tea.

I groaned my displeasure as soon as her warmth left me. "No." I wasted no time answering. I wasn't going anywhere, but I knew she'd neglected her business to stay here with me. As much as I enjoyed her company, I did feel a little guilty. "I doubt I could if I wanted to." I smiled and gave her a wink. "I was just wonderin'. I know it's been several days and you got a business to run."

I leaned back on the edge of the counter with my arms crossed as I watched her every move. I marveled at how difficult it was to take my eyes off of the woman whenever she was within view. I was still in awe of what she'd done to me. I belonged to her completely, no matter how hard I fought to resist.

"I'll go out and fix the fence today. If it rains too much it might wash out the dirt and cause the post to come down. Won't take me long."

"Well, I do appreciate it. I do have to go in later, actually. I promised Jade the night off, but you're welcome to join me." She eyed me over the rim of her tea cup with one of her teasing glances. She more than enjoyed riling me up.

I was hit with a sudden urge to put the finishing touches on our food. Her gaze made me weak and I had to turn away. "We'll see." I grinned over my shoulder.

She already knew the answer. I was such a push over for her. While I wasn't in the mood to deal with Carter again, I did want to spend as much time as possible with Jo. Our time together was almost at an end.

***

**Spokane- O'Shea Ranch**

With a spring in his step, Mike made a beeline up to the main house. He was anxious to tell his boss the new information he dug up. Since Mr. O'Shea put him in charge of finding out anything he could about killings related to his associates, he'd been scouring the surrounding towns to find something, anything. This time, however, he wasn't going to interrupt the old man's shaving hour.

Mike knocked on the front door. He didn't have to wait long before he was escorted by a young woman to the large living room where Danny O'Shea sat at his desk.

Without a glance or an acknowledgement in anyway, O'Shea spoke with a deep, throaty voice bellowing flat and cold. "Whaddya want?"

His harsh tone made Mike cower a little, breaking the confidence he brought with him.

"Sir, I have more news for ya. Another man was found dead outside Challis, Idaho. The death is a few days apart from the one in Red Lodge, but they seem to be headed in this direction."

This new information made the old man pause as he looked up from his letter and stared at the younger man on the other side of the room. "Interestin'. No word of who is behind this?"

"Only that a U.S. Marshal and another woman collected the bounty last time."

"But no bounty this time?"

"None reported sir. They found the body out in the hills there."

"I highly doubt a woman is killin' all these people and a U.S. Marshal don't just go around shootin' folks. This is curious..." Danny let his eyes drift to the ceiling in contemplation of his options.

"It's hard to tell if they're headed here, but I won't take no chances. Tell Bart to up patrols around the border of the property and to let me know immediately if there's anythin' unusual. Also, let's add a few men up around my place, since they'll most certainly be comin' for me if they come this far."

"Yes sir. Right away, sir. I'll keep an ear out for anythin' else too," Mike said. His excitement was plain as day. He turned on a heel ready to hurry from house to find Bart and relay the order.

Danny called him back with a slight grin on his face. "Mike, that's the kind of thing can help a young man go a long way with me, you understand?"

That was all the encouragement Mike needed. He smiled big and replied, "Yes sir. Thank you, sir." He wasted no time finding Bart and heading back to town in hopes of finding something more to put him in the boss's favor.

***

## Ketchum- Jo

The rain pounded in a steady rhythm on the tin roof. The pinging grew louder and louder as it intensified outside. I took a break from cleaning the house and looked out the window. There was Sarah working on the fence in the pouring rain with her trusty sidekick Clover giving her playful shoves to hurry up.

I smiled at the scene and how nice it felt to have her here, finally. The smile faded fast as I came to terms with the fact she'd be leaving me again soon. Though she never really revealed her purpose, I had an idea and wished I could convince her to give up her quest for vengeance.

Seeking revenge never gave me the satisfaction I had hoped for. I would've loved to have taught my father a lesson, but I decided to let go of my anger and find happiness instead of focusing my energy on him. I wasn't like the rest of my family. The day my sister was killed in a shootout, I ran and never looked back.

If only I could make Sarah understand how much better life was when you forgave and let go. Of course, I never had my family murdered while I watched. I couldn't begin to imagine the pain, but all I could think about was how it might end in Sarah's death. I hated to watch the woman I loved leave again, but losing her forever would be beyond devastating.

My mind drifted until the slamming of the door startled me. She kicked off her boots, hung her hat and removed her rain coat. I took a good long look at the woman I'd fallen for. She was beautiful. Tall and lean with long blonde hair, high cheek bones and honest eyes.

I'd never met anyone like Sarah before. There was a quiet intensity about her. Everything she did was so smooth and purposed, almost as if the practice was what kept her from thinking about her past. Every movement, every word, was performed with a specific intent behind it. I'd often find myself watching her and wondering what thought was behind each action.

"All fixed." Sarah smiled with the satisfied look of a job well done.

"Thank you, Sarah. You can hang the jacket in the closet. I bet you're cold. Want a hot drink?" I enjoyed the familial feel of the moment. Having Sarah here with me, the way we just fit together, it was so natural, so right. My heart ached knowing it wouldn't be long before it was over. It was eminent, I could feel it, but I was determined to keep a brave face.

***

## Sarah

I opened the door to the closet and hung up my rain soaked jacket. Something caught my eye in the back of the small room. I reached in, moving a few things aside and when I saw it, a smile crossed my face. I pulled out the old guitar and gave the strings a gentle strum. I looked up and there was Jo staring at me questioning with eyes. "Do you play, Jo?"

She looked away, horrified.

"What? I was just wondering."

She took slow steps toward me, her hand motioning to put the instrument aside. "Please put that away, Sarah," she begged with a shy laugh.

Now I was even more curious. "Why?" I darted away from her, content to let her chase me. "I'd love to hear ya, Jo." I flashed her my best doe eyes and she paused for a moment.

"I'm no good at it." After a few steps she gave up her pursuit and sighed. "I started to learn a long time ago. Let's just say it didn't go well." She laughed. "I forgot I even had that old thing."

I played with the strings and tuned it a little. "That's too bad. Maybe sometime I'll show ya. It's a lot easier than most people make it."

"You play?" Her question was one of shock and surprise, almost bordering on doubtful. She placed her hands on her hips as if challenging me to prove I could.

I shrugged. "A little. My parents liked to play and sing together quite often. I learned some, but I haven't played in years."

Her laugh was the sweetest music to my ears. She sat down with a wide smile directed at me. "You are a very talented, very mysterious woman, Sarah Sawyer."

I leaned over to put the instrument away, hoping to hide the red in my cheeks she always brought out of me.

"Oh no you don't." She shook her head and pointed at the guitar. "You don't get to tell me you can play that thing and think you can get outta here without a song." Her eyes shone with excitement.

As much as I didn't want to, I couldn't find it within myself to say no to her. I hadn't played in years and I'd never played for anyone, but my parents and Clover. My nerves got the best of me, setting off a slight tremble of my hands as they began to sweat.

She reached out and touched my arm. "Relax, Sarah. I'm not gonna to judge you. Whatever you do will be miles ahead of me, but I'd really love it if you played a little somethin' for me."

Clearing my throat, I bought time as I tried to think of any song I could remember. Only one came to mind and it made me swallow hard. The song was my parent's favorite, one my father had written to my mother for their wedding. A song he'd play for her several times a year just to see her smile.

With a gentle strum of the strings, I began to play. I couldn't remember all the words, so I gathered the courage to hum along. I was a little shaky at first, but I closed my eyes. As I relaxed, my voice grew stronger. When I opened my eyes, I locked on hers, holding her gaze as I continued on and letting the song say what I never could.

I only remembered the chorus. The words poured from me without effort. They echoed my feelings for Jo the same way they did for my parents so many years ago.

"So lucky I am, that a heart chose mine,
Till now was just a dream.
Love that lasts a lifetime,
Sounds farfetched to me.
Yet, here she is,
Holding me tight,
Freeing me from solitude,
Like a shining knight."

Her eyes were glassy and overflowing with emotion, knowing full well what I was doing. It was her special talent, to hear what I couldn't say.

Breaking our gaze, I looked down at the strings, strumming the last few chords as I hummed through to the end. There was silence as I put the instrument down on the floor and stared at it.

"That's the one song I really remember. It was my parent's favorite, but um..." I glanced back up at her through my lashes, "it describes the way I feel about you." I looked away as soon as I said it, suddenly feeling shy. I fidgeted my fingers until I felt her warm hand on my own.

Jo had tears running down her cheeks as she slid over to me. She held my face in her hands and delivered a lingering kiss. Her soft lips graced me with their presence like warm sunshine on a cold winter day, heating my chilled, damp body from the inside out. Her happiness made any task worthwhile.

"Thank you, Sarah. That was beautiful. You play very well and your voice is amazin' too."

I nodded my appreciation, fighting hard against the lump in my throat and heat threatening to rise up my cheeks once again. Unable to find words at the moment, I squeezed her hand and pulled it up to my lips, kissing her palm. Several silent moments passed before I got up and walked to the kitchen. I poured us both some of the tea Jo had made and sat down next to her, handing her a cup.

She grinned at me. "Thank you." She kissed me on the cheek and curled up into my side as we watched the rain continue to fall out the window.

This was one of the happiest moments of my life.

***

### Ketchum Sheriff's Office- Jessie Walker

Ketchum was like every other prospering town. Everyone was happy and rushing from place to place. I stepped into the entrance of the sheriff's office and looked around. There wasn't a soul in sight. I knocked on the open door and a man peeked out from a back room, looked me up and down then hid behind the wall again. His dark hair was tussled. I'd woken him up. I laughed to myself and shook my head. These local lawmen had it easy.

"Hold on. I'm a comin'," he called out. Several seconds ticked by before he walked out, putting on his best air of authority. "Hello, Sheriff Carter Hamilton, pleased to meet you Marshal...?" He tipped his hat.

"Walker, but enough with the formalities, call me Jessie. I just got into town and wanted to check in, see if there was any important news." I looked him up and down. The man was a keen dresser and not bad to look at, but I mentally cringed at his handlebar mustache. He was going to be one of those guys.

"Okay." He seemed frazzled by my gruffness. "Well, nothin' new really. There were a few killings reported a few weeks ago between Challis and Red Lodge." He pointed the direction of the towns. The same way I'd come from. "But all's peaceful here." The Sheriff smiled with pride, letting his eyes wander down my body.

I folded my arms across my chest and cleared my throat, snapping Carter out of his lust filled daze.

He coughed with embarrassment and met my eyes.

"Good to hear. I wanted to give ya the courtesy of stoppin' in since I was town. If you need anythin'..."

"'Preciate that. Will ya be staying long?" There was an eagerness in his voice.

I debated whether or not to tease the Sheriff, but first and foremost, I needed to find Sarah. I let my trademark smug grin take over and left my entertainment for later. "Don't know, depends." I started to leave, but made a quick turn back "By the way, any chance you've seen a cantankerous blonde cowgirl around?"

His brows raised in question as he laughed. "Why yes, actually. Is she wanted?" He was almost too hopeful and it made me suspicious. "I can have her here in twenty minutes."

What did Sarah get herself into now? "No, no. We're old friends. She mentioned she'd be headed this way. Didn't know if she'd still be around. Don't tell her you saw me. I always like to surprise her," I teased with a wink.

"Very well. You can probably find her at the saloon later," he said a little deflated. "I'm glad I got to meet ya. I was beginnin' to think the stories of the lady Marshal were just a farce," he followed in a shy voice.

Guess I had successfully intimidated another one. People just didn't know how to respond to a strong woman.

"See ya round Sheriff." I gave him a tip of my hat before stepping outside. I strolled through the handful of small businesses until I reached the stables. The gal there pointed me toward the saloon for food and rooms. Apparently in this town, all things led to a saloon. Good thing too, because I was ready for a drink.

I set my horse up for the night and made my way back to the saloon. Stopping outside the swinging doors, I took a long look around before entering. There wasn't much going on inside and no sign of Sarah. I took a seat and slapped some money on the counter top. "Barkeep, shot of whiskey for a weary traveler."

The tiny, Spanish-looking girl behind the bar jumped at the noise and turned around. "All right," she huffed. "Hold your horses blondie. I'll be right there." She filled a shot glass and sauntered over, leaning over to read my badge.

I made quick work of the whiskey and paused for a moment to savor the burn. "Ah. That's good stuff. I'll have another and a room if you got one."

The girl refilled the glass, watching me with curious bright green eyes as I threw back the second shot just as fast. "Never seen you round here before." She rested her elbows on the top and set her chin in her palms. "What brings you to town Marshal?"

"Didn't realize I needed to clear my travel plans with you," I answered with a snarl. "Ever heard of official business and a little thing called privacy?"

"Nope." She stood and set her hands on her hips, giving me a hard stare. "It's my business to make sure there's no trouble here and that none of my friends get hurt. It doesn't matter if you tell me or not, I have ways of findin' out."

Loved the attitude. She had guts. She was also quite the beauty with her light caramel skin, raven hair and blazing green eyes. "Not that it's any of your business, but I'm here to meet a friend. You seen a tall, cranky, blonde cowgirl named Sarah?"

The feisty girl tensed up and her eyes narrowed in suspicion. "I find it highly unlikely you two are friends."

"Ah, so you do know her?" I chuckled. "Yeah, Sarah's not much of a talker, but we go way back. Know where I can find her?" I tapped the bar top signaling another round. She seemed like the loyal type, so she'd never give me Sarah's whereabouts. But she also seemed like a smart egg, which meant she knew damn well I'd find whoever or whatever, I was after.

Leaning back against the counter with her arms crossed, she watched me with great interest. "You're in luck. I do have a room left and you might catch her here later tonight. Better not be any trouble in my place. I don't care who you are. Got it?"

"I like you." I chuckled while she poured another glass. "You're straight up, no bullshit. I can appreciate that. I'm Jessie."

"I'm Jade. Just remember, I got my eye on you."

I nodded with a smile. "I have no doubt." I finished my drink, tossed down some more cash and headed up to my room. Tonight I'd find Sarah and everything would be right back to plan.

# <u>Chapter Eleven</u>

**Sarah**

It was shortly after four in the afternoon when we arrived at the saloon. Jo was giddy as we strolled in together. Her smile was infectious and it pulled a big grin out of me. The place was beginning to get a dinner rush as patrons slowly filtered in and it looked as though it would be a busy night for them.

Not seeing Jade anywhere, Jo set me up with a drink and went to check the stock room. I took a seat at the end of the bar and sipped my beer until I was overwhelmed by a familiar presence taking the stool beside me. I didn't have to look, I already knew. The real question was what the heck was she doing here after our confrontation in Red Lodge?

Glad I wore my gun today.

I took another sip of my beer with my left hand while my right drifted down to my six shooter. "Jessie, what the hell do you want?"

***

## Jo

The storeroom door flew open and Jade stormed in behind me, scaring me half to death.

"Jo, I'm so glad you're finally here," she said in a breathless whisper. "There's a U.S. Marshal in town. She's lookin' for Sarah. Says they're old friends or somethin', but I think somethin's goin' on." She looked over her shoulder as if she expected someone to eavesdrop on our conversation.

My friend was always so suspicious of everyone. Even with her keen instincts, I stared at her like she had two heads. She was in a panic over something, but what? Why was it a big deal if Sarah had a friend? "Calm down Jade. Whaddya think's goin' on?"

"I don't know, but we both know Sarah is not miss social, so friend? I think that's pushing it." Her faded Spanish accent came through loud and clear in her panic. She let out an awkward chuckle at the idea.

"Hey, she's a lot different than you think." I crossed my arms and glared at her. She was always making negative comments about the woman I loved.

Jade waved me off and paced around the room. "Anyway, she was checkin' the place out and she's got a room upstairs for a few days. Is she really even a U.S. Marshal? I've never seen a woman Marshal. Maybe we should check with Carter?"

I shook my head. "No way. You can check with him. I don't want to deal with him. He already doesn't like Sarah. Maybe we should get out there in case the woman shows up."

I set the crate of whiskey down and walked back out into the main room, stopping dead in my tracks when I spotted Sarah and another woman sitting face to face.

*** 

## Sarah

Jessie didn't answer my question. Her silence only served to make me more irritated along with her sudden appearance. I never expected her to show up after our last meeting. The memory of her locked in a warm embrace with one of O'Shea's gang didn't sit well with me and only reaffirmed the reasons why I never let anyone get close to me. Well, except for Jo. Jessie and I shared a close relationship, but even she hadn't been privy to the parts of me I'd shared with Jo.

"I said I'd meet you here mid-September. Actually, I'm surprised you're still here. This town is pretty boring for an adventurer such as yourself," she remarked in the sarcastic tone I'd become so accustomed to over the years.

What were her motives? It couldn't be to sleep with me again and it seemed she wasn't going to kill me herself. I steeled my jaw as I braced myself for whatever was to come in the next few moments. "Why are you here? You coulda waited for me in Spokane. You know I'll show up eventually and then you could have me killed, so why all the extra attention," I seethed.

I still refused to look at her face as my anger bubbled up from her betrayal. Seriously, if she was going to lead me on so O'Shea could kill me, why take so long? Why not take me right to him?

"It's hard to resist how cute you are when you're angry."

I knew her well enough to know that smug grin was directed right at me. I gritted my teeth and kept hidden beneath my hat. I didn't want to give anything away.

"Besides Sarah, can't a girl have a sit down with an old friend?" She rested her hand on my shoulder.

"Humph, a friend," I spat through a clenched jaw and shrugged her hand off. "We seem to have differin' opinions on the meanin' of the word friend. My friends wouldn't pretend to be helpin' me while secretly lurin' me into a trap, so please, leave now before this gets ugly."

My body stiffened. She wouldn't make this easy on me. She never did. Jessie had something to say and it had nothing to do with the ridiculousness of how cute I looked. That much was obvious.

She needed to start talking and fast. I glanced down at my hand, my knuckles white from the death grip I had on my guns.

"Sarah please, you've got it all wrong. I'd never hurt you. Just let me explain," she pleaded. Jessie pulled my shoulder around so I would face her. The sincere sadness in those usually steely yes was plain to see.

What was going on with her?

Over Jessie's shoulder I caught sight of Jo running out of the stock room. She froze when she spotted the two of us. As angry as I was, every muscle relaxed when I laid eyes on her.

Jessie noticed. In an instant, her eyes were drawn to the same place as mine. She glanced between us a few times, analyzing the situation.

I focused my full attention back on my beer hoping to throw her off.

Jo was hesitant as she made her way towards us. "Anyone need a refill?"

We both shook our heads.

Jo's eyes begged the silent question, was I was all right? I tipped my head away from Jessie, shielding my face so I could give her a wink to say I was fine.

Jade stormed out from behind Jo. She had an "oh shit" look on her face that led me to believe she knew something was up. I'd have to ask her about that later.

"All right," Jo said, "but if either of you need anythin', don't hesitate to ask." Jo gave me a worried glance before she walked away. She parked herself in the corner and started polishing glasses. Funny the way she positioned herself in a place she could keep a protective eye on me.

Jade wasted no time hurrying back to her side. The two of them went about whispering and casting glances our way, in no way hiding their interest.

Jessie had long since turned her focus back to me. She didn't notice the extra attention, for which I was glad.

When my eyes met hers once again, I hardened my glare, but Jessie's pained expression made me soften. I still didn't know the reasoning behind her actions. I only knew she'd never let me down before. In a rare moment of mercy I decided to listen to her reason for betraying me. "Okay thirty seconds to say whatever ya need to say." I flipped my hat up and kept our eyes locked.

She didn't flinch or back away, not that she ever did. There was a determination in her haunted expression as she touched my arm.

Jo stared daggers at the woman from her place across the saloon.

I looked down at her hand on me and slid myself free.

"Look what you saw that night..." she paused and took a deep breath. "Yes, he is in their gang, but he joined them to help me bring them to down."

"Why would someone do that? It's suicide?" I brushed off her ridiculous explanation.

"Sarah..." she looked around then leaned in. "He's my brother." It was a whisper, but I heard it plain as day. Still, I couldn't believe my ears.

"What? Are you mad? He's gonna to get killed!" I tried to keep my voice hushed, but the surprise of the news caught me off guard. Of all the reasons in my head over the last few weeks, that one was nowhere on the list.

"Can we talk about this somewhere else? I gotta room upstairs." Jessie's voice remained low, but turned scolding.

This was not a conversation for public ears. Somewhere else would be for the best.

I signaled for Jo to come over. I knew she was worried and I didn't want to go anywhere without letting her know I was all right. "Jo, this is Jessie. She's a U.S. Marshal and an old friend of mine that's helped me over the years. We're gonna step away and talk over a few things in private."

"Nice to meet you Jessie," Jo said with a pleasant smile. She seemed relieved of her earlier worries, though her eyes still held questions. Even if she was good at hiding her true feelings from strangers, I knew the signs. She wasn't happy about the looks Jessie was giving her, but mostly, she hated the way Jessie kept looking at and touching me.

I left money for the drinks and followed Jessie toward her room. I elbowed her in the ribs when she threw a little smirk over her shoulder at Jo. My eyes drifted down the stairway. I offered a frowning Jo an apologetic smile, holding her eyes until I reached the top.

We entered Jessie's room. I picked the wall across from her and leaned back in wait for her explanation.

"The U.S. Marshals had been after him for years, even before I joined them." She began to pace as she spoke. "It was my first month on the job when the shootout near El Paso happened. We really thought we had O'Shea then, but the bastard's got a lot of clout. He's got his hands in everything. He always has someone in his pocket, even Marshals. So he got away again."

She stopped and shook her head. Glancing up at me for a second, she resumed her path around the room. "We did manage to take out a lot of the gang and even some of his family. Four years and several near misses later, I decided to go it alone. We were getting' nowhere and you never knew who to trust."

I nodded my understanding. After all, that was the same reason I worked alone. "How long has your brother been in there?"

"About three years now. After years on my own, I hit a dead end. I needed to get a man inside to pin point where the old man was at any given time since he moved around while addin' to his collection of properties. Jimmy and I try to meet in towns away from his holdin's or wire messages under fake names. He tells me where they're settin' up and where the old man will be and for how long if he can." She stopped pacing and faced me, her eyes wrought with determination.

"I've been waitin' for the right moment. Then I met you and heard your story. I hoped we could do this together. We made a plan, even though you keep tryin' to do it yourself. But, here we are and we're so close. I'm sorry I kept that from you."

A few things were clear now, things I didn't know before that led to my life falling apart. "So you guys killed his daughter?"

She nodded, a flicker of pride shown in her eyes. "Actually, I did. One of 'em anyway."

"So, I guess I have the U.S. Marshals to thank for my pain. If you didn't get into a shootout, they never woulda come to my dad for help and my parents never woulda been murdered."

Her expression changed right before my eyes. She crumbled as the realization suddenly hit her. "Oh my god, Sarah. I'm so sorry. I never realized, I never..." Jessie's words froze and she stepped toward me, her eyes pleading for forgiveness. "Sarah, no one coulda known that would happen. We were so sure we'd get him."

"But you didn't." I bowed my head. None of it meant a damn thing anymore, but it didn't keep me from being angry about the events in my life. Even all these years later, I was still consumed by deep pain and hatred.

"We didn't." Jessie stood closer, invading my personal space as she placed her hands on my shoulders and then cupped my face. Her voice softened. "I really am sorry for any pain I've unknowingly caused you."

My eyes closed tight, fighting back the hurt and anger coursing through my veins. I tried to remind myself that they were just doing their job and had no idea what the crazy old man would do. If anything, you would have thought he'd go after the ones who did the killing, not the one who tried to do the saving.

Out of nowhere Jessie's mouth consumed mine. My hat hit the floor as her body threw me into the wall and her arms wrapped around my neck.

Stunned by her actions, my mind raced to grasp what was happening. I tried in vain to push her off, but she tightened her hold. Struggling to free my mouth from her onslaught of unwanted affection, I mumbled against her, "Jessie, stop. I can't."

All of my protests were for naught. She was persistent and strong, continuing to crash her lips onto mine hoping I'd give in. Our encounters had always been passionate and sometimes rough, but now that I was with Jo, there was no one else I wanted or needed in that way.

"Why, Sarah? You know," she continued to plead between rough kisses. "How I feel about you. We're so good together." Her body pressed harder against mine in all the right places.

She definitely knew how to get me going, or she used to anyway. The guilt I had for using her came back in a flood. I had no feelings for her beyond that of a close friend. I never did to be honest. Jessie was safe and familiar and I could trust her. Now I had to end it all, clear the air between us if we were to keep this friendship alive.

She was beginning to piss me off. I maneuvered for leverage to force her back. My elbows bent and locked in place between us. There needed to be enough space to speak clear words and talk some sense into my old friend. I didn't want this to be any more uncomfortable than it already was. "We've had this conversation before Jessie. I've always been honest with you about what I could give you and that's all. I can't do this with you. I'm sorry I let it go this long, I wasn't fair to you."

The words made her stop her assault. She pressed her forehead to mine, her chest heaving. "To be fair..." She sucked in a breath. "I lied sayin' I was fine with it. I just wanted to take whatever you'd give, hopin' eventually you'd feel for me what I did for you, but I guess that's never gonna happen is it?" She loosened her hold, pulling back enough to look at me. Her eyes were glassy, a side effect of the pain inside. "It's her isn't it? The reason you can't be with me? The reason you were smilin' last time I saw you? It's Jo?"

I closed my eyes and nodded. It was so hard to look at her knowing her heart was breaking. At the same time, a gentle smile crept up my lips at the mention of Jo. "Yeah, it's Jo. I'm so sorry Jessie. I never intended to hurt you." I meant it with all sincerity. "I needed some company once in a while and I know I was selfish, but when I was with you I really did enjoy our time together. For what it's worth, I truly do care about you. You're the one person I call a friend."

I was surprised to hear the muffled sounds of crying.

Jessie turned around fast, hiding her face. She cleared her throat and straightened herself as she looked out the window. "I appreciate that more than you know, Sarah. I do want us to be friends still." She wiped her cheeks and when she finally turned to me, my suspicions were confirmed. Her eyes were red and watery as she looked right at me. "I still have every intention of helping you take down O'Shea. Lemme know when you wanna leave."

"All right. It means a lot to me, Jessie, your friendship and commitment to this plan. Really it does. I was thinking another day or so. I'll come and get you when I know for sure."

She nodded in silence.

"I'll be down stairs for a while if you wanna come back down for dinner." I turned and opened the door. As I stepped out, she called me back.

"Sarah? For what it's worth, she's beautiful. You sure know how to pick'em." She forced a smile.

I didn't know what to say, so I tipped my hat and smiled back, pulling the door shut behind me. I didn't know if she would come back down tonight, but I hoped so. We'd been friends for years and even though this was an awkward time for us, I'd still like to have her in my life. I knew I could rely on her to have my back. That was a rare find these days.

As I made my way down stairs, I spotted a relieved Jo smiling at me from behind the bar. I grinned wide and bright like an idiot, the way I always did when she looked at me that way. I took a seat across from her and lost myself in those hazel eyes I adored so much. "Hey pretty lady," I purred.

Her already brilliant smile stretched to the ends of her face bringing those dimples out to play. Just the reaction I was hoping for. "Hello to you. What can I get ya," she returned and leaned over the bar to rest on her elbows.

I let my eyes drift to her chest before meeting her sparkling gaze once more. I scooted closer and whispered, "I had my mind set on a breathtakingly beautiful brunette. Got any of those around here?"

Jo chuckled as she teased back, "Easy cowgirl, this ain't a brothel, but if you don't mind waitin' a few hours, I think I know one you'd enjoy." She winked at me.

"Then I guess I got some time to kill. How 'bout a beer?"

"So, you gonna tell me what that was all about?" She quirked her brow and slid me a full glass.

One thing about Jo, she had no problem speaking her mind or going after what she wanted. She didn't like her life, so she changed it. She wanted me and damn if she didn't get me. The damn woman even got me to admit to myself how much I wanted her. She was brave and strong and those were just some of the things I loved so much about her.

I had to be honest with Jo. We were way past me hiding and I didn't want any suspicions about me and Jessie. "Yes." I took a swig of beer. "Like I said, she's an old friend. We met years ago. I made a few mistakes and ended up on the wanted list."

For some reason I expected a reaction when I said the words even though she was well aware of my past. There was nothing but the usual softness and genuine interest present in the eyes staring back at me. It helped to ease the tension I was holding as I told her about the only other woman with a special place in my life. One I knew would also give her all for me.

"We were forced to re-evaluate our relationship after I saved her from a couple of outlaws who got the jump on her. She helped me clear my name and put me on a new path. Ever since then, we'd meet up and occasionally do some business together. She's the only person I trusted, until you."

Jo blushed a little when I looked at her with honest emotion in my eyes. "Um, Sarah, I hate to be the jealous type, but she seemed a little too friendly. Are you sure there's nothin' else going on there? I mean, I know you don't owe me any explanations, I just..."

"Jo, its fine." I covered her hand with mine. "I won't lie to you. Yes, Jessie and I have been together on occasion over the years, but I was always firm about my intentions. Nothin' more than sex. She was safe and comfortable. She understood what I was going through and was the only person I'd felt remotely close to. My only friend or family besides Clover."

"She looks at you with more than friendship in her eyes."

There was no putting anything past Jo. As a bartender she observed people every day and knew well what hidden desire looked like. Even so, her blunt questioning made me a little uneasy. This whole sharing thing was still a little new to me.

"Yeah, uh...she did want more. I explained I couldn't give it to her. I do care for her, but not the way I do for you. When she saw us today, she knew why." I was uncomfortable talking about this. I cleared my throat and continued, "Everything's fine though. We talked it over. She really is a good person and a strong woman, just like you." I smiled to break the tension between us. "This stays between you and me, okay."

"No problem and thank you. I'm glad you trust me enough to be honest with me." She reached out and placed her other hand over mine. "She is quite the looker. I'd be jealous if I didn't already know your heart was all mine. Seems you have a thing for the strong, pretty ones, huh?" She joked and winked at me.

"Apparently that's my type. I've never been complemented twice in one day on my ability to get beautiful women." I laughed until I noticed the perplexed look on her face. "Jessie said the same thing about you," I clarified. "And Jo," I held her eyes, "my heart is yours and only yours as long as it continues to beat."

Jo turned away, pulling her hands from mine. She looked up at the ceiling and took a deep breath before turning back around with tears in her eyes. Her reaction set my mind to worry. What did I do or say to upset her?

"Jo, what's wrong? What did I do?"

"Nothin'." She shook her head. "Nothin'," she repeated with a deep breath, running her fingers through her hair as she collected her thoughts. Jo struggled to find the words to match whatever was in her head. "I um... I love you, Sarah and I know you're leavin' soon. I don't even know where you're goin' or if you'll be back. Will I ever see you again?"

She sighed and brushed her hair back over her shoulder. "I know I said it's my burden to bear. It's so easy to love you, but it's also the hardest thing I've ever done." She grabbed a towel and wiped her face.

I looked around the room to see if anyone was watching. Only Jade had her eye on us. Always the protective friend. I reached over and touched Jo's arm, wanting her attention on my next words. We locked eyes, my own beginning to sting as they threatened to well up. "I know what ya mean, Jo. I feel like all I do to everyone is apologize for makin' them feel bad. Lettin' you in is the best thing I've ever done for myself and the worst thing I coulda ever done to you." I took a deep breath, choking down the emotions building inside. "But you've changed everything for me. I know what I want when I find my peace and it's you. You asked me once if it was 'can't or won't' and I didn't know, but now I know. It's can't. Not yet, but soon. All I ask is for your patience and understanding."

I was begging her to keep loving me. That was a first.

She seemed as dumbstruck at my open admission as I was. She placed her hands back atop mine and ran her thumb across in slow, soft strokes.

Since when was I the type to discuss my feelings? She definitely changed me. I was becoming more human. Something I'd lost in all the time since my parent's deaths. I'd let myself go to the darkness, enslaved by this concept of revenge, but I was seeing the light now and I needed to finish this as fast as possible and get back to Jo.

Jade moved in closer, approaching with slow steps and gauging my reaction with every step. "Hi there! You two love birds all right? Looks a little intense over here."

Jo smiled and glanced at me and back to her concerned friend. "We're fine, thanks. We're more than fine actually," she said as she caught my eye.

The satisfied expression she wore told me she spoke the truth. We were fine and the exhaustion from all of this emotional outpouring was catching up to me. Beer seemed like a good idea. I chugged the remainder of the glass and wiped my face with my hand. The two laughed, my unease obvious to them both.

Jade slapped me on the shoulder. "Quite the day for you, huh? Old friends, socializin', feelin's," she teased.

Jo hit her in the arm and scolded her like a mother. "J!"

"Ow! What?" The girl looked at Jo, then me.

I chuckled and agreed with her assessment. "No, she's right. That's gotta be a record for me."

The three of us fell into an easy conversation. Jade finished working for the night and stuck around as we shared some war stories from the bar and the trails. I marveled at how comfortable I was around the pair. The tiny Spaniard was one of the most intimidating, yet genuine women I'd ever met. Her loyalty to her friend was visible.

The pair looked up and fell silent as the sound of boots on the wooden floor stopped behind me.

"May I join you," a hesitant voice asked.

I was relieved she decided to come back down. I turned and gave her a warm smile. "Of course old friend. You're always welcome."

A bit of tension sizzled between the three ladies at the start, but Jessie soon fit right into our little group. I was happier for it. So much time had passed since I had anything like a family, but sitting here with them right now, that's what it felt like. Amazing how life could change in just a few weeks.

Could it be like this when it was all said and done?

# <u>Chapter Twelve</u>

**Carter**

Carter was drawn by the sound of laughter. The distinct sound of several women to be exact. It wasn't something one would hear coming from such a place very often. He looked inside to the four ladies perched on bar stools carrying on like old friends. The Sheriff stepped inside quietly, but hung back against the wall.

He didn't escape Jade's keen eye though, as she excused herself and headed right for him. She gave him a curious glance, then turned back to see what he was staring at with such interest. The only thing she could find was Jo and Jessie focusing their attention on Sarah as they spoke. Jo was sitting right against the cowgirl's side with Jessie close by.

"Hey Sheriff? Whatcha doin' all the way back here. They won't bite," she joked.

Carter creased his brow at the scene before him. "What's goin' on there?"

She shrugged. "Old friends. New friends. Just a bunch of girl's having a good time. Why?"

"I don't know, it looks more," he paused, searching for the right word, "intimate?" His tone questioned whether that was the appropriate description for what he was witnessing. Seeing Jo hanging on Sarah was disturbing for reasons he couldn't seem to understand. And the Marshal? Really, her too? What was it about Sarah Sawyer that had them so mesmerized?

Jade smirked, amused by his confused expression. "Well, as an insider I'd say it's a pissing match over who gets Sarah, but I'd bet my perfectly proportioned bottom Jo's already won that competition."

Carter's eyes fell to the floor. Even though he was married, he kept holding out hope that one day Jo would come to her senses. Maybe it was his ego, as Jade liked to tell him, but it seemed like time to put his dream to rest. He sighed. "I don't get it."

The small girl gave the tall, stoic sheriff a supportive pat on the back. "If you were around them together, you'd get it. Que esteban destinados a ser."

"What does that mean?"

"They were meant to be. Carter, Jo is happy. So be happy for her."

He looked down at her and smiled. She was right. "Thanks Jade. You're a good friend."

She laughed. "I'm the best friend! Goodnight Carter." She stood on her tip toes and gave him a consoling hug which he returned just as strong.

When she left, he stood silent in the corner watching Jo carry on with her arm draped around Sarah's shoulders. She looked so happy and alive. That really was all he ever wanted for her. He just always thought he'd be the one to give it to her.

Jo took notice and nodded her head in acknowledgement.

Carter smiled and tipped his hat. He walked out of the saloon deflated, but a weight had been lifted at the realization that Jo was never going to want him.

***

## Jo's Ranch- Jo

Usually Sarah would be the first to rise, but today I beat her to the punch. After she tossed and turned, whimpering throughout the night, I was happy to see her resting well. Several times I held her tight hoping to chase her demons away. Sarah never had a moment's peace. In daylight, she battled her past and her future, struggling to make a life the best she knew how. At night, the recesses of her mind came to life, torturing her repeatedly with reminders of events that could never be changed.

I wanted to wake her, save her from her merciless subconscious. More than that, I wanted to help her escape her past and embrace a future with me. But she was so guarded. She kept everything locked tighter than a bank vault. There were tiny peeks behind the closed door, only for it to be slammed shut in my face. Sarah Sawyer was strong and stubborn, kind and tortured, beautiful and deadly and I loved her more than anything. If only she would let me show her how my love could conquer her anger, her fears. If only she would throw the door wide open and let me in.

Sarah rolled away from me. The sheet hung low around her waist leaving her torso exposed. I'd never really seen her back, at least not in the daylight. The sight made my throat clench. Tears threatened to fall as I scanned the many scars on her delicate skin. Old scars, most of them white, serving as a painful reminder of a past she couldn't seem to escape.

Only the devil would do those things to a girl. Several long marks resembled whippings and a few small round ones almost looked like burns, maybe from a cigar. Her flank was healing well, but that would scar as well.

I reached out to run my fingers over them, but stopped short. I didn't want to wake her. Even worse, I was afraid to stir up the bad memories that kept her running day and night.

My hand hung in the air over her body. A sadness crept up inside knowing the memories had such a strong hold over her. Each mark held a horrible story and I wanted to hear them all.

I pulled my arm back and tucked it under my chin as I continued to stare. Whoever she was chasing, she hoped that finding them would stop her pain. It wouldn't, but maybe she could find closure.

The memory of my own struggle years ago left me to ponder telling Sarah the truth about my family. Opening a new can of worms might scare her away and that was the last thing I wanted. I had enough trouble getting over my own past. To ask someone like Sarah to take on the task would probably be the end of us. She had enough to deal with on her own.

My family was not good people. The last memory of my father ten years ago still gave me chills. The look in his eyes haunted me even today. As I stared him down, it occurred to me that I never understood the madness driving my father to hurt people in the pursuit of money. I thought you could be successful and powerful without stepping on the less fortunate or being outright cruel.

Somewhere deep down I wanted to believe he was really a good man and that everything he did was for us to be happy. I didn't understand the workings of the world. Heck, I was barely eighteen. Maybe it took his brutal mentality to survive in the world, but I hoped not. I didn't want to be like him.

Not knowing much about life didn't keep me from standing up to the man I called "Daddy." On more than one occasion I'd hoped he'd see my point of view. Each time my suggestions would be shot down and quite often, I'd be physically put back in my place. While he was kinder to my sister and me than my brother, his gang or the people living on our property, I wasn't lacking in scars on my body or in my mind.

## Ten Years Ago- Amarillo

*"Daddy, ya sure ya wanna do this? Is business really worth taking lives?"*

*He narrowed his eyes at me and approached with slow, intimidating steps. Short and stout with a well-kept beard, my father oozed the aura of power, even to his family. No one dared question him without experiencing the wrath. I was no exception.*

*He strolled around me with a sadistic grin while I sat frozen in place. When my father acted like this it usually resulted in someone's torture or death. He would size them up and decide how best to break them.*

*I remained still, puffing out my chest in an effort to seem brave, but he knew better. I'd challenged him before. He came back around to the front and smacked me hard across the face, drawing blood from my lip. I was quick to cover the red mark left behind by his palm, but I didn't make a sound. I glared at him with my other hand balled into a fist and tried to choke down my own anger.*

*"Margaret Josephine O'Shea." He sighed, crossed his arms and looked me dead in the eye.*

*He was searching me for any sign of fear, but I wasn't afraid. I was mad.*

*"Why must you always challenge me, girl? Don't I provide for you? For your sister? For your brother? Hell, for all the rest of the people under my employ?"*

*His voice rose as he began to pace, taking the opportunity every few steps to glare back at me. "Some people need to be an example for others to see what's best for themselves. This will help all of them and only two families stand in the way. They must be shown why the good of the many is the best option. Besides, no one says they have to die, they just need to make the right choice," he said with an evil grin and crazed eyes that made my skin crawl. He stopped pacing and once again stood right in front of me.*

*I shook my head and spat, "Don't you mean the good it will do you? You don't care about the others."*

*He laughed at me. "My business helps them grow, Margaret. I can't let a few closed minded people place a burden on those who want to better themselves. You'll come with me, Maria, Myles and the boys to see firsthand how I take care of this problem and how it'll benefit everyone in that damn town."*

*I released a breath of defeat. He was a lost cause. I bowed my head in submission, saving my fight for another day. My answer was soft and obedient, my stomach turning at my own cowardice. "Yes, daddy."*

Over the years I'd learned to let go of the anger towards my family, but I still thought of that day quite often. That was a turning point for so many things, both good and bad. Sometimes I wished they'd killed him, but mostly, I was happy to be free. I'd made a life of my own here, a good one, and with Sarah, I felt complete.

The feeling wouldn't last long. She'd leave soon, though I still held out hope of convincing her to stay. Maybe I could help her defeat her enemies without leaving. Maybe, just maybe, Sarah would finally let down her walls and I'd be able to fix everything.

Yeah, it sounded like one of my fairy tale books, but Sarah made me believe the princess really could be rescued and live happily ever after. I wanted nothing more than to do that for her. I slid in close and wrapped my arms around her, content to enjoy the few precious moments we had left.

**\*\*\***

## Ketchum- Jessie

Sarah may have found some peace with Jo, but there was no way she would give up this fight now. Not after being haunted for ten years by her past. The day was coming soon, very soon. Sarah and I would face our demons and the man who brought them to our door. The man who left us with a lifetime of nightmares and unanswered questions.

## 10 Years Ago-El Paso, TX

*I stood in a room full of US Marshals and town sheriff deputies. We were all armed and ready as the plan was laid out. Marshal Smith had been the man in charge of bringing the O'Shea gang to justice for the last three years. Today was the first time he felt confident this hunt would come to an end. He had it on good authority Danny O'Shea himself would be here to oversee the activities. Dead or alive, we would get him today.*

*I leaned against the back wall in silence. I'd only been a U.S. Marshal for a few months, having joined because I had my own reasons for wanting the man dead. This seemed like the best way to make it happen without ending up an outlaw myself.*

*The meeting broke and we planned to reconvene the next day before heading to our destination. I walked back to my room with the memory of my own loss filling my mind as it had so many times before.*

*Three years earlier, Danny O'Shea had been ramming some new business venture down the throats of the people in my little town. Most of the township voted to accept the payout and let the bastard have his way, but my father held fast. He was convinced it would only end up destroying our happy home, rather than helping it grow.*

*Blinded by the money being thrown at them and the pressure to conform, our family and friends turned on us. We soon began receiving death threats and our business wasted away to nothing. Finally bowing to the pressure and praying he was wrong, my father agreed to the offer. Our farm was important, because it was one of the larger ones right along the edge of the property to be used for the trade depot.*

*Following a face to face meeting with O'Shea one afternoon, my father seemed different, afraid. He kept hugging each of us and saying how much he loved us. Despite what anyone said, I always believed there was a reason other than peer pressure that caused my father to cave, but I could never prove it.*

*The town went downhill fast afterward. The depot brought all types of unsavory characters that plundered the businesses and murdered people. A few months later, my brother Jimmy found our father hanging in the back yard. Maybe he felt responsible for giving in. Truth be told, he'd been dead sooner if he hadn't given in to O'Shea. That was the day swore I'd make the evil bastard pay.*

***

## Jo's Farm-Sarah

Sleep was hard to come by last night. My dreams drifted from losing my parents, to losing Mary and Henry. I laid still with

eyes wide open on yet another perfect morning with a sleeping Jo
wrapped around me.

A content little smile pulled at her lips, making me wonder
what her dreams held. I envied Jo. I longed for that kind of
peace. My upcoming plan only set me more on edge and I
dreaded the conversation we needed to have later when I'd tell
her I'd be leaving tomorrow. I hoped she'd understand why I
needed to finish what I started. More importantly, I needed her
to believe with all her heart how much I did want to come back
to her when it was all said and done.

Tracing lazy circles on her hand, she stirred beneath my
touch. I wasn't ready to lose the possessive hold she had on me
yet. The way she clung to me made my heart swell. There were
no words to describe the way she lit me up inside. So strange. So
unexpected. So completely welcomed. Jo managed to lasso my
heart despite my best efforts to fight her off.

I pulled her hand up to my lips and placed a soft kiss to
her palm then pressed her warm hand against my chest. Jo's
body moved in tighter against mine, like second nature. Gentle
breaths interrupted before evening out again, letting me know
sleep still had her in its clutches. Every time I was amazed at
how she reacted to my touch. Everything about her was like the
perfect dream and she fit me like my favorite pair of boots.

My body sank further into the bed. Was this what true
relaxation felt like? In a rare moment of peace, I allowed myself
to be happy. My lips turned up into a smile as I closed my eyes,
trying like hell to imagine what a life with Jo would be like when I
got back. For me, picturing such happy endings was difficult. I
had yet to see one. The world seemed more wrought with

suffering than happiness and sometimes I wondered what the point was to it all.

Jo stirred once more. Something inside me sang in anticipation of a new day with the woman I'd fallen for. Her beauty held me in a trance as her eyes slowly fluttered open, adjusting to the light.

Despite my deep feelings for Jo, I still hadn't said those words to her. Even though she'd spoken them aloud to me, I wouldn't let myself return them. She said it was fine, that she didn't expect me to say them back, but I knew better. It was plain as day in her expressive eyes pleading for me to let down one more wall. I might not be experienced in love, but I knew what Jo wanted to hear. Those three little words meant the world, but when thrown around callously, they only caused pain.

I refused to be reckless with her, at least no more than I had already been. She deserved better than empty promises and spoken half-truths. Jo knew I cared for her, even if I found it impossible to say those particular words aloud. I didn't need to make things any harder on her when I left.

The truth was, no matter what my plans for the future were, I might never make it back. Death was a real possibility. I wasn't a romantic soul. I'd seen the dark side. Jessie and I knew what we were getting ourselves into and had long since accepted whatever fate lie ahead.

Jo's hand slid up my arm and came to rest on my cheek. She gave me a delicious, sleepy smile.

I closed my eyes and soaked up her warmth even as I filled with anxiety and despair. She was awake and our conversation was inevitable. "Jo," I whispered in a raspy morning voice. The adoration in her eyes made everything more painful, but it was hard not to smile. She made me come so alive inside.

"I know." She pressed her hand to my face and forced a smile back through her sleep filled haze.

I couldn't bring myself to tell her yet. I wanted to enjoy our day together first, so I feigned ignorance, hoping beyond hope she had something else in mind. "What do you know?"

She closed her eyes, not wanting to look at me when she answered. "I know you're leavin'."

The tremble in her voice was noticeable and it broke my heart. "Oh." My eyes cast down, hiding guilt from my attempted lie.

She lifted my chin, not allowing me to hide from her. "When?"

Tears threatened to fall and I swallowed hard in an effort to control them. Damn emotions. The lack of control I experienced around her was so frustrating. "Tomorrow."

She sighed and forced a smile as she brushed the hair from my face. "I knew it would be soon."

Grabbing her hand and holding it close to my heart, I gave her a pleading look, asking for understanding, for patience. "I was gonna tell you. I made you a promise. I thought we could enjoy our day first."

"I trust you, Sarah. I just wish you'd tell me who you're after or where you're going." Now it was her turn to plead and while it was nearly impossible to deny her anything when she looked at me that way, I refused to break this time.

"I don't wanna get you involved. Does it really matter?" I released her hand and rolled to get out of bed, but she grabbed my arm, halting my escape. I didn't look back at her. I couldn't.

She loosened her grip. "Of course it matters. I love you, even though you're as hard headed as a damned goat." She spoke soft words draped in sadness. "I wish I could get you to stay here, but I know why you can't. I understand, I do. I...I just wish I finally knew where and who. Is that too much to ask?"

I shook my head unable to keep her completely in the dark. "No, I suppose not." I lay back in the bed and rolled to face her. "I'm headed to Spokane. Jessie's comin' with me. We'll finish this together." She wanted a name, but this would have to suffice.

Silence followed while my words were processed.

With no expression to read she responded, "While I'm glad you're not gonna do this alone, I hope your former lover will keep her hands to herself." Now sporting a glint in her eyes, she smiled and leaned in, pecking me on the lips.

Even a gesture as simple as a small kiss gave me chills. Her jealous side was amusing. How could she ever think anyone could hold a candle to her in my mind? "She will. She can be trusted on all accounts and we'll keep each other safe."

"Who're you after Sarah? You've been chasing people all around the country."

She was persistent, I'd give her that, but again I shook my head and rolled out of bed. Let's just enjoy our day Jo, please?" I may not have been able to see her face, but I knew what disappointment looked like. I'd seen it on others before. I hated to be the cause of hers, but I had no choice.

She said it herself. She knew what she was getting into when she fell for me. I, on the other hand, had no idea what was in store falling for her.

Sucking in a deep breath, I ran my fingers through my hair and let the air pass out through my lips. I dropped my hands on my lap and pushed myself up from the bed and leaving her there alone. I sensed her eyes on me until the light patter of footsteps against the old wooden floor boards carried out of the room.

This was so hard, harder than I ever imagined. I never should have stayed this long, but I couldn't tear myself away. Tomorrow would be worse.

I washed my face and threw on some clothes, looking out the window to find Clover waiting by the fence, anxious for a ride. My loyal friend always made me smile.

I made my way to the kitchen. Jo was sitting at the table with her hands over her face. The sight froze me in place. My stomach dropped and I feared the worst. "Jo, you all right?" I kept my voice soft even though I knew the answer.

I was an ass and her tears were all my fault, but knowing who I wanted to kill wouldn't bring her any comfort. He was only the most evil, corrupt man in the country and no one had ever come close to bringing him down. Why I believed Jessie, me and two others could do any better, was beyond me, but we had to try.

"Um, yeah. I'm fine, Sarah." She sniffled. "Some old memories, that's all." She wiped her face and gave me a sad smile.

She wasn't selling me on her story. "Anything I can do for you?"

She laughed at my offer, more of a huff actually, like she wondered how I had the nerve to ask when I knew damn well what I could do.

"Other than the obvious?" She shook her head. "No. But promise me you'll be careful Sarah. Revenge can make one weak and stupid. I don't think you really know how bad I want you to come back to me."

With quick strides I closed the distance between us. I stopped behind her, placed my hands on her shoulders and gave them a squeeze. "There is nothin' I want more than to come back to you."

"Seems there is one thing you want more," she uttered with a harshness. Her muscles tensed, then softened beneath a sigh. "I understand. You wouldn't be happy here without closure. I do hope you get what you need, Sarah. I really do." She looked up at me with glassy eyes over run with such sincerity my chest began to ache.

I swallowed hard and cleared my throat. "You wanna go for a ride? It's beautiful outside. I'll pack us a lunch." Without waiting for a response I picked up two apples and started to pack. I peeked up at her through my lashes.

Jo put on a brave face before nodding her head. She excused herself to the bedroom to get ready.

As soon as she left was I released a hard breath. This was going to be a long, trying day.

# **<u>Chapter Thirteen</u>**

**Jo**

    I walked past Sarah's room and into my own. I needed a minute alone to clear my head. Sarah made me feel so many things. Frustration being a big one. She wouldn't let me do anything to help her and that drove me crazy.

    My thoughts drifted back once again to my past. I understood Sarah's pain and suffering. Our experiences may have been different, but I knew what it was to hate so strong I could taste it and how hard it was to start a new life while holding onto the hate and pain.

    I looked at myself in the mirror and recalled a time when my own anger ruled my life. The day my life changed forever.

    Ten years ago I stood at a ranch outside El Paso. I thought it odd when Daddy suddenly had more pressing things to tend to than accompanying us to this all important meeting. Instead, he sent my brother, sister and me to take care of the business. All he'd done the last few days was talk about this big deal and now he had something else to do? It didn't make any sense. That was all I could focus on, right up until the first shots were fired.

The lawmen ambushed us. Everything became clear. My father knew what was coming. He had insiders everywhere. It was one of the reasons he was so unstoppable, yet he still sent all of his children into harm's way, saving his own ass. What kind of father would do such a thing?

Furious didn't describe my emotions when Marie was shot down right beside me. I couldn't find Myles, but men on both sides dropped like flies. I held my sister in my arms, helpless to do anything more than watch as she bled. I screamed and begged amid a torrential rain of bullets for help that never came.

I made the decision on the spot to disappear for good. This was not a life I wanted for myself and if I didn't act soon, I'd end up like my sister.

For years afterward, I wanted to make him pay, but lost opportunities and the fear of revealing myself, kept me at bay until I finally let go of the hold he had on me and embraced life.

**\*\*\***

**Sarah**

The ride to the lake with Jo was filled with pained glances and uncomfortable silences only broken by forced small talk such as the weather and business. She had every right to be upset. Truth be told, I was so nervous that my chest weighed heavy as if Clover were sitting on it. Each attempt to fill my lungs was met with extreme resistance.

This was beyond painful and not at all what I had in mind when I finally laid eyes on her again a few weeks ago. I meant to have a quick visit, a fix for a longing to see her beautiful face once more. Her face got me through those long nights on the trail and would have to get me through many more as I traveled to my date with fate. I never planned on speaking to her, only to watch from afar in order to protect her from the burden that was Sarah Sawyer.

How was I to know she'd been hoping for my return, wishing every new face in town would be mine? She must've been a glutton for punishment if she was praying to reconnect with this lost soul. How could she ever think that having feelings for someone like me would end well for her? The one comfort I had was knowing I'd given her fair warning and offered her an out.

She knew what would happen, but it didn't deter her actions. Maybe she thought she could change me or I'd decide to stay. Maybe she just couldn't resist a hard luck case. Either way it was bound to be hard on her, yet she held the line and made her intentions be known.

In all honesty, she still changed me despite my resistance. If things were different, I would stay here with Jo. But... seemed there was always a "but" or an "I wish"...but, things were not different. They were still the same as when I rode into town each of the times we'd met. The only difference was now my journey neared its end. Well, I hoped so anyway, because I finally had a reason to care how my story ended.

They said hope and faith were the big difference makers. Whether or not it evened the odds of thirty plus men against four was a mystery to me, but I was gonna hope it did and have faith I'd find my way back to Jo.

She rode beside me, all lost in worrisome thoughts. I tipped my hat back, tilted my head to catch her eyes and offered her a warm, confident smile. My heart pounded and the corners of my mouth stretched up to the brim of my Stetson when she returned the small gesture. When Jo smiled, time stopped and everything around me illuminated. A warmth that always defied explanation spread through me and multiplied tenfold when her smile was directed solely at me.

As I lit up, she did as well. Within seconds the tension lifted and we were left grinning like fools, unable to peel our eyes from one another.

"The lake is up ahead. I don't know about you, but I'm starvin'." I rubbed my belly as it growled on cue. We probably should've eaten some breakfast, but I was anxious to get out of the house after the way our morning started.

"Definitely ready to eat and I can't wait to see the lake again. I don't come up here often, but it's my favorite place. The clear blue water against the dark gray mountains is just magnificent."

"That it is." I smiled, turning my focus to the narrowing trail ahead as my excitement grew for how much more beautiful the scenic area would be with Jo beside me.

Yet another memory to burn into my mind.

***

## Ketchum Saloon- Jessie

"Hey blondie."

Jade's enthusiastic greeting was unexpected. I growled and narrowed my eyes in response to the new nickname.

"Whoa, easy now," she chuckled and waved her hands. "I was just being friendly." She slapped her hand on the bar top, directing me where to sit. "What'll ya have?"

"Beer would be good. Have you seen Sarah today?"

"Nah, but Jo should be in this afternoon, so my money would be on her showing up too. They've been pretty much attached at the hip, literally and figuratively, if ya get my drift," she winked.

I rolled my eyes. I was happy for my friend, but still struggling to come to terms with the fact I was never in the running for her heart. Sure, Sarah was always upfront about not being able to give more in our relationship. For a while she was too closed off emotionally, but I guess Jo was the spark she needed to live again and not me. That's what hurt the most.

"Yeah, I get it. Thanks for the visual though."

"Anytime." Jade leaned across the bar. Her expression turned serious as she spoke low so only we could hear. "Tell me, and tell me the truth. Things are about to go to shit, right?"

"Whaddya mean?" I tilted my head and squinted, my eyes questioning her intent. The girl may have her ways of finding out information, but only Sarah and I knew the plan. The question was, why'd she want to know? The alarms in my head went off, but I kept my cool.

Jade slid a little closer. "I mean, you and Jo's little cowgirl got somethin' goin' down and by the serious conversations you two been havin', I'd say it's soon."

I folded my arms, scowled and answered her with a harshness tone. "What if we do? It's none of your business."

Done with the whispering, Jade stood back up with fire in her eyes and huffed, "Yeah well, it affects my best friend, so I'm makin' it my business. She's ridiculously over the moon for Sarah, who I do think cares for Jo in her own strange way. I don't want Jo getting hurt."

"Yeah well, they're both big girls. They can take care of themselves." I dismissed her concern with a hint of bitterness I couldn't hide.

She set her hands on her hips. Her smile hinted she knew otherwise. Jade was a sharp one and picked up on it in a hurry. "Oh, I sense tension. You got a thing for the cowgirl too, don't you?"

"You're being ridiculous."

"Am I?" She challenged me with her words and her hard gaze.

"Yes, you are," I asserted without question and matched her challenge with an aggressive move forward.

She shrugged with indifference. The moment was over and she appeared content to have irritated me. "Well, be that as it may, I hope you won't be tryin' anything because there's lots you don't know about Jo. She'll fight for anyone she cares about and it can get ugly."

She threw out the last comment as fair warning. Jo wouldn't roll over and let me take Sarah, as if that were even a possibility. There was no doubt Sarah and I were through.

I could read people as well as my foe. Her intent wasn't lost on me. Still, I could respect her for protecting her friend. I'd do the same. I was satisfied that the whole point to this interrogation was solely about Jo and not at all about what Sarah and I were about to do.

"Cool down will ya. Yes, Sarah and I have been together and yes, I have feelings for her, but she has made it very clear repeatedly. We're just good friends."

Jade cringed. There was a look of regret as she stared at me, but it didn't stop her from talking. "Ouch! That's gotta hurt."

I was completely done with this conversation. Talking about it didn't make my predicament any easier. All I wanted was my beer. "Humph. Thanks. If you're done with the inquisition, can I get my beer now?"

***

## The Lake- Sarah

Even the horses seemed to enjoy the trip. They both perched by the lake edge drinking down the cold water and gorging on fall's last remaining sweet, green delicacies.

The afternoon air was crisp, a sure sign winter was well on its way. Snow wouldn't be too far behind, especially here in the mountains. One more reason why Jessie and I needed to get a move on or we'd be stuck until spring.

Not that being stuck with Jo would be a bad thing, but as special as our time together had been, I was ready to finish off O'Shea. I readily accepted what "being done" might mean. Death could be the end result, but if that was my fate, I was determined to take the old man with me.

For the first time in ten years though, I possessed an inkling of doubt about continuing. For the life of me, I wished I could let the hatred go and stay with the amazing woman lying by my side in the plush green field at my favorite place in the world.

The grass rustled as she rolled on her side to face me. Her hand reached up, coming to a gentle rest along my cheek.

My eyes drifted shut as soon as the warmth of her skin met mine. I might never get over how much comfort the simplest touch from this woman brought my soul.

"Sarah?"

"Hmm?"

"Tell me somethin' about your childhood. A happy memory."

Her voice was soft and soothing as she asked me to do something I hadn't done in far too many years. Long since forgotten was the happy life of childhood, painted over with the pain and anguish of my new existence.

"Please? I'll tell you one of mine." She fidgeted beside me.

My silence made her nervous. Unlike most of the other times she asked me a question, this lack of response wasn't due to her innocent request. Instead, my loss for words came from the fact that those days, those memories, were more like a fairy tale from my youth. One I struggled to recall anymore. It finally struck me how long those ten years had been.

Funny how time could go so fast, yet so slow. Seemed like only yesterday Jessie wanted to arrest me. I'd beaten a man for giving his horse a savage whipping, then took the horse, Clover, as my own. Wow, that was about four years ago, but at the same time, it seemed like Clover had been with me for ages, like family.

Kind of like Jo. Each day with her flew by, making me wish for more hours in the day, but it also seemed like much longer than a few weeks that we'd been reunited. Jo felt like home, like someplace I belonged, someplace that existed inside me waiting to be embraced.

Would a good memory be harder for her to recall than me? I was happy until my life was ripped away from me. Jo on the other hand, seemed to have it rough going all along.

I didn't look at her. I kept my eyes on the mountains, soaking in the serene surroundings of my second favorite view, the gray peaks against the blue sky with white puffy clouds skirting by. "Okay, but I haven't thought of those days in a long time. Why don't you go first?"

Jo had a troubled past, but she'd been sparse with any details. I knew she'd left her family, so I was curious to hear anything at all about her youth.

"All right," she said and laid back flat on the grass.

I turned my head to her as she started to speak.

"I was ten, I think. I'm the youngest of my siblings." She slipped her hand into mine and intertwined our fingers, letting her thumb rub back and forth along the top of my hand. Her eyes fell shut as she continued, "I have a brother and a sister. Anyway, they went on a trip somewhere. I think it was something for my daddy, but I was left at home alone with him. Even the woman who took care of me was gone for some reason. Daddy never paid too much attention to me. He was always working with important meetings and running somewhere with the boys. I didn't know what he did, only that he did it a lot and he made a good living to take care of us all. As a kid though, all I really wanted was an ounce of attention from him.

While they were all gone, he caught me watching him in his study. I was pouting hard, trying my best to make him feel guilty for ignoring me. I guess it worked, because he finally glanced up at me with a puzzled look on his face before he patted his lap for me to come over. I ran over fast as my legs would take me and hopped up. He asked me what was wrong. I still can't remember a time he ever expressed any concern over my feelings besides that day."

Even though she chuckled a bit at the memory, sadness tinged her words. I tilted my head more to get a better look at her expression as she spoke. No emotion shown on her face, a complete contradiction to the tone of her voice.

"I told him I wanted to spend time with him, but he was always too busy. I don't know if it was just because there was no one else in the house with us, but his eyes softened and he smiled and he took me to the kitchen where he scooped out some fresh whipping cream and apple pie. We sat together and he made a smiley face on my slice then dabbed some cream on my nose as I giggled." Jo turned to meet my gaze, her brows creased in pained reminiscence.

Though she tried to force a smile, her eyes gave her away. My heart broke for her.

"Anyway, that was the best day. I never shared another even remotely close to it with him. In fact, I don't think he ever so much as looked at me after." She rolled on her back and stared up into the bright blue canvas above. Her hand left mine to wipe the stray tear that found its way free.

We laid in silence for a few moments.

"Your turn."

I swallowed hard with guilt. My memories were much happier than hers. I didn't want to come across as someone who didn't appreciate what I once had. "Um, I was probably eight years old. It was my birthday and I wanted a horse." I laughed. Of course I did. All little girls wanted a horse.

She rolled to face me again, her elbow on the ground to prop up her head. Jo's smile grew as she tuned into my memory. She was extra excited for me to reveal a piece of my past, something I rarely did for anyone.

"Well, my father was an intellectual with no horse sense. My mom had never been around them and was a little scared of horses. I know it's a bit odd for Texans to not have a horse, but they weren't native Texans and my father was a doctor who spent much of his free time trying to learn new ways to help people. In many ways, I wanted to be just like him, so I did the same, except I really wanted a horse. So for my birthday, since we didn't have a barn or fenced pasture, he found an old man in town with a gentle horse no longer being used much. He traded medical care for the family in exchange for me to get some lessons and ride whenever I wanted.

I still remember how excited I was the first time I climbed up in the saddle. I've been in love with horses ever since. That was a great day."

I closed my eyes and took a deep, shaky breath. The memory was so fresh in my mind as if it were yesterday. The joy, the warmth associated with a family that loved one another filled me. But soon my smile faded. I opened my eyes knowing it was a whole other lifetime ago.

Her finger brush lightly against my face before she leaned in, pressing her soft lips with the utmost tenderness to mine. She pulled back and gazed into my eyes with such adoration, filling my heart to the brim with her love. So much so, I thought the small organ might explode.

When I studied her adoring eyes, I was struck by more than just the love she held for me. Hope, warmth and the possibility I might embrace joy again someday shone bright. I slid my arm around her back and pulled her closer, parting her lips with mine as I deepened kiss. I wanted nothing more than to stay right here with her in this moment forever.

# **Chapter Fourteen**

Sundown approached faster than either of us liked. Jo and I were greeted at the saloon by an odd sight, Jessie and Jade carrying on like old friends. I'd never seen Jessie so open with anyone. It was quite the sight to behold, her laughing and smiling with so little effort.

So often I forgot that Jessie, like me, had a life before the pain. For all I knew she was the most popular girl in town. No matter how things ended up for a person, there'd always be a time they wondered what their life would've been like if things went a different way. Almost as if we were never happy with what we had unless the things we had now were merely a shell of what they were once.

Jade looked up as we approached. "See? I told ya so," she poked fun at Jessie who shrugged unimpressed.

"Howdy ladies," Jade said louder than necessary. "What have you two disgustingly happy love birds been up to today? Ya know, besides..."

"J!" Jo crossed her arms and frowned when her friend began to act out a rather intimate gesture.

I turned away, embarrassed yet again by the girl's frank nature of all things I held private. Jessie reached over the bar and pushed her off balance. The three of us laughed loudly as she stumbled and her butt landed in the water bucket used to clean the glasses.

I tipped my hat to my old friend who grinned and returned the gesture.

Jo looked to me, asking without words if I was all right. Jade liked to have her fun, but that kind of teasing did make me a bit uncomfortable. I gave her an easy nod, letting her know I was fine. She took my hand in hers and led me to a stool.

Jessie offered a smile, but the hurt in her eyes still lingered as she tried to accept my new relationship. She spun back to the bar as I took a seat beside her.

I took pleasure in watching Jo walk away until she disappeared into the storeroom. Quite frankly, it was a mighty fine view when she was leaving. The view was mighty fine when she was coming too, in more ways than one. The passing thought caused a grin to spread across my face despite my best attempts to stifle the darned thing.

Lost in my own delicious thoughts, Jessie brought me back to reality by clearing her throat. She caught on to me and for the thousandth time since I'd gotten here, I scrambled to hide the red tinging my cheeks. Boy was I getting soft.

Jessie said nothing. She brought her hands up to cup both sides of her mug and kept her eyes on her beer. "So," she said low enough only I could hear, "looks like things are going well between you two." She lifted the mug to her lips and took a hearty gulp.

I couldn't quite read her tone. Dealing with her feelings for me wouldn't happen overnight, but she did want me to be happy. I glanced at her for a brief second then lowered my eyes to my folded hands on the bar top. With my voice low to match hers, I said the only thing that came to my mind. "I'm sorry. I didn't mean to make you uncomfortable."

Jessie shook her head and let out a huff. "Sarah," she said a little louder as she turned to face me. Her fierce eyes met my hesitant ones as she continued, "I'm not uncomfortable. Sure, I have my issues to deal with, but I'm truly happy for you. I envy you. What you and Jo have is what everyone hopes to find. You deserve to be happy. Hell, if I were in your boots, I'd be strongly considerin' hangin' up my weapon and makin' a life with that pretty little thing you got there."

Her words made me smile. My attention drifted over to Jo when she came out of the back room. I couldn't say I hadn't considered quitting, but hearing my old friend say the same thing made the idea more than a fantasy. Happiness almost sounded tangible. Almost. But it couldn't really be possible for someone like me.

"Thank you, but I don't deserve her." Those were words I believed to my core. I was more than blessed at having Jo's love and was honored to hold her heart, even if I wasn't worthy of such affection. No, I didn't deserve her, but I would cherish her love till the end. It killed me knowing what tomorrow would do to her, but no matter how much I might want to, I couldn't hang my guns up. Not now.

I brought my gaze back to Jessie. Curiosity got the best of me and I allowed myself to play in the fantasy once again. "Would you really quit now and stay with her?" My voice came out timid, shaky, nothing like she was used to hearing. I even surprised myself.

Her brow raised at my reaction. She didn't expect me to ever consider the possibility and truthfully, I never expected to either. "I'm not sayin' I would or wouldn't, only that I'd have to think long and hard about giving up happiness." Her eyes focused on me hard, like she was trying to yank the thoughts from my mind.

The purposed intent of her statement hit its mark, but as quickly as I'd entertained the idea, I let it pass again. I had to see this through. I sat up straight and fixed my hat, the telltale sign I'd made up my mind.

Jessie frowned. "You're lucky if you ever get one chance. Most people don't get a second. And what? You think just because you had a shit deal that made you hide from life while you ran off in search of revenge for your family, that it makes you a bad person?" Her words were spoken with harsh determination aimed at making me see the light. She kept silent and waited for my response.

I gave her none. I cast my eyes down. Jessie saw right through me, but she missed the fact that I was a killer. I was no better than the ones who killed my parents, other than the fact I wasn't killing innocent people. A life was still a life though and I was raised to treasure all life. The person I'd become was a far cry from the gentle, caring little girl who made my parents so proud. Only Jo was able to bring some of that back as I strived to become a better woman for her, to be worthy of her gift.

Jessie placed her hands over mine. Her eyes shifting into a softness I'd not seen before. "Sarah, you're not a monster. You're good and decent and deservin' of wonderful things. We both are."

That was the first time I'd ever heard her speak of life and love with such passion. I had no idea she was even capable of such profound emotion. I sure as hell struggled with the concept and we always seemed similar in that way. But now I found new respect for this woman I called a friend.

Her eyes welled up. "Look," her voice cracked. "We both got the shit end of the stick and we're doin' the best we can to make ourselves whole again." She spoke fast, trying to get the words out before emotion took over. "Intent is the difference between good and bad. Believe me, I know. You and I, our intent is to bring bad people to justice, one way or the other. To help those who are wronged. The O'Shea's, they have an intent to harm, cheat, steal and manipulate anyone and anything as long as it benefits them."

The sound of breaking glass startled us both, our hands going on instinct for our guns. My eyes darted up to the disturbance.

Neither of us had noticed Jo pouring a beer not three feet away as we spoke. She turned white as a ghost. Her face dropped in sheer horror as she squeaked out a question in the form of one word, "O'Shea?"

There it was, the truth landed like a sledgehammer. The name O'Shea hung heavy in the air as a moment of eerie silence engulfed us. Jessie cringed at the icy daggers I shot at her. My heart pounded in my ears. My body tensed in anger at my friend while my gut wrenched in dread at Jo knowing the truth.

Since I came back to this sleepy little town, my relentless mission plagued Jo's mind. She had tried in vain numerous times to drag the details out of me. I avoided her questions on purpose. The last thing I wanted Jo to hear was how my whole existence revolved around bringing down the most notorious man in the country, Danny O'Shea.

She made no secret about worrying over me and this news would do nothing to ease her fears about my leaving tomorrow. The burning in my stomach grew worse with every passing second as her panic began to spill over.

Her eyes fell shut, her hands covered her mouth as she started shaking her head. "No...no,no,no,no,no,no, no, Sarah. You can't go after them." She opened her eyes. They were red and glassy and pleading with me to reconsider.

The desperation in her voice shattered my heart.

Jo crumbled forward, the bar serving as a prop to keep her from falling to the ground. "That's a gang and you two are going to do what together exactly and against how many?"

"We have two more to help us," Jessie blurted out in an effort to soothe Jo's fears.

Her assertion only served to set Jo more on edge as her face grew redder. Jo glared, not at all impressed by the news. "Oh, well that's just great. I feel better now," she spat back. "Four against what, thirty? Maybe more? You have no idea what you are riding into."

The unexpectedness of the situation sent me stumbling over responses as I struggled to intercede. I wished I could make her understand. "Jo I-"

"It's suicide, Sarah! You wanna die don't you?" Her words were full of venom, attacking me instead of persuading me to stay. "I thought you'd found a reason to live again, here with me. Opening yourself up little by little. I was so sure you'd begun to accept you could be happy, but I guess you truly are so miserable in this life that you're ready to end it all in a blaze of glory, aren't you?"

Her eyes locked onto mine and I couldn't pull away from her penetrating gaze. Deep sadness emanated from her soul. All remaining fight dwindled as if I had squeezed the life from her. The twinkle in her eye usually reserved for me dimmed.

I'd never experienced anything more uncomfortable. I'd rather have been shot or burned with a branding iron, than suffer the look she gave me ever again.

Her shoulders slumped in defeat. Just when she seemed to be finished, Jo steeled her jaw and threw out one last jab. "Well, congratulations. I'm pretty sure you'll get your wish, Sarah." Jo stood up and slapped the towel from her shoulder hard on the counter in frustration before bolting.

Her words stung in a way I never expected. Did I want to die? I never thought about it to be honest. I never gave much thought at all to the outcome of the battle until I came back to her. For the longest time finishing this was merely a dream anyway, like something so far in the future it didn't even seem real. Now, I was resigned to the fact that it was a real possibility

I might die. It wasn't what I wanted to happen, but there was a good chance it would.

I'd always been a fighter, even before I met Jo, but she did give me one thing I never really had, hope. I always fought to stay alive, but I never had those positive feelings of joy and wishful thinking. I let them slip away years ago. Jo made me want to live the life I'd long since given up believing was possible.

I sat in stunned silence as she stormed off with tears beginning to fall down her face.

Jade ran over to check on her best friend, grabbing both of her arms as they whispered heated words back and forth. Jade glanced at us, her jaw slack open and shock all over her face. She struggled to keep Jo with her, but the smaller woman was no match as Jo powered past and ran outside.

Jade's eyes alternated between her two options, chase Jo or confront us. Apparently she choose us. Her shock gave way to a steely glare as she walked with determination towards me and Jessie.

I swallowed hard and looked at the Marshal. The stoic woman I knew so well stood pale and expressionless, still regretting her earlier slip. Rooted in place, I had no idea what my next course of action should be. The pain in my chest told me I needed to move fast, but the hardened look in the eyes of the tiny woman with the big temper nixed my first inkling of movement with a sharp motion of her hand.

Her green eyes burned with even more intensity than usual as she commanded my full attention. "Sit!"

For half an hour, Jade gave us an emphatic piece of her mind. To my surprise, the young girl was also quite understanding of our mission, even offering to lend us her skills. Seemed she had a knack for getting into places she shouldn't and was leading quite the interesting life when Jo met her.

I didn't want anything else on my conscience though. I refused to have any more blood on my hands than necessary and I sure didn't want any innocent blood. Jade needed to be here for Jo and she assured me she would. Still, an uneasiness rolled deep inside. I couldn't explain why. Maybe because tomorrow was the day. The day I took the first step toward facing the man who ruined my life.

Jessie walked me out, shaking her head with a smile. She winked at me, saying something about taking all the time I needed for a proper goodbye. I didn't want to think about leaving Jo and as much as I enjoyed having her in such an intimate way, another night of passion wasn't the best way for us to proceed given her reaction to the news. I only hoped for one more night of her arms around me. To feel what it meant to be loved by her would be enough.

I hopped onto Clover's back and squeezed her flank, signaling her to get a move on. I needed to get back to Jo sooner rather than later.

Galloping into the barn, I dismounted and unsaddled Clover and the released her into the pasture so fast you'd think it was a rodeo event. I sprinted to the house in record time, bounding up the three steps until I came to a full stop at the doorway. The brief pause gave me a second to catch my breath and collect my thoughts.

One small light illuminated the inside, but the house was quiet. I didn't see Jo through the window. I wasn't even sure what to say at this point. She was well aware of my feelings on the topic and that this had been a long time coming. Now I knew how she really felt too. This was uncharted territory for me. I never had to explain myself to anyone or consider their feelings regarding my actions. The situation was both frustrating and heartwarming to have someone care so much they'd do anything to save you from acting rash.

While Jessie and I were indeed far undermanned, we did have a plan. Her brother and a trusted friend from the U.S. Marshals would help us finish the fight. I wasn't running off half-cocked. I had a plan. I always did and tomorrow I would finally set the plan into motion.

My hands fidgeted and I swallowed hard as I gathered the courage to walk through the door. There was no sign of Jo in the living area. A hundred not so pleasant possibilities raced through my mind. I had to find her. "Jo," I called out. Her name carried a slight tremble of panic. My steps quickened through the house. My shouts were louder than intended, but my emotions got the best of me.

"Sarah?" Her voice cracked. She sounded like she'd been crying and I hated being the reason for her sadness. "Be right out," she called from her bedroom. She didn't keep me waiting long. Jo met me by the fireplace where she offered a sheepish smile and waved me to join her.

We sat together and talked, but to my surprise, we didn't talk about anything related to O'Shea. Our conversation covered our trip to the lake and plans for the future. Making plans with Jo gave me more reason to see this through in one piece. For the first time in my grown up life I was making a plan to be happy. The idea of a real future with someone I cared for and who cared for me was frightening, yet somehow enlightening.

As the night wore on we moved to the bed where I drifted off to sleep with our limbs entwined. Her gentle breaths on my neck brought me comfort from my harsh reality and offered the hope of better days to come.

# Chapter Fifteen

*Another warm summer day in El Paso and I sat on the porch swing with my mother. We watched my father stitch up old man Johnson's arm. He never seemed to get the hang of barbed wire. This was at least the third time he ripped himself open mending fences and my father told him he probably needed to start hiring a kid to do it for him.*

*I always liked the times I got to help my father treat people, but as I watched him right now, I didn't know if that's what I really wanted to do with my life.*

*"Mom, what if I don't want to be a doctor like daddy?"*

*The question took her by surprise. She always quirked her brow when she was caught off guard. "What do you want to be dear?"*

*"I don't know." I shrugged. "A cowgirl?" I half expected her to tell me it was a silly idea.*

*"A cowgirl?" She didn't laugh at me. Mom reached up and ran her hand over my hair, putting a few strands back in place.*

*"Yeah, I want to ride horses all day." All I associated with the job was riding. I wanted to spend all my time with horses*

*riding across the country and sleeping on the trails. It seemed exciting and each day there would be new sights to see. I'd already grown tired of this dusty old town at my young age and wanted more.*

*"Well, you're only twelve, so you have plenty of time to decide, but whatever you do, we just want you to be happy. That's the most important thing in life, Sarah. Remember that."*

*Mom kissed me on the head and slid her arm around my waist. She was so warm and smelled like fresh linen, everything you'd associate with home. I smiled and cuddled up closer to her. I could have stayed right there forever.*

My eyes snapped open, thrusting me back into the pitch black bedroom of Jo's farmhouse. I reached for Jo beside me, my heart stopping when I found nothing but cold sheets. The emptiness made my stomach turn and my throat clench.

What time was it? Where was Jo? How long had she been gone? She was upset, but she did come to bed with me, soothing me with her comforting arms around my waist until I fell asleep.

Rolling over with a groan, I pushed up out of bed and tiptoed to the door. The cold chilled my skin sending a shiver through my body. A soft light carried through the crack under the door. I peeked out. Jo sat staring into nothingness with a shot glass in one hand and a bottle in the other.

The thought of talking to her passed as quickly as it appeared. She was locked in an intimate moment alone with her thoughts. A moment she should be allowed to keep private. Though she hadn't said anything aloud, something else troubled her. Something more than me. Maybe some of those bad memories resurfaced. One thing was certain, the uncomfortable things circulating through her mind were all my fault.

For another moment I stood transfixed by her beauty. The soft light shimmered off her creamy skin. Pushing down the guilt burning in my gut, I returned to bed. Sleep avoided me as a million things ran through my brain. More of them revolved around Jo and her worries than my own destiny with the man who destroyed everything I held dear.

At least that's how I'd looked at it over the last ten years, but as I lay here, I realized I'd probably never have met Jo if my life had gone a different way. Not that I wouldn't want my parents back and my life to be different, but Jo gave me something I never imagined having.

Even as a child I never dreamt of a family or a farm. I wanted to travel and roam, but with her...

I sighed and rolled on my side unable to get comfortable. I wanted her to come back to bed for the few hours we had left, even if it was only halfhearted. My body craved her warmth and my soul yearned for her presence. Only time would tell how my story would end, but I was never more sure that I wanted her to be a part of my future. Well, if I had a future and if she would still have me.

Like me, Jo had her secrets. She had pain. But unlike me, she'd dealt with her past. Supposedly. But from what I witnessed moments ago, she hadn't let it all go. She still struggled with something and it begged the question of whether or not we could ever really be free of our past. The picture of her sitting in the other room like a shell of the woman I knew made me wish I could help her the way she helped me.

Footsteps approached the door. I squeezed my eyes shut and pretended to be asleep even though she couldn't see much as dark as it was. The door creaked as she stepped into the room. Her steps fell as soft and quiet as possible as she slipped back into bed. The sound of a weighted sigh escaped once she stilled her body.

All I wanted was to roll toward her and wrap her in my arms, but I didn't. I wanted to know what she would do. Would she still slide her body in close to mine even when she thought I was asleep or was she too frustrated with the whole ordeal and in need of her own space?

She did come back to bed with me rather than her own room. The small gesture made me hopeful, but with every passing second she laid stiff, my heart sank a little more. The darkness of night turned a minute into an eternity before she snuggled in behind me. Her heated body melted into each curve of my own like a puzzle. My breath caught as a soft hand snaked up under my arm.

"I love you, Sarah," she whispered into my ear.

A rush of relief and happiness filled me. I said nothing, afraid I'd upset her again. A tear trickled down my cheek and it took all the strength I had to maintain the façade of sleep as emotions overwhelmed me. In only a matter of minutes she was out cold. The gentle rhythm of her chest rising and falling against my back and her adorable sleepy snorts gave her away.

I smiled wide. Even without seeing her I knew how peaceful she looked. I'd seen it before. The picture was etched in my brain. Jo was still by far the most beautiful thing, inside and out, I'd ever seen in my life.

With her beside me, my mind fell silent with the answer to my question. I focused on the fullness in my heart, doing my best to ward off sleep. I wanted to savor every second of lying in her arms for what might be the last time.


The morning was full of unspoken emotions as I packed my things. Clover seemed excited for another adventure, but for the first time in our life together, I didn't share her enthusiasm. She kept nudging me with her nose as I saddled her up.

Fed up with her behavior, I placed my hands on my hips and confronted my old friend. "You know this would go a lot quicker if you'd hold still. What's your problem?"

Clover whinnied and tossed her head toward the house, drawing my attention to Jo watching us from the porch swing. I took a deep breath and exhaled hard. The dreaded moment was nearly upon us. Soon I'd be leaving her and riding toward an uncertain future. "I know, but she's not comin' with us. I promise we will try and get back as soon as possible."

She whinnied again, letting out a little grunt. Jo waved at her and Clover quieted right down.

I laughed and shook my head. Even my temperamental old friend was attached to the woman. I stroked her neck and gave her a kiss on the nose before tying her to the hitching post.

Turning my attention to Jo, I could almost vomit from my nervousness. As the seconds ticked closer to our goodbye, I was thankful for my cowboy hat to hide my eyes. The wide brim gave me more time to collect myself during my approach.

She stood up when I stopped an arm's reach away from her. I tipped my hat back and gazed into her radiant eyes that shifted between green and brown. The ones that made me both weak and strong. At the moment, I was definitely weak. I cleared my throat to start, but she went first.

"Sarah, I'm sorry. I didn't mean those things... at least not the angry ones. I don't think you wanna die, but was I wrong to think you'd finally opened yourself up to livin' again, here with me?"

I shook my head. "No, you weren't wrong, Jo. You really did show me so much and I do want more with you. I promise to be as careful as possible to get back to you in one piece." With a soft smile, I reached up and brushed a lock of dark hair from her face.

Jo closed her eyes and sighed at the contact. She moved her hand up and held onto my wrist as I cupped her cheek. "Sarah, I wish I could talk you out of this. I wish I could explain all of the reasons this is a bad idea, but I know you won't listen. At least let me go with you. I can help you."

I pulled my hand from her face, breaking the hold she had on me. I hardened my gaze before the words came out. "Absolutely not. No way. This is my fight and I won't risk your life. I can do this, Jo. I need you to trust me. Do you trust me?"

There was that look in her eyes again, the one I couldn't place and it confused me. Her lips began to quiver as she fought back sobs. "With everything I am and everything I ever hope to be. I trust you and I love you. Please come back to me. I just found you."

Before any words could be spoken, she lunged forward. Her hands slid behind my neck with fingers tangling through my hair as she pulled me down hard onto her lips.

The force knocked my hat from my head and made me stumble backwards. She may have split my lip, but I didn't care. The only thing I cared about was Jo and her heart pounding like a hammer for me against my chest. Thankfully, I was able to catch my balance before we fell down the porch steps. Pulling her in tight, I lifted her up off of the ground and erased all space between us as I pressed her for more.

She obliged with parted lips, attacking my mouth at a feverish pace as we poured all of our emotions into one passionate release until the lack of air forced us to part.

I was dizzy. My heartbeat echoed in my head. Through heavy breaths, we smiled at one another. Her face was flush and her lips swollen, making me want to taste them again. I gave her another squeeze before setting her back down on two feet.

Placing one last lingering kiss on her delicious, soft lips, my face fell. "I gotta go now."

Unable to speak, she choked back more tears and nodded her head in understanding.

"I will stop at nothin' to get back to you, Jo. You are my heart now." I took her hand and pulled it to my lips. I kissed her palm and placed her hand over my chest, wanting her to feel the pounding beat of the piece of me she now owned.

Letting our hands drop, I took slow steps backward. Without another word, I turned and descended the steps. I picked my hat from the dirt, dusted it off and placed it back on my head. With a quick tip of the Stetson to her, I took off for the barn.

How did I manage to stay strong in her presence? I'd probably never know, but I had a job to do and I had to see it through. My insides threatened to explode the farther I got from her. A heavy weight bore down on me, making breathing a chore. I was desperate to look back, but I couldn't bear to see her upset. I did manage a quick glance as I climbed into the saddle.

Jo did her best to hold herself together too. I had no doubt we'd both lose it the second we lost sight of one another. Anxious to get the distance between us, I asked Clover for speed as I raced away from love and toward an uncertain future.

***

## Jo

In a matter of seconds Sarah disappeared over the hill, leaving only a trail of dust and my breaking heart behind. Choking back tears, I walked back into the house, slammed the door hard in frustration and kicked over chairs. My anger at not being able to keep her here safe with me spilled over.

My heart was numb. I shifted my focus to the job that lay ahead as I stormed my bedroom and pilfered my closet. In the far back behind several boxes were guns and knives I'd kept hidden; remnants of a life left far behind. So many thoughts flashed through my mind. The life that once was, the life I had now and the one I wanted to have for years to come with Sarah.

The day I hid from my father's men so many years ago was the day I made the decision to run. I had peeked out the window of the small room where I'd sought refuge. Out in the yard was a mother and her young daughter embracing with huge smiles on their faces. Tears stung my eyes. I had wished I had that kind of life, that kind of happiness.

I had sworn to leave all the death and destruction behind me and find that life. The longing to have the same love and happiness I saw in them still pulled at my heart today. I was finally close, but in order for my wish to come to true now, Sarah had to come back to me. Years had passed since I'd killed anyone, but keeping her safe meant more to me than anything. More than any promise I'd made myself. More than my own life.

I found myself in the kitchen with no memory of walking here, nor did I have any idea how long I'd been staring out the window. Sarah's cloud of dust had settled, leaving the clear horizon and an empty hole in my chest.

My gaze drifted to the far cabinet and a healthy helping of amber liquid that could numb my mind to match my heart. I pulled the whiskey out and took a swig straight from the bottle. Tears began to fall once again. Helping her wasn't even a question. I was going after the woman I loved, even if it meant having to see my father again.

**\* \* \***

## Somewhere West of Ketchum- Sarah

"Whoa! Whoa!"

I pulled back on the reins and struggled to catch my breath. I hadn't gotten far. An unbearable pain gripped me from the inside causing me to stop. Tears streamed like the mighty Salmon River down my cheeks. Something left unsettled gnawed at my gut telling me to go back. I struggled to leave her at all, but I knew for sure I couldn't leave her that way. She deserved more and I wanted to give it to her.

With a sharp pull on the reins and a swift kick, Clover and I raced back to Jo's house. Within minutes we arrived at her front porch. I flew out of the saddle before Clover even came to a full stop.

Bursting through the front door, I found Jo in a state of shock. Heavy, red eyes hit me with a blank stare as she took a moment to register my presence. Her face shifted into a mix of surprise and concern at the recognition that I was standing before her once again. She wiped her face and blinked rapidly in disbelief. "Sarah? Wha--? What're you doing back here?"

I had to get this out. No more hiding. No more covering. No more leaving things left unsaid. I didn't know how this would all end, so there was no way I could go to my grave knowing I never said those three little words to her. Even if they were implied, it was never the same as hearing them aloud. I may have hidden my heart away for years, but I wasn't completely cold. Only an emotional coward.

I loved Jo and it was way past time she heard me speak those words. Maybe it would give her something to hold onto while I was gone. Something to let her know our time together was real and I hoped, lasting.

"Jo, I love you." I blurted the damn words out. My blunt declaration wasn't the grand gesture she deserved, but it served its purpose. She gasped, but I powered through, afraid to lose my nerve at being so open and vulnerable. "I love you. I don't know why I haven't told you yet, but I couldn't leave without you knowin', without you believin'. No matter what happens, you need to know for sure...you have my heart, mind and soul. You, Jo Porter, have me in ways I never imagined I was capable of. I love you and never, ever doubt how all I want is to start a life with you when this is all over."

There it was. I finally let it all out and it was amazing, freeing.

Her tears of sorrow changed to tears of joy right before my eyes as my sincere confession overwhelmed her.

For the life of me, I didn't understand why I couldn't tell her sooner, but I was damn sure glad I did now. Just saying the words aloud made me lighter, stronger.

I stood rooted to my spot as Jo strode toward me with the most brilliant smile I'd ever seen. Her smile shamed the sun and warmed me inside and out. Her dimples came to life and for a few more moments, all felt right in the world.

Our mouths met roughly in a powerful, passionate dance. I gripped her hips and pulled her in tight as her arms snaked around my neck like a boa constrictor and kept me locked in place. The kiss was unlike any other I'd ever experienced. Time stood still. The only thing I was aware of was our lips moving as one, pouring in every bit of emotion between us. I was lost in the swell of sensations that left me breathless.

We broke apart with chests heaving and rested our foreheads together. I was close enough to see the tiny specs of light brown in her otherwise green iris as I took a good look deep into her eyes. What I found there screamed her love for me. This was the most perfect moment of my life so far.

"Stay," she whispered with a shaky breath, her lungs still gasped for air. "Please stay."

Her gaze begged me to submit to her wishes. I closed my eyes to cut off the connection and the heartbreak began all over again. I was right to come back and profess my feelings, but now I had to leave her all over again.

My legs were lead and breathing? Impossible. Every bit of strength that I had was needed to move as I slowly backed away.

She held onto my hand as long as possible. The desperation shone in her glistening eyes. Her grip was firm to show her intent, but not overpowering. The tears pouring down her cheeks once again were no longer happy ones. "Please stay, Sarah, for me."

# **Chapter Sixteen**

**Spokane, WA**

Danny O'Shea sported a devious smile as he headed to the main bunkhouse. Winter was on its way and it appeared, so was his long awaited guest. He'd waited years for this and it seemed the time was nearly upon them.

"Buck," he called out into the old wooden structure.

"Yeah boss, be right there." Several moments passed before the large, older cowboy emerged from his room, his shirt splattered with tobacco stains. "What can I do for ya?"

"I've been keepin' tabs on a certain U.S. Marshal for some time now and my insiders tell me she's finally heading our way. I'm surprised it's taken her this long, really."

O'Shea fingered through a selection of books on the table, stopping on the bible. The only part of the book he concerned himself with was the part reading "God helps those that help themselves." He chuckled at the old text before turning his attention back to Buck. "Keep an eye on that brother of hers. I wanna know if he leaves the farm at all. Got it?"

Buck nodded. "You want me to take care of him?"

"No, no. I want you to keep me informed. When the time comes, I'll deal with them both. Anyone who thinks they can infiltrate the O'Shea family has got another thing comin' to 'em."

"Yes sir, Mr. O'Shea. You expect her to try somethin' with just her brother? She'd have to be crazy."

"She may have some help, but nothin' official through the U.S. Marshals. I've looked into it thoroughly. Anything she's got planned will be a few rogue guns that won't even scratch the surface of what we've got."

All these years O'Shea knew the Marshal and her brother blamed him for their father's death. Why should it be his fault some old fool decided to off himself? It wasn't like he had him killed. He nearly did several times over, but the man finally came to his senses. O'Shea figured it must have been easier for some people to blame others for their problems.

"Anyway, keep on him. Lemme know about anything he does off property."

O'Shea took his time walking back to his house. Winter was his favorite time of year and the chill in the air made him feel more alive. An evil smile pulled at his lips. Won't be long now till there were two less foes to deal with.

***

**Ketchum- Jessie's Room**

Sarah would be here anytime now and she'd expect me to be ready. I'd admit I was a little tense, a bit off my game. If I was honest, it was nerves, but I'd never say it aloud. U.S. Marshals were supposed to have nerves of steel and I usually did, but this was different.

My reflection told the story of wear and tear from a hard life. Long periods on the trail, plus stress and worry about my brother and Sarah all took a toll. I didn't think of myself very often. Maybe I didn't expect a happy ending, lord only knew why.

It might've been early, but I felt a shot was in order. After all, it would be a while before we got to Spokane, so why the hell not? Filling the glass with the last of the light brown liquor, I lifted it to my nose and inhaled its oaky scent. My eyes drifted shut as I smiled. I threw back the shot and savored the burn.

Damn that's good.

I took one last glance around the room for good measure. All my stuff was packed. I had promised the fiery little girl, Jade, I'd say goodbye before I left. She was good people and one of the few who understood me, kind of like the sister I would've wanted. All I wanted before I left though, was ten more minutes in the comfort of that soft bed. I'd be spending tonight and many nights to come on the ground and that wasn't something I was excited about.

I lay back, allowing my body to sink into the softness and my mind to wander back ten years ago. The day we'd created a ripple, which had turned into a tidal wave that was still pulling Sarah Sawyer under to this day.

We had watched from a distance as the O'Shea family arrived at the meeting place outside El Paso. We were certain he would be there. We were wrong. He never showed. Instead it was his three kids. No one had ever seen the youngest girl and I didn't get a good look at her then either, but they all had the same dark hair.

Everything happened so fast. I saw the son run off. The older girl stood still so I took my aim. My bullet hit her square in the chest. The moment still gave me a deep sense of pride at having taken her down and knowing I took something away from him. Though considering he was willing to send his children to slaughter, I often wondered how much it really hurt him.

The younger sister stood crying over her. I lined her up in my sights, but hesitated, wasting a chance to take her out as well. I never figured out why I'd paused. Was it a moment of weakness or was it sympathy? Either way, it would never happen again.

Bullets were flying and after a moment of panic, she carried her sister away and disappeared. I couldn't tell if the younger girl had been shot by anyone else during her escape, but later I'd heard that she'd died from wounds sustained in the raid.

I should have gone after her. I should have kept her from ever leaving that property. No, what I should have done was pull the damn trigger.

That was even more of a regret now after learning what her bastard of a father did to Sarah and her family. It crushed me to the core knowing our failed attempt led to her life being stripped away by that madman. It hurt almost as much as knowing she didn't love me the way I did her. The one thing I took comfort in was the special bond we had; a deep respect and kinship I wouldn't give up for anything.

I slowly returned to the moment at hand. Where was Sarah? Maybe she took my advice and gave up this suicide mission to live out happier days with Jo. I couldn't fault her if she did, even if I would be disappointed in some respects.

With one last deep breath, I hopped up and grabbed my bags. Spying the empty bottle on the table made me frown. I'd have to grab one last shot from Jade before I hit the trails. I was gonna miss that kid.

***

## Jo's Farm- Sarah

Jo's voice trembled and her knees weakened the farther I moved away until she collapsed on the floor in a heap.

I wanted to rush back to her, to hold her and comfort her, but delaying the inevitable would solve nothing. No, she'd get over it in a little bit. I hoped our separation would be brief and then we could get on with our quiet life on the farm.

"Jo please, get up," I choked out, holding back tears of my own. I tried to put up a strong front. She didn't need to see that I was scared too. Not scared of dying, but scared of never seeing her again, never holding her in my arms, never feeling her warmth against my skin.

"No. You don't know what you're gettin' into, Sarah." The desperation in her voice was deafening. "Why won't you let me protect you?"

Protect me? How could she protect me? I was the one keeping her safe. The only way to protect her was to keep her far away from it all.

I grew irritated. I did my best to remain calm, because had the roles been reversed, I'd be doing the same thing trying to keep her from danger. "We've been through this already, Jo."

"I know whatever they did to you must have been beyond horrible, but why can't you put this behind you? He's a madman and he won't just kill you, Sarah. He'll make you suffer."

My focus stuck on her asking me to drop it and my anger began to build up inside. The irritation was gone, chased away by rising rage. I couldn't hear anything else she said. Ten long years I had suffered in one form another at their hands and there was no way in hell I was letting this go now. Not for anyone or anything, no matter how much I loved her.

I steeled my jaw in disgust at the notion. I couldn't brush it off now. After all I'd been through, to all of a sudden just be happy here like none of it ever happened...

"He'll make me suffer?" I huffed with disdain. "Jo, you have no idea what they did to me and my family and how much I have suffered over the last ten years. I can't, not now. Not this close to giving the son of a bitch what he so richly deserves."

"Killin' him won't change a damn thing, Sarah. It won't bring them back. Believe me, I know."

She didn't know. How could she? She didn't live through what I did. A shitty family life didn't compare to my tortured past. Her constant insistence pissed me off even more.

I seethed. My fingernails dug into my palms from the force of squeezing my fists into tight balls. "You think I don't know that, Jo? You think I haven't realized that nothin' has changed even after killing some of the men responsible for my pain? Well, I do know. I'm well aware that no matter what I do, my parents will always be dead and I will still bear the physical and emotional scars of being his slave for three years. A thirteen year old girl beaten and tortured and for what? Because my father tried his best to save his daughter and failed."

My truth hit her hard, as I hoped it would. Jo whimpered, doubling over as if someone stabbed her in the gut.

"From what I heard, she was pretty much dead when she got there, but did O'Shea go after the ones who shot her? No!" I was shouting now, throwing my arms up as I spoke. My entire body shook with pent up anger. "He beat me and my mother while my father watched helplessly. That wasn't good enough for them though, so they murdered him, then her, while I watched. I tried with all I had to escape, but I was helpless. I was held captive for three agonizing years being burned, groped and beaten as a god damn slave to him and his family of degenerates."

I struggled to catch my breath. The full weight of my past finally hit her full bore.

Her eyes went wide and darted around the room as she processed my words. As the hard truth settled in, she began to tremble. She opened her mouth to speak, but no words came out.

Probably better off. There was nothing she could say to make it better. There was no reasoning I wanted to hear. My mind was made up, had been for a long time. Those few moments of hesitation were due to my love for Jo, but this deep hatred and need for retribution outweighed everything and anything. I could never move on without my closure. I would die trying.

My eyes burned with unshed tears as they drifted to the floor in a moment of deep resolution. When they fell on her again, I knew they were cold and filled with hate, just like my heart. My words fell out in a growl, "If I get the chance, I'll kill every damn member of his family."

For some reason my last words hit her the hardest. Jo fell apart even more at my hate-filled pledge. She probably came to the realization that she really did fall in love with a monster. The love she had for me may have died after my hate filled admission. They weren't words spoken by someone worthy of such love and compassion.

She tried to speak, but I couldn't make out her words until finally, she found her voice through heavy sobs. "I hope you don't mean that, Sarah. That's not you. I know it's not. You can't blame them all for his sins."

When did she become a preacher? His whole family in one way or another either brought or carried out my pain.

"And why not?" I stood over her and continued my verbal assault. "He blamed us for somethin' we had no part in. Why are you defending him, them? I thought you said you understood, Jo."

"I do understand and I know what they did was despicable, but you're not like him and killin' just to kill ain't you. You'll regret it." Her voice softened, though she still plead for me to stay.

"I'll have to live with it, the same as I've lived these last ten years. I gotta go now. Jessie's waiting for me." I left no room for negotiation and hoped we'd reached the end of the conversation.

I headed for the door, but she grabbed my arm, preventing me from walking away. My blood boiled over. My body strung tight. All I saw was red. When I turned around Jo was in my face. Fed up with the bullshit and ready to get the hell out of here, I couldn't control myself. I shoved her backward. The force pulled a yelp from her as she hit the wall and in an instant, I regretted my actions.

Jo gritted her teeth and creased her brow. Her right arm pulled back, hand balling up in anger. Her fist approached in slow motion. I was powerless to stop her as she hauled off and punched me in the jaw.

I guess that was my first look at the old Jo.

It wasn't supposed to be this way. I never expected this from her. The two of us stood toe to toe in a stare down. I rubbed my face and gave her a lopsided grin before I charged her again. Her eyes flashed with rebellion when I pinned her hard against the wall with my body.

Quick, exasperated breaths danced against my neck. Nose to nose we held fast, until something clicked in my mind. I finally paid attention to the hints she'd been leaving. There was something she'd been alluding to and I managed to ignore it all this time. She had a past. She said she understood, she knew what I was going through. How?

Exhaling hard, I softened my throbbing jaw. It was so hard to stay mad at her. She meant well, but what was her secret?

"What aren't you tellin' me, Jo?" None of this made sense. There was more to this argument than she let on.

"I can't, Sarah." Her body relaxed against mine and the anger melted from her eyes, replaced by sorrow. "I'm afraid you'll hate me."

Whatever she was hiding, it must have been important, otherwise we wouldn't have been having this argument. I reached out to touch her and she flinched. Tears began to bubble in her eyes once more. It killed me to get that response from her, but given my actions, it was warranted.

I ran the back of my hand down her cheek and pushed a strand of hair behind her ear. With a loving touch, I cupped her jaw and smiled as she closed her eyes and pressed into my hand. Even after a heated argument, we could melt into one another.

Amazing.

Keeping my tone low and calm, the same way I always did during intense situations, I tried again. "Can't what, Jo? What could be so bad? After everything I've told you, what can't you tell me? Talk to me."

The sight of her shaking her head at me in defiance only caused my anger to resurface. If she wasn't going to tell me, why the hell were we going through all of this? She should have let me leave.

"Dammit Jo. What the hell is going on?" I was yelling at the top of my lungs again. If she had neighbors, they'd have come a running at the disturbance. "Tell me," I shouted as I pounded my hand against the wall in anger. My sudden outburst made her eyes go wide in panic.

"He's my father," she blurted out. Her hand covered her mouth the second the words escaped as if she could pull them back out of the air so I'd never hear them. Fear grew in her eyes as she watched my reaction to her confession.

My heart dropped. I fell silent. There were no words. I struggled to process what I just heard. "What?"

My mind and body went numb in response to the explosive confession she threw at me. My gut twisted and turned. I had to get away before this got any worse, if worse was even possible. I operated on instinct. Vaguely her voice echoed in the background as I stumbled out the door toward Clover like a drunk from the saloon.

Her hand gripped my arm tight and pulled back, hoping to make me face her.

I callously yanked myself free in disgust. I couldn't look at her. A deep hole burned through my insides. I glanced down at my chest as I swiped my hand across my heart. I was certain there'd be blood since it felt like I'd taken a gun blast at close range. But there was none.

Climbing into my saddle, I spurred Clover hard. She groaned, but obeyed my command, taking me as far and as fast as she could, until she could go no more.

# <u>**Chapter Seventeen**</u>

**West of Ketchum- Sarah**

Zero to forty in a matter of seconds. I asked Clover for every ounce of that speed as we left behind another trail of dust. Tears streaked my face yet again as my world shattered.

Jo screamed out for me in vain. I refused to look back. I didn't even take note of the direction we traveled. My only concern was putting a ton of distance between me and her as fast as possible. Spokane would still be there when my head cleared.

At the moment, I couldn't think at all. My mind continued to reel as the words "he's my father" echoed in my head. I couldn't wrap my head around it, not one bit. Was this some kind of cruel joke? What did I do to deserve this?

I pushed Clover to her limit. I'd never asked her for this much and I continued to spur her without shame knowing her legs and lungs were burning. I had to get away, far away and fast.

Minutes later, Clover's protests brought me back to reality. The grunts and groans coming from deep within her served as warning that I was hurting my one true friend.

I slid her to a screeching halt and tumbled out of the saddle, collapsing to the ground like a sack of feed. Air seemed impossible to find as I gasped in a desperate attempt to fill my lungs. With my chest constricting and body shaking, I had the overwhelming need to vomit from what could only be described as a knife twisting viciously in my stomach. Choking back sobs of anger and heartbreak, I squeezed my eyes shut and screamed with every bit of breath I could muster until dizziness took over.

My fists pounded into the dirt over and over again attempting to rid the overflowing rage and pain within. I couldn't even begin to express how much I wished I was striking O'Shea instead of earth.

Bastard.

I finally found someone to help piece together my life and he even had his hand in that? How could this be true? Why did he ruin everything I loved? Was I not allowed to escape his hold and find happiness? Was it really possible to want to kill the man even more than before?

Sure felt like it at the moment. I didn't just want him dead, I wanted him to suffer. I wanted him to suffer the way I had, but that would be impossible. He would be out of his misery within seconds. I didn't feel a single ounce of guilt about wishing him harm. I was only sorry I couldn't make his pain last ten years.

Then there was Jo. What about Jo? She probably hated me for what I did, what I said. I would hate me. I did hate me. The problem was, I meant it at the time. I meant it with all my being. I still did. The hatred and anger for her family ran deep, pumping through my veins with every beat of my heart. The same heart I surrendered to Jo, only to have it ripped out. I could do without that damn organ. Opening it up has only ever brought me pain.

My chest still ached, as did my jaw, as I cried myself out. I curled up into a ball where I lay while Clover nudged me with concern in her big, brown eyes.

When I had no tears left to shed, I opened my eyes. The light of day was blinding. How long did I lie there? Long enough for Clover's sweaty coat to dry, leaving behind a white crust along her chest and neck. I pushed up into a seated position and wiped my face on my sleeve.

My own words haunted me as much as Jo's confession. I said I would kill them all. She was one of them. I loved her. God help me, I loved her so much. Maybe she would find it in her heart to forgive me if I survived.

Could we go back to where we were? Even with the love I had for her, something in me was disgusted at fact his blood flowed through her veins. If I found a way to push past those thoughts and be with her again, would she be able to forgive my words and actions? How about after I killed her father? Sure, she ran away from him for his vile deeds, but they were still family. Would it all be too much to overcome?

I almost considered a prayer to the same god that allowed all of this to happen in the first place, but my pride and anger refused such a suggestion. I sat up and ran my hand over my old friend's muzzle with a loving stroke while I begged the universe for strength to finish this task.

***

**Jo's Farm- Jo**

"Sarah!"

I screamed her name from the front porch so loud into the heavens that I didn't even recognize my own voice.

"Sarah!"

What happened? One moment Sarah was saying the words I'd longed to hear. The ones representing what I already knew to be true, but yearned to be serenaded with in that silky, smooth voice of hers. The long awaited "I love you" was music to my ears and my heart.

The next moment, she was gone, leaving me shell shocked at the sudden turn of events. My body began to tremble, unable to hold the weight of my world. I fell onto the porch swing squeezing my head in my hands, fingers pulling hard on my hair in frustration. The fragile thing in my chest that beat for her was crushed. I was too paralyzed to even cry right now.

The way she looked at me when I told her the truth... I was dead to her. In my worst nightmares I never could've imagined such disgust and contempt in her eyes directed at me. I'd only ever seen softness, love and hope in those soulful, amber eyes.

They say the eyes are the windows to the soul and despite her tough cowgirl exterior, I'd always been able to read Sarah like a book. I saw past her fear and hesitation and found her true feelings for me, for us? I read those feelings loud and clear today. What once was a romance, now resembled the scariest book I'd ever read; one I never wanted to open again.

Even now I shivered at the memory of her icy glare ripping through me as I broke her heart. I was the one who ripped away any semblance of happiness from the woman I loved more than life itself.

I understood why she was the way she was and why she believed she had to do this. After hearing her story, my insides crumbled. It was painful to listen to and I couldn't imagine how horrible it must have been to live through. My father was a diabolical man, but I never thought he was capable of such evil. It was unfathomable to believe what my family had done to her; what I had done to her.

I didn't know what hurt more, losing her or knowing my family and I were to blame for her pain. Well, I knew for certain my damn hand hurt. I punched her. I couldn't believe I hit Sarah, the woman I would give my life to protect.

When was the last time I let my anger control me? Years and years. I thanked the heavens the physical fight stopped right there. With our combined tempers, we would've torn down the house. We're both very passionate people. Sarah with her quiet intensity and loyalty and me wearing my heart on my sleeve. The same passion we had in love or pursuit of a goal, spilled over into the side of anger as well. Thank goodness we didn't go to my bedroom. All of those guns and knives would certainly have made things worse.

Sarah had no idea I planned to go after her. That was the plan before she left and despite her biting words, it was still my intention to go after her now.

First, I needed to get to Jessie as soon as possible. She was no doubt waiting for Sarah and probably wondered why she hadn't arrived yet. Plus, she knew the destination and plan of attack. I could help them with my insight into my father's habits. They would need all the help they could get. Both of them wanted him dead. I couldn't blame them, but my goal was solely to bring Sarah back alive.

Going after her was full of risks, but I was in a bind either way. She deserved the truth. I had no choice but to tell her when I did. If I'd waited until Spokane, my identity would've become known anyway. I'd rather she heard it from me now, than him in the heat of battle. The problem was, I was hiding more than my real name, but I would risk everything for her.

Whatever happened to me or us after the fact, so be it. Sarah Sawyer deserved to be free from this need for vengeance, from her haunted past and I was going to give it to her. She would have her life back. She was owed that much after what the O'Shea family had done to her. If luck was on my side, and I prayed it was, then maybe she would still find room in her life for me when this was all over.

I took a deep breath and looked to the horizon. The sun was shining bright at ten in the morning and the subtle remnants of dust still hung in the air from Sarah's hasty departure. A new found determination settled in my gut as I gritted my jaw and strode into my bedroom.

While I packed my bags with weapons, food and warm clothes, Sarah's story of abuse by my father's gang filtered through my memory. I drifted back to the days of my youth and after all these years, some things finally began to make sense.

Growing up, I had never knew my mother. Daddy didn't pay much attention to me, I rarely went to town and I had no friends besides my siblings. The maid took care of me most of the time. She was a pretty, dark haired woman who I pretended was my mother. She gave me the closest thing to love I ever experienced as a child.

I would spend hours sitting and staring at the bunkhouses where my father's workers lived. I saw women and children quite often. I only knew them to be the families of his men. I wanted to play with the other children, but was forbidden to socialize with the help. They looked as miserable as I felt, but unlike me in my big house, they were filthy looking and lived in tiny shacks.

As time went by, I began to assume that all families were unloving and cold. I thought myself a bit of an outsider for wanting to have the warmth of a parent's arms around me like those story book families I read about.

"Margaret Josephine," my father would say, "those are made up stories, like monsters and happily ever after. That's not real life. This is real life. No one has time for make believe. Now try to be more like your brother and sister."

For the longest time I believed him. At least until the day I saw the mother and daughter in the yard. They looked so happy. There was so much love between them that I cried at the sight. I cried because it proved those story books held truth. Instead of having the warm, happy life like them, I was the girl locked in the tower destined to know only coldness and contempt for others. My refusal to accept my fate only fueled my desire to run even more.

I now knew that the people in our bunkhouses were slaves. It was also clear now that it was the first time I had ever laid eyes on Sarah Sawyer. She was the vibrant, smiling girl with her mother. The girl whose life I trampled with my selfish actions.

My stomach twisted in disgust at myself and an anger rose deep inside me with this new revelation. Sarah being ripped from her loving family and forced as a young girl into those conditions enraged me even more. It was true. My father was evil and deserved the fate coming to him.

If I knew anything about him though, he wouldn't be an easy fight. Heck, he probably already knew someone was coming for him. That made time even more precious as Sarah was already well on her way.

I ran to my horse and saddled him as quick as I could. Danny O'Shea would be more than surprised to see me and while I was a little more than nervous about the reunion, part of me couldn't wait for the expression on his face.

I spurred my gelding hard as we galloped toward town. I had to find Jessie and fast.

"Time for your reckoning, Daddy."

Twenty minutes later I arrived in at the saloon hoping Jade had come to work early. I couldn't go anywhere without making sure everything was taken care of and the one person I considered to be family was always there when I needed her.

I tied Jet up to the hitching post near the water trough. He better get rested up, because he was gonna need his energy on this trip. My boy was spoiled and not used to going too far, but there were no more lazy days for him in the foreseeable future. He was gonna be hating me tonight.

I chuckled to myself about my temperamental friend. Horses were so loving, but could be as moody as an adolescent girl.

I pushed through the swinging door to find Jade behind the bar polishing glasses and to no surprise, stealing a shot of liquor. She always brought a smile to my face with her craziness. "Ain't it a little early for that?"

She perked up when she heard my voice and her eyes sparkled with mischief. "In my family we believe one should never deny themselves wonderful things regardless of the time of day."

Nothing I said ever changed her ways anyhow, but I could see her point there. What the hell? It was gonna be a long trip. I motioned for her to pour me one as well. I rarely ever drank this early, but this day already seemed three days long and it wasn't even noon yet. She poured me a shot and I slammed it down in a hurry.

Jade looked at me with concern. "Somethin's going on. What happened?"

With a deep breath, I shrugged and looked around my empty saloon. The emotions were still raw as I fought back some tears. The look of disgust in Sarah's eyes before she left still hovered in the forefront of my mind.

"Yeah, that's not gonna cut it Jo. I know Sarah's leaving today, but I see no Sarah with you, so out with it," she said in a demanding, yet sympathetic tone. Abandoning her duties, she moved around the bar and took the seat beside me. She placed her hands on my thighs and looked right into my eyes.

I couldn't lie to her, about most things anyway, and she knew it. She got me every time too, especially when she raised her brow knowingly like she just did.

"Yeah, she's leaving. She left already, pretty quickly actually." I really didn't want to relive the morning drama, but I had to tell her. On the brink of riding off into a rather sticky situation, my fate could end any number of ways, most of them poorly.

We'd been honest with one another during our relationship, as far as she knew. I had things to hide, things I was ashamed of or tried to forget. It was finally time my good friend of nearly seven years heard the whole truth about me.

"What? When? Jessie's still here." Jade leaned back with a look of surprised confusion.

As if on cue, Jessie entered the saloon and made a bee line for us. She was all business and seemed a bit annoyed.

"Where's Sarah? She's never late."

The Marshal took a seat next to Jade and gave me a glare. She expected an answer fast.

I sighed hard, not wanting to tell her my identity as well, but on the other hand, it was probably best to have it all out in the open. If she wanted to fight it out when she found out my blood was O'Shea, then it was better to do it here and now. We

all needed to be on the same team on this trip and a surprise like
that wouldn't be in any of our best interest.

I pushed back from my stool and began to pace while the
two of them exchanged confused glances. Jade shrugged and
mouthed an "I don't know" to Jessie. I swallowed hard, ran my
fingers through my hair and started in a shaky voice. "Okay, so
there's a couple of things I need to tell the both of ya and I need
ya to hear me out, all right?"

They nodded and waited for me to continue.

I gathered my courage, gritting my teeth as I prepared to
confess yet again today. Was this what church was like? No
wonder why Daddy never took us. There was a shit load of sins
on his back, and well, mine too I guess. Jade's reaction wasn't
my concern, but Jessie's possible response to the news had my
stomach in knots.

"Sarah left. We had a fight and she was gone like a bolt of
lightnin'."

They looked at one another and then back to me, waiting
for the rest of the story, but before I could continue, Jessie broke
in with a touch of worry in her voice. "When? She didn't come
here so that means she runnin' off to do this alone. She's gonna
get herself killed, Jo."

My hands fidgeted with my growing nervousness. She was
right and I knew it, giving me even more reason to spit this out
so we could get a move on already.

"You think I don't know that?" My tone was harsher than I
wanted. "I know we have to get outta here soon if we're gonna
catch up to her. She left not more than an hour ago."

Jade jumped up with her hands on her hips and tilted her head to make sure she heard me correctly. "You said we. Are you goin' after her Jo? You could be killed too."

I looked at the ceiling, willing myself to go on, to make her understand how I cared more for Sarah than I did myself, especially knowing what I knew now. "That's a risk I'm willin' to take. I love her J. I had every intention of going after before, but now I have to go. It's my fault she ran off. I'll do everything in my power to bring her back alive."

She wasn't happy with me and I couldn't blame her. If the roles were reversed, I'd be just as concerned for my friend.

Jessie narrowed her eyes. Her keen senses read between the lines and demanded more answers. "Why do you have to? What aren't ya tellin' us, Jo?"

My voice trembled as I explained Sarah returning to express her feelings, how I begged her to stay and how things escalated as our tempers flared, ending with her hasty retreat.

Jade focused on every word, her discomfort showing as she shifted in place.

Jessie's stare bore a hole through me. She cared a lot for Sarah, like family, more than family. The news would strike a chord in her and I wasn't sure I could handle her response.

I paused to catch my breath and readied myself to deliver the big news. I glanced from my best friend to the frowning U.S. Marshal, keeping my eyes locked with hers to monitor the reaction as I delivered the news.

"I told her that Danny O'Shea is my father."

Silence.

Jade's eyes grew wide. Her hand shot up to cover her mouth and stifle the gasp that escaped her lips.

Jessie glared at me as she jumped up with her hand on her gun. "What did you just say?" Her words were more like a growl. Her muscles contracted and her body readied to pounce at any moment.

The tension thickened as Jessie and I stared one another down. I tried to maintain a passive stance, showing I meant her no harm, but she had other ideas.

Jade stood still in shock, processing the information. The expression on my best friend's face served as proof of her disappointment. We shared everything, yet I didn't trust her with my secret.

Stuck in our own little world, staring one another down, a deep voice startled us all.

"Jo, is it true?"

Of course Carter would have to show up at this exact moment. We all turned our attention to him. He had his hand on his gun, but he wasn't looking at me, his focus was on Jessie.

I slumped my shoulders in defeat and mustered the courage to repeat myself as I choked out, "He's my father. I'm an O'Shea."

My eyes cast downward as I said it with sadness. I said it with shame. I didn't want to be one of them. I'd spent the last ten years trying to get away from them and thought I'd made it to freedom.

"Why didn't you tell me?"

I expected Carter to respond, but instead it was the small trembling voice of Jade; her expression solemn and eyes riddled with hurt.

I was over whelmed with guilt for betraying her trust. We were sisters, maybe not by blood, but sisters all the same. She told me all of her horrible truths. From the abuse as a child, to stealing for a living and even her arrest. She told me everything and I loved her just the same. I told her nothing really. Some fabricated stories of my youth ending with running from a crazy guy I'd slept with a few times right before we met. My actions made me sick to my stomach.

No matter how much I tried to escape my past, I was unable to run from the monster I was bred to be, hurting everyone and everything I cared about. That was the blood, the curse that ran through my veins. I was content to wallow in my shame. The weight of the three of them staring at me, with lord could only imagine what running through their minds, was crushing. I would understand if they looked upon me with the same disgust Sarah did this morning.

Without warning, I was pulled into a tight embrace as she whispered, "You're my sister. I understand why you hid it from everyone. I still love you, Jo." She squeezed me hard, harder than you'd think possible for a woman of her size.

I wrapped my arms around my best friend, my sister. I fought back the tears pooling in my eyes. One escaped and ran down my cheek while I kissed her on the head. "Thank you, Jade. I love you too."

Turning to Carter with fear in my heart, I prepared to be arrested for some crime from ages ago. I was still guilty by association, but I couldn't help Sarah from a jail cell.

He tipped his hat instead. Carter didn't think of me as an O'Shea. "I guess now I know why you were always askin' me about any news to report," he said with a gentle smile.

A wave of relief washed over me as the two people I was closest to recognized I wasn't my father's daughter. Granted, neither of them had the pleasure of his torment, but their support was comforting all the same.

When I met Jessie's gaze however, it was a whole new ball game. There were a million thoughts running through her mind and from the looks of her, most of them weren't favorable for me.

The fear on Jade's face and concern on Carter's left a warm spot in my heart knowing they cared for me for the person I was now. They didn't care where I came from or whose blood ran through my veins. I made a choice to better myself and that was my life now. My focus, however, was only on the woman whose fingers were tickling the handle of her six shooter.

Jessie's anger spilled over, just as Sarah's did. Her jaw clenched, her nostrils flared, as she took heavy breaths in an attempt to control herself.

"You. Me. Outside now," she barked and stormed past me, hitting my shoulder as she left.

# **Chapter Eighteen**

I assured Jade and Carter that I'd be fine, even though doubts of my own swirled like a bad summer squall. The old saying "it's gonna be one of those days" said it all. I was knee deep in shit and it was definitely one of those days. There was no way around the truth. My reveal had sent Sarah over the edge. I was the reason she ran like hell to an uncertain fate.

The light blinded me as I stepped through the swinging doors of the saloon and out into the street. The sun sat at the perfect angle as it rose higher in the sky forcing me to shade my eyes. I balled up my fists and walked with purpose into the street. My willingness to face her would show Jessie I wasn't afraid to face her wrath. She was a fighter. If I was to earn her respect while accepting my blame in all of this, I needed to be a fighter as well.

The moment seemed like one of those high noon showdowns. I cringed at the idea of our little confrontation escalating to such a degree. Straightening up my shoulders and putting on my best killer stare, I planned to let her get anything and everything off her chest. That was the only way we'd make any headway toward forging a working relationship. Besides, I deserved any and all ill feelings she harbored. I wanted her to bare her feelings in full, but I had no intentions of getting into a brawl with her.

Carter surprised me when he let me walk out of the saloon. He had always tried to play the hero, but I guess he finally got the hint that I didn't need his help.

The fuming Marshal paced back and forth in the street mumbling to herself. She stopped for only a second to glance up at me before returning to her ramblings.

I creased my brows, gauging her intentions. I held strong to my defensive stance, but I didn't want to fight. This day was exhausting. Nothing like all of the things you'd thought you had escaped coming back to haunt you all at once. Well, almost all.

Jessie's few moments of silence ended when she turned to face me. I stood my ground as she closed the gap with aggressive strides, not stopping until we were nose to nose. I refused to back down. If the red in her face wasn't sign enough, Jessie's warm breath hitting my skin in a rapid rhythm certainly let me know she was struggling to control her anger.

My jaw clenched and my muscles tensed, ready for whatever came next. The only thing I knew of Jessie was her fierce protectiveness of Sarah. I hoped we'd find a quick and peaceful resolution for our differences and get on to the task at hand, saving Sarah from herself and my father.

As beautiful as the Marshall was from a distance, she was even more so up close. Like many of the deadliest creatures in nature, her beauty masked her ability. I wasn't fooled by her looks. I had a front row seat for that snarl of hers and those searing eyes could intimidate anyone. Jessie's glare sent a chill jolting through me, but I wasn't one to cower. I pushed in a bit closer and returned a deathly stare of my own.

Her lips pursed tight. They barely moved as she spoke through clenched teeth. The words came out filled with venom. "I should beat you down. Everything your family touches turns to shit and now, after all she's already lost...if she dies, so do you."

My breath caught at the mention of Sarah dying. My defenses faltered.

Though only for a second, Jessie caught the change. The look in her eyes shifted like the sand in a desert storm. Her fist raised into the air.

I braced for impact, but it never came. She thrust her fist back down by her side in frustration. This emotional push and pull exhausted me. I didn't want to get into another fist fight today, but if punching me was what Jessie needed to do, then so be it and we could move on.

I stepped back and dropped my hands, leaving myself open to whatever attack she planned. Resolving to accept the punishment Jessie deemed fit, I offered myself up for her to release everything she'd been holding onto.

Her expression gave away her own dueling emotions as she debated her next move. There must've been a million things she wanted to say and do to me, but she seemed to be fighting her instincts. Jessie stopped fiddling with her gun and rested her hands on her holster.

I exhaled hard, letting every strained cell in my body fall slack in relief.

With a stern expression she huffed, "No. Sarah would never forgive me." She backed away, eyes casting downward as she shook her head. "Just when I was startin' to like you, ya know? I can't imagine what Sarah's thinkin' right now, but I'm certain it's a whole lotta what the hell."

Her blunt choice of words made conversations with the Marshal an interesting affair. I'd come to appreciate this trait from her over the short time we'd known one another, but it sure was intimidating to be on the receiving end. I opened my mouth to say something and she waved me off.

"I'm not finished yet. Of all the people in the world for you to be related to..." She stopped and looked to the sky. We both took a deep breath and then her steely glare returned to me. "I won't bore you with more horror stories of your father's evil doings, but let's just say he's hurt me greatly as well. Not to the degree of what he did to Sarah, but unforgivable nonetheless."

I nodded and softened my stare. I wanted her to know I understood what she meant.

"I could have killed you ten years ago, ya know that?" Jessie shook her head again and added a light unbelievable laugh.

My eyes grew wide. What did she mean? How had our paths crossed before?

"I had the chance. No one really knew what you looked like, but when I saw you, the younger O'Shea girl bent over her sister after I shot her, I knew. I almost pulled the trigger. Still don't know why I hesitated, even to this day."

I hung on her every word as she told her side of that fateful day.

"I often wondered how things woulda been different if I did shoot. I mean, my failure, and that of the U.S. Marshals, to bring down your father led to the demise of Sarah's family. Our failure led to her life being forever changed."

She rolled her eyes and laughed in disbelief. "What a tangled web we weave, you and I. What are the chances? And poor Sarah...well, she keeps getting the shit end of the stick."

Unbelievable. Unimaginable. The way our lives connected in such horrible ways made my head spin. My family and I were at the center of everything and it sickened me. I grew nauseous again at the mention of Sarah and her parents. How would I ever be able to look her in the eye again? None of it changed the way I felt about her or what I had to do to make sure she survived. I'd have to figure it all out when she was safe.

"Look, Jessie. I know an apology from me means nothin' and changes nothin', but I want you to know how very sorry I am for what happened to you, Sarah and all the others affected by my family. You have to understand I'm not like them. I ran because I didn't want to be like them and I've spent all this time leavin' them far behind...until now anyway."

She focused hard on me, clenching her jaw before she spoke. "You're right. Your apology changes nothin'."

She paused and I braced myself for a sudden volatile shift in attitude. Instead I got nothing.

Jessie relented, letting her hands fall slack at her sides. "But I accept your apology, Jo. As much as I hate your family and as much as I want to hate you right now, I almost feel like I knew you were different. Maybe that's why I didn't pull the trigger. You weren't fightin' back. You wanted out."

The look in her eye and the weight of her words hit me hard. I remembered El Paso so clearly. I had replayed the scene many times in my head. I never saw who pulled the trigger that led to my sister's death, but I was thankful I didn't join her. If I'd fully understood all the things my family had done though, I may have wished to join her. But I didn't die. I ran.

I spent several years hating my father for what he did to us, even wanting to make him pay, so I was well acquainted with what Jessie and Sarah were feeling. Over time, I let go of my hatred, but I wasn't going to let go of Sarah.

I spoke with confidence, with certainty, leaving Jessie no doubt I meant every word. "I got out and I found Sarah. I'm not gonna lose her to them. We need to get to her. We both love her and want her to be safe. Regardless of our feelin's for one another, regardless of whether or not you think you can trust me, trust that I'll do anythin' for her, even face the past I've tried so hard to leave behind."

Jessie studied me, looking into my eyes, into my soul, before nodding and extending her hand for me to shake.

Waves of relief rolled through me as I let down my guard and took a deep, calming breath. My last real breath seemed like an hour ago amid the tense standoff. I grew lightheaded as oxygen finally flowed back into my brain. A small smile curled at my lips.

Releasing her grip, she patted me on the shoulder and returned the gesture. "Well, I guess we better get a move on if we're gonna get your girl back."

She surprised me with her sincerity. We exchanged a glance that said more than words ever could. A powerful alliance had been forged, one that would put an end to the O'Sheas and bring the woman who owned my heart back home safe.

Jessie needed to take care of a few things before we left town, so I headed back inside to finish up with Jade. She'd be upset with me leaving, but I didn't expect her to understand. I had to go. I had to get to Sarah regardless of how she might feel about me. Lord only knew what she was thinking right now, wherever she was.

I spotted my friend alone and bent behind the bar. Carter must have slipped out while Jessie and I were having our little chat. "Jade, I need ya to look after the saloon and my house. We're going after Sarah."

She popped up, her eyes blazing. "No way! I'm goin' with you."

I knew this was coming. She was as stubborn as the day was long. "No, you're not. I'd never forgive myself if anythin' happened to you." I kept my tone firm and even, looking her right in the eye to show I was serious. Too bad she was just as strong willed as me.

Her hands shot to her hips and she stared me down. "Yeah? Well that goes both ways and besides, you need me if you are sneakin' into places. You know that's my specialty."

She had a point. Sure we could use more help, but no. No way. I couldn't risk it. "Really, this is dangerous. No way J."

She walked right past me like we weren't even having a serious discussion right now. "No more debate. Nick can take care of the place. I'll be packed in ten minutes."

I stood there shocked. My jaw dropped open at her complete disregard for my words. She had spunk. As much as I wanted to keep her safe and away from this mess, it was pretty evident that once again my good friend played by her own rules.

She turned abruptly before exiting the saloon. "What about Jessie? You two good?"

The conversation was still so fresh that I hadn't processed it all yet. Were we good? I believed we were. I saw the pain in Jessie's eyes. The sincerity in words went right to my heart. I knew the woman would be true to her word and she'd go to the ends of the earth for those she cared about. She loved Sarah too and I had no reservations about her as we prepared to meet the devil himself.

Realizing I'd been stuck in my own head for several seconds, I looked up to Jade staring back at me awaiting my answer. "Yeah, we've come to an understandin'. She needed to send her brother a telegram before we left. You wouldn't believe how messed up this whole thing is, J."

She narrowed her eyes at me in the way she always did when she wanted the whole story. "Whaddya mean?"

The whole thing was too crazy and heartbreaking to be true, but as the saying goes, "real life is stranger than fiction." I rolled my eyes and thought of the irony of the situation. The three of us were stuck in some screwed up circle of pain and attempted redemption.

"Apparently, Jessie, Sarah and I...well, let's just say our pasts are intertwined and not in a good way." I tried to leave it at that as I brushed past her and out toward my horse. The quickening click of boots behind me said that wasn't going to happen.

She tugged on my elbow, pulling me back around to face her. "Jo, you can't say somethin' like that and not tell me the whole story. I'll let you explain while we go grab my pack."

Walking to her house, I took my time describing my connection to Sarah, Jessie and how I came to be here, well, most of it anyway. I did leave out a few details that had come to light. I doubted I'd ever admit those to anyone, especially since I could barely admit it to myself.

Her eyes shot open wide, a gasp falling off her when I told her Jessie killed my sister and could have taken me out with a swift pull of the trigger, as well.

"Holy shit, Jo! That's crazy." She pulled me in for a hug that squeezed the air from my lungs. "Jo, I'm also glad Jessie froze. I can't imagine how my life would be right now if ya hadn't taken me under your wing."

Her words brought a smile to face and my heart. Truth be told, I could say the same thing about her. I hugged her back just as strong and placed a kiss on her head.

People always told me that things happen for a reason. I never bought into that saying. I'd never been able to find a viable reason for the harm I'd done or for the things that happened in my life. One thing was for certain however, Jade and I were meant to cross paths and I could only hope that would carry us both through this mess in one piece.

\*\*\*

## Somewhere outside Ketchum, Idaho- Sarah

Despite the nip in the air, the sun warmed my body as it climbed higher into the sky on a mid-September day. I got to my feet, finished wallowing in my self-pity and dusted myself off as I tried to regain my bearings.

Where was I? With all the craziness in my head earlier, I had no idea what direction we ran when we left Jo's. Looking at the sun, west was to the left. There weren't many ways to get to from Ketchum to Spokane by horseback, but I didn't want to go the way Jessie and I had planned. She was sure to be headed out soon, if she wasn't already. She wouldn't let me do this alone. Jessie and her brother wanted O'Shea dead as much as I did and they'd be there waiting by the time I made my move.

I'd push to reach Spokane as fast as possible, but I'd use alternate trails to buy me some extra alone time. I needed to clear my head, sort through my thoughts and regain my focus. I needed to be alone. This morning with Jo threw me right off track and I couldn't afford to be preoccupied with her. Going into battle with your mind unclear and a lack of focus on your goal was ill-advised. That's when bad things happened. My mind was still a mess, as was my heart. All I was sure of was that I needed to finish off O'Shea.

I climbed back onto Clover and headed west, wishing I'd taken Jade's advice. She had said her mother always preached to never leave home empty handed. She was referring to a nice stiff drink. That's why Jade always carried a flask of Jo's finest liquor with her at all times.

I chuckled at the spirited girl. I didn't think Jo knew what was in the flask, but the point was I never wanted a drink so bad in my life. I wished I had a flask of my own to dull the ache spreading from my heart to the tips of my toes. It was gonna to be a long trip.

Starting this ride all alone made me realize how much I'd grown attached to not only Jo, but her good friend as well. Many years had passed since I had a friend besides Jessie. The sad fact was becoming painfully obvious at how much it meant to me. I missed the companionship. I liked to believe I was a loner, but having people in my life that cared about me, people I could trust, meant more to me than I could understand. I was beginning to feel like I was part of a family again and losing them hurt almost as much as losing Jo.

What was Jo doing right now? What did she think of me? Was it weird to be worried about those things after what happened between us this morning?

Jo probably wouldn't tell anyone else her true identity, not after the great lengths she'd gone to hide it. Somehow I doubted even Jade knew the truth. I could only imagine what Jo told her about me and a brief moment of sadness for the loss of our friendship washed over me. In spite of our tentative start, our common love for Jo led us to several enjoyable talks, forging a solid friendship.

By now Jessie would be well aware of something amiss since I hadn't met her. She knew me well. Regardless of anything anyone may have told her, Jessie was keenly aware that there was nothing more important to me than finishing this mission.

She also knew my pattern. I would clam up and push on toward my goal. She would be correct.

"Hah!" I gave Clover a light squeeze in the flank to hurry her along. There was lost time to make up. We were a few days from civilization. Several small towns lined our path, so at least we'd have places to refuel and clean up. Maybe I'd even find a little something to clear my head.

# **Chapter Nineteen**

**Spokane- Jimmy**

Hurrying over to the Western Union telegram office, Jimmy hoped to get in and out without the other men noticing. When his name was called out, he shuddered and came to a halt. Plastering a fake smile on his face, he turned around to find the older cowboy waddling as fast as he could across the street to meet him. The old cowboy seemed intent on sticking to him like glue since they'd left the ranch. Butch was acting suspicious and it left him with an uneasy feeling in his gut.

"Jimmy, where ya goin' son?" Butch caught up with him.

The younger man turned and headed toward the general store instead. Were they on to them? He sure hoped not. Maybe he could throw them off with a good lie.

"I need a few things from the store and I wanna send my mother a telegram. Her birthday's coming up." Jimmy needed to get Butch off his back so he could find out if Jessie sent any word yet of her arrival. He'd been checking every few days, using different excuses to head to town.

"Well, that's a good boy. Always take care of your mama. I'll come with you. I gotta message to send myself." Butch didn't budge as he followed along.

Jimmy did his best to hide his discomfort with a smile and a nod even though he was nervous as hell inside. "Yes, sir."

Picking up a few things at the store, they both walked to the office where the teller greeted Jimmy with a smile. They were almost what you'd call friends with as often as he stopped in. The teller pulled out an envelope and Jimmy shot him a look that froze him in place.

Rather than ask for the message, Jimmy said, "Bob, I need to send a message to mom. Please say Happy Birthday, mom. I love and miss you very much. Please wire the message to Abigail Walker in Dallas."

Bob nodded with a cautious smile, glancing at Butch who watched their interaction carefully. Jimmy set his money on the counter and Butch turned to leave. Seizing his window of opportunity, Bob quickly passed the letter to Jimmy who shoved the paper down into his jacket with haste.

As the pair left the office and headed back to their horses, Jimmy noticed the tremble in his hands. With a swift move he buried them in his pockets, his right hand scrunching up the letter even more. He'd grown more and more nervous as the time crept closer to attempting the feat of taking down the O'Shea gang. Jimmy knew what was on the line and it was everyone's head.

\*\*\*

## West of Ketchum- Off the beaten path- Sarah

With my first intentional movement of the new day I became more than aware of the soreness throughout my body. The first night back on the cold, hard ground was always a killer, but it didn't even come close to the deep ache from being in the saddle all day. Night of rest my ass. I found it hard to recall a time I hurt this much after one day on the trail.

Didn't take long for the body to get soft when you slept in a comfortable bed every night next to a warm body. The same warm body I yearned to sleep beside despite the pain in my heart and the doubt in my mind. There seemed to be an undeniable force pulling me towards Jo. Though I tried to push her out, she still seeped into every ounce of my being and expunging her would not be an easy task.

Was that even what I wanted? Did I want her gone?

There was something to be said about love and loss. I'd experienced both and regardless, I didn't think it was a matter of wanting to forget her. No, I just didn't want to feel anything for her anymore. The truth of her identity cut me deep, as if she purposefully betrayed me, but deep down I accepted that she didn't ask to be born into a family of murderers. She ran. She didn't want to be like them and here I was punishing her for something out of her control. Shouldn't I be punishing Jessie for her involuntary part in my parent's murder as well? Seemed only fair, yet I brushed it off for my old friend and held Jo's feet to the fire.

Jo could be just as angry at me for dragging her back into the very thing she'd worked so hard to get away from. Maybe she was angry. I didn't know. How could I when I bolted the moment the words left her lips? I didn't want to hear anything else, so I ran. The confession set my blood to boil and all I wanted was to kill the man who brought so much pain to so many; who was still bringing me pain today.

Killing him was all I'd wanted for the last ten years. Maybe I was punishing Jo, because she was the one thing that could derail all of my plans. If I let her soothe my anger, let her calm the beast within, then how would I finish it? How would I ever find peace?

Taking in a deep breath, I rubbed my stiff neck and glanced over at my friend who stood watching me in silence. Clover was missing her cushy little barn right now. She didn't seem too pleased with me and given my behavior yesterday, I owed her an apology. "Don't look at me like that. I already know."

Ugh! The creak in my bones and my stubborn muscles made getting to my feet quite the hassle. I made my way to her with slow steps to pet her on the muzzle and hug her muscular neck. She gave me a nudge and let out a snort, her breath visible in the cold morning air. I brushed her out and gave her a few carrots I'd packed to keep her happy.

I wasn't hungry, but I forced myself to chew on some jerky I'd made to keep up my strength. We made better time yesterday than I thought after the trials of the morning set us off schedule. Maybe we could get to the next town in two days or so. The quicker the better. Clover would be ready for another taste of the easy life and I'd be more than ready for a warm bed.

***

**Ten years ago- Amarillo, TX**

    *The thunderous sounds of hooves brought Danny O'Shea running out his front door. Three of his men galloped their horses right up to the front porch before skidding to a halt.*

    *"What's the meanin' of all this?" The old man's eyes blazed as he demanded answers for the sudden intrusion.*

    *"Sorry sir, but something went wrong in El Paso yesterday and um...," the oldest cowboy swallowed hard and gripped his reins tight.*

    *O'Shea grew impatient as he snapped at the man, "Yeah? Spit it out Jeff, what happened?"*

    *"Well," he looked to the other two men who shied away. None of them wanted be the one to speak. That was never a good sign. With no other volunteers, Jeff took a deep breath and spoke once again. "We received a telegram. There was a raid by the Marshals. Marie's dead and Margaret, well, she was shot and now she's missin'. Ben followed her, but no word yet. Your son is fine. He should be on his way back as we speak. I'm sorry sir."*

    *Danny O'Shea's face dropped. Both of his girls could be dead. He'd sent them into a hornet's nest, but had confidence his inside men would be able to protect his family. He turned red with anger and his hands rolled into tight fists. "We're goin' there right now. You have twenty minutes to get more men and supplies. Meet me at the train station."*

    *He stormed back into the house, slamming doors and yelling profanities as his maids ran for cover. Closing the door to his master bedroom behind him, the realization hit hard as a sharp pain shot through his chest. He fell into his chair as his world spun around him.*

*He loved his kids. They may not have understood his methods or had warm fuzzy childhood fairy tales, but the world was a hard place and he was raising them to succeed in it. He had created an empire so they'd never want for anything ever again. All they had to do was understand how to run the business. All he ever wanted was for them to continue on in his place, was that so wrong?*

*Margaret. He cried for her most of all. She always fought him tooth and nail, but he saw so much of himself in her. With her fire and determination, he was certain she would've been the one to run the business. She was so young and just needed to understand why things were done the way they were. He truly believed the two of them were on the verge of breaking down their barriers.*

*Now, all Danny had left was regret. He knew good and well what would be waiting in El Paso, but his confidence in others cost him dearly. Someone had failed him. His family should have been safe. He pounded his fist on the table. Everyone would pay for his loss.*

***

## Somewhere along the main road to Spokane- Jo

Jade was not made for camping. There I said it. She might've been my best friend and I loved her, but we would never, ever rough it together again. We were half an hour into our second day of riding and I knew she was driving Jessie crazy, because she was annoying the heck out of me and the Marshal was used to traveling alone.

Well, alone or with Sarah. I'd bet a bottle of whiskey on a complete lack of riveting conversation when they rode together. The two of them and their grand plans were probably locked deep inside their own heads the whole time. Some long days of silent riding those must've been.

Those were some of the little thoughts I entertained to distract myself from Sarah.

Jessie was just as worried about Sarah even though she said my cowgirl could handle herself. Before we left, Jessie said, "Even when Sarah runs off half-cocked, she ain't really half-cocked. There's always a plan. That's how she operates." Whatever their relationship, it was a deep connection forged by their shared hatred of my family.

Jessie sighed and frowned at J as she groaned once again, commenting about how she had none of the cushioning we did to protect her precious little ass from the rigors of riding all day. I wasn't clear if she was calling us fator not, but she really could use a little more meat on her bones.

"J, quiet please. I hurt as much as you do. I haven't ridden anythin' this long in years."

With her snicker, I could only imagine what thoughts were running through her mind. Whatever it was, it made Jessie crack a smile too. It was amazing how those two got along. Who'd have guessed they'd hit it off as suspicious as they were of others. Made me wonder how they ever got to know one another when they were always being so secretive. Then again, they were like two peas in a pod and my friend's uncanny ability to break down walls amazed me.

Let's hope she still had a knack for getting in and out of places unseen. One thing she'd never been good at was staying out of trouble. If anything happened to her, I'd never forgive myself, but I had confidence in Jessie's ability to lead us through this in one piece.

There would be so many things in play when we reached my father. A confrontation was imminent unless Sarah killed him first. He'd be more than shocked to see me and if I found him first and I hoped I did, I wouldn't kill him. Sarah or Jessie deserved that satisfaction, but I wanted to face him none the less. If everyone else was getting closure, then I deserved it as well.

Jessie had more on the line than any of us and I was sympathetic towards her plight. There was nothing I could do or say to take her mind off of Jimmy and Sarah, so in long periods of silence I offered a distraction with idle conversation. Lucky for us, Jade was pretty entertaining on her own.

Anytime I let my thoughts wander they landed on one person. There was no helping myself. Was she still angry? Was she riding alone, stewing in her hatred of me and my family? Would she drive herself mad on the long road to Spokane?

Sarah did need her space, I agreed with Jessie on that, but I wished we'd gone the same way in case something happened to her.

Loud laughter erupted from the other two. Smiling along with them as if listening in, I was only intent on answering one question; was there any way Sarah and I could work through this? Most of all, I worried that one or both of us wouldn't survive and that love we had together would end in heartache. The air between us needed to be cleared before we faced my family.

"Jo, you alright?"

"Hmm?" Turning toward the sound of the voice I found Jade looking at me with concern in her eyes. Most of the morning I'd been quiet and that was unusual around her. "Yeah, I'm fine thanks. Just worried about Sarah."

Jessie glanced at me over her shoulder. We didn't need words to read one another's mind. She maintained a brave mask for the world, but after our conversation, there was no question how deep her feelings ran or that her loyalty to friends and family would be unmatched.

A small nod of acknowledgement was all we needed. We both turned our attention ahead. This early part of the trip was the hardest and slowest as we navigated the mountainous terrain.

Afterwards would be smooth sailing. It was hard enough to do this in a group and yet, Sarah was out there somewhere going it all alone. She was more than capable of taking care of herself, she'd done so for many years, but my concern centered on her state of mind. One mistake, one slip out in these parts could be fatal. If my callous actions cost Sarah her life, I'd never forgive myself.

Never.

Our situation could've been handled much better. The whole thing was a whirlwind. Everything happened so fast. I didn't mean for the words to come out the way they did. As soon as I learned my father was her target, I had to tell her. I just wished I'd done it a different way. But no matter how many times I replayed the scene in my head, it always ended the same.

Was there really a good way to tell someone that's fallen in love with you that you ran away from your family, changed your name and your father was the one who destroyed their life? It was incomprehensible. And then there was Jessie. How she fit into the story still made my mind spin.

No matter how hard I tried to put myself in Sarah's shoes to try and figure out what she was thinking and feeling, it was impossible for me to understand. She'd had everything ripped away from her and yet, she had fought back and found a purpose for her life. She had kept her heart under tight wraps until she gave it to me and look what I did.

I never wanted to be an O'Shea. They destroyed everything. Despite all my hard work to distance myself from them, it all came full circle when Sarah rode into my life. Now I had to face him and her; explain myself to my father and show Sarah I wasn't one of them.

All I cared about was her, Sarah Sawyer. Not because of what my family did to her, but because of what she did to me. She gave me the fairy tale life I'd dreamed of as a child. The one where the princess gets saved and finds true love. Turning around wasn't an option and I wouldn't settle for anything less than her love. Finding her fast and getting our happily ever after was my only goal.

With a gentle squeeze of my heels, I urged Jet to pick up the pace as the others followed my lead.

# **Chapter Twenty**

**Spokane-Jimmy**

Finally finding a moment alone, Jimmy locked the bedroom door and opened the telegram from Jessie.

*Your Aunt Jane will be traveling to Spokane and would love to see you. Expect her in the next few weeks. Love mom.*

He lit the message on fire and set it in the ceramic basin until it burned itself out. Closing his eyes, he leaned back against the edge of the counter. It was almost time. His heart beat a little bit faster. His nerves had been on edge more and more as of late knowing this message would be arriving soon.

Now, ready or not, the day of reckoning was soon upon them. Even with his sister's best laid plans, he couldn't help but fear his days were numbered. If all their efforts resulted in the end of the O'Shea Empire and justice for everyone they'd scorned, then he'd die a happy man.

**\*\*\***

## Boise, Idaho- Sarah

I'd never been so excited to see a town in my life. My time with Jo was the longest I'd been off the trails in years and every muscle I had was expressing its discomfort. I'd left four days ago and not only was my entire body screaming out for a hot bath, but my mind hadn't stopped spinning. All of this solitude was driving me mad as I rehashed our time together, over and over and over again.

Something or someone, would have to numb the pain for the night. With Clover set up for the evening it was time for me to find a place of my own. Where was the damn saloon? Whiskey had been on my mind since I left Jo. This time I'd be sure to take some with me for those nights soon to follow back out on the trail.

I stepped through the swinging doors into a quiet little place. A piano player sat in the corner, a couple of ladies served the patrons and one man stood behind the bar. Not sensing any danger, I settled myself in the back corner where I'd be free to lose myself in a bottle in private. Nothing had gotten Jo off my mind and I was really hoping that at least for tonight, alcohol would do the trick.

The pretty little dark haired girl across the room might just help too. She was smiling at me. Tipping my hat to her, I offered a small smile in return. She blushed. Even though she tried to hide it by looking at the floor, her shy smile gave her away.

If I was being honest, she might look a bit like Jo. A bright smile, large breasts and a nice body. No dimples though and her eyes lacked Jo's warmth, but attractive none the less. The minutes kept passing and she kept sneaking looks at me. I was enjoying the attention.

The server left me the bottle and a glass, as requested. Undoing the top, I savored the scent of the brown liquor. My nerves calmed having the bottle in my hand, watching as the liquid filled the glass before my eyes. With just one sip, the burn on the way down made me sigh in relief. I knew it was impossible that it already had an effect, but mentally, I was right on track.

A few more shots and I began to relax. Exchanging a few flirtatious glances with the pretty little thing still taking an interest in me, my mind once again drifted to Jo, reminding me how I needed another distraction. Alcohol alone wasn't getting it done. Holding up my empty glass to her in a silent request to join me, she stared intently as she weighed her options.

After a moment of indecision, she approached me with cautious steps.

Once more I filled the glass. She had a fantastic smile up close that lit up her face and for a moment, that was all I could see. I pulled out the chair beside me and offered it to her. She nervously glanced around the room before settling on me again. Not coming up with any last minute objections, she accepted the seat.

I slid her the shot and flashed a knowing grin. She was putty in my hands. Even though I didn't enjoy the company of others often, I was well aware of my attributes and had no problem working my charm when it suited my needs. Was I using her? Of course, but she would enjoy it.

"Thank ya." She downed the drink sitting before her. "I'm Jackie. Haven't seen ya round here before." Her voice was raspy, just like Jo's first thing in the morning.

"Hello Jackie. I'm Sarah. I'm only passin' through." Resting on my elbows, I leaned forward to take in her soft features. High cheekbones and full lips, a diamond in the rough for these parts.

"Oh," she said in a soft tone, deflating at my response.

Even if I did stay I wasn't looking for anything long term. I needed a brief distraction. Maybe it wasn't a distraction I was looking for. Maybe I was clinging to the hope that a night with someone else would prove what Jo and I had wasn't so special. Maybe with all the other women, I just hadn't been open to anything more yet. Maybe now that I'd been shown something else, I could recognize it in another person. Maybe I could have an amazing night with this beautiful woman and never give Jo another thought.

That was a lot of maybes.

I needed to quit thinking about Jo all together, because comparing this girl to her just made me think of her more. More whiskey. That's what I needed. I took a swig straight from the bottle.

"Are you from here, Jackie?" Some small talk might get my mind off other things, but I really didn't care about her response. Pulling the glass back from her, I refilled it and slid it back over. She seemed to appreciate my speaking to her like an actual person. If I had to guess, she didn't get treated very well. Her brown dress and jacket were a bit tattered, even though she was well kept. Her nervousness led me to believe she was afraid.

Would someone punish her if she got caught? A husband?
Boyfriend? Owner?

"Yes, born and raised."

Maybe I should stay clear of this one. Sure didn't need
any trouble, but with the mood I was in, the hint of danger did
make it more fun. Scanning the room in my inebriated state, I
found no signs of trouble.

"Who ya looking for?"

"Mama. She don't approve of me spending time in here."

So much for the danger, but that didn't change my plans
for the evening. "Ya think she'd approve of you drinkin' with
me?" Words were getting harder to form. I funneled all my focus
to the girl before me.

"Probably not." She shrugged with indifference.

So she was afraid of mama finding her, but not of doing
the deed. Interesting. "How 'bout if you came back to my room?"
My hand covered hers and the glass, allowing my thumb brush
over the back of her hand. Her breath caught. I was satisfied my
message had been received. "Do you think she'd approve?"

She looked down at my hand on hers. "I don't think she'd
like that either," she whispered and looked up at me through
dark lashes.

"You're a full grown woman, a pretty one at that. What
would you like, Jackie?" My hand went to her knee and I flashed
my sexiest grin. It hadn't let me down yet.

She tossed her hair back over her shoulders. Her
confidence grew knowing where I stood. The glint in her eyes left
no question. She was more than happy to disobey in search of a
little fun. "I'd like you to take me to your room."

"Why Jackie, are you propositionin' me?" With a laugh, I finished off another round of whiskey.

Her eyes sparkled as she giggled and bit her lip. Her gaze drifted from my eyes to my mouth and back up again. "Maybe." She slid her hand into mine. "Why don't we go somewhere more private?"

My eyes narrowed, studying the girl. She couldn't be more than twenty or so. How many times had she done this before me? Was it more of a rebellion against her mother or boredom from this one horse town?

Eh. I did enjoy the inner workings of the mind, but either way, she'd serve my purpose. Several minutes had just passed without thinking of woman who broke my heart. Yes. Jackie would do just fine.

With a squeeze of her hand, I stood and pulled her up with me. The effects of the whiskey hit me as I got to my feet and steadied myself on the edge of the table. She laughed at me and helped me up the steps in silence. The reminder of my aching bones was present after the trip up the stairs. I wished for a moment that I had taken a hot bath to relax my muscles. A hot body would have to suffice for now. There was always the morning.

When we reached my door, I could sense her eyes all over me. We stepped inside and my hat found a place on the table, as did the bottle. I set my holster on the chair beside the bed.

She studied my every move, unsure what she should be doing.

I smiled a soft smile then circled behind her, slid her jacket off of her shoulders and hung it on the hook with care. I didn't want to look into her eyes. This didn't mean anything to me and I didn't want her to think otherwise. She was just an encounter, a night of release, a poor attempt to distance myself from past day's events and nothing more.

Erasing the space between us, I pressed against her back and ran my hands up and down her arms. I buried my face in her hair and took in her lilac scent. She tipped her head to the side, letting me trail soft kisses along her warm skin. Her body shivered beneath my touch and it excited me.

There was power in possessing someone. Jo had that power over me and now I was enjoying the domination of this complete stranger.

She tried to turn, but I held her still, my fingers sneaking up under the hem of her dress to graze her thigh. She gasped and reached her hand up into my hair, pulling me down into her. My tongue glided along her lobe as I let my hands roam her waistline. Her stomach was taut and skin soft. Her desire spiked with a moan as I slid my hand down between her legs. Holding her tight, I caught her when her knees buckled.

There was almost an inkling of my own fire beginning to burn. I'd wondered if I'd be able to touch anyone else, if I'd be able to enjoy anyone else. I wasn't sure I was enjoying this. It was more the idea of being in control than anything else.

Ever since Henry taught me to shoot and punch, I'd been the master of control, that was, until I met Jo. She made me lose control of everything; my emotions, my fears, my desires. For a few minutes, here with this poor girl, I was back in control of my thoughts, feelings and actions.

Her arms rose allowing me to pull her dress up over head. The worn cotton garment was quickly discarded on the floor. Jackie turned to me, unbuttoning my shirt with slow, determined fingers as I stared at her. I felt nothing; neither excitement, nor warmth for her. She was beautiful and kind, but she wasn't Jo.

She pressed her lips to mine and her tongue slid along my top lip. In an instant I became sick to my stomach, disgusted with my actions. Shoving her away, I pulled my shirt closed. I looked at the floor, not able to deal with the hurt in her eyes and backed away when she came closer. "I can't. I'm sorry, I thought..." I shook my head.

Buttoning my shirt, I ran out the door without another word, ignoring her pleas for me to stay. I didn't stop until I was out in the street. The cold night air prickled at my skin and burned my lungs. My warm breath turned to mist before my eyes as my chest heaved in uncontrollable gasps. Dizziness set in and I tried not to pass out.

Shivering from the winter temperatures, I leaned my hands on my knees and focused on my breathing, trying to push down the anger inside at not being able to do something as simple as satisfy my carnal desires.

I wanted to scream. I wanted to hit something. Dammit, I wanted Jo.

***

The hot water enveloped my body and soothed my aching muscles, but it did nothing to ease the pounding in my head or the ache in my chest. Finishing the second bottle last night wasn't one of my better ideas. Whiskey seemed fitting at the time and did serve its purpose for a short while, but now I was awake with all the same problems and a bonus, I had one hell of a hangover.

When I'd gotten back to my room last night, Jackie was gone. Not surprising after my inexcusable behavior. What I attempted to do and how I was willing to use her just like some of the disgusting men did with the girls at O'Shea's repulsed me. They treated them like playthings to be used and tossed aside.

Had I really sunk so low? Had I become the very people I despised?

Here I was, a pathetic, broken drunk of a woman crying over a crushed heart in some sorry excuse for a town. Instead of sitting on my horse headed toward Spokane, I was soaking in this bathtub, drinking from the flask I filled the night before in a vain attempt to drown out my consciousness. Drinking again wouldn't solve anything. In fact, if this was how I planned to spend my day, then I'd be repeating all of this again tomorrow.

My father always preached about the never ending spiral of shame that came with indulging in whiskey to avoid your problems. There was a time when I stuck to his advice like glue, but that was another life, another Sarah Sawyer. The sweet burn of liquor dulled my headache and quieted my soul if only for a little while. My only hope laid in this flask. Would it have enough to put me out for a few more hours?

The closer I got to O'Shea, the more I seemed to lose control. Maybe I needed to indulge in my dark side. Maybe I needed to admit that I could be as bad as them. Perhaps the only thing separating us was conscience and intent. My intent last night was to ease my own pain using someone else, not caring how they felt. My mind, my heart told me it was wrong, so I ran. I ran from what I was capable of, from what I could become if I did it to humiliate or possess for fun like they did.

That damn voice telling me what I could and couldn't do was only feeding my frustration. The constant badgering from my conscience had driven me to drown it out with liquor last night. This morning I hoped to do the same.

A soft knock at the door kept me from achieving my goal of slipping back into a drunken stupor. Who could it be? It was rarely a good thing when I didn't know and I was in no mood, or shape, to deal with surprises.

With an exhausted groan, I tried to regain my bearings. The tub was slick and hard to get out of when the room was spinning around you. Trying to be silent proved a difficult task as I stumbled my way out of the tub and fumbled around for a towel. I wrapped myself up tight and picked up my gun.

The knock came again, a little harder this time. Not wanting to give them any advantage, I refused to reply. If only I could get a peek at who was waiting on the other side, but I was in the blind. Positioning my body behind the door, I undid the lock with a gentle turn. With the doorknob in my right hand and the gun in my left, I swung it open and jumped back ready for action.

# Chapter Twenty-One

**Outside Idaho City, Idaho- Jessie**

"Okay ladies, rise and shine, up and at 'em."

Jo and Jade were burrowed deep into their blankets. They looked haggard. We were only a few days into this trip and it was already glaringly obvious this would be more of an adventure than I had set out for. Groans emanated from their bodies, but there was no real movement yet.

Before walking over to the two of them, I made sure the fire was roaring. My stomach was rumbling and I wouldn't let their slow morning routine ruin my breakfast. I bent down and poked at them. It was impossible to resist a smile as Jo's face scrunched up, her agitation obvious. I kept prodding her. "Come on ladies, we gotta move. Never gonna catch Sarah when you're busy snugglin' in your blankey."

"Dammit Jessie," she threw back her top blanket with a hiss. "Give me a damn minute. I'm not miss mornin' sunshine like you."

A muffled voice followed Jo's groans. "Yeah, what Jo said."

They're irritation made me snicker. Life wasn't easy out on the trails, especially with winter fast approaching. The temperature dropped at night and the cold ground took a toll on your body. They'd be happy to get to town, hopefully tonight if I could get them moving sometime soon.

"If ya'll wanna sleep in a warm bed tonight, I suggest you get moving. I'm makin' oatmeal and if you're not up by the time I'm done, you miss out." A girl's gotta run a tight ship if things were gonna get done.

The pair started to move around, but not before hissing a few curses under their breath. We needed to get back on track as soon as possible. I smiled at their grumpiness and focused on getting breakfast ready. Teasing them was fun, but once out of bed, they were pretty efficient. In only a matter of minutes they were dressed and packed up.

"I gotta take a hike," Jade said, motioning over her shoulder.

The girl was like clockwork in the morning. Guess that's a good thing. She was holding up much better than expected, well, after she finally quit complaining about her ass hurting. Jo and I were excited about the lack of bitchin'. After so many years on my own or with Sarah, it was taking a little getting used to riding in a group.

As Jade disappeared behind a bush, Jo took a seat next to me and smiled. "Good mornin'."

"Mornin' Jo. How ya feelin'?"

"Oh," she laughed and stretched. "I'm sore in places I never knew I could be sore."

I didn't mean to laugh at her, but I'd been there and was quite familiar with what she meant. "It'll work itself out."

"I can't believe you and Sarah spend so much time out here." She helped herself to a bowl of oatmeal and settled into her spot.

"Sarah loves it more than I do, though it is pretty nice to wake up near the river when the sun is rising with the color is reflectin' off the water."

Jo nodded as a distant look fell across her eyes. It didn't take a genius to know she had questions about Sarah, about me and about our relationship. Jo wanted to understand more about the closely guarded woman she'd fallen for, but couldn't decide whether or not she should ask. It was a position I'd been in once, wondering about Sarah and all she kept hidden.

There was a time I'd have let Jo drown in her thoughts, but I knew how deep their connection went. I cared for Sarah and I wanted her to be happy, so maybe I could help Jo find the answers she sought.

"It's comfortin' to many." My gaze followed hers, settling on the horizon. "Specially if you're runnin' from somethin'. A new place, a new adventure every day, with nothin' to remind you of whatever you're tryin' to forget, ya know?" I turned my attention back to her.

She shrugged. "How long you two been doing this?"

"For the most part of four or five years."

"I see. I didn't realize it was so long." Jo picked at her food. The wheels were turning in her head, a slight frown on her face.

"I'd take time off, go see family. She'd usually head back down toward Texas in the winter, lookin' for leads on any of the gang or what the O'Shea's were up to. We've been puttin' together this plan for quite some time now, lookin' for the right moment to strike."

Jo didn't look up from her bowl. She kept pushing the food around without actually eating. "She didn't take a break?"

"Usually only a night or two every so often. You know, you saw her a few times over the years." As soon as the words came out of my mouth I cursed at myself.

Her eyes closed and her spoon fell hard against the edge of the metal bowl. "So, she'd find a town and someone to sleep with then move on?"

*Shit! How did I get into this?*

"No. I mean sometimes, but not every time, Jo and it was few and far between. Believe me." It wasn't like that. Sarah would get lonely, hell we all did, but it wasn't the way Jo made it sound.

She ran her fingers through her hair and looked back out to the horizon. "Do you think she'll find someone now? I broke her heart Jessie, but the thought of her with someone else..."

"No." My tone was firm. "No way. The one thing about Sarah is she's loyal to a tee. She loves you and she'd never be able to do that to you, even if you're not together."

She looked into my eyes. Hopefully she'd find the truth in them. It was something I believed down to my core. Sarah loved Jo and even if she never went back to Jo, she wouldn't be able to give herself to anyone else, even me.

Jo cleared her throat and changed the subject. The pain in her eyes, I could only imagine matched what was in her heart. "How does she survive? I mean, alone for so long and you need money at some point too."

"Don't forget, Sarah's a survivor. She's one tough cookie, a dangerous woman."

She let out a soft chuckle. "Yeah, I know. This seems different than a gunfight."

"It is and it ain't. There's a will to survive and an intuition. She's really smart too. Did you know she could read somethin' once and recite it back almost word for word?"

"No." Her brow shot up. This new insight into Sarah's life definitely caught her attention.

"And she can look at instructions for somethin' and do it like she's known it her whole life. It's damn amazing. I think part of the appeal for her on the trail is she needs the constant challenges Mother Nature throws her way. She's not meant to do somethin' mundane."

My answer stirred something inside. Her face fell and she focused on her bowl once more. "Does that mean you don't think she could ever settle down, stay in one place?"

"I didn't say that, Jo. She's already done things with you I never thought I'd see from her. I think you show her all the things she's forgotten she could do and I've never seen her more happy or alive than when she's with you. We just have to get through this and I think you'll see a whole new Sarah Sawyer."

"I hope so." Jo sighed and looked up at me with a sad smile.

All of this weighed on her, probably more than she would admit. She was lucky she had such a good friend. Jade's loyalty to her was evidence of the kind of woman Jo had become. Witnessing her for who she was and not who she was related to, made me hope one day soon I could count myself among her friends.

"Oh, and as for money, she's got no problems there. We've done plenty of bounty work, plus she got a nice sum for the old couple's farm she sold before hittin' the road. Of course, you don't spend too much out here besides an occasional trip to town."

"The farm? Oh yes, the one who taught her to shoot and fight. Why did she sell it?" Jo straightened herself and finally forced a spoonful of oatmeal into her mouth.

"For the reasons I already told you. She didn't want the constant reminder. They were good to her and left her the place when they died. She stayed there a little while. That's where she was when we met, but she was consumed by the need for closure, so she roams."

Jo stood up. Her discomfort at the mention of her family's treacherous deeds plainly visible. "I hope she can forgive me. I hope you both can forgive me."

Pushing up from the rock I was perched upon, I stood beside her. We both stared out to the bright light rising over the horizon making everything look new again. I placed my hand on her shoulder. "She will. As for me, I don't blame you, Jo. None of this is on you."

Jo shook her head. There was something more bothering her, but she wouldn't say and it wasn't my place to ask. Maybe it was her family, or Sarah, or something unrelated, but it clearly cut her deep.

She set the bowl down and walked away, speaking low under her breath, "If only that were true, Jessie."

*  *  *

## Boise- Sarah

Jackie almost dropped her tray at the sight of my gun. A small squeak fell from her lips.

"Shit. I'm sorry Jackie." I lowered my gun in a hurry and moved toward the door.

"What're ya doing here?" Waving my arm, I gave her the okay to enter and shut the door behind her. My senses were sharper for the moment. The adrenaline pumped hard and fast, giving me the clarity to watch the girl's every move.

She placed a tray on the table and sheepishly glanced back at me. "I uh, I thought you might be kinda hungry. I know you didn't eat." She removed the cover allowing the delicious aroma of bacon, eggs, grits and biscuits to waft through the room.

My stomach growled on cue as proof I hadn't eaten anything since breakfast yesterday. Her gentle smile made me feel bad once again for my actions last night. I placed my gun on the table and fixed my towel, I gave her an appreciative smile and sat down. "Thank you. You didn't have to do this. Please, sit with me."

She did the same thing as last night, like it was ingrained in her to check if anyone was watching even though we were in a room by ourselves. She took the seat while I tore through my meal like a wild animal.

My hunger hit a high with warm food sitting right in front of me, so I threw etiquette out the window.

"See? I knew it," she grinned with pride. "I made it myself, too."

I choked down the wad in my cheeks and leaned back, taking a momentary break from shoveling food into my mouth. "It's really good. I appreciate you thinkin' of me." My eyes drifted toward the window to avoid her gaze. "I um...don't deserve it after last night, though. I'm so sorry."

"Thank you for that." Her nervousness was evident as she cleared her throat and shifted her weight. It was a common tell when something was on a person's mind. "I'd be lyin' if I said I wasn't sorry you ran off. Who is she?"

"Whaddya mean?" She caught me off guard with her question and I tried to recall what exactly I said to her last night.

"The woman you're in love with. The reason you couldn't spend the night with me. What happened?"

"Who says there is someone? Maybe I just don't think young girls should be taken advantage of, especially by a drunk looking for a good time."

"If it makes ya feel better, I didn't feel taken advantage of. You're the first person who treated me nice, talked to me like I was someone, but I could tell there was somethin' you were hidin' from by the way you were drinkin'."

Saying nothing, I took another bite and peered up at her through my lashes. The whiskey sitting nearby served to wash down the food. Whiskey sure did go well with eggs. "I'm not a good person, Jackie."

"I don't know about that. You couldn't go through with it, so that's gotta count for somethin' don't it? Whoever she is, she's a lucky gal."

"Humph." The greasy food was doing its job. The more I ate, the better I felt. Her words took root in my mind and heart as I cleaned my plate. My heart belonged to Jo that much was true. Little did Jackie know, I wasn't a blessing, but a curse.

"I ain't never seen a woman with guns like you. Why do you carry them?"

Ceasing all movement, I stared at her hard. She needed to understand what I'd been trying to tell her, so I said it plain and cold. "Like I said, I'm not a good person." She didn't seem at all intimidated by the words. Actually, she appeared almost sympathetic. My eye twitched. Her lack of fear bothered me. I didn't know why. Guess I was used to a different reaction.

"Well, if you say so." Her voice was soft but sincere as she continued, "But I'm pretty sure you care for someone somewhere and I'm gonna bet they care for you too. I can see it in your eyes. You're no monster. I know monsters."

Her eyes flickered with unspoken pain. It was obvious she'd lived much in her short time on earth, much as I had at her age. Her words echoed Jo's and I let myself believe it once, but not again.

Not a monster huh? If she only knew. Maybe not the kind she had encountered, but one just the same. Still, I saw a bit of myself in her and I pitied the poor girl. She was me back when I felt powerless, when I'd given up and accepted being a slave to the whims of evil people. Jackie was me before I took control over my life.

My expression softened and I set my fork down. I wanted nothing more than to point her in the right direction after her kindness. "Ya know, you can leave here, start a new life. Not all women end up mothers, maids or punchin' bags."

She flinched at the last one, but I brushed it off for now. It was none of my business anyway. The last thing I needed was to go looking for a fight.

She sighed and shook her head. "With what? How would I survive?"

I pushed my plate away and sat back in my chair. Her words hinted at disbelief, but her eyes flickered with hope. "Trust me. It can be done if you want it bad enough."

"Is that what you did?" Intrigued, she leaned forward, resting her elbows on the table top.

"You could say that. It's a long story, but yes, I finally took back my life. Now I live by my own rules."

"Wow, you're very brave." Her smile was bright and she sat up straighter. Her stare held a sense of wonder and awe.

"No, I'm a coward," I admonished myself. It was true in so many ways. "But I'm workin' on it."

"Are ya leavin' today?"

I shrugged without a care. "Well, that was the plan, but it seems I'm in no shape." I couldn't help chuckling at my own dysfunction. So much for keeping to plan.

"But you're still drinking?" She studied my ragged physical state.

The girl was more intuitive than you'd think at first glance. My hand held the silver flask which called for me to partake in the mind-numbing goodness. I closed my eyes and sighed, laying it down on the table. I slid it over to her, pulled my hand back and opened my eyes. She watched me curiously, unsure what my actions meant.

"It's yours. Enjoy it. There's some really fine whiskey in there."

"No." She pushed the small container back to me. "It's yours. I can't take it. Besides, if mamma found it..."

I slid it right back in front of her and placed her hand on top. "I insist. Where I'm goin' I need a clear head. It's my gift to you for helpin' make that happen."

She handled the shiny metal object with care, opening the top and sniffing the contents. A light smile tugged at her lips as she nodded to me.

"Keep it safe. Mamma doesn't need to know everything." I offered her a small smile, making her own grow tenfold, but she was still trying to figure me out. "Jackie, how bad do you want to get out of this town?"

"What?" Her concentrated gaze turned to surprise.

"I can tell you're curious, maybe even wantin' to tag along, which you can't by the way." Her shoulders sagged at the news, telling me I had called it right." You wanna get out of here, but don't know how, right?"

She nodded, still listening to me with a look of confusion.

"How badly do you want out?" I leaned across the table and narrowed my eyes at her, attempting to feel her out. "I'm assumin' you think you deserve better. Are you willin' to do what it takes to get out if you had a way?"

She didn't even pause. Her immediate and intense answer of "yes" while she held my gaze told me all I needed to know. She was more like me than I expected. A smart, caring girl stuck in a bad situation she didn't think she could get out of. I stood up and walked to my bag. She studied my every move as I pulled my clothes out. "How soon could you leave," I asked over my shoulder.

"I don't know, by the weekend I guess. I'd need some plannin'. Why? I thought I couldn't go with you?"

"You can't."

"Where ya headed?"

I continued to sort through my pack, avoiding her stare. "That's none of your concern. What is your concern is gettin' on the train to Ketchum, walkin' into the saloon, tellin' Jo and Jade I sent you and you need help starting over."

"I can't afford a train ride."

"Let me worry about that. Swing back around dinner time if you're serious." When I turned back around, her eyes were wide. Was she scared or surprised? Probably a bit of both.

"I don't...I don't know what to say." She pushed her chair back and stood tall. Her eyes glassed over as she fought back tears.

I hated to see a woman cry, even in the name of joy. The sight brought up my own painful memories where crying was all I could do for days. I looked away, focusing on the items I'd pulled out of my pack. It served as both a distraction and to let her know we were done for now. "Don't say anything. Just go make a better life for yourself."

Not long after Jackie left, the weight of the greasy meal in my stomach and the remnants of my hangover made their voices heard. Sleep sounded like the best thing to do, so I put myself back to bed.

Laying in silence, I stared at the ceiling for an indiscernible amount of time without thinking about anything. I couldn't remember a time I didn't have something burning in my mind, be it O'Shea, justice, the gang, Jessie or Jo. My brain always seemed to be occupied. Now here I was in a moment of complete solitude, locked away from the world and myself. My body felt almost weightless. Was this what relaxing was like?

Being with Jo offered me a great degree of freedom from myself, but something about this seemed different. It may have been the liquor or the talk with Jackie, but it was almost like I'd reached an acceptance of self. A sudden clarity of all I'd been through and the strength of will I had to make a new life despite the circumstances sunk in.

An uncontrollable smile pulled at my lips as I closed my eyes and drifted off to sleep.

***

The waning rays of afternoon sun woke me with a gentle caress. I was more rested than I had been in years. The day was shot. I'd have barely enough time to buy the train ticket, stop in the general store to replenish my pack and feed Clover before the sun went down. I hated wasting the day, even though it was best I didn't try to leave given my state this morning.

Guess I was most upset at allowing myself to get lost in the bottle and now I was a day behind. We'd have to leave earlier than usual tomorrow to try and make up some time. One good thing did come of it though, well two actually. One was I felt lighter, mentally and physically. Maybe this was my rock bottom, nowhere to go but up. Two, I found a girl I could help. A life I could change. A girl who didn't just say she wanted more, but whose eyes shined with the deep down desire to achieve it once the possibility presented itself. I had no doubt she'd use the ticket, just as I had no doubt Jo and Jade would help her.

The passing thought of Jo gave me an idea. The way I left things with her made me sick. She deserved better and possibly closure if I never got to do it in person. I'd come to accept the idea I might not come back from Spokane, but we couldn't end on a sour note. There had to be something around here to write with.

So many emotions and words flooded my being, looking for an outlet and their eventual destination, Jo. I wrote as eloquently as possible, what might be my very last words to the woman I loved. The back of my hand wiped away tears as I poured my heart out on paper. A few strays landed, smearing the letters. Thankfully they were still legible. I didn't have the strength to write them again. All I needed was an envelope from the store.

With a quick, neat fold, I tucked the letter under my pack. Before it got much later, I dressed and headed out on my to-do list so I could be back by dinner.

Six thirty rolled around and I heard a knock on my door. This time she announced herself, probably wanting to avoid a repeat of the gun in her face from this morning. She had a tray once again, which she set in the same place.

"I didn't mean you had to bring me dinner." Even though I laughed, her thoughtfulness was appreciated.

"I know, but it's the least I could do." She smiled and took an awkward stance near the table. She uncovered the food to reveal homemade pork chops with potatoes and greens.

I did miss home cooking. And a comfortable bed. And a warm house. And Jo.

With a sigh, I took a seat, tapping the table for her to sit with me. "This looks great, Jackie." I met her eyes and smiled.

She beamed from the compliment.

What was her situation? The last thing I wanted was to intrude, but she was far too sweet to walk around in fear looking like a beaten pup. Her curious behavior on display once again made me even more certain I was doing the right thing. "Did you eat already?"

"Yes. I ate with mamma and George."

"Who's George?"

"He's mamma's guy friend. He's been around for years."

She seemed uncomfortable talking about him. Her hand was bandaged. I didn't remember seeing it before. Maybe she had been hiding it, but the injury was plain as day now.

"I see." I took a few bites before deciding to inquire further. "What happened to your hand?"

"It's nothin' really. I'm clumsy."

"Did he do that to you?"

"No." Her reply did little to convince me, but there was no sign George was the culprit.

"Did she?"

Jackie peeled her eyes away, ashamed of her situation.

"Hey." My hand covered hers and I caught her eyes with mine. "It's okay. You don't have to live like that anymore." I put down my fork and stood up. Moving to the bedside, I pulled out the ticket and the sealed letter to Jo and held it out to her.

She stared at the items wide eyed. "I can't believe you really did this for me." She fell into me hard, pushing me backward from the weight and embracing me with such force I could hardly breathe. The appreciative gesture made sent a warmth through me, different than the way I felt with Jo. As I held her, my mouth pulled up into one of the widest grins I'd ever had in my life. This was all the thanks I needed.

Her body shook as she sobbed into my shoulder.

My fingers combed through her hair and I rubbed her back hoping to comfort her. I placed a soft kiss on her head out of instinct. I never thought of myself as the mothering type, yet this came so naturally it caught me by surprise.

Jackie struggled to collect herself as she pulled away. She wiped her eyes with her arm and offered me a shy smile. "I'm sorry. I um...I guess I didn't think you'd do it. People don't do nice things for me often."

"I guess it's time you had new people in your life." I handed her the letter and ten dollars for food. "Give this to Jo when you get to the saloon. I promise they're good people. I wish you a wonderful and happy life."

"I can't thank you enough. Will I ever see you again, Sarah?"

Her sincere joy and appreciation for my deed choked me up. Meeting Jackie showed me I'd been lucky in many things I'd never acknowledged. I'd known the love of a mother and a father, a true love and a true friend. I'd had blessings in my life, never realizing what they truly were because I chose to focus on the pain.

I had allowed the horrific events to plague my existence and consume my life. Until now, I never knew how much it meant to have had love. In the presence of this broken girl, still full of life and hope despite her situation, who'd never known any of the good things in life, I felt like an ungrateful asshole.

"I wish I knew, Jackie." I smiled sadly. "I wish I knew."

And that was the honest truth.

# Chapter Twenty-Two

**Sarah**

Spokane was on the horizon. After two weeks of travel, I hoped to be there by nightfall. My nerves were beginning to get the best of me. Those few moments when you realized your destiny was waiting and it was only a matter of time before everything you'd been planning collided with reality. In this case, it would probably be a shit storm of epic proportions.

Would Jessie already be there and ready to go? I hoped so. Oddly enough, after all these years with this as my only purpose, I sometimes wondered if I was really and truly ready to do this, to take him down. In the back of my head lingered the nagging question of what I would do when it was all over and if Jo would even be in my life.

Part of me wanted to do this alone, no more lives needed to be lost, besides Danny O'Shea's anyway. Despite my promise to Jessie, I was feeling antsy and my irrational swirling emotions had me wanting to run into something bigger than I could probably handle. I saw it, recognized it and yet I had a difficult time controlling the urge to rush in.

Then there was the part of me that wished Jo was here. The mere thought of her brought me to a place of serenity like I'd never known, even as I fought myself and the obvious feelings I had for her. I would've preferred to clear the air between us first, but it was better this way.

I was certain Jackie would deliver the letter and I was relieved to have Jo out of harm's way. This would've been much harder if I had to worry about her well-being the entire time. There was a reason she ran from her family and I saw no reason she should have to face them again because of me. She should enjoy the life she made without them. When I was through here, well, then we'd see if Jo and I could have a life together as well.

***

## Spokane- Jo

"Jessie, you seen her anywhere? She should be here by now. You don't think she already went after my father, do you? Oh my god. I hope she hasn't done anything stupid."

I paced the room running my fingers through my hair, my body humming with nervous energy. Sarah and Jessie were about to confront the person who had brought them so much unimaginable pain and for me, the family I had never wanted to see again. So many emotions swarmed me. I was all wound up and not in a good way, not like the way Sarah did to me.

This was painful. Breathing was nearly impossible and nausea was the reigning feeling of the moment.

Jade had gone to grab us some food, but hunger was the last thing on my mind. The sun was setting and it looked more and more like Sarah wouldn't be arriving tonight.

"Jo, breathe, please. You need to relax. No, I ain't seen her yet and no, I don't think she's gone on without me. I'll give her another day." Jessie walked to the window and looked down the street. "Maybe she needed to cool off, take some extra time to get here. That's what I'd do. She'll need a clear head to do this, although when she sees you here, that'll all go out the window."

Jessie was being supportive, but I could hear the frustration in her voice. She insisted Sarah wouldn't go against her nature and do something impulsive and suicidal, but I had my doubts. Telling me to relax only seemed to make me not relax even more. There was this deep, nagging fear that something was wrong. I couldn't explain it, couldn't justify it and damn sure couldn't shake the feeling. It had taken a hold of me the moment we arrived and Sarah was nowhere to be found.

What would happen when Sarah saw me here? Would she run into my arms or come at me with fists flaring? Whatever her reaction turned out to be, I'd accept it. She was allowed to have her feelings. This was all too much for even me to wrap my head around, but here we were and we had to move forward somehow.

I was about to face my father. Never thought I'd say those words again. Even so, coming face to face with him or my brother again was the farthest thing from my mind. I couldn't even imagine what their reaction would be when they saw me, but my biggest worry was what Sarah would do when she learned the whole truth.

"I can't relax Jessie. This is all my fault. If she...I'll never forgive myself. Never." I didn't even want to think that way. I couldn't. Those kinds of thoughts only made me panic even more. A rising ache in my hands made me shake my arms out. I'd been wringing my fingers so tight they were getting sore. My whole body was wrought with anxiety and it was wearing me out.

"It's not your fault Jo and it's gonna be fine." She grabbed me by the arm and pulled me to face her, those damn penetrating eyes of hers bored deep into mine. Determination radiated off her, reinforcing what I already knew. She was a fighter. "I promise. We will all face your father together and we will all come out alive." She said it with such certainty.

As much as her confidence made me want to believe, the odds were stacked against us and I knew my family better than she did. "Don't make promises you can't keep, Jessie." My eyes remained locked with hers. I wanted her to realize the full weight of what she was saying and to see the desperation swelling within me.

"I never do." She maintained her confidence and if possible, was even more than before.

The Marshal had already proven to be a tenacious woman of the law and an unwavering friend, but she might also be the best bluffer on the planet after that performance. Could she really believe her own words? The promise was impossible to keep, yet the strong aura around her would rally a hundred men.

There was a twinge of relief, but the doubt remained. If it were just me, I'd follow her off a cliff, but with Sarah an unknown, her words weren't enough. I let out a breath and walked to the window, keeping a lookout for the woman I loved.

***

## Jessie

"Look Jo...just have a seat and take a deep breath, will ya? Jade will be back in a few minutes with some grub. Please eat. Sarah's gonna be mad at me if I let you waste away under my supervision."

Jo smiled, finally making me feel a little better about her state of mind. It was a good idea to avoid the topic of Sarah killing me for letting her and her friend come along, but really, who was going to stop them? If they didn't come with me, they'd be out on their own, which was far more dangerous.

At least this way I was around to take care of them and I planned to do exactly that. As I promised Jo, I would do everything in my power to get us all out alive. At the very least, I wanted those two safe. It was my job to protect and be in the line of fire, not theirs. I'd accepted the reality of a lawman life without protest ever since I became a U.S. Marshal.

"I'm gonna go meet Jake and tell 'em we're ready to move tonight or tomorrow night depending on Sarah. Jimmy left me a message. He'll be workin' the west side the next few nights, so that's where we'll strike."

Jo finally left the window and laid on the bed. She closed her eyes and let out a deep breath. At least she was trying, so that was a step in the right direction. In a matter of seconds, Jo had drifted off to sleep.

I was every bit as worried about Sarah as she was, but I couldn't let it show. I had to believe she would stick to the plan. Her common sense always prevailed and my confidence was the only thing holding us together.

Fresh air seemed like a great idea, so I took the long way to Jake's door. He was a good man, a little older with a "been-there, done-that" for nearly any story you could tell. I met him back in El Paso. He had caught the two U.S. Marshals who worked for O'Shea. Jake never got over all the good men that were killed by their actions. I had a world of respect for him and he was the only one besides Sarah I would trust my life with.

"Hi Jessie. Come on in."

His deep, soothing voice was always a calming force. Jake's hair was beginning to gray, no longer the jet black from when we first met. He was ruggedly handsome still, with a strong, angled jaw and soft, whiskey eyes that could warm your heart when he wanted them to. The years had only added to his looks instead of taking them away.

I smiled, removed my hat and entered his room, noticing his Remington's were laid out for cleaning. A certain blonde I knew liked to do the same thing before every fight as well. I shook my head and chuckled to myself.

Sarah would be an excellent lawman, so meticulous and precise. So much black and white in the laws, but my favorite had always been the way she adapted to those around her, even when she said she didn't want to be around people. She could be hard as nails or soft and warm, depending on what was needed.

Sarah belonged to Jo now, but she still held a special place for me inside and it meant everything to me. I'd spend my last breath being worthy of that place, giving me one more reason to get this right.

"So, you ready for this, Jake?"

He nodded. "You?"

"Beyond ready. It's time to lay this to rest and get on with our lives. I know I've already given him too much of mine."

Jake could relate to what I was saying and if Sarah were here, she sure as hell would agree.

*Dammit Sarah, where are you?*

* * *

## Jo

"Jo? Jessie?" Jade's voice carried from outside the room as she yelled at the top of her lungs.

The rapid pounding of feet in the hallway set me on edge. Whatever it was, it must have been urgent. Jessie was gone so I jumped from the bed, grabbed my gun and ran to the door to meet her. "What's wrong? Are you okay?"

She pushed her way inside. "I'm fine, but I just saw Sarah and she was about to leave town. Didn't seem like she had any plans to get Jessie. I didn't want her to see me and run off, so I ran as fast as I could." She looked around the room, panic in her eyes. She seemed to be searching for something. "Where's Jessie? We gotta go."

Before I could even get a word out, Jessie came bursting in. "What's wrong? I heard yelling."

Jake followed close behind with guns drawn as he surveyed the room for trouble.

"Jade saw Sarah. She's leavin' without you. We gotta go now." My nightmare became reality and it was dizzying.

Jessie ran to the window looking both directions. "What? Are you sure?"

"Positive. A few minutes ago at the general store," Jade said, packing her gear with lightning speed. "I didn't let her see me. Come on. Less talkin', more movin'." She was frantic, grabbing at bags and pulling me out the door.

Jessie and Jake were two steps behind.

In all the years I'd known her, Jade had never moved so fast. On any other day, I would've had to make a smart remark, but like someone flipped a switch, we were all business. Whatever plans Jesse and Jake had in store were scrapped until we caught Sarah.

When we reached the street, I made out the faint silhouette of a single horseman heading out of town. It was her. I could feel it in my bones. While the others raced to saddle the horses, I could only stand and watch the figure recede from view, my stomach churning with dread.

Amid all the panic, a sudden calm settled me as a whisper escaped my lips, "Sarah."

***

## Outer Border of O'Shea's Ranch- Sarah

The oddest sensation swept through me as I rode out of town toward the purple and orange horizon.

Calm.

Even with the craziness and my careless march toward certain death, I was calm. The clenching muscles relaxed. My thoughts stilled. My soul...peace.

Strange.

Calm's been nonexistent for me since the night before I left Jo. What about the conversation with the girl at the general store? Was it possible I missed human interaction more than I thought? Doubtful. I had denied myself the simple pleasure for years, so why miss it now? Hard to tell. After I had met Jackie, I avoided all towns with the sole purpose of steering clear of people. The only reason for me to ever stop was a hot meal, to clean up or restock.

The only place I ever felt more at home than the trail was in Jo's arms. Was it possible my calm stemmed from allowing Jo back into my heart? The thought of the woman sent my memory sifting through images of her and me. My body warmed, spreading a flush through me in the usual way I responded to her touch.

"Jo." Her name floated from my lips in a breathy whisper. One word, only a name, but it held the power to fill me with a steely determination. This quest ended tonight.

The edge of the O'Shea ranch came into view as night claimed the sky. I took my time riding the border in search of the perfect entry point. The key to making this work would be surprise and efficiency. The cows on the west side would serve as a cover. Clover and I kept far enough away to remain hidden by darkness, but we didn't have long. The moon would be up well ahead of my approach. On a night as clear as this, I might as well be riding in at high noon.

There was no going back, no changing my mind. I was tired and O'Shea had lived long enough.

The faint rumble of hooves echoed through the stillness of the night. The sound grew louder. They were closing on us fast. In a flash, I dismounted and pulled Clover behind a large brush. We'd be well hidden until they passed.

Four riders on horseback slowed to a walk twenty paces away. I couldn't quite catch the conversation, but their low voices carried clear enough. One in particular stung my ears.

Could it be? Why?

I'd never mistake the voice of the only person who possessed to ability to build me up and tear me down. The same honey voice that weeks earlier had whispered words of love in my ear, screamed my name in the heat of passion and cursed my death wish. With no chance of stopping myself, her name rolled off my tongue, falling out with more volume than I wanted, "Jo?"

The horses stopped.

Scolding myself under my breath, I hoped my mind hadn't play a trick on me, because the alternative had the potential be a very bad thing. My mission would finish before even getting started with one little slip. But, no. That voice belonged to Jo. My gut told me so.

I stood and walked out from my cover unarmed and completely vulnerable. "Jo." I stated her name again, this time with certainty. My heart no longer allowed my brain to question what it knew to be true. The sight of her made me happier than ever. Also livid.

She shouldn't have been here. Jessie should've never let it happen. Truth be told, they both pissed me off with their actions, but I couldn't ignore the relief accompanying my anger. They saved me from charging into certain death.

"Sarah?" A mix of apprehension and comfort intermingled in one tiny spoken word.

Internally, I struggled. How was it possible to be so drawn to someone, yet still battling the demons of our combined pasts? Two completely different sides that seemed impossible to coexist.

"Jo, why are you here? This is too dangerous." The act of stepping towards her overshadowed my halfhearted protest. The sight of her in the flesh negated my fear for her safety. All thoughts of life, death, worry and plans evaporated. I only wanted one simple thing, Jo.

"There was no way I wasn't comin' after you, Sarah. I was already packing when you left the first time, but after...well, you know... I caught Jessie at the saloon waitin' for you."

I glared at my good friend who lowered her eyes.

Jo intervened. "Please don't be mad at her. I told her I was goin' after you one way or the other so we might as well stick together. Jade and I had no intention of lettin' you do this alone." She swung her leg over, dismounted her horse and moved toward me with purpose.

My heart still battled my better judgment. I couldn't decide if I should scoop her into my arms and kiss her hard or scream at her for doing something so impulsive and dangerous. Once she and I were face to face though, my body made the decision for me. The moonlight reflected in her eyes and I melted.

The fastest hands in the west did me proud, cupping the sides of Jo's face before she batted an eye. This time, instead of killing, they were used for healing. I pulled her in hard, taking possession of the moan that escaped her, savoring the way it made me hum all over. I kissed her like my life depended on the silky caress of her tongue against mine.

In some ways, I guessed my life did depend on her. I lived for Jo now and as much as I wanted her safe, I became whole again with her by my side. With Jo I believed I could conquer anything.

Jo's hands copied mine. She clutched me tight, daring me to try and pull away. The want, the need, the passion she conveyed with only her lips shattered any wall I'd ever built.

I'd never pull away from her again. She lit a fire in my soul and I needed her like a flame needed air. My arms slid around her back removing all remaining space between us. The heat from her touch, her body, her love, chased the cold from my skin and my heart. I poured everything into these few moments, maybe our last ones like this.

The clearing of throats brought me back to reality. A reality so easily forgotten in her loving embrace. My eyes fluttered open. A broad smile forced its way across my face. I leaned back and recognized the same unconditional love reflected back at me in Jo's blazing eyes.

I held the most beautiful creature on this planet in my arms, flushed and breathless. The mere fact I'd been privileged enough to have a woman like her for even a second, never ceased to amaze me. For a solitary minute, I considered leaving with her right then and there. I could abandon this self-destructive need for justice and live happily ever after with Jo, couldn't I?

Why didn't I before? All of this could've been avoided.

Who was I kidding? The wheels were already in motion. They had been for ten long years. We'd made our beds and the time had come to see this through.

"Um, ladies?"

I hated to pull away, but forced myself to acknowledge the voice. Jessie gave me a stern look. Not the right time or place for romance I'd admit, but how could I resist? Rolling my eyes, I grumbled, "Yeah, be right there."

The intense need to keep her near dominated my senses. Jo and I groaned as we pulled apart. Hard to believe we had the strength to separate. The warmth from seconds ago dissipated in the cold night air. Nothing like the chill of reality to bring you back from what might have been. In one last desperate attempt to stay close, I leaned in and whispered, "To be continued."

The moon's rays betrayed the secrets of darkness, hitting her in a way that she couldn't deny the effects of my words. I'd seen it enough. Her chin dipped down, eyes falling away to hide the glint of shyness. Had we been under the bright rays of day, the light pink blush traveling up her neck and to her cheeks could've be witnessed by all.

Jo sucked her bottom lip between her teeth and nibbled while I continued to smile, waiting for her gaze to return to me. Her hand slipped into mine as we walked over to the rest of the group. A gentle, tingling sensation spread up my arm from her touch and reached every part of my body.

"Sarah, I don't even want to think about what you had goin' on in that head of yours, but we made a plan and now we're gonna to use it, all right?"

I didn't think Jessie owned a stern, mothering tone, but point taken. Enough of my stupidity. There was so much more on the line with them here. I had to consider the others and we all needed to get out alive.

"Yes, Marshal." She flashed a grin when I answered her.

The awkwardness between us passed and Jake took control, outlining the plan for all to hear. "Here we have cattle, the perfect cover to get close to the bunk houses across the way. To the left is O'Shea's place. He usually only keeps a maid there at night. Jo and Sarah." He pointed at us. "You ladies flank either side of the small house on the end, clear it and then move in toward his house."

He turned to Jessie. "You're the only one who knows Jimmy, so you'll take the house in the center where the lookout sits. That's where he's supposed to be tonight. Jade will go with you. I'll go right and take the last two buildings. Let's all do our best to stay quiet if we encounter the enemy so we can keep our presence a secret as long as possible. That means no guns if you can help it."

He met us each eye for eye, pausing until he received nods of understanding. "Good. Now Jimmy says we can expect ten to fifteen men, but be ready for more. Let's take the place down and go home in one piece."

My eyes locked on Jessie's. The glances we exchanged said all that needed to be said. She was well aware of how I cared for her and what the moment meant to us both. An eerie silence fell, interrupted by nothing but the pounding of my own heart in my throat.

The revelation of the task we were about to attempt sunk in for us all. Shared nods of respect and recognition were exchanged between every member of the group.

I took a deep breath and stood, leading them toward an uncertain fate. We snuck through the cow field far too easily my liking. Easy always made me nervous. Too easy reeked of a set up.

"You're sure we can't tip any of them?" Jade's crazy question in a time of high tension made us all smile. What made it even funnier was her slight Spanish accent.

"No." Jessie spat back a quick answer with a frown fixed to her face.

"You sure? I always wanted to do that."

"Do I look like I'm jokin'?"

Jade studied Jessie's stern expression and then shrugged. "How would I know? You always look like that."

Jessie chuckled and shook her head. "Maybe on the way out. Just stay close to me and keep out of trouble, okay?"

"Deal."

With one last nod, we all acknowledged there was no going back. Anything could happen. Lives may be lost.

I swallowed hard as Jessie and Jade broke off first. Jake followed soon after, leaving only Jo and I squatted behind the water trough with the cows.

"Jo," I whispered.

She faced me. The moonlight caught the flicker of concern in her eyes.

I took her nearest hand in my own. "No matter what happens out there, never doubt that I will always love you with everything I am."

She smiled a soft smile, albeit a forced one. Her hand slipped free of my grasp and moved to my cheek. The endearing look in her eyes filled with something I couldn't place. "You remember those words, Sarah and know that I will always love you too."

I'd take those words to my grave. I placed a chaste kiss on her lips and ran off. My past, present and future met at a crossroad in Spokane and I hoped I had it in me to not die today.

# Chapter Twenty-Three

**O'Shea's House**

The stillness of the night didn't sit well with Danny O'Shea. Most nights at least the cows and horses held conversations, but tonight even they were silent. He didn't like it when the tiniest whisper could be heard five acres away. Those kind of nights always ended up being trouble.

He kept to his usual routine of sitting in a rocker with a glass of fine whiskey. Tonight though, instead of reading, his hardened hazel eyes fixated out the window. The Marshal would arrive soon. When she did, he'd bring her insistent pursuit of vengeance to a close.

This moment had been building for years. After a certain someone inquired about his activities, he put the feelers out. Not long after, O'Shea learned all about one U.S. Marshal Jessie Walker. He gathered as much information as possible until all her snooping came to a head and landed on his doorstep earlier in the year. One of his contacts had tipped him off about her brother. A quick strike seemed certain, but they were far more patient than he would've ever been.

"Nobody's gonna beat me at my own game," he said with a sneer as he refilled the empty glass. The upper hand belonged to him. Jimmy and Jessie were clueless and soon their misguided quest for revenge would meet a sad end. "Especially for something I didn't even do." O'Shea shook his head with a laugh.

He had engaged himself in the same conversation every night for months. If Jessie and Jimmy wanted to blame him because their father couldn't handle what life threw at him, then they'd suffer the consequences.

Life hadn't been an easy day in the field for him either. He'd lost family, suffered financial losses and weathered attempted takeovers. Building an empire took hard work and sacrifice and even more to keep it together, but losing Margaret was one of the hardest moments of his life. Still, here he stood, strong and persevering. He had never once thought to hang himself.

The longer he sat, the more something nagged at him to go outside. An unexplained pull drew him out into the darkness. Nothing justified the calling, but his instincts rarely let him down.

He set his whiskey aside and walked toward the door. His holster hung around his waist. The ritual checking of the pistol commenced before leaving the house. The first rule of survival in the west was to keep your guns fully loaded and in working order.

With caution, Danny pulled back the edge of the curtain. Still nothing unusual drew his attention besides the dead, unnerving silence. Through the door, off the porch and into the yard he went, stopping at the sight of a dark haired woman not thirty feet away. Hers was not the face he'd been expecting, but she possessed a familiar presence.

"Hello Daddy. It's been a long time."

The stranger's tone was a curious one. Not one of anger or love, but almost unrecognizable, except for the subtle tremble of nervousness. The soft voice filtered through his memory, striking a chord O'Shea couldn't quite put a finger on.

"Daddy? Who dares call me that? I've got no daughters. Who are you?"

"Look closely and I think you'll know."

O'Shea squinted and stepped closer. The moonlight illuminated her face. She couldn't be...it wasn't possible.

"Margaret Josephine?"

***

## Ketchum- Jackie

"Hello," Jackie said from the saloon entrance causing the tall, dark haired man with a hat to turn in his seat and a giant man to pop up from behind the bar.

"Howdy ma'am, I'm Carter," the cowboy replied with a smile. He took in the sight of her in an old blue dress and a brown bag in hand. "What can we help you with?"

"Well um," she began, hoping to hide the nervousness in her voice. Dark eyes scanned the room while fidgeting hands stuffed themselves into jacket pockets. The envelope crinkled beneath her fingers. "I'm 'sposed to see a Ms. Jo or Ms. Jade. She said I'd find them here."

The large man towered over the wooden bar and laughed hard. "Ms. Jade? That's a good one."

Carter grinned at him, then turned his attention back to her. "Who sent ya?"

Jackie shifted her stance. An uncomfortable sensation filled her body under the weight of his gaze. "Sarah. She said they'd help me. I uh, shoulda been here a few days ago, but um, I couldn't leave as soon as I planned." She folded her arms around her waist and looked away.

"Sarah?" He stood up and approached with slow steps. "When did you see her?"

"Last week." She tensed up as he reached her, but softened as he took her bag. Jackie shielded her arm, hoping he didn't take note of her injury. "Any idea when Jo or Jade will be back?"

"Afraid not. They're on their way to Sarah, but we hope soon. The big ole lug over there is Nick, Jade's boyfriend. Please, come and sit. Wanna drink?" Carter kept his voice soft and soothing. He offered a warm smile as he waved his hand toward the stools.

"Yes, thank you. I'm Jackie." A shy smile for their kindness perched on her lips as she followed behind. She flinched when Carter made a sudden move, an involuntary reaction to the repeated beatings plaguing her memory.

He narrowed his gaze and slowed his pace as he finished setting the bag on the floor. Carter took a seat, leaving a space between them.

Nick flashed a heartwarming grin and extended his massive hand. "Hello Jackie. Pleasure to meet ya."

She took it with some apprehension, but smiled at the gentle touch. The man looked to be seven foot tall and wide as a hundred year old tree trunk. His tenderness came as a surprise. "Nick, you gotta be the largest person I've ever seen." A little embarrassed by her declaration, she averted her eyes to the old hardwood floor instead of him.

The men shared a laugh at her statement, but they didn't make her feel uneasy. Quite the opposite actually, but she hadn't been able to trust anyone in so long that she wasn't about to assume they were good guys. The giant, however, exuded warmth and safety.

Carter continued to chuckle as he tried to speak, "I agree, Nick. You are a giant, but a gentle one at that."

"Thank you." He nodded to the Sheriff and then turned to Jackie. "Where'd you meet Sarah?"

Jackie paused. How would she explain without including the part about almost sleeping with her? She didn't know the whole story, but one of them had to be the reason Sarah couldn't go through with it. Probably Jo, since she held a letter for her.

The worry that kept a tight hold of her since Sarah had left, eased. Someone cared enough to try and stop whatever the cowgirl was set on doing and from her behavior, she feared the worst.

"I'm from a little bit outside Spokane. She came into the saloon and she um, helped me out."

The Sheriff studied her every move, focused on every word and it made her nervous. "Does it have anything to do with why you're hurt?"

Jackie's eyes met his. Her cheeks heated with shame as she nodded. "Sarah said I didn't have to be nobody's punchin' bag. She gave me a train ticket and some money for food and told me to come here. She said they'd help me." She began to tear up as she continued, "I was gonna leave last weekend, but mama caught me packin'. George was 'sposed to keep an eye on me, but he said to get out while I could, so here I am."

Nick's eyes turned glassy as he placed a supportive hand on her shoulder. "I'm so sorry, but you're safe now. We'll look after you 'til they come back."

He glanced at Carter, worry etched in his expression.

What were they hiding?

Jackie smiled at them anyway. She pushed fear aside and embraced relief. Her heart swelled with hope. "Do you think Sarah will be back? She was so good to me. I want to thank her for saving me."

"Hopefully soon." Carter said, offering a comforting smile. "Did she say anything else?"

"No, but um, she seemed sad, like she was tryin' to forget somethin' or someone."

He stood up and took her bag again. "Why don't you come with me? There's an extra room and my wife can check over your injuries."

"Oh, I don't want to be a bother. I got a few dollars left. I can get a room or somethin'," she protested.

"Really, I insist. No problem at all. When they get back we can go from there, but this way we're sure you're safe. Sarah would never forgive us if you made it here and we let somethin' happen to ya."

His genuine smile brought her more comfort than she remembered feeling in a long time. She followed him down the road, saying a quiet thanks to the cowgirl who gave her another chance at life and praying that one day she'd be able to thank her.

***

## O'Shea Ranch- Jessie

Jade and I fell silent as we moved in tandem around the small house the night guard usually occupied. The door swung wide open with no sign of my brother. A flood of bad images flashed through my mind, sending a bitter chill through my body.

"Where the hell did Jimmy go? He should be here." I managed to keep my voice low enough to hide my growing concern. "Jade, keep watch on the main house. Keep out of sight, but signal me if you see a short, fat man come out." I held my hand up shoulder high and then twice as wide as me. She raised a brow. Did she take it for some kind of joke? "I'm serious, that's O'Shea."

"This I gotta see." She shook her head. "Okay, quiet like a bunny. Be careful yourself. If you need me, I'll be right over..." She motioned to a general vicinity to which I nodded in agreement.

We exited the building and Jade hurried to a place she could see both me and the house. Stealth was easy in her tiny little body. Jade wasn't one for doing what she was told, but hell, there was always a first time. Why not tonight?

Before I continued on, I checked once more to be sure she was safe. I didn't want anything happening to her.

Jade threw me a thumb's up, then shooed me away.

Across the yard, Jake entered a bunk house and Sarah headed toward the barn. Where'd Jo go? I didn't see her anywhere. She seemed like she could handle herself, so I focused on other things, like the burning feeling in my gut telling me I needed to find my brother and soon.

With my gun drawn, I listened at the next door. Too quiet. This whole thing stunk more and more the deeper we went. Please let Jimmy be alive. What would I do if I lost him? He insisted on helping me, but I could've stopped him. Now the cards were on the table and I had to live with whatever hand was dealt.

A deep breath and a gentle push opened the first of three doors. There was nothing but emptiness inside the tiny room. The same for the other two. Each time I struck out, my chest tightened a little more. One of these would be the mother lode of bad guys and it scared the heck out of me. Facing a few at a time would be much easier than all hell breaking loose at once.

Was everyone else coming up empty too? Where were these fifteen plus guys we were supposed to deal with? Perhaps I just got lucky. I needed to hold on to something and that thought kept me calm as I crept along.

I moved to another building resembling a small storehouse and nodded to Jade. So far, she'd listened and remained on the lookout. Surprising. She signaled there'd been no action yet, so I moved on. My uneasiness grew with every step as I closed the distance to the tattered wooden shack. My gut churned. Seldom did it steer me wrong. Jimmy had to be near.

Please be alive.

My ear smashed against the wood and my heart raced as muffled voices resonated through the cracks. A dim light shone from underneath the floor boards. What was going on in there? How many men were inside? Even more important, who?

Searching the perimeter, I found a window cracked open and slipped below to listen. A man's voice carried over the echoes of painful groans and sharp cracks of fists hitting flesh. The brutal sounds of a beating left me with a dreadful feeling.

"You're gonna die," the victim inside coughed out. "If she don't kill ya, I will," he continued. His words were slurred but confident.

I'd recognize that voice anywhere. My breath caught in my throat. My greatest fear realized. "Jimmy," I croaked out in a hushed voice, forcing back tears and rage. "Hang on Jimmy, I'm coming."

I braced myself to charge in fists blazing, but a familiar sound stopped me in my tracks.

"You're gonna pay for your little stunt. You and that sister of yours are gonna die just like your father."

The deep, twang in the voice of the other man and the mention of our father triggered flashes from my past. I'd eavesdropped on my father's conversations several times after things went bad. Through all the threats and negotiations, I never once heard defeat in James Walker's voice. His steadfast strength made his suicide even more shocking to me. I never to this day believed he took his own life. Never. The voice with Jimmy was the last one I remembered hearing with him. It couldn't be a coincidence.

"Buck, you don't know a damn thing about my father and if you touch my sister I'll kill you." Jimmy's words trembled from the pain, but stood strong with defiance.

I could picture him in there beaten and bruised with his jaw steeled as he spat blood back at his attacker. My brother would fight to the death, just like the rest of our family.

Buck laughed obnoxiously hard again as another slap rang out. My fists balled in anger. The only thing I could hear was the hammering of my heart in my ears.

"Jimmy, let me tell you somethin'. I know your father better than you think. Yeah, James was causin' us all kinds of trouble. Old man O'Shea said to ignore 'em since we got what we wanted, but he just wouldn't let up. After a while, I quit tellin' the old man. Myles told me to deal with 'em myself. So, one day I'd heard enough. Some town's people started to side with the self-righteous son of a bitch, so I took care of 'em."

A sickening roar of laughter and another thud echoed through the air, both causing my stomach to twist in disgust. White, hot fury enveloped me at the pride in Buck's voice. I bet he wore a smug grin on his face too and I couldn't wait to wipe it off of him.

"Wha...whaddya mean you took care of him?" Jimmy couldn't hide his suffering anymore. He cried and I broke down with him as the words sunk in.

"I hung the aggravatin' son of a bitch." Buck let out a cold, hard laugh.

The scrape of boots across the wooden floor neared the front door. Time grew short. I needed to make my move. The element of surprise would be key for me taking him down without a scene.

Jimmy let loose a heartbreaking scream and I squeezed my eyes shut tight. The sound of it sending a piercing pain through my chest like a dagger to the heart.

"Noooo! I'm gonna kill you! Jessie's gonna make you suffer, you son of a bitch!"

How I remained silent would always be a mystery. The unparalleled agony of the truth ripped through my heart and soul. I found it hard to pull myself away from the man's voice. Were there more secrets to be revealed?

"Oh and that pretty little sister of yours?" Buck snickered. "Yeah, I kept an eye on her. I know she enjoys the company of her own kind, but I'm gonna show her what it means to be with a man before I let O'Shea have her." He let out another harsh laugh. "He's been waitin' a long time for this. Maybe I'll let her watch you die first."

More sounds reminiscent of a side of beef getting slugged echoed from the shack. Jimmy moaned in agony. The legs of the chair scraped along the floor from what I imagined was Jimmy struggling against the ropes to get free.

Buck's cackle boomed with joy from the torture.

Sheer determination and hatred replaced the nausea that overwhelmed me moments ago. "Enjoy it while you can, Buck. In twenty seconds you'll be a dead man," I sneered.

I pulled my knife from its sheath. With blade in hand, I made a beeline for the front door. Shooting would've been my first choice, but I didn't want to warn O'Shea. I kept to plan, giving us the best chance to survive.

One last deep breath pulled into my lungs. Every muscle tensed in ready for the fight. I kicked the door in with more force than I ever thought I possessed. Buck's cold, dark eyes widened as the edge of the door clipped his face. He fell back, giving me a head start in my attack.

My voice sounded foreign to me as I growled out, "Die you son of a bitch." The adrenaline pumped through my body like there was no tomorrow and that was a good possibility. One of us would walk away and it damned sure wouldn't be old Buck.

Charging hard, I stabbed him in the chest over and over again with lightning quick speed, driving him to his knees. I aimed for his lungs and hit my mark. Buck's weathered old face twisted from the pain and he gasped for breath. A strong shove of my foot sent him to the ground.

No other detail of my surroundings registered in my mind. My entire focus was set square on killing Buck. I moved closer to his body, hovering above while the sticky, red liquid squirted out from the stab wounds and oozed down onto the wooden floor.

He lifted his hands towards me in a last ditch effort to fight. Like child's play, I shoved them aside and smirked at his suffering. Such wonderful satisfaction I took in watching his life fade into a pool around his body.

"This is too good for you, Buck. There are so many things I want to do, but it's your lucky day, because I've bigger things to tend to." I smiled wider and set my boot on his throat, staring down at him lying helpless with eyes open wide in shock.

Blood spat from his mouth as he tried to speak, but only managed gurgles. Buck's strength grew weaker by the second, but he still struggled to push my foot away. I barely made out his murmured whisper, "See you in hell."

I pressed down harder. The fragile tissue in his neck slowly gave way under the pressure. Oh, I'd love to do this for hours, but I didn't have the luxury of time and I held neither an ounce of pity, nor mercy for the man.

"Yeah, well when I get there, I'm gonna kill you again you piece of shit." The fatal crunch of his throat didn't prove as satisfying as I'd hoped. Like I told him, he deserved worse.

The last of the color drained from his face and with it, every bit of anger I'd held onto since our father's death. A tremendous weight had lifted with the vindication of our father.

My eyes found Jimmy, softening the instant I saw him safe and alive. He didn't seem at all shocked or disturbed by my behavior. Instead, his battered and bloody face melted into a smile full of pride.

I hurried over and sliced through the bindings with my bloodied knife. Tears flooded my eyes as his hands fell free.

Jimmy engulfed me with those long, strong arms that always made me feel safe as a child and gripped me with the same sense of relief.

The nightmare of our father giving up and leaving us to fend for ourselves came to an end. A sweet redemption for us that meant nothing in the grand scheme of things. No one knew, nor did they care. Just us and mom, who'd suffered the worst. For years she beat herself up thinking she could've done more or somehow changed his mind. She did nothing wrong.

In the safety of Jimmy's warm embrace, I found myself daydreaming about how happy mom would be when we came home and she finally learned the truth.

* * *

## Jade

That's gotta be him. A short, fat old guy, walking around like he owns the world. How many could there be? Was he really Jo's father? How did she come from him? They had the same dark hair, but really? She had to look more like her mother.

Wait, what the hell? Jo? What was she doing? Why would she confront him alone?

Sarah? Jessie? Jake? Jimmy? Anyone? Not a one was near. I couldn't panic. Jo needed me and I'd never let my family down.

I surveyed the area for options. There had to be a way to get to her without being seen. I snuck around the side of the building. When I caught sight of the yard again, Sarah was standing across from Jo and her dad. This had all the makings of getting real bad, real fast.

Words were exchanged and whatever was being said, O'Shea appeared to be enjoying the hell out of it.

Closer, I needed to get closer. I clung to the wall like a spider, inching my way along the back of the next building in hopes of a better perspective.

Jake's body came flying from out of nowhere, missing me by a hair. He landed with a hard thud on the ground. All breath left his body upon impact in an audible "oomph."

Before I even thought to move, another man pounced on him, pounding his fists to his face hard and fast. Everything happened in a flash. Jake wouldn't last long. I needed something, anything that would help me take down the larger enemy.

A pipe, perfect. My pulse quickened as I dashed for it. With the metal rod gripped tight in my hands, I turned back to Jake. He was still flat on his back and taking the brunt of force from the behemoth above him.

Power surged through me. With Jake's life hanging in the balance, I raced toward the fight. With all my might, I swung the cold metal down onto the brute's head, ending with a nauseating crack. His body fell slack on contact, coming to rest atop Jake's. I recruited all my strength and then some to roll the guy off of him.

"Jake? Jake?" I panicked. "Talk to me. Are you all right?"

The man was a bloody mess, but he let out a pained groan. Slow, cautious movements followed as he staggered to his feet. He patted me on the shoulder. "Better now, thanks to you."

I couldn't believe he was conscious after that beating. "All in a day's work." I smiled as he cleaned himself up, dusted off his pants and picked up his hat. "I'm glad you're okay, but I gotta run. Things are about to get ugly out front. Be safe."

"You too, Jade."

I hurried off once again to find my way to Jo. Without blowing my cover, I moved closer, but how would I ever be of help from over here?

Things seemed even more intense than five minutes ago. Whatever the old man said didn't set well with Sarah. I'd never seen such a crazed expression on her before. She teetered on the edge of control with fingers tickling the grips of her guns. Her focus was locked on Jo, but her usual look of reverence had shifted to vile disgust.

My skin crawled. I'd heard Sarah's hands were deadly, but that look could lay waste to an army.

What did he say? Why wouldn't he shut up?

Sarah gripped her pistols. She wouldn't. No. She couldn't.

Damn manipulative old man. Shit!

The air grew thick. My chest squeezed so tight that breathing was a chore. The tension of the situation weighed heavy on every part of me. Seemed O'Shea liked to play mind games and Jo and Sarah were sinking fast.

Help. I needed to help. I ran as hard as I could to the next barrel.

BANG!

The echo of the shot sent me cowering to the ground and set my ears to ringing. I scrambled to my feet and made my way to cover. When I peeked out into the yard, my heart stopped at the sight of Jo on the ground writhing in pain.

"Oh my god, Jo."

# Chapter Twenty-Four

**Moments Earlier- Sarah**

Jo stood ten yards from her father. The years had turned his hair from jet black to salt and pepper and his skin had weathered, but he was still the same. Hard angular face, neatly trimmed beard and pear shaped body. He was dressed to the hilt and still fond of his black derby hat, matching black buttoned up shirt, black leather vest and silver pocket watch. Patrick Daniel O'Shea had a presence ten times larger than his five foot, five inch stature. He looked every bit a gentleman. The man was anything but.

The family resemblance was obvious. The hair. The eyes. The rounded shape of their noses. I stared at the two of them, still unable to wrap my mind around the fact the woman I loved was the daughter of the man I hated more than anything in the world.

Jo shifted her weight, a sign of her discomfort. She had several physical cues linked to her emotional state, none of which she ever seemed to control. The simple movements and her eyes never lied, at least not to me. Those were just a few of the things I'd picked up on during our time together. They helped me navigate our early relationship and now they spoke volumes without ever making a sound.

What were they saying?

The tension was palpable, even from a distance. What else would be expected when someone returned home after running from their family for so many years? For the briefest of moments my heart went out to a father finally seeing his daughter again. A very brief moment.

I shook the thought away, remembering who stood a few short yards away from me and the purpose of my visit. Reminiscing was not on the list. My legs threw caution to the wind before I could think it through, carrying me into the clearing and creating a triangle between us. With wide eyes, I'd thrown myself into an unknown situation with no understanding of how to navigate it. All plans went out the window as I glanced between the two of them. From here on out it would be all instinct. My nerves rolled in my stomach and my hands stood at the ready for any sign of a threat.

They both froze, tore their eyes from one another and focused on me.

Jo's eyes held more dread than when she confessed the identity of her father.

O'Shea arched his brow. He didn't recognize me. The last time I'd been near him was almost a decade ago and even then, he had never truly looked at me.

"And who might you be darlin'?" The pitch of his question hinted at humor, as if my presence was comical to him.

I didn't answer. I just stared him down. The man's air of arrogance reminded me of more reasons I hated him, besides the most obvious ones.

Jo replied for me and it made me cringe. "One of the many whose lives our family destroyed in your quest for money and power." Her voice trembled with fear and anger.

I didn't want her to answer for me. She should be quiet and let me finish what I'd waited ten long years to do, but something didn't seem right. The tension in the air made sense seeing as how someone would be dying tonight, but this weighed heavier, more personal.

Jo appeared sick to her stomach and I shared her nausea. Why?

O'Shea enjoyed her anguish. His lips pulled up into a wicked sneer. "Oh don't be so vague, Margaret. I got a darn good memory, but this one draws a blank." He eyed me up and down as if sifting through the years of ruined families stored in his mind.

I refused to say a word, not wanting to give him any satisfaction. My silence seemed to make Jo more nervous. She shifted her weight again, appearing shakier now than when I first arrived. She took small steps between us, tightening the triangle while I studied them with caution.

"Well daddy dearest, maybe she's the one with the most right to be angry at us." Jo's eyes turned glassy, darting from me to him and back again.

I knew all her tells, committed each one to memory. Something needed saying and she couldn't figure out how to say it without hurting me. She sure didn't save me any pain the last time. What else did she have to hide?

My stomach dropped and I feared the worst.

"Maybe a doctor's daughter whose family you murdered and then let your men treat her like a dog," she said. Her soft voice held an edge.

"Ah, your Doctor Sawyer's little girl? Well this is interestin'," Danny drawled. He rubbed his beard with one hand, the other hung near his gun. He moved closer to me, so I took two steps back, maintaining our distance.

"Daddy no!"

"No?" He huffed and rolled his neck. His glare never left Jo. "She's here to kill me right?"

Jo said nothing. Her eyes fell to the ground giving him his answer.

He smirked, turning his attention to me. "It would seem we've a bit of a misunderstandin', Ms. Sawyer."

"There's no justification for what you did," Jo's voice wavered.

He remained fixed on me for another moment then turned to Jo. "Oh, but there is for what you did?" His voice rose in challenge her as he bowed up and strode toward her in anger.

Questions swirled in my mind. What did he mean? What did she do?

Jo stood paralyzed like a child being scolded, forgetting she wasn't the little girl who obeyed her father anymore. Did she still hold feelings for him? Not surprising. No matter how much you might despise your family, there'd still be some kind of emotional connection, wouldn't there?

Would it make her hate me when I killed him? Why hadn't I killed him already? My gut said I'd missed something. After suffering all these years of pain, I deserved the truth and tonight wanted to hear it all.

The two of them were engaged in a conversation of their own. I stood by in silence as an outsider in a family squabble I'd somehow gotten involved in, but didn't know my place. Why would he say Jo caused my family's death? There was no misunderstanding on my part. He killed them. I was there, so he couldn't deny the fact.

"I don't know Margaret. You think findin' out your baby girl was dead wasn't a good enough reason to go a little crazy?"

What did this have to do with Jo? She was alive. Her sister was dead, killed the same day. My hand paused at my gun. My muscles tensed and eyes narrowed. I struggled to connect the dots and wrap my mind around their conversation.

The tension between them grew even thicker until Jo stood tall and let her anger take over. "But he tried to save, not kill. Marie didn't make it. We tried."

"I guess that's one person's perspective my dear. Obviously he did save you, because here you are. The spittin' image of your mother, I might add. Marie, well, she wasn't so lucky..."

O'Shea turned sharply back to me. "Ms. Sawyer, did my daughter here tell you I thought she was dead?"

I shook my head in a daze, jaw agape as this drama seemed to get more and more unreal. Jo said she ran away, never anything about being dead, but what did that have to do with...

A not so pretty picture began to form in my head, one I didn't want to see fully realized. I should end this now. Some things were better left unknown, because once released, you couldn't stuff them back into the box.

Jo yelled out, her body erect and arms bowed out in a defensive stance. "I am dead. Dead to you. I couldn't be around you anymore. I couldn't be like you. That's not who I was."

"Well then, you can quit callin' me daddy you ungrateful little bitch. After all I gave you? I treated you like royalty while your brother and sister went out and did all the hard work. I saw so much of you in me. I had big plans for you. Then Marie got killed and you were gone. Well, I was a little bit upset."

"An innocent family destroyed all because you were a little upset?" Jo managed to rasp while fighting her emotions.

I didn't acknowledge him. My gaze shifted to Jo. Her anger dissipated, replaced by desperation and fear. This was about to come to a head and my gut feeling said would be ugly, mostly for me.

"You have no one to blame but yourself Margaret. You could've prevented all of it."

A tear rolled down Jo's cheek as her head shook with fervent passion. "Sarah, I'm so sorry..." She reached out to me with a trembling hand.

O'Shea interrupted, "Oh yes, she's so sorry."

My attention drifted back to the smug old man staring back at me. The air of fear and pain he'd created pleased him.

"She's sorry she pulled your family into this, ain't that right Margaret?" His dark, soulless eyes danced from me to Jo. "Sorry that your selfishness got them killed?" His lip twitched with pride as he directed his words back to me. "I have to say, I'm quite impressed your father managed to keep my daughter's little secret while he watched his wife being molested and beaten, his daughter being taken and a gun to his head. A very loyal man. Very foolish."

Her eyes popped wide in shock and horror as the full realization of her actions hit Jo as she listened to the gruesome details.

Memories flooded back to me as fresh as the day it happened and I was drug out from under the house by my ankles all over again. The last memory of my loving parents was them lying bloodied and dead in a heap on the ground as if they were nothing more than trash. The anguish hit me like a tidal wave. I wanted to curl up in a ball until the gripping pain in my heart subsided, but I didn't have that option. Not today.

"You," he continued, "well, you're well aware of the rest of your story, Ms. Sawyer. Margaret? Would you like to share so she can get a true understanding of what it means to put one's needs above others?"

Jo stood frozen like a tree in the dead of winter. Not a word was uttered in forgiveness or defense.

Was it all true? Was it all her fault?

O'Shea smirked and continued, "She convinced your father to pronounce her dead so she could run like a coward from the horrible, comfortable life she'd been livin'." His tone turned condescending. "Poor Margaret. And here we mourned your death for ten years. As long as you're happy though." The corner of his mouth pulled up into a sick grin, enjoying our torment.

Jo's lip quivered, her knees buckled. "Yes Sarah, I begged him to tell the boys I'd died. I was wounded, it was perfect and I'm so much more than sorry." Heavy sobs began to wrack Jo's body. "You have no idea how sorry. There's nothin' that would ever make up for the unspeakable things I've done, but I had no idea what he did, Sarah. Please believe me."

I stared at Jo, speechless. Her words hung in the air causing my gut to wrench so hard I nearly collapsed. Multiply my feelings by a million from when she announced O'Shea was her father and it still couldn't touch the kind of vile disgust and anger I was experiencing right now.

How many times would my heart be ripped out? How would I ever trust her again? Why did I believe I could get over her heritage in the first place? All O'Shea's were cut from the same cloth. They destroyed everything good.

Tears streamed down her cheeks as she trembled. Her mouth continued to move, but nothing came out. Jo appeared as if she'd fall to the ground at any second and beg for forgiveness.

Forgiveness was something I was neither willing, nor able, to give. The blinding rage bubbled to the surface and I tightened the hold on my revolvers.

Jo shook her head, holding her hands up. She wouldn't deny it. She wouldn't fight me over it and it made me even angrier.

I wanted her to go for her gun. Something, anything to justify the actions playing in my head, but I reined in my boiling anger, unsure who I should be more focused on right now. My eyes bounced between the two of them before settling on Jo again when she took a step towards me.

Once again she drew me in, only to tear me apart. Was it some sick game of hers? I loved her, but she repulsed me. There was no other word to be used. As much as it pained me to admit, I held deep contempt for Jo and I didn't think it would go away.

I squeezed the grip of my pistol so tight I thought it would shatter from the force. So consumed in a tunnel of blind rage, I didn't register my surroundings or my actions. There was only me and Jo and the need to release this venom poisoning me. All these years I had blamed him. He had killed them, but she had brought him to my door.

"Sarah," she plead. The light from the moon glistened in her glassy eyes.

BANG!

I stood frozen in time, a helpless spectator as Jo's body fell backward in slow motion, twisting like a rag-doll. The bullet went clean through. Droplets of blood splattered on the dirt as she fell to the ground.

\*\*\*

Hate consumed me for what Jo's actions had caused my family, but in that moment it all washed away. Those hazel eyes I loved to lose myself in shot open wide with shock and anguish as she was thrown from the force of the bullet ripping through her.

A pained scream echoed into the night. Was it hers or mine?

The briefest of moments after her body landed seemed like an eternity to me. Any memory of the last few milliseconds sat blank. My trembling hands still gripped my guns with all my might. My eyes dropped to the pistols, not entirely certain whether or not I was the one who pulled the trigger. I hoped beyond hope I didn't. Seeing both weapons still in their holster, a ragged breath pushed through my lips. But all relief faded fast when I remembered Jo on the ground with a bullet in her. Everything inside me screamed run to her. As I took a step, a red, hot heat grazed my shoulder and bullets whizzed past.

More popping sounds filled the air. Where'd the shots come from?

The world around me blurred. My only choice was to scramble, leaving Jo vulnerable where she lay. I shifted into survival mode. Drawing my gun, I fired back in the general direction of the gunfire, hoping to provide some cover for my escape. I ducked around the corner of the building, gasping for breath.

Jo still lay in the dirt where I'd left her. She writhed in pain, but was alive. Thank the heavens. I wanted to reach her, help her, but that would have to wait. "Hold on Jo."

Movement on the front porch drew my attention. A dark haired man in a white shirt ran around back. I took careful aim in hopes of hitting him, but my efforts fell short. The distance outmatched my gun.

More shots rang out into the night.

My hands moved quickly to reload the pistols without much thought. All those hours of dedicated practice paid off as it allowed me to scan the area for other shooters amid a hail of bullets. There was no safe way for me to get to her.

All of a sudden, Jade popped into view. She was trying to make her way to Jo. She just needed a clear path. She was close, but the hidden gunman made it too dangerous to charge into the open. I waved to catch her attention. She made eye contact and I signaled my plan. With a simple nod, we were set.

My fingers in the air counted down to action. Three. Two. One. Go!

***

**Jo**

"Nooo!" The word flew from my mouth on impact. A deep burning pain cut through me as it knocked me off my feet.

What the hell? I lay dazed on the ground recounting the last few seconds. My father connected the dots on how I came to be standing in front of him. I wanted to confront him alone and tell Sarah my dark secret in private. Maybe never tell her at all. I didn't think things out that far. Only one thing in my mind lacked any doubt; I didn't want the meeting to go this way.

The look on Sarah's face upon his reveal said it all. I had ripped her heart out all over again. I should've said something, but what? No words would change the truth. I was desperate. In my need to escape, I had failed to consider the potential danger to her family. My actions had ultimately caused the gruesome murder of her parents and dragged her into this nightmare. Who could forgive such a thing? My love for her wouldn't change the past. Somewhere deep inside I wanted her to kill me. Maybe then the debt would've been settled and we'd both be free of the pain.

Our eyes were locked and I witnessed firsthand the dangerous glare of a woman scorned. My wish was granted, but not by her. The bullet had come from an unknown hand and that pissed me off. The only person here with the right to take my life was Sarah.

How many times could my family cause her complete devastation? Talk about torture, her words the other day rang true. We tormented Sarah Sawyer over the course of ten years, but I believed this to be the last straw. She'd be lost to me for good. I could find a way to deal with that, but only if I got my ass up and made sure he didn't kill her. I couldn't live with myself if Sarah died at the hands of an O'Shea. I wouldn't allow my family to destroy another good person.

Moving was excruciating, but after running through a quick check, I figured I'd live. The round pierced clean through my right upper chest. Whoever pulled the trigger missed my lung. My arm would be useless, but at least I could breathe. If their goal was killing me, they failed miserably.

"Jo!"

My name rang out over the sound of gun fire.

Who? Where?

I tried to push myself onto my belly. Shit! Not going to happen. I maneuvered my body to see the house. A man in a white shirt ran around back. He almost looked like Myles. Did my own brother try to kill me? Guess I couldn't be too surprised. I doubted there was any limit to their madness.

"Jo, I'm coming."

The woman's voice called out once more over the gunfire. The voice didn't belong to Sarah. Was she okay? I had to find her. She needed to be safe.

A wave of panic rolled through my body taking precedence over the pain. I worried more about her than myself and whatever the consequence of the bullet would be later.

Jade came into view, hiding behind a wagon to get a good glimpse of me. Dammit, she shouldn't be in the line of fire. My best friend owned a stubborn streak every bit as bad as mine. Her presence pissed me off, but at least she was unharmed at the moment. She better stay that way.

Jade communicated with someone across the way, but I couldn't make them out from my spot on the ground. She nodded and not a second later a barrage of shots flooded the area. She sprinted to me with all her might, grabbed my arms and somehow found the power to drag me to safety.

The girl might be tiny, but she had more strength than most men. When she set me down, the seated position made the ache spread across my chest. I was thankful to be alive and hidden, but still mad at her. "What are you doin'? Get outta here, J."

"No. Not without you, Jo." Jade's glare bore a hole through me. She wasn't going anywhere.

I nodded and shifted my focus elsewhere. "Where's Sarah?"

"She's over there."

Jade pointed to the building across the yard, but I didn't see anyone. "Where? I don't see her."

"Well, she was a second ago. She covered me so I could get you." Her hands roamed my upper body assessing my injuries. "Are you okay? There's a lot of blood, Jo. We gotta get you--"

"No. No way." I was firm. Leaving was out of the question. As long as I could move, Sarah would be my priority. "We gotta get Sarah. She's gonna go after him and he'll kill her."

*** 

## Sarah

With Jade taking care of Jo, I moved on to search for O'Shea. He could be anywhere. I stepped through the next doorway and couldn't believe the scene. Several dead men lay on the floor and a couple unconscious ones sat tied to the old anchors in the wall. No wonder we hadn't met much resistance yet. We still had a long way to go, but I was grateful for this small reprieve and whoever was responsible.

Footsteps approached at a fast rate. I slipped inside the closet, leaving the door cracked to see who entered. My fists curled tight, ready for a fight if need be. When a familiar figure entered the room, my breath seized and my body froze. I struggled to believe my eyes.

There stood not a man, but the woman who saved me from hell. The years hadn't been kind to her and I knew the old man hadn't been either, but she was still beautiful and thankfully, still alive.

I remained hidden as she silently roamed the room. The fact she wasn't at all concerned or shocked about the men struck me as odd. Was she the one responsible? I wouldn't doubt if she did pull that off. The woman always possessed a certain inner strength. Guess he never broke her.

"Ann," I called out softly as I pushed the door open.

She jumped back startled and drew her knife.

I threw up my hands, showing her I meant no harm. She probably wouldn't recognize me. Heck, I didn't recognize me most days.

"Sarah?"

I nodded. A small smile on my lips at her easy recognition. Her wide eyes turned soft and dare I say it, teary? "Hello, Ann"

"Oh my god, Sarah!" She took big steps, closed the distance and pulled me into a tight embrace." I always wondered if you made it safely and what you were doin' now," she said into my ear. Pulling back, she held me by the shoulders and looked into my eyes, searching for something. "What are you doin' here?"

"What shoulda been done a long time ago."

"It's too dangerous. You shoulda never come back."

"I had to and believe me, you don't even know the half of it." I laughed at the crazy reality of my situation.

She stared at me with her brows creased in confusion.

If only she knew what a mess things were with Jo, O'Shea, me and Jessie. The truth was too much to fathom sometimes. "A story for another time." I stepped out of her embrace and scanned the room. "What're you doin'?"

"Well, I heard some rumblin's of a Marshal comin' to seek kill the old bastard, but I never expected you. Anyway, the guards stepped up the last few days, so I knew it was close. I figure it was my only chance to get free, even if he wins tonight, I'd be gone."

"He won't win." I said it with stone cold certainty and I believed it right down to my very core.

"I hope not, for your sake, Sarah." She offered a sincere smile. "When I saw Buck take Jimmy with his hands tied earlier, that's when I knew tonight was the night. I got as many as I could and sent the other women and children to hide."

"Well." I took her hand in mine, pushed back my fears for Jimmy and stared her right in the eyes with unwavering confidence. "You're right. Tonight is the night you'll be free. I can never repay you for savin' me, but I hoped, selfish as it may be, that you'd be here when I did come back to kill him. I wanted to thank you by getting' you out; givin' you back your life, just like you did for me."

Ann let her gaze drift to the floor and took a deep breath. "Sad part is, after all these years, I don't even know where to go or what to do. I just need to get out of here."

"You can always come to Ketchum. That's where I'll be when it's all done, with Jo." So I hoped. Even after all we'd been through, my heart remained with Jo. If we made it out alive, I wanted to spend the rest of my days by her side.

"Let me help you," Ann said as she picked up a shotgun.

"No. Get the girls and get out. Run. Don't look back. You know where to find me." I smiled, leaning in for a last hug.

She kissed me on the head and whispered, "Please stay safe. He's taken so much, don't give him the rest."

I knew exactly what she meant. "I--"

The thunder of hooves and wheels caused the building to shake as they passed. I rushed out the door and caught the tail end of O'Shea fleeing in a horse and buggy. Bet the old coward had it in the barn ready for his escape. The ride gave him a good head start. So had the firefight that had kept me busy, but he wouldn't get away that easy.

I took one last glance back at the house and thought about Jo. Jade would take care of her, but deep down I still teetered between finding her and chasing him down. I'd come too far to quit now, so I pressed on, searching for options. I needed a way to pursue him, something fast. Clover was across the pasture, but this was a ranch and somewhere there'd be a horse.

Looking around for anything with speed, I spied several horses tied to the fence line. I ran as fast as my legs would allow. My chest heaved in a desperate attempt to grab more air. How kind of them to be left saddled and ready to go. I untied the reins from the post, pulled myself up on the fittest looking one and took off like a bullet.

Damn, did he have race horses pulling that buggy? He'd put quite a gap between us in a short amount of time, but I could reach him before he got to town.

A whistle blew in the distance. The train would be leaving soon. Such a perfect getaway for the elusive little bastard.

How important were the next few minutes for my past and my future? For Jessie and Jo? The last ten years had all led up to this point. The grip of tension clamped down on my lungs. The anxiety inside me grew, pulsing my nerves from head to toe as I sped toward the buggy.

What if I missed? I'd be forced to hunt him down again. Every day would be more difficult with him expecting me or worse yet, hunting me in return. Not just me. Now he knew all of us. I couldn't miss. This ended tonight, for all our sakes.

With the train in sight and O'Shea within reach, I spurred my steed for everything he had. O'Shea pulled alongside the tracks, standing as he searched for a jump point. No way. I couldn't lose him now. The light from the moon lit his silhouette, making him an easy target even in the darkness. I drew my gun, waiting for the right moment.

The buggy struck a bump, knocking him back down into the seat.

I smiled. He was right where I wanted him. So close now. All I needed was a little more from my horse. Ignoring the animal's groaning and gasping, I cared for nothing else but killing Danny O'Shea. I pulled close enough for a clear view of his head. Standing up in the stirrups to steady my aim, I zoned in on one small point at the back of his skull.

A puff of white smoke from the back of his buggy caught me by surprise. My pride and foolishness had just cost me in the worst way. I got off two quick rounds before the bullet ripped me from the saddle. The shot tore through my flesh, knocking me to the ground. I landed hard, rolling with violent force. My body became a twisted mess. One eye hazed over, but the other saw everything with perfect clarity.

I had handed myself to him on a platter. A second man laid in wait in the back of the buggy. His white shirt stood out in the night, the same one from the house. He threw O'Shea's body out as he drove away. The lifeless mass rolled several times before coming to rest face down.

The sight of his body thrown unceremoniously away like trash, crept a smile to my lips. A wave of deep satisfaction crashed over me. Despite my pain, I couldn't help but laugh, cringing with every heave of my chest. I managed to roll on my back, taking in the bright stars in the crisp, clear night sky. For the first time tonight I took notice of the cold air. A shiver ran through me and I winced at the sharp, shooting pain the slight movement elicited.

I scolded myself for being reckless. For so long, I took pride in never making vital mistakes. So stupid, so driven by hate and rage that I had just committed a fatal error. Deep down, I never really thought I'd die. Well, someday I would, but not by them, not tonight. Even through all of my passing moments of doubt, the picture always ended with me standing over his dead body in victory. I was a survivor, a fighter, but I guess even they had their day. At least I could rest in peace knowing I completed my journey.

Tears trickled down my face. In no time they turned to a steady downpour. I tried my hardest not to sob. Each one paralyzed me with pain, but I wept anyway. I wept for the family I lost and the future I wouldn't see. I wept from the sudden weightlessness of freedom from his tyranny. Most of all I wept because Jo wasn't here as I fast approached my last breath.

# Chapter Twenty-Five

**Ketchum, Christmas Day- Jo**

*Sarah? Where's Sarah?*

*A sense of urgency grew with every passing second.*

*The old familiar rumbling of my father's racing buggy shook the ground as he made his escape. I wouldn't allow it to happen this time. He would never hurt anyone ever again. I needed something with speed. This was a ranch, so where were the horses?*

*Another round of thundering of hooves rooted me in place. My stomach dropped and a chill went straight to my bones. I knew the second horse would be carrying Sarah.*

*I needed a damn horse and fast.*

*Running with all my might, I raced across the yard toward a single saddled stallion. He had better be built for speed, because we had a lot of catching up to do. My heart leapt into my throat, hammering with a force that made swallowing almost impossible. I climbed on and dug in, spurring him hard. As I* reached the end of the property, the whistle of the train called out into the night.

Faster, we needed to go faster.

Long ago my father mastered the art of the backup plan and I feared for Sarah's life as she chased after him. The light of the moon set a subtle outline of the locomotive in the distance. Out of nowhere, a bright flash appeared in the night, followed closely by two a little farther back. Several long strides from my horse passed before the popping sound of the shots reached me. The burning in my gut at what it all meant was almost too much.

The stallion couldn't run fast enough for my liking as I urged him harder toward the fight. The silhouette of a body on the ground brought me to a screeching halt. A horse stood nearby. My intuition said the body was Sarah's. My Sarah.

Like a knife through the chest, my next breath led to pain like never before. Fear gripped me tight at the thought I was too late. On instinct, I bolted from my saddle and ran to her. She didn't move a muscle as I fell to my knees beside her.

"No, no, no, Sarah, look at me. I got you. Please stay. Stay with me." The woman I loved lay in a pool of blood. Heartbreak ripped through me like a tidal wave at the sight. My body shook. My stomach knotted. The sharp ache gripping my lungs continued to prevent full breaths.

Helpless. That was the word of the moment. My head spun on a swivel for help, but I was on my own.

Precious warm, red liquid pumped without mercy, continuing to seep through the cracks between my fingers despite my efforts. Tears flooded my eyes, blurring my vision.

*"I'm right here, Jo. I'll always be with you." Although her voice lacked its usual strength, her words were still clear as day. Her gaze lingered at my lips then continued a slow path to meet mine. The haze of bitterness clouding her eyes when last I saw her faded out, replaced by earnest affection.*

*Those were the ones I loved to look into, to lose myself in and I wanted to do so for many years to come. She held no fear in those eyes, only love, acceptance and peace. She couldn't accept this fate, could she?*

*The place where my heart once beat ached as if someone reached in and ripped the frail organ out at a slow and agonizing rate. I cradled her to my chest with one arm and struggled to keep pressure with the other. My efforts were fruitless. Her life essence continued to stream from under my palm. Hot tears streamed down my cheeks as I searched for anyone at all. Time grew short and every second that passed she fell further from my reach.*

*Where the hell was everyone?*

*"No. I need you here with me. Hang on. Fight for me, Sarah please."*

*"I'll always fight for you, Jo. I love you and I don't blame you for anything. I want you to know that." She tried to sit up, but I held her in place. The smallest movement might be her last and the risk was too great to attempt alone. "It's bad though, isn't it?" She attempted to reach for the wound, but I grabbed her arm.*

*"No--a little," I couldn't lie. "But you can make it. Promise me, Sarah."*

*Her cold, blood soaked hand cupped my cheek. Her smile fell from one of joy upon seeing me, to a subdued satisfaction. Her eyes rolled around in their sockets. "It doesn't hurt anymore...my heart." She was slipping away, yet she summoned the strength to speak. "Not since I found you. You saved me Jo. You gotta know what that means to me. I finally have peace and happiness and that's all because of you."*

*She was fading fast. The blood loss took a heavy toll on her. I couldn't let her go, wouldn't let her go. A gentle nudge kept her conscious while I stroked her hair and begged God for mercy.*

*"Don't you dare." The words choked out between breaths. "Sarah Sawyer. You stay with me. Promise me."*

*"I only ever made you one promise, remember Jo? I'm sorry. I wanted to stay, but I couldn't." Heavy eyelids fluttered shut and her voice grew weaker, more of a whisper now as her hand fell from my cheek.*

*The conversation still lingered fresh in my mind. At the time I took comfort knowing she meant "couldn't" and not "wouldn't." When the dust settled, I hoped we'd be together. Now the meaning changed. My heart broke all over again as the "couldn't" she referred to meant the rest of my life without her.*

*I held her tight against me. Her body went slack as Jessie came running with sheer terror in her eyes. Jade trailed close behind.*

*With my lips pressed to her ear I whispered, "You saved me too, Sarah. More than you'll ever know. I need you with me. Please come back to me."*

Jessie glanced over at me with panic and fell to her knees sobbing. "No, no it's not fair. She can't be dead. Pick her up. Let's go. We need to get help."

Jade put her hand on Jessie's shoulder. Tears streamed down her face at the sight of Sarah's lifeless body lying limp in my arms. She avoided my eyes. "Is she...?"

No words came out. I only shrugged. The answer to the most important question eluded me. So many things came to mind. I wanted to scream, curse the world, punch holes in a wall. Instead, I knelt by her side motionless, speechless and numb. Every muscle fell into a state of paralysis as I continued to hold her.

Jessie crawled over and cupped Sarah's face, then checked for a pulse. Pure anguish shone in her eyes. Her one true friend and the only person she'd ever loved might be gone.

"Damn you and your stubbornness, Sarah. Why couldn't you wait?" Jessie spotted my father's abandoned horse and buggy. She jumped to her feet and ran. She didn't even glance at his body as she sprinted with all her might. "Get her up. We can't give up. There's a doctor just across the way," she yelled over her shoulder.

Jade and I stared at one another confused, but she hopped up and pulled at my arm. I was still in shock, cradling the lifeless body of the woman I loved.

Jessie kept shouting at me to put pressure on the wound and get her into the buggy. The determination in Jessie's eyes gave me new hope. If Sarah wasn't already dead, she was knocking on the door, but a sliver of hope was better than none at all. We had to try. The Marshal drove us full speed into town.

*I checked once more for any sign of life. Tremors rocked my body yet again when I was met with no response. I did the only thing in my power, held pressure to the wound and whispered words of love, wishing so very much I was the one at death's door instead.*

I shot up in bed, my body drenched in a cold sweat. My heart raced, my hands shook. The disturbing images were still so fresh in my mind that waves of nausea rocked my body. A ray of light shone through the window into my otherwise dark and quiet room. Averting my eyes from the empty spot beside me was impossible. A shiver ran down my spine.

I had become accustomed to the sight over the last few months. The nightmares of my memories came almost every night since her breath fell shallow, her life slipping literally right through my fingers. The memories still shook me to my core and I wondered if I'd ever get past them. Worse yet, would I ever forgive myself for getting to her too late, for not keeping her safe?

My fingers slid through sweat soaked hair as I struggled to settle my nerves. With a deep breath, I fell back into bed. I hated waking up alone. I wished she were here with me.

My jaw clenched as I rolled out of bed and walked to the basin to wash my face. Today was Christmas and chores needed to be done before everyone arrived.

The repetitive crunching of snow beneath my feet soothed my frazzled mind. The holidays would be rough, especially after all we'd been through. As I thought back to that day, I wouldn't lie, it was the worst day of my life. Now and again, the anguish would still sweep through me, stopping me dead in my tracks, even in the middle of the day. Seemed the memory of her lying in her own pool of blood wasn't only reserved for my dreams. They flashed through my mind randomly and without warning. The trauma would take time to get over. At least they were occurring less often as I adjusted to a new life.

I'd faced my past, nearly gotten killed, lost my father and Sarah...

Running my fingers over the bullet wound in my chest caused me to flinch. That was a hard day, nothing else could be said. I didn't even give my father a second glance when I ran past his body lying in the dirt. My thoughts had rested solely on Sarah and my rising anger that once again my father took away any chance for happiness in my life.

The one good thing was, Sarah had finished her fight.

We all stayed in Spokane for several days to heal before attempting the long ride back. Jessie tied up all the loose ends of the mess we'd made. They were all wanted men, so everything went smoothly. She agreed to never reveal my true identity. For all intents and purposes, Margaret Josephine O'Shea was dead and I was more than happy to leave her in her grave.

Bringing Jade with us had made me nervous, afraid she'd get hurt or I'd lose my best friend along with the love of my life. Turned out she was invaluable. No one could ever doubt her loyalty or ability again. As much as we argued about how to proceed during the battle in the days leading up to it, listening to her had saved my life and she took care of all of us even after we got back home. She often joked about being like a mother to me. I had to give it to her, more times than not, the girl was right.

Jimmy turned down a job with the U.S. Marshals to become a deputy under Carter. He was every bit like his sister in his fierce loyalty to friends and family. We were lucky to have both of them on our side.

The livestock seemed glad to see me today. Why kid myself? They'd be excited no matter who fed them. Clover seemed content as she enjoyed the hay I put out. I stroked her muscled neck. Her whinny brought a smile to my face knowing Sarah's loyal companion had found a home to spend the remainder of her lazy days.

That's what Sarah had wanted. Heck, she spoke of that dream more than any she ever wanted for herself. I was happy to oblige. Only a few months had passed, but staying put seemed to agree with her as she indulged in the fresh hay.

"Even without the summer grass you're getting plump. Didn't take long for retirement to settle in for you."

Clover gave me a hard stare, flicked her ears and then resumed eating. She made me laugh. I bet she cursed me for calling her fat. What a character.

A light chuckle escaped and I slid over to pat Jet on the butt a couple of times. He sure was glad to have a girlfriend. Must've gotten old only socializing with cows.

I took a good look around. Hard to believe how much changed, yet how much remained the same. Unbelievable how your life switched from moment to moment. From the time Sarah Sawyer walked into my saloon almost two years ago, or to more be accurate, from the time I first laid eyes her and her mother through their window ten years ago, my life did nothing but change. She had opened my eyes to so many things. Thanks to her and her parents, I'd made a new life and faced my demons. I thought, no I knew, I did the same for her. Sarah and I had found our peace, but in different ways.

Voices back at the house pulled me from my musings. My makeshift family had arrived for our own little holiday tradition. We started a few Christmas's ago. Me, Jade, Nick, Carter, Maggie and their kids would eat dinner Christmas night over here and the children opened their gifts from Auntie's, Jo and Jade. Took me until now to realize the things I'd always wanted had been right in front of me. A loving, albeit mismatched, family of my own.

This year, Jessie, Jimmy and Jackie joined us. Seemed only right since they were part of us now. Jessie took a liking to Jackie and now spent more time here than she did away. Jackie worked for me at the saloon, giving me more time to be here. I planned to make this a working farm, so I had plenty to do, even in winter.

The crunch of boots in the snow meant the time to head back inside had come, but I couldn't help staying a bit longer. The cold weather invigorated me. Even though snow covered the ground, the sun shone bright and warmed us enough for just a sweater.

"What's on your mind?"

The question shifted my happy smile to one of sadness, because my answer was always the same. It had been the same every time since we got home. "You already know the answer."

"I brought Jessie and Jimmy from the train station. Sounds like their visit with mom went well."

I didn't turn around, wanting a few more moments of peace before I joined my family for the holiday craziness that was sure to ensue. My focus lingered instead on the animals enjoying their meal, envying the way they found joy in such small things. I envied them. Now that I was free of my secret identity, my purpose became making the best life possible and appreciating the little things just as much as the big ones. Gratitude for my blessings was something I no longer wanted to ignore.

Her strong arms wrapped around me from behind and her warm breath tickled the crook of my neck, bringing a ridiculous smile to my face. Those storybook endings, the one the man I once called Daddy told me didn't exist? Well, like so many other things in life, my father was wrong.

Sarah and I both suffered the same way in wondering if we deserved this happiness. I found peace in my decisions after doubting so much over the years. The agony I brought to so many would never be forgiven, but everything had come full circle. I'd helped heal the pain I'd caused, giving me penance for the lengthy list of past transgressions I'd committed over the years.

I needed to forgive myself for giving up on Sarah. If it hadn't been for Jessie, she'd be dead. Jessie kept her promise of bringing us all home alive and for that, I would forever be in her debt.

The guilt washed away in Sarah's loving embrace, encircling me in her protective arms. Her body enveloped mine like a cocoon as she squeezed tighter.

Sarah claimed she never thought about whether or not I'd given up. She didn't blame me for anything and was thankful for having a second chance. So was I, but I couldn't get away from the image of her slipping away as I held her a helpless mess. My body and my mind froze. I did nothing to save her. I was a damsel in distress hoping someone would rescue us.

Thankfully, someone did.

My hands covered hers and I sighed. Every muscle relaxed with one simple touch, despite my mental anguish. It still seemed like a dream. Nothing scared me more than the idea that one day I would wake up to a harsh reality and find she didn't really survive.

As if she sensed my dilemma, she gave me a gentle squeeze. Our bodies melded into a perfect fit. She nuzzled into my hair as her fingers worked their way under my sweater.

My breath caught in my throat, both from her contact and the cold against my heated skin. A shiver shot through me as her nails drug across my stomach and she planted soft kisses on my neck.

"God Sarah, I can't resist when you do that to me."

Her lips curled against sensitive skin. "That's why I do it." She nipped and kissed her way along my jaw line, teasing me. The cold air took over where her warmth comforted me only seconds before. Nibbling on my lobe she whispered, "And I can't resist how beautiful you are when you're lost in deep thought, so I think we're even."

The wry smile pulling at my lips proved her right. I turned in her arms and allowed myself to get swallowed up by those soft, expressive eyes that spoke like a beacon to the depths of my soul. Nothing topped the tiny tingles encompassing my being when I submerged myself in them, except her smile. They were hair-raising tingles, the kind that excited every cell like when lightning struck real close. Sarah's smile was lightning and when her eyes held me in their trance, I never felt more beautiful or loved. Each time, I fell for her all over again.

They said all things happened for a reason. I never believed the words, but as screwed up as it may all seem, everything had led me to her. Despite the hurt we caused one another, we had saved each other just the same.

The letter she gave Jackie was still tucked into the corner of my top drawer unopened. Sarah survived, so I figured she'd tell me in person. In fact, she'd spoken more lately than all the time we'd been together combined. Quite uncharacteristic of the quiet, moody cowgirl I first met. Of all the things she said since she came back, only one phrase stuck in my mind. *"I'll love you till the end of time and even that won't stop me, Jo Porter."*

My eyes drifted closed, arms reaching up as my fingers weaved through her long, silky flaxen hair. Hands locked behind her head holding her in place. The thought of how close I came to losing Sarah made my heart clench.

We leaned forward until our foreheads touched, I prayed this life with her would be a long one and made a silent vow to cherish every moment together for as long as I lived.

# Chapter Twenty-Six

**Sarah**

Knowing love changes you. Knowing loss also changes you. I had experienced both in my short life and sometimes it took one to put the other in perspective. Somewhere between love and justice, I found my way. Probably at the moment of enlightenment brought on by a bullet through Jo's chest.

As painful as my past was, I could never love Jo like I did now, if I'd never lost what I did then. The thought brought me comfort.

I missed my parents beyond measure. That was a hole that would never be filled, but I often felt their presence ever since I'd made my peace with their deaths and forgiven myself.

Maybe one day Jo and Jessie would be able to forgive themselves as well. The lingering pain of my near death still rippled in their eyes and I hoped one day they'd be able to let it go. They had nothing to be guilty about. Our pasts entwined in a series of missed opportunities and unfortunate events, all out of our control. Only one thing mattered, that we were here together.

Everything I'd shut down in myself over the years reawakened. Every idea I held onto about myself, rewritten. I thought loving Jo would make me weak, but I was never more wrong. She made me stronger than ever and accepting that she loved me proved anything was possible.

One of the things I wanted to change in my new life was taking time to embrace the simple joys. Little things like the delicate curve of her jaw and shimmer in her eye. I burned them into memory forevermore. Her love set my every fiber afire. Jo was simply amazing and most definitely my greatest joy.

With her arms draped around my neck, I took care of the final distance between us, stopping mere millimeters away from her mouth as our heavy breaths intermingled.

Her lips trembled with anticipation. She made no secret of what she wanted from me.

Where I once lived for revenge, I now lived to give her everything her heart desired. I wouldn't deny her. Especially not on Christmas day.

My lips dusted hers, causing my entire body to warm from the inside-out. I tugged on her bottom lip. The moan that erupted made me smile with pride. I loved to get her worked up and made a mental note any time I found something she enjoyed. Some might call it a hobby.

The glint of mischief in her eyes caused me to stop. What did she have in mind? Her eyes darted to the tack room and I could only grin in wild excitement.

I wholeheartedly agreed. "You wanna go for a roll in the hay?"

She waggled her brows, then kissed me hard. Firm breasts pressed against mine as I held her tighter and wished for these thick sweaters to disappear.

Never able to get close enough to Jo, I lifted her up and settled her body between my legs. A surprised yelp echoed in my ear as I moved us toward the door. We laughed together at our adolescent behavior. That's what Jo did to me. She brought me to life. She made me want to explore all life had to offer, a stark contrast from the Sarah Sawyer that existed a few months ago.

Impossible to get enough of her, I buried my face in her hair, inhaled the soothing lilac scent and sighed. We came crashing down into the hay when I stumbled over the feed bucket, giggling like little girls over my clumsiness. Her smile filled my heart and when those tiny dimples appeared, like they were right now, there were no words for what they did to me.

My thumb slid across her cheek, pushing a lock of dark hair behind her ear. I couldn't express the exhilaration coursing through me when she closed her eyes and pressed into my hand. Such a simple gesture that meant so much. The adoration in her expression as she brushed the hair from my face overwhelmed me.

Our lips met once more, soft at first, as we moved together in a well-practiced dance. Forget about the people in the house or the voices calling out for us. Only the sensation of her fingers tangling in my hair and her body against mine concerned me. In that moment, my only care was Jo and showing her how much I loved and needed her.

I rolled her over, pressing her deeper into the hay as our bodies began to work in rhythm. The heat radiated through our clothes, chasing the chill of winter away.

She pushed forward with the same driving desire, devouring my mouth with a needy insistence that spoke of her insecurity. Her tongue pushed past my lips as my rough hands pulled at her sweater.

Our movements grew feverish, both still grasping for something to prove this was real, that we were truly alive and here together. She needed the reassurance more than me and I did everything in my power to take a little bit more of those bad memories away.

Jo's hips pressed firmly into mine, making me groan from the contact and ache for more.

I always wanted more of her. The unbearable urge to feel skin on skin had never been greater. Every time we touched I needed her more, like an addiction, but better than any liquor or smoke and I never wanted to quit.

A breath-stopping gasp escaped my lungs when her hand worked into my pants and slipped between my legs. The proof of how much I ached for her touch brought out a deep, guttural groan of her own. The sound only fueled my need, increasing the hunger for her to take me. The silence of the small room fell victim to the tune of heavy breaths and wanton whimpers.

My hips rolled in time with her fingers, wanting so much more, but content to be at her mercy. Roaming hands teased her with light touches across bare skin.

Jo bit my neck when my fingers grazed her breasts, stopping to give them their due before trailing down her heated flesh toward their prize. Our thrusts grew more intense as I slid inside her waistband and gave her the same devoted attention she gave me. Her head pressed back into the hay as she arched up into me.

It was nearly impossible not to go crazy when she was so ready, like some primal part of me was begging for release. Time stood still as I gazed into her eyes. Our passion spilled over as our bodies tensed and we reached our peaks together.

For a moment we were wrapped in silence; the calm before the storm. I appreciated the goddess before me. Jo was truly a sight like no other. Her mouth locked open before loud moans of appreciation escaped from deep within us both.

Our names echoed amid the otherwise quiet room as we called out one to one another in the throes of passion. Crashing down together, I fell against her with my chest heaving as my lungs begged for air. The pounding of her heart synced with my own.

I brushed back luscious, dark locks from her face and smiled with total adoration until the waves of pleasure passed. "This may be the best Christmas gift I've ever gotten." Once more I savored her kiss swollen lips against mine. She tasted better than the finest holiday dish.

"It may be the best one I've ever given." She winked back at me. The mischievous grin brought the sparkle out in her eyes. "I guess we should get to the house. The rest of the gang is bound to be here by now."

My pout couldn't be contained. I wanted her all to myself for a while longer. It was so hard to have only one sampling of Jo. I likened it to getting just one bite of the best dessert on

Earth. Your taste buds would scream for another helping in hopes of satisfying the craving, but a second bite never solved anything. You wanted to indulge in the deliciousness until you were full. The problem was, I never got full of Jo.

She smiled and pulled me in for another soft, but teasing kiss. She wasn't helping any.

I pulled back to get a good look at her eyes, trying to decipher what was going through her mind. She hated waking up alone and I was late this morning. I'd hoped to get back in time, to hold her and show her I was safe; to show her that she didn't lose me. She would never lose me.

"Yeah, but I can't resist a few more minutes with you." Jo nuzzled against my neck. "It all still feels like a dream," she whispered.

"It's no dream." I pulled away, needing to look her in the eyes when my next words were spoken. "I'm here with you and will be for a long time. I'll never run again, Jo. I promise."

"I thought Sarah Sawyer didn't make promises." The curve of her mouth quirked up and she brushed a piece of hair from my eyes.

"Only to you and my family. I promise. I'm forever yours. I'll never leave your side."

Her lip quivered. A nod was her only response.

I tugged her back to me and wrapped her in a strong embrace, hoping to convey that my promise was one I'd keep till death and then some.

Jo was right when she told me revenge wouldn't quench my thirst the way I thought it would. Maybe I just didn't get to enjoy it having almost lost myself in the process. The search for payback had left me cold and bitter while life passed me by. I was drowning in my own misery.

I was lucky someone like Jo fought to drag me out of the depths, though it did bring me the one thing I needed in order to move on and live my life with her, closure. Anytime I was with Jo was always my happiest. With her I'd found everything I ever desired and some things I'd never even thought about. Without hesitation, I could say I'd love her for the rest of my many lives. Whatever part of me continued on after I died would never stop loving Jo.

Every detail about her reverberated deep within me. I'd long since given up on the idea of a god, but the powers that be had put us together by plan. The remainder of my newly-gifted days would be spent creating the life and the future I wanted, instead of wallowing in my past.

We straightened our clothes and collected ourselves in a hurry. The cold was noticeable with the heat from our passion subsiding. Laughter filled the room as we pulled hay from our hair and brushed off our backs. It didn't matter. They'd all know anyway. Jade could always pick out when we'd been fooling around.

Little things like that used to bother me. The intimate details of my life were no one's business but my own. But now, I embraced every opportunity to show everyone how much I loved Jo.

The past was at last a memory for me. And the future? Well, we can never be sure, but the present held a hard headed, passionate, beautiful woman who loved me more than she should and I was more than grateful for her.

I'd been fortunate in an unfortunate life, if that made any sense. I'd found incomparable allies when I needed them most and conquered my demons. Ann, Mary, Henry, Jessie, Jo and Jade, not to mention the rest of our bunch. Every one of them played a part in getting me here and that was a debt I could never repay. They wouldn't want me to anyway.

My hand slipped into hers with ease; like it was only ever meant for her. The people we held dear were inside waiting, but I couldn't help taking an extra moment on a special day to enjoy the greatest gift I had ever received and the only one I ever wanted, her love.

Gunslinger art provided by Rafi
@tsparklingblue / thesparklingblue.tumblr.com/
Title and border by Cindy Bamford

# ABOUT THE AUTHOR

This is the debut novel by S.W. Andersen. Having been raised by her mother, a strong female character in her own right, she has always been attracted to stories that depicted independent, capable, determined women. She has spent a large part of her life around horses and rodeos and has always had an affinity for the cowgirl lifestyle. Her love of the mountains and westerns were the driving forces behind her first novel. When she isn't working, she enjoys outdoor activities and traveling with her wife, Dianna. They share their ten acres in rural Florida with a rambunctious crew of two dogs, four cats and two horses.

Made in the USA
Columbia, SC
31 July 2019